I0760953

BLOOD BOND

DIRTY BLOOD SERIES

BOOK THREE

HEATHER HILDENBRAND

Blood Bond

Dirty Blood Series Book 3

Jacket Design by Malice & Mayhem Book Covers

Edge Design & Character Art by Samaiya

Hard Case Cover Design by We Got You Covered Book Designs

heatherhildenbrand.com

CHAPTER ONE

Wood Point Academy crawled with bodies. And even though they weren't killer hybrids or attempting any sort of attack, it made me claustrophobic. It was Thursday. Tomorrow signaled the end of the school year. Parents had arrived to cheer on their graduates. Unlike most high schools, where completing twelfth grade was the main celebration, Hunters considered it a milestone to complete each and every year of high school. From freshman to senior, everyone got some sort of ceremony. I guess when you trained as hard as we did, passing your classes *was* something to be admired.

The junior class had voted on a prom sort of thing, complete with a crepe-papered auditorium and a sound system with enough bass to induce a heart murmur. I shoved aside the flash back to the last school dance I'd attended, the one where I'd caught my ex-boyfriend, George, making out with my arch-nemesis, Cindy Adams. Listening to her smug comments over that night, I'd lost control of my temper and punched her in the nose. An action that had gotten me expelled and landed me here at Wood Point, a private boarding school for Werewolf Hunters like myself. The irony of the connection between that dance and this one wasn't lost on me.

The thump-thump of the beat as it slammed out of the speakers echoed in my ears and vibrated through my bones. Some kid with red sunglasses and a suit jacket to match bobbed his head to the beat of a remixed version of something that sounded suspiciously like reggae. I hated reggae.

"You look thrilled," Cambria said. We stood shoulder to shoulder, surveying the room.

"There's just so much to see and do, I can hardly contain myself."

She grinned. "Just because you're antsy to get home and see your sexy wolf-boy doesn't mean you can be grumpy with the rest of us."

"Did you just call Wes sexy?" My eyebrows shot up.

"Please, you have nothing to worry about and you know it." She flipped her hair, which she'd highlighted with streaks of ghostly white. It glowed in the black light. "Besides, you're supposed to be my wingman tonight."

"There's not much to choose from, unless you count that guy." I pointed to the brightly dressed kid still grooving to his own beat.

"Uh, pass." She rolled her eyes. "You're being sulky again. You've been like that all month."

"What can I say? I was ready for summer a month ago."

"No, you were ready for Wes a month ago. Do you know where he is this week?"

I shook my head. "I haven't talked to him in a few days. Last I heard they were passing through some hick town in Nebraska."

"What the hell are they doing in Nebraska?"

"I don't know. Grandma said they caught a trail that looked like it could be hybrids and decided to chase it down."

"Is he coming back to take you home?"

"Not enough time. Grandma's coming tomorrow." I shrugged, trying to pretend I didn't miss Wes so much it hurt, and bumped her with my shoulder. "Speaking of home, what are your plans?"

Cambria hesitated. She'd been trying to reach her mom for weeks now with no luck. I wasn't sure what that meant because Cambria wouldn't come out and say, but I knew it wasn't good.

"I think I'm going to become a hippie."

"What?"

"Like a nomad, a wanderer. You know, road trip. See the country."

"You don't have a car."

"A hitchhiker, then. I'd get a lot of pickups. My thumb is pretty sexy."

"What happened with your mom? Why aren't you going home?"

"She's unavailable."

"And that means what exactly?"

Her shoulder rose and fell against mine. "She's in rehab. Or so my building manager tells me. She hasn't returned any of my calls. I checked with the place she stayed at for a while last year and they 'can't confirm patient records.'" She used her fingers to air quote the phrase. "Which basically means she's there and can't be reached."

"What are you going to do?" I tried not to look sorry or pitying. I knew Cambria would hate pity.

"I don't know. She's got a van. Or she did last time I was home. If it's still there, I can use it and maybe take a trip somewhere. I think I have a cousin in Biloxi."

I didn't know much about Cambria's relationship with her mom. Conversation about it was rare, except the occasional allusion to the fact that they didn't get along when her mom *was* around—something I could sympathize with. But even with the fighting, this seemed worse. My chest ached at the thought of Cambria going home to an empty house. "Come home with me," I said.

"Are you serious?"

Disco boy moonwalked by us and winked. We ignored him.

"Seriously, Cam. You have nothing better to do and my mom is probably going to house arrest me for that crap with Miles. I would love having a friend under the same roof." I smiled. "You'd be doing me a favor."

She narrowed her eyes. "You're trying to get me to feel better about mooching off you all summer, aren't you?"

"Maybe," I squeaked, keeping the smile plastered to my face. "Is it working?"

"Totally," she agreed.

We grinned at each other until something behind me caught her eye and her expression faltered. Her eyes flickered back to mine. "Uh-oh. Trainer with bedroom eyes headed this way."

"Trainer with …?" I twisted to see who she meant, though part of me knew the moment her eyes had shifted. Alex headed this way. He wore a black suit and a white shirt that contrasted against his tanned hands and face. He would've been breathtaking except for the pained look on his face and the way he pulled at the tie knotted at his throat as he moved through the crowd.

Cambria whistled loud and low. "Trainer boy cleans up good."

His eyes fell on me and swept up and down. I smoothed the silk dress I'd stolen from Victoria. My breath caught a little and I forced it in and out evenly. We'd been training together for weeks now without crossing the line from professional to personal. Somehow, this night felt different. Maybe it was the fact that we'd be leaving tomorrow. A last chance to say everything. Not that I had anything different to say. My heart belonged to Wes.

Sometimes I wondered if my heart had selective memory.

"Tara." The way he spoke my name sent a shiver down my spine. "May I have a word?"

"Sure." I nodded at Cambria and followed him outside.

Stars twinkled overhead. People milled about in the courtyard; parents gushed over their offspring and couples engaged in a last make-out session before returning home.

"Can we take a walk?" Alex asked.

I nodded and fell into step beside him, my heeled sandals making clicking sounds on the sidewalk that wound around the outskirts of the courtyard. Soft, white bulbs strung about the shrubs illuminated the pathway. It was meant to be romantic, but instead, it left my stomach tight.

The entire month there had been a sort of resigned tension between Alex and me. After the stir caused by Miles subsided, Wes and the others had gone home. School was restored to order. Classes resumed. It all felt so *normal.* Then there was Alex.

I don't know what I'd expected my first day back at training.

Closeness over a shared near-death experience? Distance caused by the secrets I still kept? I felt neither.

Alex was business as usual. Painfully so.

It was as if none of it had happened. Or as if he'd experienced it all separate from me somehow. He had a singular focus: the hybrids were running around leaving a trail of dead humans in their wake. A fact Alex made painfully clear in his never-ending rants about how he couldn't wait for the special team selections. He was itching to hunt them. Except, unlike Wes, who'd gone searching for hybrids willing to choose peace over death and destruction, Alex would hunt to kill. No matter how hard I tried, I couldn't shake that.

"Are you enjoying the party?"

"It beats running."

Alex chuckled. "I could've converted you if I'd had more time."

More time.

Tomorrow we'd go our separate ways. I swallowed against the lump in my chest. "Alex …" I didn't know how to put any of it into words.

"Kane called me into the office today."

"Oh." I stopped. We were at the edge of the courtyard now, closer to the trees than the cobbled path. Movement caught my eye. I swiveled, muscles bunching. My body was more alert for danger than my mind, though, because it took me a moment to realize what I was seeing. "Logan?"

He broke from Victoria's embrace. Even in the dim light, I could see him flush. "Tara, hey."

Victoria glared at me. "Is that my dress?"

"My wardrobe is gone, remember? And you have more than you need. Doesn't it look nice?" I pivoted right, then left, showing off the silky fabric that ended a little higher than it should've since I was taller than its rightful owner.

"Breathtaking," Alex agreed.

"Stay out of this, Channing. What are you doing with her anyway? She's rabid."

"Lay off, Vic. Summer starts tomorrow. Kick back. Relax," Alex said.

"Evil never sleeps," I muttered. Logan shot me a dirty look. I lifted my eyebrows in mock innocence.

The animosity between Victoria and I was old news. Since the incident with Miles, and more than that, since the day she'd cried to me about her parents disappearing, there'd been no more exploding bags of dog food. No more shredded clothes or attempts to shave my eyebrows in my sleep. Although, she never missed an opportunity to insult me in conversation, which was almost daily since she and Logan were practically joined at the mouth these days. I figured wearing her clothes was an even trade.

"I was relaxing just fine until you and Barking Barbie showed up," Victoria said.

Alex laughed, and this time I shot him a dirty look. "Sorry," he said, still grinning.

"Are you guys passing through or should we pick another spot for privacy?" Logan asked, giving me a pointed look.

I opened my mouth, snarky comment at the ready.

"We were just leaving." Alex took my elbow and led me away before I could protest. Victoria said something I couldn't hear and Logan shook his head like he was too beaten to argue. "Let it go," Alex said as we headed for the woods.

A few steps in, the light from the string of bulbs faded and blackness closed in. My eyes adjusted quickly so that shadowy stalks rose around us and the trees ran closer together. Alex stepped off the path; I had to watch my step to keep from tripping over undergrowth. It didn't matter that I couldn't see past his shoulders in front of me. I knew where he was headed. My heels crunched over the gravel that led to the shed.

"I can't believe it. Logan and Victoria," I said, shaking my head.

"Definitely an unexpected pair," Alex agreed.

Something about the way he said it sent a warm ripple over my skin. Part of me wanted to confess how much I would miss him. How even though my feelings for Wes had only solidified after all we'd been through, it hurt to think about being separated from Alex. Especially when I had no idea if we'd ever see each other again. But I couldn't say that. It was against the rules we'd set, and I refused to be the first to break them.

Instead, I picked up our earlier conversation. "What did Kane want?"

Alex didn't answer until we'd reached his work-in-progress—a shabby pickup truck. Tools were strewn around the bed and tailgate, which was permanently down since the hinges were rusted out. He picked up a wrench, twirling it deftly in his hand.

"I got picked up for special teams," he said.

"Oh." It was the same response I'd given before we'd been interrupted, but I didn't know what else to say. This was the moment he'd been waiting for all month, the moment I'd been dreading.

Special teams were what they called the Hunters being sent by CHAS to search out the crazed hybrids Miles had created and then loosed. Some were capable of becoming human at will, some weren't. All of them had these weird, yellowish eyes. When you looked into them, even into their farthest depths, you were struck by their lack of humanity. But, despite their viciousness and thirst for blood, most of them had been Hunters once—some were friends and family to the very same Hunters who searched with orders to kill on sight.

Hopefully, Wes, Jack, and Cord would find them first. If they could get the hybrid to swear allegiance to The Cause, legally they couldn't be touched by CHAS. They were neutral. Or so we hoped. So far, neither side had located a single one of them.

It was a wedge between Alex and me, his wanting to join these teams. The fact that he was volunteering to kill something that represented a part of me—a bigger part than I was willing to admit—was hard.

"Which team?" I asked quietly.

"A scouting team to start, but if I do well," he shrugged, "I should be promoted quickly."

I nodded, not trusting my voice, and stared at a pile of nuts and bolts on the tailgate.

He sighed and dropped the wrench. “Say something.”

“Like what?”

“I don’t know, but your silence is weirding me out. Usually you just yell or wave your arms or something.”

“I’ll remember that for future arguments.” As soon as I said it, my eyes watered. What *future*? This was it.

“Tara …” Alex took my hand.

“Don’t,” I whispered, but he ignored it and laced his fingers through mine.

“I’ll miss you. Will you miss me?”

All I could do was nod. He leaned closer, his eyes on my mouth. His free hand traced an invisible line down my jaw and rested on my shoulder. I held my breath, sure he was going to kiss me. I had no idea what I would do if he did. My feet became anchors, holding me in place.

At the last minute before our lips touched, he exhaled. His breath was warm on my lips before he leaned away. He let go of my hand and wrapped his arms around me, pulling me into a tight embrace. I hugged him back and tried to ignore the sting in my eyes and throat. We didn’t move for a long time.

When he spoke again, his voice was rough. “This is harder than I thought it would be.”

“For me too.” It was easier to talk standing in his arms, without him looking at me. “Alex? Will I see you again?”

“Absolutely.”

“Promise?”

He pulled away, facing me squarely. His hands rested on my arms. “I’m going to tell you something, and then I’m going to walk away because it’s late and also because I don’t want you to feel like you have to say anything.”

“Okay.”

“I love you, Tara Godfrey. I love you so much that I walk around breathless from the exertion. No, don’t talk,” he said when I opened my mouth to respond. "Just listen. I don't have family. I don't get attached. It's easier that way. Which is what I kept telling myself about you, but it happened despite my best efforts to prevent it. It's not going away and it's not fading. If anything, it's gotten worse.

"I understand you have feelings for me but you *love* him. The only option that leaves me with is hunting hybrids. And even though you hate the idea, it's not what keeps us apart."

"Alex, I—"

"No, don't." He attempted a smile but it looked pained. "I'll see you again. I'll *always* see you again. No matter how much you hate what I do in between. I also suck at goodbyes. So …" He dropped his hands from my shoulders and buried them in his pockets. When they were safely tucked, he leaned in and planted a kiss halfway between my mouth and my cheek. It was quick, chaste, his expression strained. How much had that cost him?

"I'm going to head back. Get some sleep. I leave early so you won't see me in the morning. Bye, Tara."

He spun on his heel and began a long retreat down the gravel path that led back to school. I stood there, torn between wanting to respect his wishes and needing to give him what I could. The ache won out. My dress flared up around my legs as I sprinted. I held it down and kept running.

"Alex, wait!"

I threw myself into his arms. He staggered backwards before catching his balance, holding me to him and lifting my feet off the ground. He didn't complain that I'd come after him.

I wrapped my arms tightly around his shoulders, burying my face in his neck. I breathed in his scent of outdoors and bar soap and committed it to memory.

"Be careful," I said when he finally lowered me to my feet. "And—you're my family, too." His expression clouded. "I know you said not to respond." I grabbed his jacket lapels to brace myself and rushed on, not caring whether the gesture was right or not. "I just had to say that, so you know it's mutual. No matter what." I squeezed my eyes against all of the rest that I couldn't respond to and added only, "Always find me, okay?"

"Okay." His voice was hoarse. His hands closed over mine, gently removing my fingertips from his jacket front. "I have to go."

"See you later, Alex." I dropped my hands from his.

This time I let him leave.

CHAPTER TWO

I couldn't work up the motivation to return to the party. I wandered, surprised at all of the memories that sprang to mind as I passed various locations on the grounds. Vincent Hall library, where I spent more and more time these days on the computer, emailing Sam and Angela even though their responses were fewer and fewer.

The courtyard, which I still avoided at all costs because even though Victoria's torture had subsided, most other kids still called me "mutt" or tried to trip me when I walked by. I'd grown used to it enough to ignore it most days. Like an old shoe.

Then there was Lexington Hall and the dorm nestled underneath it, both of which felt like home, even after only a couple of months. It would be strange to sleep in my own bed again.

My phone rang, startling me since it rarely had a signal unless I was on the rooftop of Griffin Hall. I pulled it from my bra, where Cambria insisted all girls tucked their cells in the absence of purse or pockets, and read the incoming number.

"Hi, Grandma. What's up?"

"Just checking on you. How's your last night at school? I didn't interrupt anything, did I?"

"You didn't interrupt anything."

After the Miles-slash-hybrid fiasco, Grandma and Mom had driven up several times. Mom, so she could lecture me and hug me and shake me for scaring the crap out of her. Grandma, so she could throw her influence around with CHAS and make sure they got a new security person out here to handle the wards in Vera's place.

During their whirlwind stays, I'd felt the weight of Grandma's sharp eyes more than once when Alex was around. She suspected something more between us, and I had a feeling as much as she liked Wes, she was pleased with the idea.

"How's George?" I asked, changing the subject to the only reason I called home anymore.

"He's holding up."

"Is Fee's healing preventing the change?" I asked.

"It's slowing things down a great deal but, honey, I don't think there's anything that can stop it."

I ignored that. I couldn't think about such a scary possibility when I was so far away. "What is everyone in town saying? Have you spoken to his mother?"

"Your momma says George convinced his own that he was going away to some training camp for sports this summer."

"That's good." I exhaled.

When I'd made arrangements for Fee to care for George while we figured out his condition, I hadn't taken his family into account. As far as they knew, he'd taken a weekend road trip here to see me. No big deal. But by the time he'd gone home, he'd been the victim of a syringe-induced change that would eventually make him a Werewolf—a human-wolf hybrid creation, courtesy of the late and creepy Miles DeLuca.

If we were lucky, George would survive.

Miles had sounded certain that George's change would end in death—unless I shared my blood with him. Even then there was no guarantee. Miles had a problem with full disclosure. I could only imagine what sort of reaction George would have to an injection of my DNA. It could make him worse, or speed things up. I'd decided to hold off until we could learn more about the possible side effects of such a treatment.

"Don't worry about anything happening here until you get back. I'll see you tomorrow around lunchtime. We'll figure things out then. Oh, and so you know, Vera asked to catch a ride back with us. She's going to Fee's for the summer."

"Good. She shouldn't be driving on her own," I said.

Vera Gallagher, built like sinew, was a powerful Hunter with an extra-sensory gift that allowed her to do various forms of magic. That probably wasn't the right word, but there wasn't anything better. She could do locator spells, though they seemed to work only on Hunters, and weave wards, a protective but invisible barrier that kept Werewolves out of a designated space. Vera's official job, besides being a leader of The Cause, had been to maintain the wards that protected Wood Point from Werewolves and any other unwanted visitors. The wards also kept this place off the map for humans.

But Vera was sick. A mysterious illness had taken hold, slowly robbing her of her magic, and the wards failed. After the breach with Miles and the hybrids, everyone agreed the best thing was for Vera to step down.

"How's she feeling? Have you seen her?" Grandma asked.

"Um, I had tea with her a couple of days ago. She seems all right."

Vera was my great aunt. I'd found her name in my family tree during my lineage project and confronted her about it. She'd admitted the relation and ever since, it seemed like she was edging toward developing some sort of friendship with me. Every time I sat down with her, I felt like I was facing aristocracy. I hadn't visited often, but I didn't tell Grandma that.

"Hopefully, her strength is up. It's a long trip home and it's bound to tire her," said Grandma. "You make sure to rest up too."

"I will. Oh, there's something else I've been meaning to ask you. Who is Astor DeLuca?"

Grandma whistled, long and low. "I haven't heard that name in … wait, where did *you* hear it?"

"Oh, um." Miles had given me the name just before Cord killed him to save me. I hadn't mentioned that fact to Grandma yet. I'd decided I wouldn't until I knew who he was. It wasn't that I didn't trust Grandma—I didn't trust Miles. "I came across it during my lineage research for school. Apparently we're related?"

"Huh. Well, I guess the closest thing is uncle. He's the younger brother of your grandfather, on your father's side."

My head spun as I struggled to connect the branches. "So, great uncle then?"

"Yeah, that's the one. Anyway, he's always been a little ... detached, we'll say. Genius on paper, but not all his screws are properly tightened."

"He's crazy?"

"And unpredictable to boot. Nobody's seen him in years because he never leaves his house. Good thing, too, since CHAS would probably have a fit if he did."

"What do you mean?"

"Years ago, he was experimenting with the properties in metal that allow us to kill Werewolves. There was an accident and a girl died. Ever since then, we all steer clear."

"But if it was an accident—"

"Tara, he's bat-crazy, which is apparently rampant on your daddy's side, God rest his soul, so don't even worry about it. He's best left alone." The edge in her voice made it clear she meant it.

"Bat-crazy, got it," I said. She huffed out a breath, apparently satisfied. "One more thing. Is it all right if Cambria comes home with us for the summer?" I gave her the story about Cambria's mom being in rehab and how Cambria would be spending the summer alone otherwise.

"I'll talk to your momma to be sure, but I don't see a problem with it," she said.

"Thank you."

"Oh, 'Army Wives' is on. I have to go."

I heard rustling sounds and then the line went dead. *Army Wives*? I shoved the phone back into my bra—glancing around to see where I'd wandered. There was something familiar about these trees. My mouth went dry as I made the connection.

This was where I'd fought the hybrids with Wes. This was where I'd blacked out.

I spun on my heel and hurried back to the path and the twinkling lights of the courtyard. I couldn't get away fast enough; images bombarded me. The way hybrids had poured out of the trees toward Wes, their eyes yellow and glowing and intent on killing. The way they seemed to enjoy the violence of the fight. When they'd taken Wes down my heart stopped. I thought I'd faint or freeze up from the fear. Instead, I went mad. Something inside me snapped, and I became more animal than human. It wasn't a conscious decision and it wasn't something I could control.

When it was over, broken bodies—some wolf and some human—littered the clearing. Wes said I'd killed without mercy. He also said I smelled like a wolf.

It took us three hours to bury the bodies so no one would know what I'd done. I'd made Wes swear not to tell anyone about it and prayed it wouldn't happen again.

Professor Flaherty met me on the way inside. Her red hair hung loose down her back, like a floating flame. "Tara, you look nice. Are you enjoying the party?" she asked.

"Yeah, I just needed some air."

"I know what you mean. I was just taking a breather, myself." I moved to go around her, wanting the solitude of the ear-splitting noise, the absence of conversation. "Oh, Tara, before I forget," she called, "please use the summer to think about my offer to mentor you next year." She smiled wryly. "I'm told mine wasn't the only offer, so I understand if you turn me down. It's a hard decision. Kane usually only extends the opportunity to one student at a time. It's quite an honor."

"Um, I'm thinking about it," I said.

She nodded. "Like I said, consider it over the summer. You can let us know in the fall."

"Thanks, I'll do that."

"In case I don't see you tomorrow, have a safe trip home. Tell Vera I said the same."

"I'll tell her. See you later, Professor."

I made my way back to the party. Cambria met me at the door. She smiled and leaned in closer than necessary. "Where've you been? You're missing all the drama." Her breath reeked of alcohol and her eyes were lit—a little too lit.

"Have you been drinking?"

"Professor Kane caught Levi spiking the punch and they got into it. The DJ cut the music so all you heard was the yelling. It was hilarious."

"How does that explain the alcohol on your breath?"

"I might've charmed the kitchen lady into letting me have a cup of the punch before they poured it out."

"A cup?"

"It was a really big cup?"

"Cambria!" I hissed, glancing around.

"Relax. No one saw me. They were all too busy watching Kane ream out Levi. Demi was pissed. You should've seen her face."

"I'm quite content not having seen her face. In fact, if I never see it again, I'll die happy."

Demi became the new Queen Bitch after dethroning Victoria a couple of months ago. She'd also had her hand in helping Miles with his attempt to take over the world using hybrid Werewolves. Demi was not my favorite person. She made Victoria look like a walk in the park.

"Can't disagree." Cambria glared at something behind me. Demi, judging by the intensity of her expression. I didn't bother to turn. "Ugh. I still can't believe I liked Phillipe, or Miles, or whatever. Leave it to me to pick the psychos."

"It's not your fault. He used you."

"It's still gross. I feel weird about it."

I didn't answer. Whenever Cambria brought up the fact that she'd been briefly fooled by Miles, who'd posed as a security guard for the school to gain her trust, I bit my tongue. It wasn't her fault. He'd lied.

Still, Miles had been creepy before I'd known who and what he really was. How had she missed that?

She took a deep breath and let it out. I had the impression she was expelling the conversation with it. "Well, I'm off." She bumped me as she passed, wobbling slightly.

"Where are you going?"

"Christian Norton." Her eyes glazed over and she wore a dreamy smile.

"Who is Christian Norton?"

"He's a senior. Long legs. Tight jeans. Mmmm."

"You're half drunk."

"So?"

"So I am not letting you run off with some guy you barely know. What if something happens?"

"Um, that's the idea, genius." Her pupils dilated and I blinked, wondering if I'd imagined it. At the same time, a feeling of serenity washed over me. I had the urge to stop arguing, to let her go.

I shook my head and the feeling cleared. I put a hand on my hip. "Are you compelling me?" I demanded.

"No! … Not anymore."

"Cambria."

"Sorry. It gets a little out of control when I drink."

"Point proven. You're not meeting Christian like this. We're going to bed."

She pouted. "You're no fun tonight. Did something happen with Alex?"

I sighed. "Absolutely nothing happened with Alex, nor will it. Let's go." I took her hand and led her out.

CHAPTER THREE

The next morning, Cambria's eyes were dull and glassy.

"Did you drink enough to get a hangover?" I asked.

"For a normal person? No. For me? Yes." She scowled as she pulled her boots on and ran a brush through her hair. Her white streaks were already fading to gray as a result of the cheap dye she'd used. Her complexion almost matched.

"You look sick, Cam."

"Thanks. You look gorgeous too."

"I didn't mean—"

"I know, I know," she said, waving her hand and scanning the room distractedly. She tugged her school-issued gown from a pile of laundry and pulled it over her head. "Alcohol and compulsion don't mix. It's my own fault. Let's go before they come looking. I'm not trying to start next year off with detention."

We made it there just as the doors began to close. Professor Hugo glared at us and waved us to a seat without a word. When our names were called, we were given a certificate of completion. It wasn't the same as a diploma and seemed completely pointless to me, except it gave us a reason to cross a stage in front of a clapping crowd.

Headmaster Whitfield beamed like a fluorescent bulb, as if each student crossing the stage was a testament to his ability to lead and mold. When my turn came, I shook his hand, doing my best to ignore the glower he aimed at me.

We returned to our seats and the lights dimmed. A video began on the screens mounted to either side of the stage. It was a slideshow of pictures, yearbook style. I squeezed my hands together and prayed I wouldn't be in any. I'd rather be left out than featured during one of Victoria's or Demi's attempts at public humiliation. *Please, God, no dog food pictures.*

One of the last slides showed a picture of the courtyard. Kids scurrying to class or stopping to socialize filled the screen. I recognized the couple in the left corner just as Cambria poked me in the ribs.

"Is that—?" I began in a whisper.

"Logan and Victoria sucking face. Yes." Cambria made a gagging noise.

I heard a few snickers as the slide changed to another picture. When it ended, the lights came on and Headmaster Whitfield returned to the podium to tell us to have a safe summer.

The junior class surged into the aisles like a tsunami. I waited in my seat for the throng to exit and looked again for my family in the sea of faces. I spotted Grandma shoving her way upstream and waved.

Her sweatshirt, a throwback from some cross-stitch-meets-iron-on situation sitting atop her elastic-waist jeans made her look like the typical grandma-next-door. A cookie-baking, church-organ-playing, senior citizen—but looks could be, and in Grandma's case, definitely *were*, deceiving. She was one of the best Hunters I'd ever seen. Like an old lady version of Chuck Norris. I loved her.

"Hey, baby," she said, reaching over the chair backs from the aisle ahead of me and pressing a kiss against my cheek.

"Where's Mom?" I asked.

"Oh, she stayed behind. Flower emergency," Grandma said. "You both looked gorgeous up there."

"We did, didn't we?" Cambria slid her gown over her head and threw it over a chair.

"How long until we leave?" I asked.

"Soon," Grandma said. "I need to find Vera and load her bags and then we'll get on the road. Why don't you two meet me in the parking lot out front of Griffin Hall in an hour or so?"

"Sounds good. I need an aspirin," Cambria said.

Grandma headed off in the direction of Headmaster Whitfield. He was still hovering near the stage talking to Professor Kane. They looked up as she approached. Headmaster Whitfield smiled wide enough to split his lip. Kane's eyes flickered from her to me and held for a moment, a slight frown on his face. The way his mouth tipped downward elongated the scar on his cheek. I shuddered.

"You okay?" Cambria asked.

"Um, yeah," I mumbled. Kane turned his attention back to Grandma and the heavy feeling passed.

"Hey, you." Cambria snagged Logan's arm as he walked by with Victoria close behind. "Tara and I are leaving in an hour, so if we don't see you before then …" Cambria trailed off. Her version of goodbye.

Logan pulled his hat out of his back pocket where I'd seen him hide it before the ceremony, and yanked it securely onto his head, facing backward. Strands of sandy hair peeked out the front and sides. It looked funny with the black robe he still wore over his jeans and sneakers.

"Goodbye to you, too, Cam. I'll miss you." He let go of Victoria's hand long enough to hug Cambria. Victoria made a heaving sound.

"I might find it in me to miss you," Cambria told him.

He grinned and hugged me. "It's not going to be the same this summer without you two stirring things up," he said.

"Oh, we'll still be doing that. I'm bunking with Tara this summer," Cambria said.

Logan's brow shot up. "Huh. Well, try not to get arrested."

Cambria snorted. "Like that would ever happen. I'd just charm—" She stopped short and stared at Victoria, eyes wide.

"Please." Victoria waved her hand. "Like I don't know you did that to me."

"Logan," Cambria hissed, sending him an accusatory glare.

"I didn't say anything. She knew."

"Wait, does that mean the truce is over?" I asked. Suddenly, the idea of leaving my packed bags in my room didn't seem very safe.

"You mean the truce you managed to trick out of me under duress?" Victoria folded her arms.

Cambria shook her head. "Uh-uh. New deal. It's called the Logan truce, and you have no choice, even without being charmed."

"What the hell is the Logan truce?" Victoria demanded.

"Look, you want to date Logan, God knows why." Logan shot her a look, which she ignored. "But he was our friend first and will continue to be. Hence, the Logan truce."

"That's the dumbest logic ever. Besides, I won't even see you until fall. We can negotiate the details then."

"You're not going to see Logan until fall, either," I said, but one look at Victoria's smug smile and Logan's guilty one told me I was wrong. "Or maybe you are."

"Victoria's coming home with me for a while," Logan said. "Her parents are still missing so she doesn't really have anywhere to go."

At the mention of her parents, the evil twist left Victoria's expression. In its place was sadness and fear, and suddenly she was just a girl with no family. Guilt stabbed at me. I hadn't told her what I knew. Her parents weren't missing like she thought. CHAS had them locked in a cell so they could be studied after being turned into hybrid Werewolves. I didn't feel any loyalty to CHAS or the powers that be, but Alex was different. And I'd promised him.

"You have family," Cambria said. "In Vermont or something. I've heard you talk about them."

"Her family won't talk to her until her parents are found. There are rumors of them being turned," explained Logan. I stared at the ground.

"Well … that sucks."

I looked up, shocked at Cambria's empathetic response. She wasn't looking at any of us. Instead, she stared blankly at some plaque on the far wall depicting a wig-wearing headmaster from the seventeenth century.

Logan cleared his throat, and Victoria tugged on his hand. "Well, we're going to meet up with my parents, get our stuff together. I'll talk to you guys soon," he said.

"Call us, okay?" I gave him a one-armed hug, steering clear of the hand he'd attached to Victoria.

"You okay?" I asked Cambria when they were gone.

"Hmm? Yeah, why?" We wandered toward the door, a task made easier by the near-empty hall.

"You seem preoccupied."

"Just happy to be sprung from this place for a few months."

I nodded as we walked out into the sunshine, unable to voice any sort of agreement. The ache in my chest—the one I pretended was indigestion—sharpened at the thought of leaving.

My bags were intact. I'd been briefly worried Demi would mess with them, but she'd been leaving us alone. I think she was on some sort of probation. She kept it very hush-hush. I'd heard she'd been interviewed and released under the assumption Miles had used this "sweet, innocent, and very gullible teenager for his insane and criminal acts." I'd almost barfed when Alex told me that.

Alex.

Alex was gone. I felt numb about his absence, unless you counted the ache—which I didn't.

I mentally shook myself. Nope. Wasn't thinking about it.

"Did your grandma say anything about George?" Cambria asked as we walked toward the parking lot.

I glanced around, checking to make sure we were out of earshot of the few kids left on campus. I'd told Cambria what Miles had done, injecting George with whatever it was he'd concocted to create these hybrids. I'd also told her there was no way we could let the other Hunters, or more importantly CHAS, know about his change. They'd only lock him up—or worse.

"She said he's okay, for now. Whatever Fee is giving him has slowed everything down. But nothing can stop it." I sighed, feeling the worry come crashing down anew. "I just need to get there so we can figure this out."

"You could give him your blood and see what happens," she said.

I frowned. "You know how dangerous that could be. Miles was nuts. For all I know, he told me to do that because it will kill George instantly, or make him an even bigger monster."

"What about that Astor guy?"

I shook my head. "I asked Grandma about him. He's some mad scientist whose experiments killed a girl. She says to stay away from him. I don't think it was a request."

"Sounds like he and Miles must've got along great."

We rounded the corner and the shiny Hummer came into view, double-parked, as usual. Grandma loaded bags as a sickly-looking Vera leaned against the passenger door.

"Maybe Vera knows of something," Cambria said.

"Maybe," I agreed half-heartedly.

We added our bags to the growing pile, helped Vera into the front seat, and climbed in.

"Geez," said Cambria. "It's like an army-issued cave or something. Are there rocket launchers? I've always wanted to shoot a rocket."

Grandma laughed and backed out. "Sorry, no weapons of mass destruction. Unless you count the passengers, of course." She winked into the mirror.

I watched the buildings as they slowly faded from sight. Griffin Hall loomed larger than the others. I felt conflicted—I should've been relieved, excited to be leaving. And a part of me was. Another part felt lost, like whichever version of myself I'd brought to Wood Point was still on the grounds, left behind.

TWO HOURS LATER, GRANDMA TOOK AN EXIT ADVERTISING GAS AND burgers. "Anybody want anything?" she asked as she hopped out.

"A bottle of water would be perfect," Vera said. Her eyes were dark underneath where shadows had formed in the time we'd been on the road.

"Sure." Grandma looked at me. "Tara, anything?"

"Water's good," I said, scratching absently at the base of my neck. Since she'd opened the door, a strange feeling had crept in. Not goosebumps. This was different. Still, the threat it held was unmistakable.

"I need a restroom and I don't think you can go get that," Cambria said. She climbed out and headed off toward the station entrance.

I watched her, on edge, my eyes darting to the shadows created by the gutter overhang that wrapped around the stained stucco walls. Nothing moved. Two other cars sat parked at the pumps and a rusty pickup dripped oil onto the space by the door.

As Cambria entered, a man exited. He wore battered shorts and a shirt with so many holes I didn't see the point in the fabric. I stared as he got into his truck, trying to zero in on him—or anything that could be the cause of this strange feeling. Nothing registered. A moment later, his clutch popped and he motored off.

The feeling remained.

I scanned the lot, but nothing and no one in it seemed to be the source. I shifted in my seat, my palms sweaty; the cool air had escaped when Grandma opened the door.

"Everything all right?" Vera asked.

I looked up sharply and found her watching me through the mirror in her visor.

"I'm fine," I mumbled, feeling a little awkward. Vera always made me feel that way.

She frowned and twisted in her chair to face me, her eyes searching. For what, I didn't know. "You look unsettled."

Unsettled.

That wasn't a bad way to describe it. I opened my mouth, ready to brush her off, to tell her she was imagining things, when the feeling suddenly spiked. Something like adrenaline burst from my chest and ran through my veins. My leg jerked at the unexpected energy. My incisors sharpened and my jaw stretched forward. I clamped both hands over my mouth and stared at Vera with wide eyes.

"Tara?"

I grappled for the door handle and pushed it open. When I'd jumped clear of the Hummer, I ran. I didn't stop until I'd rounded the corner and reached the dumpster. My knees buckled and I bent over and heaved. Nothing came up but my stomach churned and roiled. My breaths came in short gasps and my lungs swelled to bursting. Was this what an asthma attack felt like?

"Tara?" Cambria appeared from the front of the building. She held a bottle of water in each hand. She watched me warily, like one might approach a wild animal.

"I'm good," I said, still breathing heavily. I wiped my mouth with the back of my hand. "I felt like I was going to be sick for a minute."

She handed me one of the waters. I took it and gulped. It was cold enough to chill my insides as it went down. I was grateful. It calmed the swirling in my stomach.

"Do you get carsick or something?" she asked.

I shrugged. "First time for everything, I guess."

"But you're okay now?"

"Yeah, I think so." I gulped more water.

"Huh." She eyed me another minute and then turned to leave. "Well, come on. Your grandma wants to get going."

"Right behind you."

Grandma was waiting at the car, arms crossed. "You all right?" she called before I'd finished crossing the lot.

"Fine. Carsick, I guess," I called back.

"You've never been car sick before," she said, though she didn't look nearly as suspicious as Cambria.

We merged onto the highway in silence. I took a few more sips of water. The tightness in my stomach loosened as the miles stretched on. Vera's face reflected in the mirror and I found her watching me. I forced a smile and then looked away, feeling exposed for a reason I couldn't even name.

CHAPTER FOUR

Mom agreed to Cambria staying with us way easier than I'd expected. She said having another Hunter my own age around would be a good influence, keep me out of trouble.

Clearly, she didn't know Cambria very well.

But, she did give us permission to go to Fee's the next morning. It shocked me, after the way she'd acted about The Cause before I left, but who was I to argue? I had a feeling her willingness had something to do with Wes's absence. Once he returned, I was sure she'd take up her usual "The Cause is the devil" attitude.

"We'll take my car whenever you're ready," Grandma said, as Cambria and I loaded our breakfast dishes into the dishwasher. I bolted upstairs to dab on lip gloss, hurrying now, and beat everyone back down again.

My mother met me in the foyer, a spray bottle of water in her gardening-gloved hands. "Oh, good, I wanted to speak to you alone," she said.

I followed her into the sunroom. I didn't want to talk. I wanted George. She went to a flat of planters sitting on a table near the window and began spraying them. I stayed near the door. "What's up?"

"You're going to be a senior next year, and it's got me thinking."

My shoulders fell. This didn't sound quick. "About what?"

"I know you think I sent you to Wood Point because I don't trust you, but that's not true. I did it to protect you. I ignored what you are for too long, and now you're suffering the consequences. You aren't trained, and it puts you in danger."

"Jack and Fee were training me, remember?"

"I know that, but you have so much time to make up for. You deserve to learn from the best. Having you so far away has been hard on me too. I just want you safe."

"I know, Mom."

"I think you and I should work on things. Try to find a common ground. I know you think I don't trust your judgment, but I do. I'd like us to start fresh, a clean slate."

"That sounds great."

Her words had been surprisingly accurate. So often my mother would lose herself in running the shop and fail to realize how little credit she gave me for how I handled the responsibility of so much freedom. We'd both kept secrets and lied to the other. Maybe that made us even. "Does our clean slate have anything to do with you letting me go to Fee's?"

"Like I said, I trust your judgment. Or I'm trying to."

"And Wes? Are you going to let me see him?"

Her sunny smile dimmed. "I'm a work in progress."

"Mom …"

"I'm not going to keep you from seeing him. I just wish you'd pick someone … safer."

"You mean someone human."

"I know that's probably unreasonable. I can't explain it to you. Maybe one day you'll have kids and understand. I need you safe, and a Hunter's life isn't ever safe."

"There're no guarantees for anyone."

"I know that. It's just …" Her expression crumpled, turned desperate. She crossed to me and grabbed my hands. "Please don't give me a reason not to trust you, honey. I'd really like it if I didn't have to worry so much."

My heart pricked at her pleading tone. I hadn't lied to her, not exactly, but there were several things I hadn't been entirely forthcoming about, either. George was one such issue. I'd been too afraid she would freak out and bring up moving away like she did the first time I'd been in danger.

"You're going to worry no matter what," I said instead of promising what I couldn't deliver.

"True, but the appliances can only take so much scrubbing." She held up the spray bottle still in her hand. We shared a smile.

Footsteps sounded on the stairs and Cambria joined us. My mother's eyes flickered to the hem on Cambria's shorts—which was short enough that the lining on her pockets stuck out the bottom—and then to Cambria's purple-streaked hair. Cambria had re-dyed it last night. My tub was stained plum to prove it.

"Are we ready?" Cambria asked, oblivious to my mother's scrutiny.

"Let's go," Grandma called from the hall. Cambria and I turned to leave but my mother's voice stopped me.

"I almost forgot, George's mother called for you the other day," she said.

I stiffened, careful to keep my face neutral. "Oh?"

"She asked if you knew any way to get a hold of George. Said she's had a hard time reaching him at that training camp he went to in South Carolina."

"No, I haven't talked to him since he left," I said. Which wasn't a lie. I'd spoken to Fee and Grandma to check on him, but not to George directly.

"Well, if you do, tell him to call his mother."

"I will," I promised, hoping he was well enough to do so.

"All right, kiddos. Let's get going." Grandma came up behind us. She'd applied a fresh layer of rose-colored lipstick. A direct contradiction to the sturdy, leather boots she'd pulled on over her pedal pushers.

"What's the deal with George?" Cambria asked once we were in the car. "I thought you guys broke up."

"We did."

"Then why is his momma calling you for his whereabouts?"

"I've known George a long time. He's the closest thing to family I've got, besides my mom and Grandma."

"Family," Cambria repeated. Her brows shot up, one disappearing into her side-swept bangs.

"Yes, family. Like brother and sister." I emphasized the last part.

"And I'm sure he feels exactly the same about you."

"He does," I said, "although, he may not realize it."

Cambria snorted and said something like "understatement" under her breath. I pretended not to hear. I wasn't going to hash out George's feelings for me when I wasn't even sure what they were. He'd seemed a little friendlier toward Wes after the attack. And by "friendlier" I meant he hadn't tried to use a handshake as a pretense for arm-wrestling him like the day they'd met.

Grandma turned down the narrow back road that led to the gravel drive almost hidden by undergrowth and tree branches. I cracked the window, not enough to combat the AC on full blast, but enough to inhale the scent of sun-heated honeysuckle hanging in the air.

Cambria made a noise like she was choking. "Can't … breathe," she said in a strangled voice, "too much humidity out there. Roll up the window." I held the button until the glass slid up, sealing us in. "Aahh," she said, relaxing against the seat with eyes closed. "How do you manage this? The humidity will kill you here before Werewolves even get the chance."

"Funny," I said.

"Your summers aren't this hot back home?" Grandma asked.

"Summer in Arizona is hot all right, just not so humid. I feel sticky."

"Have you heard anything else about your mom?" I asked. Cambria's expression clouded. I watched her try to blink it away, shrug it off, but it clearly bothered her. "Sorry, I heard you on the phone earlier and—"

"It's fine," she said, staring straight ahead. "I haven't talked to her. The nurse at the center told me a little but only after I sent them ID. Apparently, she fell at work and then blew a .14 in the ambulance. Her boss said she could either do rehab and he'd hold her job, or he'd fire her right then. I'm still surprised she opted for rehab."

"I'm sorry, Cam. How long is she there for?"

She shrugged. "I don't know. A couple of months, I guess. They said she'd call when she could. I gave her your mom's number. Hope that's okay."

"Yeah, that's fine," I said.

I was careful how I responded. This was the most open Cambria had been about her personal life since that day she'd first introduced me to the cave in the woods behind Wood Point—the perfect place to yell out my frustrations.

"I don't mean to interrupt, but we're pulling up and I just want to remind everyone here that you're going to feel the presence of Werewolves and not to panic." She eyed Cambria in the rearview. "Especially you. I know you're not used to feeling a Werewolf unless you're trying to kill it, but we're all friends here."

"I promise I won't attack anything, two legs or four," Cambria said.

"Atta girl."

Grandma turned onto the familiar gravel drive and a lump wedged itself in my chest. I wasn't sure whether I was sad knowing Wes was absent or overwhelmingly happy at being back. This place already felt more like home than my mother's. That should've been disappointing on some level, but it wasn't.

The Hummer rolled to a stop and we got out. I shaded my hand against the sun and looked up at the worn siding and peeling shutters. Fee's house looked exactly the same. It was at once both comforting and heartbreaking. Something about going back to the place where it all started and seeing it so unchanged when I was anything *but* made me want to break down.

"Whose truck?" Cambria asked, gesturing to the other vehicle in the yard.

"Jack's," I said.

"I thought you said Jack went with Wes."

"He did. They took Wes's car."

"They? Oh, right, Cord tagged along."

The name sent a shot of unease through me. I didn't love the idea of Cord—a gorgeous blond Hunter with a bad attitude and killer knife skills—on a cross-country road trip with my boyfriend, but it was better than having her here, making snarky remarks in response to my every move. And I knew any feelings Wes had for her were brotherly. Besides, Cord and I could use a break from each other. After being roommates for a few weeks at Wood Point—a role she did not volunteer for but rather had been sent by Wes as my protection from Miles—I was surprised our time hadn't resulted in injury for either party.

Cord had done more than just babysit me, though. She'd killed Miles. I still found it bothersome that she'd done it even after he'd already surrendered, but Cord had a lot of anger inside her. It wasn't fun knowing she directed a lot of it at me.

The front door opened before we reached it. Goosebumps slammed into me and I faltered. I'd almost forgotten what it felt like to have my body warn me of a nearby Werewolf. I smiled despite the discomfort and slid into Fee's waiting arms. She held me close, smoothing my hair. The scent of cookies clung to her, but underneath that: wolf.

"Tara, so glad you're home. We've missed you so much," she said as she released me.

"I missed you too. I'm glad to be back. You remember Cambria."

Fee put her hand out. Cambria's shoulders were stiff, and she smiled like she was on autopilot, but she shook Fee's hand. "Nice to see you again," Cambria said.

"And you," said Fee. "I hope we'll have time to get to know each other better over the summer. We're happy to know Tara's friends. Especially when they're as loyal as you are." She smiled bright enough that Cambria relaxed beside me.

"Thanks," Cambria said.

"Edie, Vera was asking for you earlier," Fee said as we filed inside. "She's in the library now."

"Then that's where I'll be if you need me." Grandma disappeared down the narrow hallway.

I stood just inside the front door and let my eyes soak up the richness of the cherry finish on the walls and floors. Everything glowed brown-red just as I remembered. Heat emanated from the kitchen, the air thick with the aroma of warm dough.

"Smells good," I said, wandering toward the kitchen. I stepped through the doorway and stopped. The counters were covered with sheets and sheets of all sorts of baked goods. Cookies, brownies, cakes, and pastries I couldn't name covered the countertops all the way around the room. The center island was taken up by mixing bowls, empty egg cartons, and an electric mixer. Flour dusted the floor.

"I've been stressed," Fee said, a sheepish smile on her face.

"Holy crumpets," Cambria breathed.

"Would you like to try some?" Fee asked. "I'd hate to let it go to waste."

"Would I …?" Cambria trailed off, looking around with wide eyes. I couldn't help but laugh.

"You just made her day," I told Fee. "Her favorite food group is dessert. You better get her a jug of milk."

Fee headed straight for the fridge. "Coming right up. In the meantime, George is upstairs in your old room if you want to go say hi."

"Thanks." I shot her a grateful look, but she was already bent over a cake, cutting a hefty slice for Cambria.

I hurried up the stairs, stopping outside the door and leaning against the wall. Grandma and Fee had said to be prepared for a different George, that he'd be tired and weak from the treatment Fee gave him to slow the change. Every time I called, he was either sleeping or too sick to come to the phone. I had no idea what to expect.

I took a deep breath and knocked softly.

"Come in."

I turned the knob and pushed the door back. George lay under a pile of blankets, obscured from sight. He lifted his head a little and smiled at me before falling back against the pillow. I hovered in the doorway, shocked by the changes in him, despite Grandma's warning.

"Tay, finally," he said. His voice was small, nothing like the old George. He didn't sit up again.

"George?" I wandered closer, slowly, biting back the surprise. I lowered myself to the edge of the bed and stared down at him.

His eyes were ringed with dark circles, purple bruises that extended up over his eyelids. It was more than lack of sleep; his sockets were hollowed out and his cheeks gaunt. His lips were chapped and his skin flushed pink. I put a hand to his forehead. Heat radiated from his skin.

"I'm here," I said. "How are you?"

"Okay." His eyes were glassy. We both knew he was lying.

"What's happening?" I asked.

"My body—" he began then stopped as a coughing fit seized him. It didn't let up for several moments. He pointed to the empty glass next to a pitcher of water on the nightstand and I jumped up, thankful for something to do. I filled the glass and handed it to him, then raised it to his lips when his hands shook too much to hold it without spilling. He managed a small swallow between coughs and then fell back. Finally, he quieted.

"My body," he said again, "started to change a couple of weeks ago. Fee said it was the new moon cycle. I shifted about halfway and then something got stuck and it stopped. Threw out my back and cracked a couple of ribs. Fee managed to reverse the damage, and put some sort of block on me so I won't shift again. But the block is making me sick." He coughed again and I tensed, worried it would be another episode like the first, but it subsided. "I'm glad you're here."

"Me too. I'm sorry it took so long, but we're going to figure this out. You just need to hold on a little longer. Can I get you anything?" I took his hand in mine and held it lightly, afraid too much pressure would hurt him even worse.

"No, I'm all right. Fee's taking good care of me." He smiled. "She's pretty awesome."

"She is, isn't she?"

"Fee told me some stuff. About Miles. And his dad, your uncle Leo. She said you killed Leo by yourself in that warehouse. It sounded really brave."

"It wasn't nearly as premeditated as it sounds, believe me. Mostly blind luck."

"You don't give yourself enough credit, Tay. You protect humans from Werewolves. You're amazing. Besides, it explains a lot. Finding out about your past and who you really are, that had to be tough. Not to mention the little bit of family you found turned out to be crazy and now dead. And I didn't make it any easier. I'm sorry about everything."

"You don't need to apologize. That's all in the past. Focus on staying strong, on fighting this."

"I'm trying, Tay, really, but I'm tired." As if to prove it, his eyelids drooped. It scared me and I squeezed his hand. His lids fluttered open again. "Can I ask you something?"

"What is it?" I asked.

"If I become a Werewolf, especially the monster kind that Fee says I might, will you have to kill me?"

"Absolutely not going to happen," I said.

"But if it does."

"No. I'm not going to let that happen. I would never hurt you. You're my family too, you know."

His eyes closed again. His mouth turned up at the corners and he squeezed my hand lightly. "I'm glad you're back, Tay," he said. "It feels better with you here."

"Good, because I'm staying close until we figure this out. I won't let anything happen, I promise."

"I know you won't."

George's breathing slowed and became even. I watched the steady rise and fall of his chest while my own heart hammered. I didn't love George, at least not the way I'd thought I did a year ago, but my feelings for him as a friend were deep, immovable. I wasn't willing to lose him. Not when we'd just begun to fix our friendship. I'd do anything to keep him alive.

"You're worrying. I can feel it." I jumped at the sound of his voice. His hand tightened in mine and his mouth twitched at the corners. He cracked an eye. "See?"

"Just trying to figure out a way to stop this," I said, gesturing at him with my free hand.

His expression turned serious. "I don't think we can stop it. We've slowed it, but that might be all we can do. I'm okay with that."

"You can't be okay with that. You'll die."

"I've had time to think about the possibility. I've accepted it, if it means not becoming a monster." He waited a beat and then said, "Maybe you should accept it too."

"No."

"Tay—"

"I'll give you my blood before that happens. Miles said—"

"No way." He shook his head. "Fee told me enough about Miles to know that's crazy. *He* was crazy. We can't trust him."

"I'm not going to let you die," I said. Tears sprang to my eyes, and I blinked them back.

His expression softened. "Come here."

I leaned down into his open arms and curled against his side. Heat issued through the blankets. My tears thickened. I pressed my face against his ribs and let them come.

"Please don't cry."

"I can't help it. It's my fault. If I'd just killed Miles in that warehouse, this never would've happened."

"It's not your fault. You're not responsible for another person's actions. And you didn't kill Miles because you're not a killer. It's not who you are."

George had no idea. Maybe it hadn't been premeditated, but I was a killer. Starting with Liliana the night George and I broke up and ending with the massacre of hybrids at school last month. I'd seen the carnage. I knew what I was capable of, even if no one else suspected.

I sniffled harder.

George pulled me close and kissed the top of my head. I tensed. "I'm really glad we're friends again," I said pointedly.

"Me too," he said and the conviction in his voice put me at ease. "I know we've had a rocky few months. It's nice to have my best friend back."

We lay in silence for a while after that. I let myself enjoy the steady rhythm of George's breathing as my mind wandered to possible solutions. The problem was I knew so little about Werewolves and what made them that I had no idea where to begin to look for a cure.

He shifted his head toward me and began humming. The notes were scratchy and flat but I recognized the tune instantly. Even when we'd dated, our song had been a secret—for George's sake. The song's significance stemmed from a home video of George has a toddler, singing the hit at the top of his lungs and using a broom as a guitar. Besides his family, I was the only other person to ever witness the tape. A visual I'd sworn to take to the grave. The song had been a joke before becoming something special between us.

A small smile crept over me at the memory and I added Bon Jovi's words. "It's been raining since you left me. Now I'm drowning in the flood. You see, I've always been a fighter, but without you I give up. Now I can't sing a love song, like the way it's meant to be. Well, I guess I'm not that good anymore but baby, that's just me …"

The knob turned and the door opened. I looked up to find an unexpected figure in the doorway. The bass in his voice echoed against the walls as he belted out the next line. "And I will love you, baby. Always. And I'll be there forever and a day. Alwaaayyyys."

When he finished, Wes leaned heavily against the left frame, leather-clad arms crossed over his chest. He looked at me and his brows shot up. "Not exactly how I expected to find my girl, in bed with her ex."

"Wes!" I jumped clear of the bed and smoothed my clothes, at once mortified and elated. I opened my mouth to say something else but words failed me. I was still lost in the sound of his voice … singing. I'd never heard him sing before. Hadn't known he could, but *wow*.

"Hey, Wes," George called.

"George. I see Tara's taking good care of you."

George smirked. "She's doing her best."

I ignored the innuendo and flexing of metaphorical muscles and launched myself at Wes. He caught me without missing a step. My feet lifted off the floor as his arms squeezed and held. I pressed myself against him, melding our bodies together and inhaling the crisp leather scent of his jacket mixed with the woodsy smell that always clung to him like a second skin.

"I missed you," he said against my ear.

Something cold and empty inside me filled up on his words. "I missed you too," I whispered back.

Finally, and grudgingly, I let him release me. I stared up at him, too excited to make sense of his presence. "What are you doing here? I thought you wouldn't be back for another few days."

"You're here. I couldn't stay away." He glanced at George, then back at me. "You want to take a walk?"

I nodded and let him lead me from the room. Before the door closed, I turned back to George. "I'll check on you later. Get some sleep," I said.

George sent me a mock-salute and the door clicked shut.

"Keeping the patient happy, huh?" Wes asked when we were alone in the hallway.

I fumbled for a response, feeling guilty despite the innocent circumstances. "George and I are just friends now, I swear."

"Relax." He held up a hand. "I know."

"Yeah, but it's not what you think for him, either."

"I said *I know*." He pointed to his temple, cocked his head meaningfully. "Today's the full moon. You don't have to explain anything to me, at least not out loud."

"Oh." Understanding dawned. Wes had a special gift that allowed him to manipulate—and sometimes even remove—a person's memories or thoughts. On a full moon, his gift magnified and he could read minds. Including mine. He'd failed to mention that fact on the last full moon, which led to him picking up on the fact that Alex had kissed me and I hadn't stopped it. It had been the cause for our first real fight.

"I wanted to say that before we go any further. You can tell me to leave if you want, and I'll come back tomorrow."

"No, it's fine. Stay."

"Are you sure? I don't want you to think I'm eavesdropping."

"You're not. Well, you are, but I'm okay with it." I stepped closer.

Our bodies pressed together in the narrow hall. "I want to be with you."

He looked relieved. "I want to be with you too. Now that it's settled, I need to do one more thing before we go further."

"What?"

He bent his head and pressed his lips to mine so quickly I barely had a chance to pucker. The shock lasted for a split second and then I was kissing him back and our arms tangled around each other, exploring and clinging and making up for lost time.

"Better than I remembered," he said when our mouths parted.

I sighed in answer, drinking in the closeness of his scent. It dawned on me that he could hear my thoughts, my happiness at just being here in this moment. "Are you getting this?" I murmured against his chest.

"Loud and clear."

Footsteps thumped up the stairs. Cambria appeared, licking frosting off her fingers. Her eyes widened at the sight of us, each with arms woven tightly around the other. "Oops. I was just coming to check on George."

"He's sleeping," said Wes.

"How do you know?" I asked. "Oh, right."

"Did I miss something?" Cambria looked back and forth between us.

"Today's a full moon," I told her.

She rounded on Wes, eyes wide. "You can read my mind right now?"

"Whether I like it or not."

She put a hand on her lace-clad hip. "What am I thinking right now?"

Wes burst out laughing and shook his head. "No way, I am not saying that one out loud."

Cambria grinned at me. "I believe him."

I sent them both a look and then decided I didn't want to know. "We're going to get some air," I said to Cambria. "You want to come?"

"Ugh, you mean outside? In the crushing humidity that strangles and chokes while it sucks all hydration from inside your body and then hangs it over you like a wet curtain?" She sighed. "Then again, I've eaten more pastries than the Queen of England. I should probably walk some of it off."

"That's the spirit," I said.

We stepped out the back door and started across the yard, headed for the shade of the woods. Halfway across, I was already sweating.

"You want to go back inside?" Wes asked, his brows knitted in concern.

"No, I'm fine." *I'd love a cold pool of water to sink into right now, though.*

"With clothes, or without?" he whispered in my ear.

I grinned and poked him in the ribs. *Just testing how well the connection works.*

"Crystal clear," he said. There was a decidedly mischievous look in his eyes.

"Are you guys having a telepathic convo?" Cambria demanded. "I feel like I missed something."

I linked her arm in mine as we neared the woods. "*You* miss something? Not possible." Movement caught my eye just as my goosebumps—which had dimmed to a comfortable zing while inside—intensified.

"Wes," Derek called as he jogged across the yard. He clasped Wes's hand and then pulled him in for a one-armed hug. Over Wes's shoulder, he sent me a cursory nod. "Hey, Tara."

"Hi." I kept it short and polite. Derek hadn't given me reason to think he disliked me, but he hadn't given me any reason to think he *did* like me, either. I wasn't sure where he stood. It made me nervous around him.

"I saw Cord out front," he said, his attention back on Wes. He grinned. "She's already bitching about Fee letting the grass get too long."

"Bitching makes her feel at home," Wes said. "You know that."

"You don't have to tell me." His gaze wandered to Cambria and lingered.

"This is Cambria, Tara's friend from school," Wes said.

Derek extended a suntanned hand. Cambria took it slowly. "Nice to meet you," he told her in a distinctly deeper voice.

"Nice to meet you too," Cambria said softly.

Beside me, Wes shook in silent laughter. "Uh, you want to walk with us?" he asked Derek.

"Sure," Derek said, falling into step beside Wes. I hung back with Cambria and listened to them talk. "How'd the hunt go? Cord wouldn't say much, just acted all pissed off that she didn't get to kill anything."

"We didn't have much luck," Wes said. "Every trail we found was a dead end."

Derek rubbed his jaw and the little bit of stubble he had there. "They don't want to be found."

"Yeah, but the human-hybrids aren't smart enough to hide themselves this well."

"You think someone is helping them?"

"Maybe. Either way, we're going to need help if we want to keep looking. We can't afford to waste any more time on these wild chases."

"What do you mean 'if we want to keep looking?'" I increased my pace until I matched Wes and Derek. "We can't stop. You know what will happen."

"I know," said Wes. "I didn't mean we should give up. We just need to figure out another approach." He took my hand, his thumb rubbing soothing circles against my palm.

"God, it's hot out here," Cambria said, pulling her shirt away from her body in disgust.

And it was. Even under the shady canopy of the forest, the humidity penetrated. Derek and Wes shared a look. "You thinking what I'm thinking?" Derek asked.

"Dude, full moon. I'm *hearing* what you're thinking."

"Point taken."

"What are we thinking?" Cambria asked.

"Swimming," the boys said in unison.

Wes and Derek led the way. It wasn't long before the trees thinned and a lake shone through the leaves. The water was brackish but not swampy. Most importantly, it had to be cooler than the air.

"Water never looked so good," I said, pulling my shirt away from my sticky skin. I started to take it off and then changed my mind. If it had been only Wes, maybe, but not in front of Cambria and Derek.

Cambria hesitated. "Do you think there're snakes in there? I do not swim with reptiles."

I pulled on her arm until she inched forward. "Who cares? It's a thousand degrees outside. Besides, you take down Werewolves. What's one little snake?"

"Snakes are way scarier than Werewolves," she said.

I rolled my eyes and gave her a crooked smile. "Race you."

She eyed me and began pulling off her shoes. I did the same, tensing, waiting for her to bolt. I knew Cambria. She couldn't resist a challenge. We finished pulling off our shoes at the same time. Cambria's lips curved up. "Last one there

We took off running. Behind me, Wes and Derek laughed. I reached the bank and dove in head first. The second I plunged into the cool water, my whole body relaxed. Cambria surfaced beside me, grinning.

"Who won?" she yelled to the boys on the bank.

"It was a tie," Wes called.

He and Derek pulled off their shoes. I waited for them to get in, but they kept walking, dodging roots and branches as they skirted the edge.

"Where are you going?" I called.

"You'll see," Wes said.

I spotted the rope just as Derek reached the tree and began to climb. Someone had nailed pieces of wood to the thick trunk, creating a makeshift ladder. Derek scaled it easily and made his way onto a branch that overhung the lake. He inched forward and grabbed the rope, pulling it back until his feet reached the edge, and then launched himself out over the water. He swung wide and then released, falling with a splash just a few feet from where Cambria and I treaded water.

I turned my head to keep the water from splashing in my eyes. Cambria shrieked and flailed to get out of the line of fire. I'd just finished wiping the water from my face when another body dropped, this time closer to me. I tried to get away, but Wes surfaced and grabbed my leg, grinning madly.

"Where do you think you're going?" he said.

I splashed him and spun away, shrieking when he gave chase. Cambria twisted under Derek's grip on her wrist, frantically trying to swim away. Each time she tried, Derek twisted her back and sent her a face full of water so she couldn't keep her eyes open.

"Can the sight of cliché flirting make you sick, Bailey?" Cord's voice rang out over the lake, dripping with sarcasm.

"Glad you could join us," Wes said.

Cord ignored him. "I'm serious, Bailey. Are you nauseated or is it just me?"

"It's just you," Bailey said cheerfully. He stood beside Cord, his wiry frame way too tall for his fifteen years, especially since his open smile always made him look even younger than that. "Hi, Tara," he called.

"Hey." I waved.

He nodded at Wes from underneath a mop of blond hair that he'd apparently grown out over the spring. "Glad you're back, even if you did bring *her* with you." He jerked a thumb at Cord and rolled his eyes.

"Take the good with the bad, I guess," Derek said.

"You boys are hilarious." Cord stood with hands on her hips, staring disgustedly at the briny water. Bailey peeled his shirt off and moved toward the lake's edge.

"You coming in, Cord?" Wes asked.

"No, thanks. I'll take the choking humidity over the shameless flirting."

"I see," said Wes, a glint in his eye. "Bailey, if you would?"

Bailey grimaced. "You know I'm taking my life into my hands."

"I'll protect you," Wes said.

Derek chuckled. "No offense, but my money's on her."

Bailey crept up behind Cord and grabbed her just as she realized his intention. I clamped my hand over my mouth and waited for her wild swings to connect with Bailey's face. Somehow, he managed to get her into the water. When it reached knee-deep, he let go and Cord fell under. She came up sputtering, her hair falling in strings against her face. She glared at Bailey with an expression I'd only ever seen directed at me—and Miles. Bailey was already running for the rope swing.

Cord let out a growl that could've rivaled a Werewolf and took off after him. Wes and Derek high-fived.

"She's going to kill him," I said, horrified.

"Nah, she's harmless. Watch," Derek said.

Bailey swung out and splashed down just as Cord reached the tree limb. She didn't waste time with the rope. Instead, she ran to the end and launched herself out over the water, doing a perfect dive and coming up inches from Bailey.

He tried swimming away, but Cord caught him around the ankle and yanked him back. He was pulled under—only his arms could be seen above the surface, flailing in a blind attempt to grab Cord.

She yanked him to the surface and scowled at him. "Give up! Say you're sorry," she demanded.

"Never," Bailey sputtered, half laughing, half coughing.

"Then suffer the consequences," she said as she dunked him again.

Derek shook his head, swimming toward them. "Pick on someone your own size," he said. He jumped and pressed down on Cord's head, taking them both underwater. She came up sputtering and … laughing?

"Twilight zone, right?" Wes's voice in my ear was an echo of the thought in my head.

"Exactly," I said. "Why isn't she trying to murder them?"

He shrugged. "They're family."

And for them, it was that simple. It didn't matter that Cord was a Hunter and the boys were Werewolves. Just like with George and I, being family had nothing to do with DNA.

"How did you guys meet, anyway?" Cambria asked, coming up beside me.

"Derek and Cord met in foster care," Wes explained. "They lived with the same family for about eight months or so. Then Derek was sent back to the orphanage and met Bailey. He kept in touch with Cord and the three of them became peas in a pod."

"How'd they end up here?"

"Bailey got into a fight in school and almost shifted. Foster care isn't a great place to grow up, anyway, and Cord found out about The Cause and Jack and Fee living here, so they showed up one day a few years ago and never left.

"Bailey was pretty quiet and shy when Cord first started bringing him around. He's opened up a lot now, become pretty independent, but I think he looks up to Cord like a mother. And she's just as protective of him as a mom would be, so it fits."

Cambria lifted a brow. "I have a hard time picturing Cord protecting anything but herself."

"Cord's not all bad. You have to let her warm up to you," Wes said.

"Right. Warm up to me." I shook my head. "That would be like melting the polar ice cap with a space heater."

Wes laughed. In a lightning move, he grabbed me again and yanked me under. I came up clinging to what I thought was his ankle. It wasn't.

"Ow, what the …?" Cambria yanked free and glared at me. I splashed her and Wes in one move.

Our scuffle spilled over into Derek and Bailey's war with Cord and soon it was a blur of splashing and shrieks.

Wes and I ended up near the far bank. My ribs ached from laughing. My chest heaved with the effort of breathing and swimming and defending myself from his attempts to dunk me.

"Give up," I said, ducking out from under his hold and twisting his arm behind his back.

"Never." He whirled, freeing his arm and pulling me against him. I stared at his bare chest, dripping and smooth, against my wet shirt. The playfulness vanished.

Behind me, I could hear the splashing and yells from the rest of the group as each one tried dunking the other, but it sounded faint. I couldn't focus on any of it. Something about the way Wes stared down at me made me tremble.

"I missed you," he said in a low voice. I shivered, though not from cold. I wanted to press harder against his chest, wrap my arms around his neck. I tightened my grip on his arms, waiting for him to read it in my head so I wouldn't have to say it out loud.

"Let's take a walk." His voice was hoarse.

I let him pull me up the bank. No one seemed to notice our exit. The sounds of splashing water and squealing laughter faded as the trees closed in around us. When we were out of sight, Wes spun and encircled me with his arms. Despite the droplets that clung to him, his skin warmed my fingertips as I ran my hands up his shoulders and around his neck. He pulled me tight against him and lowered his head so our foreheads touched.

"Is this how you pictured it?" he whispered.

"Almost. You're not kissing me yet," I whispered back.

"Fixing that in 3 . . . 2 . . . 1."

His kiss was gentle at first, but I pressed back, wanting more. The pull I often felt when he was near urged me on, not that I needed any extra push. My hands tangled in his hair. More. I needed more. He pulled me hard enough against him that my feet left the ground, and then he kissed me back just as hard, just as desperately.

We broke apart, gasping for air. Wes's eyes were wide. "Where did that come from?"

"I don't know." My face heated as I realized what sort of mental images he'd picked out of my head. "Sorry."

He shook his head. "Don't apologize. Is it—? Um, I mean, do you always think like that about me?"

I didn't know whether to laugh or be thoroughly mortified. "No," I said. "Well, maybe. Not usually so, uh, vivid, I guess." I shrugged, trying to brush it off. "I've missed you."

A smile played at the corners of his mouth. "I missed you too, but if it's like that, maybe I should go away more often."

I swatted him, but not before his comment incited another mental image. One that involved very little clothing. The backdrop distinctly resembled our current location. "I don't know about this mind-reading thing," I grumbled.

He laughed. "Fine, let's talk about something else. How was school?"

I hesitated, unsure whether he meant actual school or something more, like a certain trainer he wasn't fond of.

"I just mean school."

"I passed my classes," I said. "For now. No small thing considering some of the last-minute papers and quizzes Professor Hugo had me do. That guy has it out for me, I think."

"And Alex?" he asked. He turned to face me, looking guilty. "I'm sorry, but I picked up on something when you thought of him. You seem worried about him. Is everything okay?"

I eyed him, brows raised. "You don't care about him enough to want to know."

"You're right, I don't care about him, but I care about you, and if something bothers you, I want to know about it."

I sighed. Wes was the last person I wanted to vent to about this, but I needed to talk about it. And he would understand at least most of my reasons for worrying. "Alex got accepted for one of the special teams they've assigned to hunt the hybrids."

Wes didn't answer right away. I imagined he was reading all of the worried emotion that was bouncing around inside me right now. Images I'd concocted of Alex killing hybrids—some of them with familiar faces—along with images of the hybrids attacking and hurting him in return.

"Did you think he would do anything else?" he asked quietly.

My temper flared, but then I realized he was right. "I guess not. He's a Hunter and he hates Werewolves more than anyone I've ever met, but—" I broke off, not wanting to voice the last part.

"But you thought he'd be different after getting to know you," he finished.

I scowled. Stupid mind-reading thing. "Something like that." The ache that had lodged in my chest since the night of the dance, a pain that had eased since seeing Wes, flared up again, leaving a small hole in my heart. It happened so fast, I couldn't bury it. Wes's expression remained neutral, but I knew he'd sensed the truth: I missed Alex.

"I think you're wrong about one thing, though," he said quietly. "He's different for having met you."

My heart leaped into my throat before I could stop it. "You read that? In his mind?"

"I didn't have to. No one who's ever gotten to know you is the same person afterward. I know I'm not. My entire life changed when I met you, and not because you're a dirty blood. It's because of who you are inside. It's because you're amazing, and surprising, and you challenge me every day. In a good way," he added, seeing my expression. "You're strong, and fun, and unpredictable, and I'm sure he thinks the same. How could he not?"

The worry still lingered, of how Alex's choice would alter our friendship, but I pushed it to the back of my thoughts and concentrated on the moment. "Thank you," I said. "You're not so bad yourself."

A smile spread slowly across his face as his mouth dipped lower to mine. Our lips met and the earlier fire reignited. The fire burned brighter and hotter than before. I had to restrain myself from pulling him down to the ground right where we stood. He shivered as I brushed my fingers over his ribs, which only made me hungrier. A sound erupted from deep in my throat. I didn't recognize it as my voice until Wes pulled away and stared at me.

"What was that?" he asked.

"Um …" Now that the steamy haze had cleared, I had a pretty good idea, though I couldn't bring myself to admit it.

He leaned down and sniffed my hair, then pulled back abruptly. "You smell like wolf," he hissed. He looked around, as if expecting to see someone lurking, and then bent closer. "Has it happened again? You said you would tell me if it happened again."

His hands were like a vise around my shoulders. I set my jaw. Deliberately, I conjured images of us kissing, arms wrapped around each other.

"Don't try to change the subject."

Under other circumstances, I would've laughed at that. Instead, I rubbed my hands over my face. "It hasn't happened again," I assured him. "Not completely. There was an incident coming home from school, but it was nothing."

"What sort of 'incident'?" I let my mind replay the images of what happened at the gas station. It was easier than trying to explain it with words. "Geez, Tara, it almost happened," he said when I'd finished.

"But it didn't." I crossed my arms. "I'm not even convinced it happened the first time." Okay, that was a lie.

He glared at me. "I saw it, Tara. You were a wolf. Or, sort of a wolf. You were this in-between thing, like your body didn't know how to get there all the way, but you were definitely trying to shift when you killed those hybrids."

"I wish I remembered." I stepped away, needing some distance to clear my head. I hated thinking about the killing I'd done, even if I didn't remember it. And I hated not being in control of whatever was happening to me.

"I think you should talk to Fee about it, see if she can help you."

"Help stop it, you mean?" I shook my head. "If it's true, and I really am shifting, there's nothing that will stop it. And I'm not going to take one of her concoctions to slow it. Look at what it's doing to George."

"George's case is different. You have Werewolf blood in you already, though I didn't think it meant you'd ever shift. It's not like there's a precedent."

"It's not so different," I shot back. "He's becoming a monster. I already am one."

"Tara, you are not a monster. You were protecting me. You can't blame yourself. Besides, those things are dangerous."

"They could've been saved. We didn't even give them a chance."

"They had no humanity in them. They were trying to kill us."

"What about the rest of them? The ones who still have their humanity? They deserve a chance to choose a side."

He used his finger to squeeze the bridge of his nose. "We have to find them first. So far, it looks like they don't want to be found."

"Why does it seem like you're arguing with me?"

"I'm not arguing with you, I'm pointing out the facts."

"Yeah, but everything I say, you're telling me why it won't work, or it's a bad idea, or I shouldn't think that way."

He sighed and ran a hand through his hair. It was a gesture he only used when he was stressed. "Tara, like it or not, I've got a responsibility here now. Even with Jack on the mend, I'm still in a place of power within The Cause. I'm still partly in charge. I can't just go traipsing all over the place looking for something that doesn't want to be found. I've got people here who are counting on me."

"Like me," I said quietly. "I was counting on you to see it from my side. Was I wrong?"

"No, you're not wrong." He stepped toward me. I stepped back. I didn't want to make it worse, but if I let him touch me, I'd give in, let it go. And this was too important to let go of.

"The council is searching to kill them," I said. "No questions asked, no chance for forgiveness or even justice. They don't deserve that. No one deserves that. We're the only ones who can help them. I thought you of all people would understand what it means to be an outcast just because of what's in your DNA."

Wes blinked. I'd hit low. He swallowed, waiting a beat before answering. Silently, I asked him not to be mad, to understand how strongly I believed in this. How helpless I felt—about everything.

"I get it," he said finally. His voice held more defeat than anger. "But Jack says we can't keep searching blindly. We need a solid lead."

I nodded, knowing that was the best I'd get, and it would have to be enough. For now, it was, if it meant I had him here with me. There was still George to deal with. "So we'll get a lead."

He stepped closer again. This time I let him come. His arms pulled me to him. I stood with my cheek pressed against his chest, my thoughts tangled together before settling on George again.

"We'll figure something out," Wes said, picking up on it.

"Like what? Fee's already said she can't hold off the change forever." I was dangerously close to tears. Even though they were mainly out of frustration, I still refused to let them fall.

"Then we'll find a cure."

"For being a Werewolf? There's no cure for that."

"For being a monster. There's got to be a way to help him retain … himself when the change comes."

"I keep thinking about what Miles said, about giving him my blood. It might be the only way."

"No, Tara." He pulled away, far enough to look down at me. "You can't trust Miles. He was a liar, a con artist. It's too dangerous unless we know the true side effects."

"I know. I wanted to find that Astor guy he mentioned. Grandma said he's crazy. Some sort of mad scientist and I should stay away. She wouldn't say much else about him."

"Hmm." Wes frowned, his gaze far away. "I can ask Jack about him and see what I can find out." He paused and then added, "I'm on your side, you know. I can tell you think I'm being bossy or 'by the book' or whatever, but I want you to know that first and always, I am on your side."

"What about your responsibility? To Jack and the rest of them?"

"You come first," he said, his tone firm and final. "No more secrets, remember?"

"I remember."

"Good. I'll talk to Jack, see if I can get any more information." He caught my chin between his fingers and thumb. The intensity of his gaze, the emotion behind it, caught me off guard. "We'll do this together, deal?"

I shivered. "Deal."

I let out a breath. Some of the worry went with it. Together. We'd figure this out together.

CHAPTER FIVE

A few minutes later we made our way back to the lake. We didn't get far before the sound of raised voices and footsteps reached us. Goosebumps spidered up my arms, across my shoulders. I spotted Cambria first, her wet clothes pasted to her skin. She was wringing out her hair and laughing at something Derek said. Cord and Bailey were right behind them, shoving each other. As they reached us, Cord reached over and locked her arm around Bailey's neck. She pulled his head down and rubbed her knuckles over his scalp.

"That'll teach you to mess with a Hunter," she said.

I stared. It always took me off guard that a genuine smile could transform her features into something so friendly and open. She was beautiful when she was being nice. She released Bailey and met my eyes—and scowled. Derek broke off whatever he was telling Cambria and looked up as we approached. Wes cleared his throat, one brow arched upward. I wondered what sort of thoughts he was picking up from them.

"Oh, hey," Cambria said to me.

"Hey yourself," I returned. "Feeling a little cooler now?"

She shrugged. "It'll last until we leave the cover of the woods.

Then I'll probably burst into flames." Derek threw Wes his shirt. He caught it in the air and draped it over his shoulder. I took my shoes from Bailey and slipped them on.

"You guys finished trying to drown each other?" Wes said, clapping Bailey on the back as we fell into step.

"For now. You guys finished making out?" Bailey shot back.

"For now," Wes echoed. Bailey rolled his eyes.

Again, goosebumps rose along my arms—this time with a forceful tremor.

I shuddered with the intensity of the warning, and spun out from under Wes's arm, searching the forest. Had Fee come looking for us? No way would my goosebumps be this strong from only her. Not even her and Jack.

"You guys …" I began and then let it hang. The others were already fanning out. I met Wes's eyes and he nodded once before glancing away again, toward the trees. I took another step away. I knew what it meant. The moment we spotted anything resembling a Werewolf, he, Derek, and Bailey would shift.

My eyes scanned for movement. The goosebumps intensified until the hairs on my arms and neck stood so straight it stung. I caught a glimpse of movement; a spot of brown fur darting among the trees.

"Shit." Cord's curse came from my left flank. She'd moved closer, a defensive tactic.

"Agreed," I said without turning. Whoever this was, the fact that they hadn't announced themselves yet couldn't be good. More fur, more movement. All of it bearing down on us.

"Baby Jesus, there must be two dozen of them," Cambria breathed from behind me. I glanced over. She was scared but holding it together. Derek was nearby. His eyes met mine, then flicked to Wes.

"Come here," I said in a low voice, motioning for Cambria to come closer.

Behind her, Derek shifted. I didn't have to turn to know Wes and Bailey were doing the same. Cambria's eyes widened at something over my shoulder. I heard the sound of ripping fabric.

"Wes and Bailey just shifted," she said, still staring.

"I know."

Her head tilted to one side, her expression thoughtful. "Bet they lose a lot of clothes that way."

I smiled crookedly in spite of the tension.

A growl sounded from behind me. Wes. Werewolves—lots of them—had come into view and positioned themselves in a circle. We were surrounded. I swallowed hard. The surrounded part didn't bother me nearly as much as their appearance up close.

"Check out their eyes," Cambria whispered.

"Hybrids." I stared into their yellow eyes, pumping my fists open and closed to keep my hands from shaking. What if it happened again? Right here in front of my friends, what if I shifted into a monster?

"What do you want?" Wes called out, his words only half discernible through the growl that coated them.

A mangy wolf the color of mud stepped up, eyeing Wes, then me. There was something familiar about him. "We want the girl," it said.

"Is he talking about Tara?" Bailey asked Wes. He'd scooted closer, so the two stood shoulder to shoulder. Bailey always itched for action. More often than not, he was made to sit out. I could imagine the amount of adrenaline flowing through his animal veins right now. His vanilla-colored coat bunched and tensed with coiled muscles. Beside him, Wes was rigid.

"What do you want with Tara?" Wes asked.

"Justice. Revenge." Its shoulders rippled. I couldn't tell if it was a shrug or anticipation.

"You're here to avenge Miles?" Wes asked. He shook his head. Disbelief and disgust colored his voice. "He was using you. He didn't care about you before and now he's gone. Not coming back. Let it go. You still have a choice. You can choose to join us and save yourself from CHAS."

The wolf's eyes flickered at that. Had he been a Hunter before Miles changed him? Maybe that's why he seemed familiar. "We are not afraid of CHAS. Let them come." His eyes settled on me again. I shivered. "Last chance to give up the girl."

"Did Miles order this? If something happened to him, you all come after her?"

"We do not take orders from Miles." The last word dragged out, becoming a snarl. A whine went up with the other wolves. Paws stomped and scraped at the ground.

"You can't have Tara," Wes growled back, "but you're welcome to try."

He was answered by a short howl from the leader. The rest chimed in, pawing the dirt, inching forward.

"We don't even have weapons," Cambria hissed.

She was right. My hands were achingly empty. If I had nothing to use against them, maybe shifting wasn't such a bad idea. It had worked the first time. But then, there weren't any witnesses left besides Wes when I was done. I held back a shudder. What if I hurt my friends?

"Here!"

At the sound of Cord's voice, I turned just in time to grab the branch hurtling toward my head. Another was right behind it. I snagged that one and handed it off to Cambria.

"We do now," I said.

Cambria twirled the branch in her hand, adjusting her grip, testing the weight. She didn't even blink as she shifted into a crouch, branch at the ready. The confusion at being caught off guard disappeared. In its place was fierce determination. She'd transformed to a Hunter, trained and ready to face Werewolves. I tried to channel the same thing as the hybrids slowly advanced.

"Last chance to give up the girl, and we'll let you live," said the pack leader. The alpha.

"Go to hell," Derek said. He'd stepped up next to Wes and Bailey so that the three of them now formed a wall, a united front. Beside him, Bailey pawed restlessly.

"You first," growled the alpha.

Then they attacked.

The space was too small. I couldn't get enough elbow room to really do any damage with my branch. Beside me, Cambria dodged a mouth full of teeth. As it spun to keep her in its sights, drool flew from the wolf's tongue and landed on my arm.

On my other side, Cord staked one but it wasn't deep enough to entirely stop the thing. The yellow in its eyes only intensified at the injury. Bright red blood dripped from the open wound. Beyond each of them were the boys, a blur of fur and gnashing teeth. They moved so fast I couldn't tell who was who, except for Bailey. His vanilla coat stood out against the myriad of browns that surrounded him. Every few seconds I'd catch a glimpse of russet fur—Wes—right smack dab in the middle of the chaos. From inside the nucleus of the fighting, someone yelped. Then the growls took over again.

I forced myself to focus on the enemy in front of me—an even skinnier, snakelike version of the leader, with eyes to match.

"If you don't work for Miles," I said, alternating between swings and dodges, "then who?"

Instead of answering, the Werewolf continued his attack. My feet moved in an endless loop: forward, backward, regroup. Over and over, neither of us gaining ground against the other. My swings were too limited to penetrate. I needed more space. And the smell up-close, the overbearing stench of Werewolf breath, made my stomach turn. To make it worse, I sensed the part of me that wanted to shift struggling to get closer to the surface. I couldn't let that happen.

A hole opened up ahead, a break in furry bodies. If I could get through without drawing attention, maybe only one or two would follow. It would give me room to maneuver and it would give me fresh air to breathe. The scent of wolf strained my senses. My skin tightened and shrank, like any moment I might push through and emerge as something else, something not human.

I went for it.

I slashed out as far as my arm would reach, driving my opponent back with my elbow, and prayed it was enough. Then, I ran.

"Where are you going?" Cambria yelled.

A few furry heads turned. So much for not drawing attention.

"I need more room," I yelled back, dodging trees.

I didn't stop until I'd put some distance behind me. I found a relatively open space, planted my feet, and whirled to face whatever followed me out. A wolf—a different one than before—slammed into me, driving me back. I quick-stepped sideways to stay on my feet and shoved him down. As his needle-sharp claws dug in, my pants—and my flesh—unzipped as he swiped down my thighs.

I repositioned the branch in my hand and shoved it up and in. The wolf's flesh gave with a sickening slurp. I pushed again and its body went slack. Its claws retracted and it slid into a heap on the ground. I yanked the branch free and danced out of the way to avoid going down with it. Its form blurred around the edges and I waited to see if it would shift back to human or stay this way.

My own body shook with it, a strange sort of shivering where I imagined my soul detaching itself from my insides. The woods around me dimmed as if someone had turned down the light switch and the sound faded out. My lungs squeezed shut.

I let out a ragged, choking sound as I gasped for air and all at once everything rushed back. Air whooshed into my lungs so quickly I gagged, and the sound returned with a roar in my ears. I shook my head to clear my vision as my eyes refocused on the scene around me.

I caught movement and looked up. Two more Werewolves approached. These were playing it cool, slowly stalking me. They obviously thought their friend would take me down without needing their help. The look in their eyes said they weren't disappointed they were getting a shot. Their yellow pupils glowed as they crept closer.

My fingers tightened around the branch in my hand. It dripped with blood, thick and slow to fall. I could see it out of the corner of my eye. I could smell it too.

My blood heated. Adrenaline pumped through me. My breath came faster, shorter. My fingertips and toes tingled. I imagined them stretching, reshaping into something else. My mind formed the image, almost as if it was instructing my body: paws.

I squeezed my eyes shut. No. I was not going there.

A yelp, loud and sharp, startled me. The burning eased. The tingling receded. I caught a glimpse of vanilla fur being shoved to the ground and then a russet wolf waded in, snapping its teeth, catching a yellow-eyed wolf in its jaws.

I focused on the two in front of me. They were closer. I could smell their breath. They exchanged a look, full of confidence and the intent to kill. Then they leaped.

I managed to get one in the stomach with my branch but had to pull it free and leap aside to avoid the second. They were already on me again when I turned. I shoved the branch out for another flesh wound before retreating safely away from their teeth.

They came again.

I lost track of the minutes, completely engrossed in the fight and glad the threat of shifting had passed. I was me: a Hunter, a human. But I needed an advantage, some sort of foothold. These *things* didn't get tired, they just drooled more profusely. They didn't even seem winded yet, and still they came. I spun and twisted to stay away from their open mouths. I grunted with the effort of another stab, knowing it was only a flesh wound.

Movement caught my eye, and I jumped toward it, branch raised.

"Whoa, whoa, it's me." The familiar tone took a moment to register. I looked into the wolf's eyes and saw they were deep brown instead of yellow.

"Derek," I said, chest heaving.

I'd barely spoken when my twin killers lunged again. I stretched and twisted away. I didn't bother bringing the branch up. It wouldn't have done any good for all the distance I had to keep. But then one of the wolves froze in midair and was yanked suddenly back. It yelped and went down.

Derek's teeth released their hold on the wolf's back leg and found new purchase around its throat.

One down.

With my attention on the one still coming, I repositioned my body, suddenly grateful for Professor Flaherty and her unceasing instruction in defensive maneuvers. I brought the branch up, keeping my body clear of the teeth aimed at my rib cage. In a move I never could've done without Wood Point, I rolled the defensive block right into an offensive swing. My left-handed hook collided with the wolf's face just as the branch in my right hand pierced flesh. I leaned into it, shoving harder as the wolf fell away from me toward the ground. The branch slid easily for several inches and then met resistance. I pushed once more and then stopped. The wolf rolled its head side to side in silent agony before letting loose in a howl-turned-wail.

The sound of it echoed through the trees.

The wolf writhed only a moment more.

I pulled the branch free and straightened, ready to move toward Derek in case he needed my help. His prey sat at his feet, unmoving.

"Not bad, Godfrey," he said.

I shrugged, trying to pretend I wasn't affected by his praise.

A snarl sounded from behind us, where we'd left the rest of the group. Derek jumped up and took off at a run.

The sight of his furry form springing through the underbrush stirred something within. From here, I could see flashes of fur, gnashing teeth, action. Heat and adrenaline coursed through me. I doubled over, my vision blurring again.

"Tara?" I looked up at the sound of Wes's voice. He'd broken away from the fighting and stood only a few yards away, his head cocked to one side. I met his eyes and then quickly looked away. I had no doubt what he'd see. He could probably smell it on me. I could smell it on me. "It's happening, isn't it?" he said in a low voice.

"I've got it," I said between gasps. Even with the lack of oxygen, it was all I could do to keep from dropping my branch and rushing forward into the fray.

"Tara, listen to me, deep breaths. You can do this." He came closer. "Are your fingers tingling?"

"Is that bad?"

"Shit." He began pacing. Every few seconds he'd throw a glance back toward the others and let out a whine.

"Go," I said. "Help fight."

"I'm not leaving until I know you're not going to shift."

"I'm holding it back," I insisted.

"Like hell. Listen to me, deep breaths in and out. You've got to concentrate on something else. Something that doesn't raise your heart rate."

"Like what?"

"I don't know, just find something."

I thought of Wes and pictured his human face. The way he'd looked earlier, smiling, sweet, bare-chested … but that only reminded me of the kissing we'd done and how much I hadn't wanted to stop and while I didn't want to kill anything, I wasn't relaxed, either.

"Argh. Not that," Wes said, obviously reading the image in my mind. "Something else."

I searched for something else to grab onto. George: too much worry and stress. My mother: stress. Alex: worry. Stress.

"Something *else*," Wes growled impatiently.

An image of Angela surfaced, calm and collected, always-an-answer-for-everything Angela. One of two best friends I'd been able to count on for support through anything, until the day I'd learned what I was. I thought of her patience in dealing with Sam and all of her dating escapades. Of the way she handled teachers, fellow students, all of her clubs, everything really. Her calm grace that seemed unshakable even under overwhelming stresses. I did my best to channel that.

Slowly, very slowly, my breathing evened out.

Wes shifted his weight. I ignored his impatience and concentrated on breathing, on Angela.

The fighting continued. The grunts and growls were closer together now. And louder. I wasn't sure what that meant, but I didn't have a good feeling. The hybrids weren't going to get tired, but we would.

I paced back and forth, impatient to feel whole again. At the edge of the brush, a pair of boots stuck out. I rounded the bushes and stared down at the body of a man. A thick branch stuck out from his ribs. His eyes were open and staring at the canopy of leaves above. His jaw hung loose and crooked, like it had been broken, and blood leaked from his ears, which were still covered in downy fur.

"Tara?" Wes's body went rigid as he stared down at the body. "Oh."

"I've seen him before," I said. My voice sounded small and foreign in my ears. "At school, I think. Wonder why he shifted back and not the others?"

Wes didn't answer.

"I'm fine now. You should go help," I said, looking away from the bloody wound on the man's chest. Seeing him this way—as a person—shook me in a different way. Suddenly, the threat of my wolf was gone, and I felt very human.

"Are you sure?" Wes asked.

A piercing wail split the air, somewhere between wolf and human. It cut off and there was silence. It lasted only a moment before the next shout.

"Wes!" Derek's yell sent us both running back to the others.

Cambria stood closest. She met my eyes with a fatigued stare. She had blood on her branch and hands. I could tell by the look and smell it wasn't her own. I clutched the branch in my hand, searching frantically for an enemy to attack or for the source of that last scream.

"What is it?" Wes demanded.

"Did we get them all?" I asked.

Derek turned to us and very deliberately stepped aside, giving a clear view of Cord. She was bent over something—and she was crying. Other than Derek and Wes, no other wolf was standing.

I took a step forward, my thoughts still jumbled from almost shifting. Seeing Cord cry threw me off even more. At the sight of the familiar vanilla-cream coat I froze. A lump formed in my chest and expanded until my voice came out a croak. "No."

Wes rushed forward, stooping his neck and poking Bailey with his nose. Bailey didn't respond. Wes poked him again and Bailey's head rolled sideways revealing a dark stain coating his throat.

"No, no, no!" I repeated. Tears stung my eyes. I took a step back.

Cord's sobs grew louder as Wes continued to nudge Bailey and call his name. His efforts were futile. The gaping hole exposing his throat was evidence of that. Still, Wes didn't stop. A hand closed over my shoulder and I swung out with my branch. Cambria caught it in her hand before it could connect with her cheek.

"I didn't mean to scare you," she whispered. Her expression was pained. "Is he …?"

No one answered her. None of us wanted to say the words out loud.

I blinked the tears back, refusing to let them fall. "What happened?"

"I don't know," said Cambria when no one else spoke. "I didn't see it. I only saw him fall. Cord tried to help him, but she had three on her."

Cord didn't look up, but I saw her shoulders stiffen. She'd blame herself. Even as I formed the thought, guilt edged its way in, weighing me down. If I hadn't left the group …

"We need to get him back to the house." Derek's voice carried across the space, calling me back. "Maybe Fee can do something."

Wes regarded Derek with sad eyes. I waited for him to argue, to tell Derek there was no point. "All right," he said instead.

"I'll carry him," Cord said quickly, sobs coating her voice.

No one had a chance to argue before she'd reached out and scooped Bailey up in her arms. His body was bunched in her hands, his fur sticking up in some places and matted with blood in others. His head hung limp from her arm. He must've been heavy, but she looked determined.

"Let's go," she said, already running for home.

HALFWAY HOME, BAILEY SHIFTED.

One minute he was a vanilla-cream Werewolf and the next he was a lean and gangly fifteen year-old boy. Cord let out a choking sob and her steps faltered while she fumbled and readjusted him. He seemed all limbs the way he hung over each of her arms. Thankfully, I couldn't see his wounds from where I ran behind Cord. But the fact that he'd shifted pretty much said what we all feared.

Still, Cord didn't stop running.

Every so often Wes glanced over at Derek or Cord—mostly Cord—and I suspected he was reading their thoughts. Mine were probably too disconnected for him to get much. I wasn't a mess like Cord—yet. I'd cry eventually. When the guilt that pressed at the edges of my mind finally came crashing through the shock of what had happened. For now, it held back, like a dam—a cracking, caving dam. Wes' gaze flickered to me. I didn't meet his eyes. Two words played on repeat in my mind: not Bailey.

When we reached the edge of the woods, Grandma and Fee appeared. Fee had shifted into her Werewolf form, but her eyes had the same panicked look to them as Grandma's.

"Vera had a vision, something bloody and dark. What happened?" Grandma demanded. She held a metal-tipped stake in each hand. Two more stuck out of the tops of her boots. "Is everyone all right?"

No one answered. Fee caught sight of Bailey and rushed forward. "No!"

Cord lowered Bailey to the ground in front of her. Fresh tears streamed down Cord's cheeks. "I think it's too late," she whispered.

Grandma's gaze swiveled from them to Wes. "What happened?" she demanded again.

"Hybrids," he said. "Lots of them. We managed to take them down, but one of them got hold of Bailey." He squeezed his eyes shut, opened them again, met her stare. "One of them shifted back. Tara recognized him from school. A Hunter."

"Where?" Grandma was all business, her jaw set in a way I hadn't seen since the night of the warehouse fight with Leo.

"A quarter of a mile straight back," Wes said.

Grandma looked past us, into the trees. "I'm going to have to call CHAS. They'll want to come out and have a look."

Cord's head snapped up. "CHAS?" she spat. "It's none of their business. It happened on our land, our territory. We don't need them."

"CHAS will notify that poor man's family." Grandma said, ignoring Cord's disgust. "Some of those creatures used to be one of us. That deserves to be recognized, at least in death. Besides," she said, her voice softening, "CHAS will do the dirty work and dispose of them so we don't have to. Hopefully, a few more will have changed back so we can figure out who they are. Or were."

"Well, they're not touching Bailey," Cord snapped.

"Of course not," Fee agreed quietly.

Grandma looked at Derek. "I could use some help. You up for it?"

"But Bailey ..." he began.

"Bailey's gone," Fee said. She stepped back from where she'd been sniffing and examining Bailey's body. Now she watched the three of them—Cord, Derek, and Wes—with a sad sort of gentleness that made me want to step forward as the villain, just to give them someone to punish.

It's my fault. Take your vengeance here.

Wes's gaze swung up to mine.

A giant tear rolled from the corner of Derek's fur-framed eye. "I'll go with you," he told Grandma, his voice gravelly, sad.

She nodded. "Let's get going, then. Before we lose any more light. This is going to take a while." She walked over to me. "You all right?" I nodded, trying not to picture Grandma dragging bodies through the woods, a trail of blood and fur in her wake. "Good, then I'll see you back at the house when I'm done."

As soon as she moved away, Wes was there. "Can you get back to the house on your own? I'm going to help them."

"Yeah, sure," I mumbled.

His eyes narrowed. "If you need me to come with you, I will."

"It's fine," I said. "I need to check on George, anyway."

He didn't look entirely convinced. I sent him a mental *Go on, I'll be fine,* and he turned to follow Grandma and Derek.

"When Jack gets home, I'll send him out," Fee called to him.

He turned back and cocked his head at Fee. Their eyes locked. Some sort of message passed. Wes's eyes widened and then he called out a hurried "thanks" before bounding out of sight.

Cord reached down and scooped Bailey back into her arms. Her bottom lip shook with the effort to stave off tears and the sight of it pierced me. The wetness I'd been holding spilled over onto my cheeks.

"Come on, girls," Fee said. "Let's go home."

CHAPTER SIX

Dragging the bodies back to Fee's took three hours. Most of the wolves never shifted back. Grandma said it was to be expected—a sign their humanity had indeed been lost. In the end, only the familiar-looking security guard and a man I'd never seen before—his face unrecognizable for the blood covering it—shifted back to their human form. CHAS was called. Vera spoke to them first, then Grandma, both in hushed, businesslike tones.

Cord took Bailey upstairs and laid him out in one of the guest rooms. Fee threw clothes on and then went to help set him out for a proper goodbye. I stayed behind, not wanting to intrude on something so private.

I left Cambria with Grandma and Vera and peeked in on George. His eyes were closed and his breathing even like the last time I'd checked. I started to back out of the room but my hand slipped on the knob and the door creaked.

George's eyes opened and he smiled tiredly. "Leaving so soon?"

"I thought you were sleeping." I sat on the edge of the bed, studying his face.

"You weren't going to sit at my bedside and watch me sleep?"

My mouth curved despite the grief coating my insides. It was nice to pretend for a moment. "I'm not that stalkerish. That's your style."

"Oh, so now I'm a stalker?"

My smile dimmed. I took his hand. "No. You're always there. I like that about you."

Instantly, his teasing expression vanished. "What's wrong?"

"Nothing." I debated whether to tell him. He didn't need the added stress, and it would only make him worry about what he was becoming.

"I can handle it," he said. "Don't keep secrets from me."

That got me. I hated the secrets. I couldn't do the same to him. I sucked in a deep breath and pushed it out. "We were in the woods, walking home from the lake, and a pack of hybrids found us." I paused, taking my time with choosing the words. Saying it out loud for the first time made it real. I couldn't take it back. I couldn't ignore it or pretend. "They attacked and a—a hybrid got too close to Bailey. It bit him and tore …"

"How bad is it?"

I shook my head and stared at a loose thread on the blanket. "He's dead," I whispered.

"God, Tay. I'm sorry. Are you all right? Were you hurt?"

"I'm fine, I just—it's my fault, and I feel horrible about it."

"I'm sure it wasn't your fault."

For some reason, that did it. The tears I'd been holding in broke loose and streamed down my cheeks. When I spoke again, my voice cracked and came out on a sob. "You don't understand. I got distracted and then Wes came over to help me and if we hadn't been there, if we'd been with the others, I know we could've stopped it."

He pushed himself into sitting and took my hands in his. He stared at me, probably trying to get me to look at him, but I couldn't. "You can't do this to yourself, Tay. None of this is your fault. They're the ones who attacked. Those wolves are the ones to blame, not you."

"I know that in my head, but my heart isn't getting the message. All I can think about is that I let myself get distracted."

"Talk it out with me. Why'd you get distracted?"

"I can't tell you," I whispered. "I can't tell anyone."

"Why not?"

I tried to put it into words. That the shame and disgust my own kind already had for me was nothing compared to how they'd treat me if they knew what I was becoming. "Because it makes me a freak."

"Uh, hello? Do you know who you're talking to here?" He squeezed my hand. "If there's anyone you *can* tell, it's me."

Slowly, I lifted my eyes to his face. His expression was open and earnest. The urge to say it aloud came over me, and I couldn't hold it in. I didn't want to. "I'm turning into a wolf."

As I'd expected, shock crossed his face. He blinked and I could see him digesting what I'd said, turning it over in his mind, fitting it with what he knew of this world. Then his expression smoothed out, and he smiled faintly. "So, we're twins." And just like that, he moved on.

Through the sadness and loss, I smiled back.

WES AND DEREK WERE STILL OUT WHEN I CAME BACK DOWNSTAIRS. Cambria was on the couch, watching some survivor show on TV. She muted the sound and shifted toward me. "How's George?"

I twisted my fingers together. "He's looking a little better."

She gave a small smile. "That's good, right?"

"Not really. It means the stuff Fee gave him is wearing off. He's getting stronger as he gets closer to changing."

"Oh."

I wrapped my arms around myself, trying to still my fidgety hands. How long did we have before he changed? A day? A week? What would happen when he did?

I needed a plan. A solution.

After today's attack, everyone would be focused on the hybrids, not to mention Bailey. Just thinking his name brought a painful image of light hair and a sunny smile. I clenched my fingers together and shook it away as the face morphed from Bailey to George. My grief was twisted by thoughts of George, and how if I didn't figure something out soon, I would lose him just as we'd lost Bailey.

George.

The one who'd known exactly what to say to ease my guilty conscience and cheer me up in the face of losing someone I cared about, someone too young to be lost in the first place.

Footsteps clunked against the hardwood and Grandma appeared. She sank down onto one of the chairs on the other side of the room and leaned her head back against it. "Gordon will be here tomorrow with a team," she said without opening her eyes.

"Who?" I asked.

"Gordon Steppe, the director of CHAS," she said.

"The *director* is coming here?" Cambria asked, brows raised.

Grandma nodded and leveled her gaze on us. "CHAS still hasn't been able to locate the hybrids since the initial attack when Miles loosed them. He wants to get a look at them for himself."

"We didn't locate them. They came to us," I pointed out.

"Either way, Vera's given him full access to the premises. I think she's hoping to partner with them on this."

"Partner how? All CHAS wants is to exterminate them," Cambria said.

"I think she's hoping to change their minds. I don't know. She's frustrated at her lack of mobility. And her gift isn't letting her see any of them, no matter how hard she tries."

"I thought her gift only allows her to see Hunters," I said.

"Some of them used to be. But she's still drawing a blank. At any rate, I'm coming back in the morning to help them wade through those bodies and answer questions. Not sure Fee or Cord will be up to it." Grandma shot a glance toward the ceiling. "Think I'll go up and pay my respects. Then we'll go." She pulled herself to her feet and trudged up the stairs.

"Gordon Steppe is coming here," Cambria said when we were alone.

"Is that bad?" I couldn't tell from her tone if she was impressed or nervous.

"He's not someone you mess with, I'll tell you that."

"Why?"

"Let's just say if the Secret Service and Osama Bin Laden had a baby, it would be him."

"Is he that bad?"

"He's that intense. And he channels it into a singular focus: killing Werewolves."

I shuddered. Cambria scooted closer and dropped her voice. "Are you okay? I mean, seriously, that attack was no joke, and then Bailey … I'm sorry about him. I know you two were friends."

"I'm fine." I stared at a spot on the floor. If I looked at her, I'd lose my control. She slid her hand into mine and squeezed. I squeezed back.

A few minutes later, Grandma returned and herded us out the door. "Fee says she'll see you both tomorrow," she said.

I nodded at her, grateful I wouldn't be expected to go upstairs and say goodbye in person. I wasn't ready to face them yet, to face Bailey. No words seemed right for the loss. Nothing I could say would bring him back, and I knew if I tried, I'd fall apart. They didn't need that right now.

Outside, the sun dipped below the treetops, casting long shadows across the lawn. Wes, back in human form, jogged up as we walked toward the Hummer.

"You're leaving?" he asked, frowning. His words were directed at all of us but his eyes were on me. I could almost feel him probing my mind, silently checking on my mental state.

"Grandma's taking us home. We'll be back tomorrow," I said.

He pulled me into a hug without a word. I let my hand slip free from Cambria's so I could put my arms around him. His shoulders were sturdy and strong—everything I wasn't. "I'm going to wait here for Jack," he said when he let go. "He called and said he'll be back soon. You want me to come over when I'm done?"

I opened my mouth to say "yes" and then remembered my mother. I wasn't sure what I was going to tell her about the events of the day. If I told the truth, she'd probably ban me from ever returning. If I lied, and she found out, well, the same outcome applied. I wasn't sure I could handle her disapproving glares aimed at Wes on top of it all.

His hand in mine stiffened.

"I think I'm just going to crash after this," I said. Another thought flitted through my mind. One I'd been pushing aside all day. I didn't want to add another item to the list of worries.

"We'll figure it out," he said.

"What?" Cambria asked, clearly aware of a conversation taking place without her.

"The hybrids. Tara's wondering why they want her, and who they're working for," said Wes.

"I'm wondering the same. There's a new player here, only I'm not sure who," Grandma said.

"You think it's Demi?" Cambria asked.

"Demi?" Grandma repeated. "Hmm. I'll look into it. In the meantime, Tara I need you to—"

"Yeah, yeah, I know the drill. Don't go anywhere alone." I rolled my eyes.

"I'm afraid so," said Grandma.

Wes kissed me on the cheek. "I'll see you tomorrow," he said.

"See you tomorrow."

WE WERE ALMOST HOME WHEN GRANDMA SPOKE UP. "I'M GOING TO speak to your mother about what happened," she said.

"You're going to tell her?" I asked.

"I'm not going to lie. Besides, she needs to learn to handle stress better."

I couldn't argue there. Maybe Mom would hear it better coming from Grandma.

And maybe I'd win the lottery.

"She's not going to let me go back once she finds out," I said.

"I'll talk to her."

The car jostled side to side as it rolled over half the curb to get into the driveway.

"Who's that?" Cambria asked, pointing toward the front yard.

I made out two shapes against the darkness as they made their way toward us from a beat-up minivan parked curbside. My stomach twisted with the thought of faking a smile right now.

Sam reached me first. "You're home." There was an accusation in the words. "Angela said she thought it was yesterday but then you didn't call and we wondered if you got held up or maybe in trouble or something, since you know, it's *you* and I know how you are…" She took a breath and hugged me stiffly. "It's good to see you."

I smiled weakly and hugged her back. "I missed you too." I held my arm out to include Angela in the reunion. "Both of you."

They pulled back quickly and Angela frowned. "When *did* you get back?"

"Yesterday," I admitted. "I was going to call you guys."

"Who's this?" Angela asked, eyeing Cambria.

"Angela, Sam, this is Cambria, a friend from school. She's staying with me this summer."

"Nice to meet you," Angela said quietly.

Sam stared at Cambria for an extra moment and the silence stretched awkwardly. Angela elbowed Sam in the ribs. "Oh, we should all go to the mall for a girls' day," Sam said.

"Um, I don't know if I'm up to it," I said.

"Why not?" Angela asked.

I started to offer up an excuse about being sick or tired but something in Angela's expression stopped me.

"Um." I glanced away, unable to hold her gaze. "Something happened," I began.

Grandma, who'd hung back until now, stepped forward and cut me off. "How about tomorrow afternoon? You could use some girl time."

"But we have that thing," I said pointedly.

"That's early. You can be back here by lunchtime and meet up with these gals. Nice to meet you, by the way. I'm Tara's grandma. You can call me Edie."

"Nice to meet you," said Angela, offering her hand. Sam nodded.

"I'll be inside if you need me." Grandma dropped her hand onto my shoulder as she passed, giving it a quick squeeze. Angela's eyes narrowed.

"Tomorrow then?" Sam asked brightly.

"Tomorrow," I agreed. We made plans to meet at the food court, Sam doing all of the talking.

When they left, I followed Cambria inside and closed the door. My mother's voice drifted out from the kitchen and I headed for the stairs. Grandma was on her own for this one.

"Your grandma's right, you know," said Cambria when we'd made it up to my room. "You could use some girl time. Something normal."

"They've been my best friends my whole life. Before I found out I was a Hunter, I'd never lied to them about anything. Now, that's all I do."

"Yeah, but, it's for a good reason. You're protecting them. Most humans can't really handle the knowledge that there are two species at war right under their noses. Especially when humans are nothing but collateral damage or bait." I scowled at her. "I'm sorry, but it's true."

"Which is why staying away from them would've been easier. I need to keep them safe. The last time we went to the mall, Leo was stalking me. I sensed a Werewolf right there in the parking lot. What if it happens again? The hybrids want something from me." Again, Bailey's face flashed in my mind and my voice broke. "What if it doesn't stop? What if they keep coming?"

"I don't think they'd risk a public place. They barely show themselves now. And when they do, it's usually the woods or somewhere equally secluded. And you need normal right now. I know you want to blame yourself for Bailey, but it's not your fault."

I met her gaze, surprised she'd read me so easily. Sometimes I forgot how intuitive Cambria could be. "You want me to compel them to blame you so you'll feel better?" she asked.

I sucked in a breath and let it out slowly, imagining patterns in the swirls of paint on the ceiling as I stared. "No," I said finally.

"But you thought about it."

"Yeah."

"You can't protect everyone. Sometimes, all you can do is protect yourself." Something about the way she said it made me think we weren't really talking about Sam and Angela anymore.

Someone knocked. The door opened a few inches and my mother poked her head in. "You girls getting ready for bed?"

"Soon," I said. I wanted to sleep, but I wasn't sure my brain would shut off.

She eased the door open and took a few steps inside. "Grandma told me what happened. Are you both all right?" Her hands were clasped tightly together in front of her. Her knuckles had already gone white with the pressure.

"We're fine, Mrs. Godfrey, thanks," said Cambria.

"Cambria, is there anyone you would like me to call? I know you said your mother is hard to reach, but if there's anyone, I'd be happy to get in touch with them for you."

Cambria shook her head, her dark hair bouncing. "No, thank you. There's no one. I'll let my mom know when I talk to her again, but I'm really fine."

She nodded and turned to me. I was still watching and waiting for a reaction, a blow-up, the part where she railed at me to never go back. "Tara?" She frowned. "Are you feeling okay? You look pale."

"I'm just tired," I said slowly, my eyes narrowing. "You're not mad?"

"Why on earth would I be mad? It's not your fault you were attacked."

"Did—did Grandma tell you about Bailey? And CHAS coming?"

"Yes. It's such a shame." Her eyes filled with tears. "He was so young." She blinked and her jaw hardened like I'd seen Grandma do when things got serious. "Makes me think CHAS has it right. Those hybrids need to be dealt with. They're too dangerous to have running loose this way."

"Mom, they're people, too," I protested. "A lot of them used to be Hunters or even humans."

"They're too far gone if they'll attack an innocent child. Or should

I say *children*. Grandma said she already told you not to go anywhere alone?"

"Yes."

"I'll add to that by saying not to go anywhere without another Hunter."

I glared at her. This was her punch line. "Is this your way of saying I can't be alone with Wes?"

Her expression remained neutral. "I'm doing this purely for your safety, Tara. Nothing more." I rolled my eyes as she turned to go. If she saw it, she didn't react. "See you in the morning. Try to get some sleep."

I waited until the door was closed and then let loose. "She's so full of it! She's only using what happened to keep me from seeing Wes. That's why she's acting so cool about everything."

"Well …" Cambria drew out the word. I looked up. There was a glint in her eye, a wicked smile curving her lips. "I'll make you a deal. I'll cover for you and your Werewolf if you'll cover for me and mine."

I sat up. "You mean you and Derek? You like him?"

Her grin widened. "What's not to like? He's got that whole dark-hair, dark-eyes, total hotness thing going on. I can't help myself. And have you seen his biceps?" She fell back on the pillow and stared into space. "I sort of want to lick them, see if they taste as good as they look."

"But he's a Werewolf," I said, ignoring her attempt to take my mind off the events of the day. I couldn't help my shock, even after the flirting I'd seen between them earlier. I'd assumed it was just that—harmless flirting. Cambria was a Hunter and even though she wasn't nearly as prejudiced as the other kids at school, she was still raised to believe Werewolves were the enemy.

Cambria sat up and shrugged. "We all have our flaws."

"Cam, it's not a flaw, it's who he is."

She rolled her eyes. "Geez. I'm joking. Do you seriously think I'm that judgy? You should know by now I'm not the hate machine Wood Point tries to mold us into."

I couldn't help but think of Alex. "You're right, you aren't like all of them, but where can it go, Cam? You'd be going against everything they stand for. You'd be thrown out."

She snorted. "Like I'm not already. You think they don't know about my mother and her preoccupation with the bottle? Or how I've been kicked out of more schools than most of them have pairs of socks? I'm destined to be the loner. Besides, it's not like I said I wanna have his puppies or something."

"You just gave me a mental picture of a bunch of wolf babies with Cambria heads."

Cambria grinned. "Cute, right?"

I threw a pillow at her.

CHAPTER SEVEN

The next morning, Grandma, Cambria, and I made our way to Fee's door, weaving in and out of black Town Cars parked haphazardly in the grass. Some still had a driver inside, replete with white gloves and a bow tie. Most, however, were empty.

Gordon Steppe was early.

"How many people did they send?" I asked.

"Looks like the entire council," said Cambria.

The last three vehicles were black cargo vans, no logos or emblems visible. "What are those?" I asked.

"Refrigerated transport vehicles," Grandma said, glancing over. "RTVs, we call 'em. They'll take the bodies back to CHAS headquarters in DC for dissection."

"Sucks to have that guy's job," Cambria said.

The front door swung open before I could knock. It was Jack. Despite the circumstances, my eyes lit up. So did his. "Tara."

He waited until Grandma and Cambria passed and then reached out and pulled me into a hug. His massive arms were like lead grips. He didn't squeeze hard enough to cause discomfort, but I had no doubt he could flatten me if he tried. I inhaled the scent of pine that always clung to him and something frazzled inside me settled into place. I finally felt like I was home.

My fingers brushed the cane clutched in his hand. The way his body leaned on it brought tears to my eyes. Bittersweet. Bailey's face floated in my mind but I shoved the image aside. Crying was for later.

"Jack, it's good to see you." I spoke the words against his shoulder. He gave me a final squeeze and then released me.

"Same. And you don't look any worse for wear after almost becoming queen of the hybrid underworld."

"Funny. You don't look so bad yourself. How's the leg?"

He tapped the cane against the ground. It made a *thunk* against the hardwood floor. He bent closer and lowered his voice. "Between us, I only use this thing at home so Fee doesn't nag me. I feel great."

I laughed, but it sounded hollow. "I bet. Wes says you're all over the place."

"Ssh." He glanced around. "Don't let Fee hear that."

"I won't. Where is she, anyway?"

He gestured upward with the cane. "Trying to keep Cord upstairs until Steppe leaves. She happened to answer the door when they got here and let's just say he knows where she stands now."

"They're in the back?" Grandma asked.

Jack nodded. "Out by the shed, taking stock. Wes and Derek are giving their statements." His eyes flickered to the clock on the wall. "They should be done soon."

"I'm going to head out, run interference," Grandma said, starting for the back door.

"Interference?" I repeated.

"Steppe isn't known for his love of Weres," explained Jack.

"You mean Wes and Derek? But we're helping them. We're giving them hybrids—dead, just the way they wanted them."

"Doesn't change the facts," he said.

"Trust me, it doesn't matter whose side you're on with Steppe," Cambria said. "If you're furry, you're the enemy."

I shook my head, disgusted. Cambria and I started down the hall behind Grandma. “You coming?” I called back when Jack didn’t follow.

“I’ll wait here until they’re done. Might be better that way.” He disappeared into the living room.

“I can’t believe we missed Cord going off on Steppe,” Cambria said as we walked. “I would’ve paid money to see that.”

“This guy cannot be that bad,” I said half-heartedly. Cambria arched a brow and I didn’t argue further. If Jack and Fee—the ultimate peacemakers—were hiding inside, maybe Steppe *was* that bad.

I pushed the back door aside and stared at the scene before me.

Dozens of people, all dressed in an identical uniform consisting of dark suits and sunglasses milled about the yard. Here and there, groups of two or three huddled, exchanging whispers and consulting clip-boards. A couple of suits passed by, carrying black, zip-up bags between them as they disappeared around the house. Some sent glances our way but most seemed completely wrapped up in their own purpose. True to Cambria’s description, they reminded me of Secret Service agents.

“Whoa.”

“Ditto,” Cambria said.

I sent her a sideways glance. “Have you seen this sort of thing before?”

She shook her head. “Not like this. I mean, this is calling in the big guns. Usually it’s just a team of two or three. Five at most. Plus Steppe is here. This is big time.”

“He doesn’t normally come to this stuff?”

“The director?” she said, heavy on the sarcasm. “Uh, no. He hides in a cave and plots evil. He doesn’t come out in public much.”

“You ever met him?”

“Not directly, thankfully, but if you wonder where our prejudices come from,” she paused to gesture with her arm at the scene before us, “look no further.”

We made it halfway to the shed where a small crowd was gathered when a stern voice rose above all the others. The tone was both sharp-edged and slippery. "I don't give a rat's ass about immunity or peace or whatever the hell. They will be caught and killed, understand?"

I caught a glimpse of a deep scowl set on a face much younger than I'd imagined and shifted my position for a better look. The man standing at the center of the suits wore soft gray that set him apart from his minions. His face was angular and lean but even through the layers, I could see wiry muscle. The entire picture was intimidating enough to make me sorry for whomever he was laying into. I strained my neck to catch a glimpse of his victim, but the suits made it impossible to see.

"CHAS has a singular mission, and that's to keep monsters like these away from the human population. No one's going to get in the way of that." He poked a finger at whomever he was speaking to. His eyes were thundercloud gray.

"Wow," I said under my breath.

"Told you," Cambria shot back.

"Is that Steppe?"

"Yup. Who's he talking to?"

I shrugged. We crept closer as Steppe spoke again, straining to see. I caught sight of a broad shoulder and tanned bicep and kept moving until the face came into view. When I saw him, I pulled up short and Cambria ran into the back of me.

"What the …?" she trailed off as she caught sight of him too.

Wes spoke, responding to Steppe's outburst in a low voice. Dangerously low. I couldn't make out the words from this far but whatever they were, they definitely had a negative effect on Steppe. I shoved forward as Steppe spoke again.

"I don't care what they want or who's in charge of them. You run your operation your way, I'll do the same. The Hunter community is not going to stand for this. If we don't hunt them down, the enemy will only use them against us."

Wes's jaw flexed, his voice strained. "Sir, with all due respect, they deserve a choice."

"They made their choice when they attacked you, wouldn't you say?" Wes opened his mouth, likely ready to argue, but Steppe went on. “I don’t have to defend my decision to you. Your organization is lucky to even be recognized after everything you’ve done.”

Wes’s eyes widened. “Everything *we’ve* done? We do nothing but support you, even though you’d rather kill us than work with us.” Steppe didn’t argue that point, and Wes’s hands balled into fists. “Just tell me they get immunity if they join us.”

Steppe’s eyes narrowed to slits and he leaned forward so they were nose to nose. “Fine. If they join you, they’re spared. For now. You just better hope I don’t find them first.”

Wes didn’t blink. “You couldn’t hunt down a Werewolf if he left a trail of breadcrumbs behind.”

Steppe’s lips pressed into a hard line. “Your disrespect is noted. One of these days, you won’t be surrounded by your gang of misfits, and we’ll settle this.”

“We can settle it now,” Wes shot back. “This is between us. They won’t interfere.”

“Loyalty’s overrated,” he sneered. “Isn’t that what got your little friend killed?”

“Don’t talk about Bailey. He was ten times the man you are, even at fifteen,” Wes said.

“Yet he’s the one you’ll bury tomorrow. Maybe you should put him next to your parents, with the other failures.”

Wes’s fists tightened. I watched the decision being made in his expression. Steppe must’ve seen it too, because at that exact moment, Steppe moved back, leaving one of his guards exposed in front of him. Either the switch didn’t register to Wes, or he didn’t care. He cocked his fist back and smashed it into the guard’s face.

The guard staggered back at the blow. I held my breath as he stumbled, waiting for him to fall and for Wes to leap—or worse, shift. Somehow, the man managed to stay on his feet. He dabbed a hand gingerly against his lip. It came away with red on it, where the skin split at the corner. He rounded on Wes, eyes hard and set. Without a single spoken command, every single one of the dark-suited minions produced a metal-tipped stake and held it at the ready toward a shaking, convulsing Wes.

"Shit," Derek said from beside me. His arms were taut at his sides, his expression grim. "If he shifts, this'll get ugly."

"Uh, I think it already is," Cambria said.

I ignored her. My heart was pounding. Steppe was an ass. That had officially been established. But Wes couldn't fight him—guards included. Not with this many stakes pointed his way. I took a step forward, ready to push my way through, but Derek's hand on my arm stopped me.

"No way, you can't go up there," Derek said in a low voice.

"I have to talk sense into him," I hissed.

He shook his head. "Steppe will just use you to bait him again. You'll only make it worse."

"Fine. Can you make him stop?" I pleaded with Derek.

"I can try. No promises I won't change my mind and help him." Derek shoved through the crowd as Steppe marched toward Wes. The rest of the crowd stood, stakes drawn but making no move to intervene. By the expression on their faces, they were enjoying the show.

"Wes, dude, let's take a walk," Derek said.

Wes glared past the guard at Steppe. "I'm not done," he said.

"Yes. You are." Grandma appeared in front of Wes, her mouth set in a hard line. "You can take a walk with Derek or with me."

Wes turned away, shaking with the effort of remaining human.

Then, Steppe smiled, his upper lip curling back from his teeth. It distorted his smooth features. "One day," he said so low I barely caught it, "you and I will meet alone. And I will remember this."

Wes said nothing.

Derek tried putting his free hand on Wes's shoulder, but Wes shrugged it off and stomped away, pushing through the crowd, his expression furious. He walked right by without even seeing me.

"Wes," I called, running after him. "Wes!"

He didn't stop until he'd rounded the corner of the house. "What?" he growled, whirling.

I pulled back, bumping into Cambria. I opened my mouth and closed it again, unsure what to say. I'd never seen him lose control like that before. It wasn't like him.

"We've got to calm him down," Derek said.

I looked back at Wes. He was still shaking—violent, convulsing shivers—and his pupils were dilated. His eyes met mine and he took a deep breath, held it, blew it out.

"Wes?" I kept my voice low and even, hoping it would be soothing.

"What?" His voice was slightly calmer, though he was still shaking.

"What just happened?" I asked.

He ran a hand through his hair so it stood on end. "He makes me crazy," he said. And he did look it, with his disheveled 'do and unfocused gaze.

Derek and I exchanged a look. "Hey, Cambria, do you want to take a walk or something?" he asked.

She nodded. "Walking sounds fabulous," she said solemnly.

I watched them head in the opposite direction of the CHAS crowd. "I would've punched him too," I said when we were alone.

That got his attention. His breathing slowed and he attempted a smile. "I would've had to peel you off him." His expression was less manic now; the shaking had almost stopped.

"I almost decided to join you," I admitted. "After that crack he made about Bailey and your parents." His expression clouded, and I decided it might be better to change the subject. "What's your deal with him, anyway?"

"Well, for starters, he's an asshole, in case you missed that."

"I noticed it."

"Add to that the fact that he hates Werewolves, and those of us who stand for something besides 'slaughter now, ask questions later,' and you've got yourself an accurate picture of Gordon Steppe, *director*." The last word came out on a wave of sarcasm.

"And is it safe to say this isn't the first time you guys have had this argument?"

"Not the first and not the last." He sighed. "I'm sorry, I shouldn't have lost it. He's not worth it, and I have a responsibility."

"You don't owe me an apology. I get it. Like I said, I almost joined you, dark-suited minions or not."

"Yeah, but Jack would've killed me. He still might. I'm supposed to be setting an example as a leader for peace." He laughed. "There's some irony for you."

"Don't beat yourself up. You're doing a great job." He arched a brow at me. "Okay, today excluded," I amended.

"I don't know," he said, looking over his shoulder at the corner of the house that led to all things CHAS. "I feel like I'm losing it. I'm supposed to be proving myself capable, levelheaded, responsible. All I did was prove to them I'm nothing more than a hot-headed kid."

"You're all of the things you're supposed to be. Smart, wise, and definitely responsible. You're always so by the book these days." I scrunched up my nose and made a face, like the idea of him being good offended me. It got him to smile. "And your dad would be proud," I added softly.

His gaze sharpened. More than anything, that mattered to him.

I hugged him and he relaxed against me. Any trace of tension or scent of emerging wolf melted.

"Thank you. I needed this." He spoke with his mouth against the hollow of my neck. I shivered where his breath tickled my skin.

"Me too," I whispered. I tried relaxing into his embrace, the way he'd done with me. I wanted so much for this to be all I needed to relinquish some of the stress that weighed me down. But, it only lifted for as long as the embrace lasted. When I pulled away, it re-settled itself against my shoulders.

"Are you okay?" I asked.

Wes ran a hand down my cheek, smoothing my hair back from my face. "I'll be fine," he said. "Thanks to you."

"You're a horrible liar."

"It's that obvious?"

"You don't go around punching people just because you're having an off day."

"It's … everything, really. Bailey." He closed his eyes against the pain that contorted his features. When he opened them, the agony was muted behind his lids. "George. The hybrids. Whoever this is coming after you. And I can't do a damn thing about any of it." I waited for him to add my whole "shifting, then killing" drama to the list, but he didn't.

"Wes—"

"Don't say it's going to be okay, because we both know it isn't. Not unless we fix it ourselves." There was a gleam in his eye I wasn't used to seeing.

"What are you saying?"

"I talked to Jack about that Astor guy."

"And?"

"And he shut me down the minute I asked. No information, no details, no reason why he wouldn't talk about it, except to say the guy's unstable and leave it alone."

"Same thing my grandma said."

"Right, and normally I would say we need to listen to them but …"

"But what?"

"If there's one thing I've learned about you, it's that you take what most would consider an order and turn it into a suggestion." The gleam in his eye deepened. "And in this particular case, if you wanted to do it your way, I'd have your back."

"What are you saying? We should run away? Find the guy anyway?" I couldn't believe this. It was so unlike Wes to behave like this. "Jack and Fee would kill you. I can't even imagine what my mother would do to whatever Jack and Fee left behind. And you're supposed to be a leader."

"Yeah, you're right. Shit." The gleam faded. He ran his hand through his hair, then shoved his fists into his pockets. "I'm sorry. I don't know what I was thinking. I hate having so many problems and no solutions. I'm sick of the diplomacy, the politics, the talking. I want to do something. For us. For Bailey …"

"I know it's frustrating. We'll figure it out," I said. I cocked my head to the side. "You know what's funny. Any other time, I'd be the one venting to you about the lack of options and you'd be reassuring me that we'd figure it out."

His mouth quirked upward. He dropped a kiss on my nose. "You're right. We make a good team. As long as we don't both lose our cool at the same time. Speaking of losing your cool, what's the deal with you and your mom?"

"What? Oh." I'd almost forgotten he'd read that last night, back when I didn't have to speak aloud for him to hear me. "She wants to be able to trust me, but I get the feeling she wants me to earn it."

His brows lifted. "Sounds reasonable."

"Right, except that haven't I been earning it my whole life? All those times she left me on my own while she worked? And all of the decisions I had to make without her? Meals I had to microwave? It's not like I ever got into trouble before all the Hunter stuff started. I mean, doesn't that count for anything?"

"I guess maybe you should ask her that," he said.

"Yeah, I guess. When did you start sounding so much like a grown-up?"

He grinned in a way that heated my insides. "What can I say? I'm wise beyond my years." I stuck out my tongue and he laughed. "That's not helping *your* case for being a grown-up."

"Funny, because it sure feels like grown-up-level stress. Between George and the hybrids and my mother, I don't even know where to start."

"We're going to find the hybrids."

My voice dropped to barely a whisper. Not because I was afraid of someone overhearing, but because thinking about it made me desperate. "Will it even make a difference if we do? What if they can't be saved? What if they won't? And what if—" I broke off and bit my lip.

"Say it."

"What if they keep coming after me, and I end up killing everyone?"

"You won't."

"You don't know that. I couldn't stop myself before. It could happen again."

He ran a hand through his hair. I knew this conversation frustrated him. As did the fact that I wouldn't let him tell anyone, but I couldn't bring myself to open that door. Not yet. Once I said it out loud—even to Fee—it would be real. There would be no going back.

"I don't know the answer to that without help. I know what it was like to shift as a kid, but I'm more Werewolf than Hunter. And I've been able to shift my whole life. I've never heard of someone waiting this long to start the process."

"Right, I mean how am I able to shift at all? You said the mother's side was the dominant one, and that's why you could, and I couldn't."

"It was a guess, Tara, I didn't know for sure."

"Miles couldn't shift," I said, feeling defensive, though I had no idea why. It wasn't Wes's fault this was happening.

"Miles couldn't shift," he agreed. "The important thing right now isn't why. It's how. You need to get a handle on it so you can control when it happens. The best way would be to—"

I held up my hand, silencing him. "Don't say talk to Fee. I can't do it. Not yet. They've barely accepted what happened to Bailey, and George is the priority now. I'm not opening up that can of worms, not yet."

"Fine, but sooner or later, you have to tell them."

"I will. Eventually."

He sent me a look that said he wasn't quite buying it, but he let it go. "I've been thinking about your shifting tendencies, the times that seem to have triggered it, and the main thing they have in common is a sense of danger."

"You think it's more likely to happen if I'm threatened?"

"I'm basing this entirely on my own experience, but yes. As a kid, we're taught to shift at will. But it takes a while to get that sort of control. A threat always triggered it spontaneously. Still does if I'm not careful."

"Huh. I thought it was temper."

"Not necessarily. Although, for some, the two go hand in hand, so it may seem that way."

"With Steppe, you just seemed so angry … Wait, you feel threatened by him?"

"I feel … a fight is inevitable. And so is my victory, if The Cause is to survive."

I frowned. "What do you mean?"

"He's made it clear his mission while in office is to disband us, or at least to reverse CHAS's decision to formally recognize us as a neutral third party."

"Why? We're willing to work with them. And what's so wrong with wanting to end conflict?"

"Because that end doesn't involve one side standing over the other's dead bodies. And because we fill our ranks with Werewolves."

"So that's it? It's that simple? Because The Cause has Werewolves in its group, he hates us all?"

"That's enough for him. So, yeah, I feel threatened by him. He has power. A lot of it. And I don't want him to use it to drive us apart."

I took his hand and squeezed it. "He won't."

"That's why I'm taking this position so seriously. Jack and Fee and Cord and Derek … they mean everything to me. I won't let anyone take that away from me. This is my family."

"I get it. That's how I feel about—"

"George?"

I hesitated, scared he'd read more into it than was there. "Um, yeah."

"It's all right. I understand he's important to you. And for the record, he feels the same for you."

"How do you know?"

"I might've seen something yesterday."

"You know, it's really rude to go nosing around in people's brains like that."

"I know. Trust me, I've got the karma-sized headache to prove it. But in my defense, he was sending out some strong thoughts when I walked in."

I frowned. "Like what?"

"He cares about you a lot more than I realized. And it's mostly friendship."

"Mostly?"

His lips curved. "He's getting there."

I sighed. "Mostly" was better than nothing. "In the meantime, he's getting healthier by the minute. He's like a ticking time bomb of monster."

"We'll—"

"Figure it out," we said in unison, our words blending into one voice.

He smiled at me, that same smile that always made my stomach flip-flop and land somewhere in my throat. When he bowed his head, I rose on my toes and met him halfway, closing my eyes as our mouths met.

I couldn't help but draw a parallel between that action and the state of our relationship. Ever since our talk at Wood Point, our promise to no longer keep secrets from the other, things between us had been much better. Even when he'd been hunting the hybrids, the loneliness hadn't affected me nearly as bad as those first few weeks.

Sharing my problems didn't come naturally for me—a family curse spanning generations, it seemed—but I was learning. And Wes was trying too. His crazy idea to run away and find Astor ourselves was proof of that. He trusted me now. Not just to make my own decisions, but to carry them out. I knew it terrified him to see me put myself in any sort of danger, but he was learning.

THAT AFTERNOON, CAMBRIA AND I MET SAM AND ANGELA AT THE mall. We spent three hours walking, shopping, and generally pretending Werewolves didn't exist. Sam talked a mile a minute, filling me in on everything I'd missed while away. She also made sure to fill Cambria in on everything she'd missed, well, ever. There wasn't much need for conversation from the rest of us. Still, I couldn't help but notice Angela's pointed stares.

"What?" I asked.

The first couple of times she shook her head and wandered off. Somehow, that only increased my guilt for the secrets between us. I'd come close to telling her many times but I couldn't ever quite bring myself to do it. What kind of friend would I be? Bringing her into this world would only put her in danger.

Still, it had become harder and harder to fake it, to pretend everything wasn't different. Because it was. Not only had I learned of an entire underground world filled with supernatural creatures, but there was an entire race of superhumans created to protect those like Sam, and Angela, from the animals that roamed the night. On top of that, every time I closed my eyes, Bailey's face floated in my mind—happy, blond, smiling—and I had to bite my cheek to keep from crying. A shopping mall seemed pointless and stupid and insulting, but here I was.

So, I forced a smile onto my face and pretended to hang on Sam's every word. As if parties and boys and clothes and gossip were the only things that mattered.

We were gathered outside the main entrance, parting ways to head home, when I caught Angela giving me the eye again.

"What?" I asked for the fourth time.

She looked at Sam and Cambria, who were locked in a heated "leather versus lace" debate that didn't look to be ending any time soon, then back at me. "I can tell something's bothering you," she said, steering me away and keeping her voice low. "I want you to know that you can talk to me about whatever it is. I'm here for you."

"I'm fine, Ang, really."

Her eyes narrowed and she stepped closer. "Cut the crap, Tara," she snapped. My eyes widened at that. "We both know you're not fine, and we both know you've been lying about it for months now. What the hell is going on with you?"

"I don't know what you're talking about," I mumbled.

She went on as if I hadn't spoken. "Ever since you met Wes, things have been different. You've been different." Her expression crumpled from anger to pained. "We used to tell each other everything. What happened?"

"Nothing happened," I said, fumbling for what to say. The truth wasn't an option, but I couldn't bring myself to tell another lie right now. A tear slid down my cheek. "I have a lot going on right now."

Angela sighed. "Well, if you change your mind, I'm here. I can keep a secret." She shot a meaningful glance over her shoulder and added, "From *everyone,* if need be."

"Thanks," I said, "but there's nothing to tell." I didn't meet her eyes and she didn't argue again.

We said our goodbyes soon after. Angela hugged me tighter than normal. When I pulled away, she wore a set expression. "Call me … when you're ready to talk."

I swallowed the lump in my throat, trying to ignore the growing fissure between the us of now and the us of then. It made my heart ache and my eyes burn.

"Thanks. I will," I mumbled before heading for the black Hummer parked at the curb.

Angela shrugged. "Well, if you change your mind, I'm here. I can keep a secret." She shot a meaningful glance over her shoulder and added, "From the others, I mean."

"Thanks," I said, and meant it. [illegible]

[illegible] nothing [illegible] again.

We said our goodbyes soon after. Angela handed me [illegible] When I pulled away, [illegible] "Call [illegible]

[illegible]

CHAPTER EIGHT

Time was officially the enemy. Hybrids no longer mattered—finding them or figuring out why they wanted to find me. Not even my fear of shifting concerned me. All that mattered now was George.

I awoke the next morning to a terrifying phone call. First, the sound of the ringer somehow melded with my dreams, becoming my own screams as I thrashed and flailed against a change I could no longer fight. I woke confused and breathless and desperate to feel human, to feel in control.

I fumbled with the screen until my fingers somehow made the right strokes.

"Hello?" I mumbled.

"Tara, oh, sorry, did I wake you?"

George's voice was clear and strong and full of life. The sound of it, vibrant and energized, brought me wide awake. "What happened?"

"Nothing happened, relax," he assured me.

"You sound really good." I couldn't help the note of accusation that crept into my words. I felt bad. It wasn't his fault he was changing into something monstrous. Still, I needed him to take longer doing it. I needed time. I hated time.

"I *feel* really good," he admitted. My heart sank even further. "I know that's going to freak you out. Sorry about that. It's just that I've felt sick for so long, I can't help but enjoy this a little bit."

I swallowed the lump in my throat, freeing my vocal cords. "Have you begun to change yet?"

"No, nothing yet. I feel strong, healthy. Like me … on Red Bull." The relief in his voice was unmistakable. No matter what he'd said before, he didn't want to die rather than turn. "You're freaking out, aren't you?"

I'd been quiet too long. "Maybe. It's happening too fast. I need more time."

"We might not have much left."

"Don't remind me." I buried my face in the pillow.

Cambria stirred from her place on the air mattress. I kept telling her she could share the bed but she insisted she was a kicker and she preferred to sleep alone. I could see her tossing and turning, trying to cling to sleep despite the noise.

"Are you still taking the meds?" I asked.

"Yeah, a little while ago. Fee's tripled the dosage, but we think my body is burning it off. Something about a higher metabolism as a Werewolf. All I know is I'm starving and I can't sit still." There was some rustling in the background, muted male voices. "Derek's going for a run with me."

"You feel well enough to run?"

"Um, yeah." He sounded apologetic.

I should tell him to enjoy it, that I was happy for him that he'd recovered so far, so fast, but I couldn't do it. It terrified me. The better he felt, the fewer our chances of finding a solution in time. "Where's Wes?"

"He went with Cord to the funeral home to buy Bailey's casket. Fee's planning a service here at the house day after tomorrow."

My eyes welled automatically at the mention of Bailey. "How's Cord?"

"Holding up, I guess. Fee gave her something last night to help her sleep."

"I'm surprised she took it."

"She didn't at first. Jack had to practically hold her down. Wes wanted to hide it in a brownie."

My stomach tightened at the thought of George hanging out with them at Jack's. One big, happy family. It was a little surreal. And for some reason, it made me a tiny bit jealous.

"We're going to head out, so I'll call you later," he said.

"Just be careful, all right? Oh, and do *not* go into town."

There was a pause. My fingers tightened around the phone.

"I'm serious, George. All we need is for someone to spot you and tell your mother. Oh, speaking of, you should call her while you feel good. She was asking my mom if I'd talked to you."

"She's worried."

"I know. Which is why you should call her. Especially if—" I broke off, too horrified to finish what I'd been about to say.

"Just say it, Tay. If I die. You're right. I should call her, just in case."

"How can you be so calm about it?" I demanded. I shot a glance at Cambria. She was still except for the steady rise and fall of her breathing. I kept my voice low. "You're not changing into something you can control. It could kill you. Or worse, you could try and kill someone else."

"The operative word there being try," he said. "You'd stop me before it came to that."

I squeezed my eyes shut. "No, I won't."

"Yes, you will. I know you, Tay. You'd do anything to keep your friends safe. In the end, you'll protect me. Even from myself. Always … like the song."

I squeezed my eyes shut, but a hot tear escaped and slid down my cheek. "Like the song," I whispered.

I DIDN'T WANT TO ASK VERA FOR HELP. FIRST, THERE WAS HER adamant claim that I was destined to take her place as a leader of The

Cause, straddling the line between two sides that'd only ever known war. Second, she was dying. And third, and this one made the other two much more complicated and therefore became the real reason for my not wanting her help, she was related to me.

Great Aunt Vera.

It still confused me on an empathetic level. Was I supposed to bond with her before she died? Spend extra time getting to know her, simply because we were blood, only to have her die just as a connection was formed? Is that what she wanted? A relationship?

It's not like she made it easy for me to figure out. The few times I'd seen her before leaving Wood Point had been purely business. She'd questioned me extensively after everything happened with Miles and the hybrids. Sometimes she'd take notes. Sometimes Kane would be present or Headmaster Whitfield, not that he ever had anything to add.

Since that night at school, when she'd admitted to me she was, in fact, dying, she'd been only polite and formal. It felt fake to me, but I suspected it was part of her personality. Only now I needed her. There was no one else—and I had no idea how to break through her wall of icy formality.

I managed to escape without Grandma and the Hummer as an escort. I suspected it was another one of my mother's attempts to show she trusted me. Cambria rode shotgun. It felt really good to be driving my own car again. It wasn't much, but it felt comfortable. It felt like me.

"Does the sunroof work?" Cambria asked, already pushing the button on the console.

"Yup," I said as she slid it back, letting in a swirl of warm air. It teased my shoulders and the ends of my hair. Humidity wrapped in summer sun. Even the wind was hot this time of year.

Cambria held the button to lower her window and leaned back, hanging her hand out of the car and riding the wave of air. She slid her sunglasses onto her face and smiled over at me. "This finally feels like a vacation, Mission Impossible."

I glanced at her. "Why are you calling me that?"

"It's your name, remember?"

"That was back when I was putting together missions."

"Uh-huh."

"I'm not running any missions right now," I said.

"Uh-huh." Her voice dropped an octave, a sound that said, "I know what you're up to." I looked over at her again, trying to read her expression. Large-rimmed glasses covered her face.

"Fine," I said finally. "We're not going shopping. I need to talk to Vera."

She pulled her hand back inside the car and twisted toward me in her chair. "I knew it. We have a mission. What is it?"

"I'm hoping she knows a way to help George."

"And if she doesn't?"

I shrugged. "Maybe she knows about this Astor guy. If we can't find another way …"

"I don't think he's a good idea. He killed that girl."

"But, if he's our only option?"

She shook her head. The ends of her hair bounced along her shoulders and the purple fabric of her shirt. "If Miles was your only option, would that *even* be an option?"

"It's not the same."

"You don't know that. By all accounts, this guy is crazier than Miles. And just as capable of causing death. We can't trust that. I made a bad judgment call once. I'm not going to do it again."

I sighed. So much for an ally. Cambria was too wrapped up in her guilt about Miles's attempt to use her to be swayed. "Yeah, okay," I agreed.

She slid the glasses down her nose to look at me. "That idea is the epitome of Mission *Impossible*."

When we pulled up, Jack's yard was empty of other vehicles. It made the house look bleaker and lonelier than usual. I wondered briefly where Jack's truck was. Had George said something about him going on the run?

Fee answered the door. Her eyes were red-rimmed and she clutched a bundled tissue in one hand. Her hair had come loose from her usual classic twist. Stray strands hung around her face and collar. "Girls," she said, smiling through fresh tears. She looked genuinely relieved for company. "Come in."

She waved us inside and closed the door, washing the entryway in murky shadows. No lights shone and only filtered sunlight, spilling in at the edges of the drawn shades in the living room lit the way.

"Are you hungry?" she asked, starting off toward the kitchen. I nudged Cambria with my shoulder and she took the hint.

"Starving," Cambria said, following Fee toward whatever newly baked goodies awaited.

I veered off down the back hall toward the library, keeping my footsteps light. Fee's voice drifted back. I listened as she offered Cambria a cookie and asked where I'd gone. I heard Cambria mumble something about the bathroom and then ask for a glass of milk. I smiled. Cambria wasn't even playing a role. She'd have gone with Fee into the kitchen even if I hadn't asked her.

I knocked quietly on the library door and after a low-spoken, "Come in," poked my head inside.

Dim lighting greeted me and several blinks later, the room took shape. I was surprised to find that it had been made over since the last time I'd been in here. Against one bookcase-covered wall stood a narrow bed. It was higher off the ground than most, reminiscent of a hospital bed, the way the back adjusted at an angle and the stark white sheets held their crisp folds at the edges.

In the center of the room someone had swapped the rickety wooden table for a set of armchairs, deep-cushioned and worn at the edges of the upholstery. Vera sat in the one facing me. Her slender fingers held a steaming teacup near her lips. The china shook slightly as she tipped it up, took a sip, and lowered it again. Her sweater hung on her already petite frame—the fact that she was wearing sleeves in this climate was a huge indication of her illness progressing.

I felt a pang in my chest in the same place it hurt when I thought of Bailey. I wasn't used to losing people.

"Are you coming in?" she asked.

"Yes." I stepped inside and nudged the door closed with my heel. Even after the soft click of the latch, I stayed where I was.

Vera took another sip of her tea, eyeing me over the rim of her cup. "It's nice to see you again," she said as set the teacup down. Her movements were stiff, her frame rigid. I couldn't tell if that was part of her normal posture or if she was in some sort of pain. "Come. Sit." She motioned to the chair opposite hers.

I shuffled forward. "It's good to see you too," I said, sinking into the offered chair. "I'm sorry to barge in on you like this. I was hoping we could talk."

"You can barge in anytime," she said with a wave of her hand. "My illness has become more monotonous than anything else. I'll take vicarious adventure over none at all." She smiled and her expression struck me as surprisingly genuine. It eased the tension some. "What is it you'd like to talk to me about?"

"Um, how are you feeling?"

"I have good days and bad days. Today is the former, or I wouldn't be in this chair. But you didn't come here to talk to me about my health."

"No, but I … I can, if you want. I mean, if you need someone to talk to."

She coughed, a deep, throaty sound. "That's very kind of you, Tara, but I'd rather you distract me with what's going on with you."

"It's George. Miles's serum is working quickly. He's getting stronger, which means he's close to changing, and I still don't have any idea how to fix him."

She folded her hands in her lap, calm and collected. "And you think I do?"

"I think you know things I don't." I tried to keep the frustration out of my voice. Talking about George's fate so rationally made me want to scream in desperation. There wasn't time to be calm.

"There's no way to stop the change, Tara," she said gently.

"I know that," I said impatiently. "The thing is, before he died, Miles said the only way to help George is to inject him with my blood."

"And you believe he was telling the truth?"

"I don't know. I think he was capable of it. And he really wanted the hybrid thing to work, so I think he would do anything to see it happen, even after he's gone. He said if I wanted to know for sure, I should talk to Astor DeLuca."

"Yes, I'd heard he'd mentioned the name."

Something about her expression made me sit up straighter. It wasn't a deep frown or a scowl like Grandma gave when I'd mentioned the name to her. It was interest, curiosity, and something else … excitement?

"Do you know him?" I asked.

"He was a good friend, once upon a time. Now, I doubt there's anyone who really knows him. He's a recluse, which would've been his fate whether he chose it or not."

"Because he killed a girl?"

"It wasn't so much her death as the decisions leading up to it that infuriated people."

"What do you mean?"

She took a deep breath, like the story she was about to tell weighed on her. "Astor was, or is, a brilliant scientist. Gifted beyond any I've ever seen. His work back then focused on metals. How and why metals affect Werewolves so absolutely. Mary Beth was his partner. She was just as brilliant as he was but better with the practicalities." She smiled wryly, adding, "Mary Beth made sure Astor recorded his research and didn't burn the place down."

"Mary Beth was the girl who died?"

She nodded and went on. "Astor was engaged in an experiment: the effects of metal on Werewolves in human form versus wolf form, and the best and worst material to use against each. He'd mapped out a great deal for us about the second spirit of a Werewolf, and how metal was such an absolute killer. Some of our best weapons against Werewolves come from his research and discoveries. Well, his and your father's."

"Astor worked with my father?"

"For a time. After the accident, Astor pulled away, but your father kept going. It was just as well. Even with the priceless discoveries, CHAS never would've accepted it if it'd had Astor's name on it."

"Why? What exactly happened to Mary Beth?"

"As I understood it, Mary Beth offered to be a guinea pig of sorts. They injected each other with a serum Astor developed. It gave her all of the characteristics of a Werewolf, so I'm told."

"Like the serum Miles gave George?" I asked, trying to keep the excitement out of my voice. I didn't care how unstable or loopy this guy was if he had answers.

"Similar, except Astor's version made sure Mary Beth retained her humanity and control over her shifting. I don't know the details. After the injection, Mary Beth offered to test some of the metals they were working with. There was an accident in the lab and Mary Beth was killed."

"How did she die?"

"I don't know the details. The entire thing was kept quiet. CHAS investigated but they couldn't do much because of the conflict of jurisdiction. Astor was under contract with them, to provide findings for his weaponized use of metals, so they voided the contract, but they couldn't charge him under CHAS law, since he's a Werewolf.

"After the noise died off, he retreated from the public eye. His lab was shut down and no one heard much out of him. I think CHAS might've issued a hit on him for what happened to Mary Beth, except that his victim had been a Werewolf at the time of her death. Again, not under CHAS's jurisdiction. And Werewolves have no laws governing each other like we do, so he was largely ignored from that point on. Still, there are stories of his, shall we say, quirks and eccentricities. It's said he is unstable. And as a Werewolf, that is never a good thing to be."

"Why are you telling me all of this? I mean, I'm grateful, but no one else would say anything except tell me to stay away and warn me what a horrible idea it would be to seek him out. They made it sound like he killed Mary Beth in cold blood."

"Some say he did. That the metals drove him crazy and he lost his mind."

I remembered what Logan said about the side effects of using metal as a Hunter without proper training. I never thought of the adverse effect it could have on a Werewolf handling it over time. "You still haven't answered my question," I reminded her, "about why you shared all this with me."

"It's always wise to understand all of your options."

"According to everyone else, this isn't an option." My eyes narrowed as I tried to decipher the real meaning of her words. "You think I should go see him, don't you?"

"I think you're going to do what you think is necessary to save your friend, consequences be damned." She shrugged, her petite shoulders rising and falling fluidly. "At least that's the Tara I've come to know."

She sounded amused, affectionate almost. It reminded me of our conversation at Wood Point. She'd opened up and told me she wanted to spend time getting to know me before her illness overcame her. She'd told me then how strong she thought I was, how I'd make such a great leader, if I didn't screw up and choose the wrong path.

I thought of my conversation with Wes the previous night and his insane idea. The same one Vera seemed to be suggesting. "You think I should go see him, regardless of what everyone else thinks? Regardless of how mad they'll be?"

"I think you wouldn't have asked me if you weren't already considering it."

I cocked my head. "And if I asked you where I could find him, what would you say?"

"DeLuca Manor is in Nevada, about 100 miles outside Las Vegas. A small town called Garth."

"How do you know he's there?"

"He hasn't left the house in fifteen years. He's there." Her eyes twinkled with something unspoken.

"You still haven't told me why you're encouraging me to do this."

"I'm simply giving you the information necessary to make a decision. I believe a good leader is self-reliant and is able to decide for herself, even when it means going against the majority."

I bit my lip. "You think I'd make a good leader?"

"That depends entirely on the choices you make."

"I hate it when you talk in riddles. Wait. When you talk like this, it usually means you've had a vision about me."

"Not a vision, exactly. I've had... images," she said slowly.

"Isn't that the same thing?"

She frowned. "Your future has holes, dark spots, moments where the picture is no longer clear. We both know my gifts are no longer reliable, but my instincts tell me it's something else that blots you out."

"Like what?" I asked, my fingers picking at the edges of my shorts.

"I can't say." Her eyes landed on mine and held in a piercing stare. I was too afraid to look away; to do so felt like a confirmation of guilt. I wondered, though, with the way she looked at me if she didn't already know. "The holes have always been there, but they are growing larger, darker. Is there anything you'd like to share with me? I could help you, if you let me."

I shook my head. "No," I whispered.

A long moment of silence passed, and still Vera held my gaze. The clock on the wall ticked out a rhythm that seemed to get louder and louder, until the deafening *click* made me blink.

"Well, then. You might be interested to know, Fee is preparing a burial service to be held two days from now," she said, finally breaking the silence. "Immediately following the service, the pack will shift and run. It's a ritual in the death of a pack member. No one else is invited."

"Um, okay, thanks for telling me." I was trying to catch up, unsure what had brought on the sudden change in topic.

"The house will be empty of all Werewolves at that time. That will leave only the two of us, Cordelia, and your two young friends."

I sat up straighter as her implied meaning dawned on me. Did she really mean for me to take George and run away? To the doorstep of a mad scientist who might've killed a girl?

Then I remembered: "Grandma will be here. She'll want to come to the service."

"Edie received a call from CHAS this morning. They need her to come in and consult on some sort of school fundraising business. She'll be back next week."

"Oh." I sat back, my head spinning a little with the possibilities. I couldn't believe it. Vera was the last one I'd suspect of sneaking around behind the others' backs. The last one besides Wes, that is. And hadn't it been his idea in the first place? Had he actually been serious? I chewed my bottom lip, contemplating the chances of it actually working. I sighed at the futility of it. "They'll know."

"Pardon?"

"As soon as I disappear, they'll know where I've gone. They'll only follow me and haul me back."

"Hmm. Yes, that could be a problem. Unless, of course, they think you went somewhere else. Somewhere they wouldn't easily question or wouldn't be able to easily verify."

"Like a diversion?"

"Precisely."

It wasn't the worst idea. Okay, it probably was. But I couldn't think of anything better. And that was the problem, wasn't it? Besides Wes, I was the only one even trying to do anything about George's impending shift.

To be fair, the rest of them were a little preoccupied. Bailey's death hit them hard, and I couldn't exactly demand they stop mourning to help me fix my own problems. It was up to me. And this was the only option I had. And though I'd like nothing more than to crawl into bed until I could blink without seeing Bailey's face in my mind, I wasn't going to let George down. I'd made a promise and I intended to keep it.

"A diversion," I repeated, my thoughts wandering as I considered possible scenarios. "But where else would I want to go? Everyone I care about is already here …"

Vera's eyebrows rose. That was it. She didn't have to say a word. The answer came immediately.

Slowly, I got to my feet. "Thank you for your time."

A smile ghosted Vera's lips. "Of course. Happy to help."

Halfway to the door, I turned back. "Vera, I, um, I know we haven't spent a lot of time together, but you've been a big help. I couldn't have done this without you. Maybe when things calm down, we could spend some time together?"

She smiled. It lit her eyes in a way that diminished the shadow of illness that hung on her. "I would like that very much."

"Great. I'll see you soon, then." I turned the knob and was almost out the door when she stopped me.

"Tara?" She waited until I looked back at her. "To be accepted, one must first accept oneself."

I blinked and slipped out.

I MADE MY WAY BACK TO THE KITCHEN AND FOUND A PLATE AND CUP by the sink, but no Cambria, no Fee. I wandered from room to room, each one empty and still. It was an odd sound, the quiet. Jack and Fee's house always seemed so full—of bodies, conversation, motion. Silence was something new.

I decided to take advantage of the alone time and test the waters on my developing plan. I slid my phone out and dialed a number I'd been convinced I'd never dial again. As I listened to it ring, I slipped into the storage room and closed the door.

Alex picked up on the fifth ring. For a second, I thought it was his voice mail. "Make it quick, I don't have long." He was breathless and grunting. The beep-beep of some sort of machinery sang in the background.

My heart pounded at the sound of his voice, gruff and terse as usual. "Um, sorry, I can call back if it's a bad time."

"Tara?" The beeping stopped. His breathing slowed a little. "No, it's fine. I'm just getting in a workout before patrols. Is everything okay?"

"Everything's fine." I hesitated. Part of me wanted to tell him I missed him, to ask about his new job, what he'd been doing, everything that'd happened since we'd been apart. I couldn't bring myself to ask, though, when the answers included his love for hunting Werewolves. "I, um, need a favor," I said instead.

"A favor," he repeated. He didn't exactly sound thrilled.

"Yes." I held my breath, sure he'd say no, sure I was the last person he wanted to hear from right now.

The background noise died off abruptly as if he'd closed a door on it.

"What is it?" he asked warily.

"I need to get away for a while, and I can't let the others know where I am. I'm going to leave word that I went to see you. I have no doubt they're going to call you to verify, and I was hoping you could sort of mislead them for a bit."

"You want me to lie so you can run away?"

"It sounds really bad when you say it like that."

"If there's a better way to say it, I'm all ears."

"I'm not running away, I'm running *to* someone." I winced as I realized how that sounded and hurried to explain. "It's for George. He was injected with the hybrid serum by Miles before he … you know, and now he's turning. I know of someone who might be able to help him, but everyone else thinks it's a lost cause."

"You mean, they think it's too dangerous."

"I wouldn't be going if I had another choice. I know I'm the last person you want to hear from right now, especially after the way we left things—"

"Why can't you tell Wes?" he demanded. "He's your boyfriend. He's supposed to be there for you, helping you, standing by you."

"Wes knows. It was his idea."

He didn't respond right away. Maybe he'd been hoping for a different answer.

"Look, if you can't—"

"I'll do it," he said, interrupting me.

"You will?"

"On one condition."

"What?"

"Tell me everything."

"Alex, I have—"

"Don't lie to me, it's insulting. I want to help you, but I can't do that if I don't know the whole story. And don't try to tell me you had no idea about George's predicament until you got home. This has obviously been going on since before you left school. Start from the beginning and tell me everything."

"The beginning of what?"

"Of you."

"Um, that's kind of a long story."

"I have time." He sounded smug. I could easily picture the smile he'd be wearing: self-assured, more than a little condescending, and reveling in the win. I wished I were there to see it—and knock it off his face. "I'm waiting."

Somewhere in the house a door slammed.

"I don't have time," I said, dropping my voice to a whisper. "Please, Alex. I will, but not now."

"Fine, tell me this. Where are you going?"

"To see a relative. Astor DeLuca. He lives in Nevada." I could hear Wes calling my name. "I gotta go."

"Tara!"

I snapped the phone closed and returned it to my pocket just as the storage room door opened and Wes stuck his head in. His hair was flattened and a sheen of perspiration coated his face and neck.

"There you are. What're you doing in here?" he asked.

"I had to make a call," I said. "What happened to you?"

"Cord decided she wanted to build her own casket, which translates to me chopping wood." He held out his calloused hands.

Grief pricked at me like a thousand tiny needles. "Wow. She's going to build it herself?"

He shrugged. "She needs to channel her energy somehow."

I thought about that. "Yeah, better woodworking than harassing."

His brow lifted. "Anyone in particular you're thinking of?"

"Nope, just concerned for the general welfare."

He shook his head and started to leave. "I'm gonna hit the shower."

"No, wait!" I yanked him back inside and closed the door as quietly as I could.

"What is it?" Alarm colored his features and he looked me over more closely, as if searching for damage.

"I'm fine," I said, waving away his concern. "I need to talk to you. I had an interesting conversation with Vera earlier."

"About?"

"Astor DeLuca."

That got his attention. "What did she say?" he asked, lowering his voice.

I repeated the conversation, making sure to tell him the about the girl, Mary Beth, and the serum. "He found a way to turn her into a Werewolf without making her a monster. He's got to be able to help us," I finished.

"She told you to just go there and see him?" he asked.

"Basically." I shrugged. "She even told me where he lives."

"Wow." He blew out a breath and leaned against the wall. Outwardly, he looked calm, but I could see the racing thoughts beneath the surface. His eyes scanned the shelves of equipment, not seeing any of it, I was sure.

"I want to do it," I said softly, "but only if you're okay with it."

He met my eyes and nodded very deliberately. "I'm glad you talked to me about it first," he said. "I'm in, but there's something else."

"What?"

"Cord was telling me about a friend of hers who works at CHAS headquarters."

"Cord is friends with someone working for CHAS?"

"They were in a foster home together at some point and the girl owes Cord a favor. Apparently, she works in the research office and told Cord she could get her hands on some sort of hard drive that holds information about DNA samples they've gotten from some of the hybrids."

"DNA samples?"

"CHAS took them from the group recovered at the school. I guess they're studying them, trying to figure it all out."

I frowned. "Even if the hard drive could help us, I wouldn't know a thing about it. I don't speak 'science geek' and neither do you."

"But this Astor guy does, right?"

"Right." Adrenaline coursed through me. I had to fight the urge to pace. There wasn't room for that in here. "We need to get that hard drive, and we need to get George out. Vera says the best time will be during the pack run. Everyone will be gone."

He nodded. "She's right. They'll be out for at least a couple of hours, which will give you a head start."

"Me? Aren't you coming?"

He hesitated, as if it pained him to say the next part. "I don't know if George has that kind of time. It would probably work best if I drive north for the hard drive and you head west, to Astor. I'll be right behind you."

I bit my lip, knowing how hard it was for him to let me go on my own, even for a day or two. "Are you sure?"

"No," he said on a sigh, "but it's the best thing for George."

"What about the run? You'll miss it."

"Bailey would understand, especially since your plan holds the possibility of a good fight." He smiled, sadness tugging at the edges. "He hated missing the action, you know." He shrugged. "I can run for him when I get back—if Cord doesn't kill me first for bailing."

I stared at him, not wanting to break the silence when he seemed so far away. I waited until he blinked, clearing the shadows in his expression, and looked at me. "We're really doing this?" I asked. "You're not going to tell me it's dangerous or a bad idea?"

"It's incredibly dangerous and a horrible idea."

I smiled and threw my arms around him, not caring about the sweat and dirt that coated his skin and clothes. "I love you, Wesley St. John."

"I love you too, Tara Godfrey. Now, how exactly are we going to do this?"

Wes and I spent the next twenty minutes whispering a plan. There were still a lot of angles to work, and he didn't love the idea of my involving Alex, but I'd already made the call. "Besides," I told him, "it's the one excuse my mother will buy. I can tell her I've gone for some summer training thing for a few days and she'll be mad, but she won't keep me home."

His jaw hardened. "Because he's a Hunter," he said. "She approves."

I didn't answer.

"How are we going to convince the others?" he asked.

"Cambria," I said. "I'm going to ask her to charm them."

"They're going to be pissed when they find out, but I guess it's our best option." He frowned. "Speaking of, you should probably check on her."

"Cambria? Why?"

"Cord and I found her at the edge of the woods. I think she was crying."

"Cambria was crying?" My eyes widened. I'd never seen that one. I couldn't even picture it. I skirted around him, heading for the front door. He caught my wrist as I passed and leaned in, an evil grin on his dirt-streaked face.

"A kiss before you go?"

I made a face. "You're filthy … but sexy." I planted one on him.

"Filthy? Is that what you really think of me?" I opened the door but he blocked my path. He leaned down so his lips hovered just above mine, tempting me. "I'd kiss you if you were sweaty." His words came out rough, a threat that sent chills of anticipation up my spine. For a moment, I forgot about Cambria. And George. And the plan.

"You would?" I whispered. He nodded, still staring at me. Heat speared through me. Like the other day in the woods, my hormones went wild and my body temperature spiked at the thought of what I wanted to do.

I wasn't sure who closed the distance, but by the time our lips met, I no longer cared. Nor could I remember why I hadn't wanted to. Something animal inside me was awake—and hungry. I wound my arms tight around Wes's neck, pulling him closer. He spun us around so I was trapped against the wall of the storage room. I heard the distinct click of the latch as he pushed the door closed with his free hand and then his palm pressed against the side of my body.

The kiss was hard and frantic. Where I pushed against him, he pushed back. The pressure of his body against mine left my skin tingly beneath my clothing. I needed more. As if Wes could sense my thoughts, his lips left mine and trailed down my throat and across my collarbone. My skin lit at each new contact. My breathing became shallow. I slid my hands underneath his shirt, dug my fingers into his back.

"Why can this never happen to us in a bedroom?"

His voice was muffled against my shoulder, but it was enough to bring me to my senses. I felt submerged, like I was slowly breaking the surface of an ocean. Vaguely, I became aware of the presence of others somewhere else in the house. I sucked in air, blinking away the euphoria.

"Um, I was going …" I managed in a shaky voice. "I can't remember where."

Wes grinned down at me. "You, kitchen. Me, shower."

He pulled the door open and eased out. The tension in the air dissolved. It left behind a bite in the absence of passion.

"Wes?" I called as he started down the hall. He turned. "We make a good team."

He winked and bounded up the stairs.

CAMBRIA CAME IN THE FRONT DOOR JUST AS I REACHED IT. DEREK hovered beside her, looking helpless but concerned.

"Cam?" Even before I reached her, I could see her cheeks were streaked with black tracks where her makeup had mixed with tears. "What happened?"

"Hey, Tara." She was dry-eyed now, but I could see it was an effort to remain that way.

"I'm going to see if Cord needs any help. Why don't you guys hang in the kitchen, eat a brownie or something," Derek said. He was already steering her that way with a gentle hand on her shoulder. He and I exchanged a nod, and I fell into step beside her, taking his place as he disappeared outside.

I heated brownies for us both and set the plates on the bar. Cambria waited, making invisible patterns on the wooden countertop with her fingers. I joined her and we sat in silence, the food untouched.

"Do you want to talk about it?" I asked finally.

After a moment, the finger-tracing stopped. "It's my mom." Her voice sounded dull, like she'd already emptied herself of emotion.

"What about her?"

"She's been arrested."

"For what? I thought she was in rehab."

"She started ranting to her therapist about Werewolves and secret political groups. He made some calls, started asking around. CHAS got wind of it."

"How?"

"Who knows. They have ears everywhere."

I sat back. I wasn't sure what I'd been expecting, but it wasn't this. "How'd you even find out?"

"I called Logan to see how his summer was going with the ice queen and he said he'd just heard it from his dad. I guess he's on some board or council or something and was there when they brought her in."

"Cam, I'm so sorry. How long will they keep her?"

Tears rose in her eyes. "They're holding her indefinitely."

I frowned. "Can they do that? Without charging her, I mean. It seems a little--"

"A violation of the Sixth Amendment?" George stood in the doorway, rubbing his wet hair with a towel. The shadows underneath his eyes had faded to almost nothing and he moved with the surety of someone who hadn't lain in bed for the past month. He crossed to the bar and broke off a piece of my brownie, barely chewing before swallowing. I stared at him.

"What?" he said finally, looking back and forth between us. His expression fell when he saw Cambria's tear-streaked face. "Sorry. Did I interrupt? I can leave."

I hesitated. "Cam?"

Cambria sighed. "Whatever, it's fine. You can tell him."

"Cambria's mom got arrested by CHAS."

His brows crinkled. "What's CHAS again?"

"Council for Hunter Affairs and Security. They keep the peace," I explained. Cambria snorted. "And they enforce the law."

"What law did she break?"

"She said some things, publicly, about the existence of Werewolves. CHAS found out."

"Huh." He swallowed another bite of brownie. "So they're like the police of mythological creatures?"

"Sort of."

"They were the ones here for the hybrids, right?"

"Yes."

"Then scratch that. They're like Men in Black, except the aliens are Werewolves."

Cambria's lips twitched. I smiled at George, grateful for the way he'd lightened the mood. Derek reappeared in the doorway. He watched Cambria from across the room with the same worried expression as before. Cambria spotted him and he straightened. It was kind of cute the way he seemed to stretch to his full height whenever their eyes met. And it made him seem friendlier, even though it wasn't directed at me.

"Hey," he said.

"Hey," she returned. From the corner of my eye, I saw George's brow rise.

"Cord's good for now. There's some old Van Damme flick on TV. You guys want to watch?" He only looked at Cambria as he said it.

"Sure." She slid off the stool and headed out. "You coming?" she asked me.

"I'll be there in five. I think I'll eat your brownie."

"I know, I know, it's like the apocalypse or something, me passing up dessert. I'll make up for it later."

"I know you will," I called as they left. George moved to follow but I grabbed his arm.

"What's up?" he asked.

I held my finger to my lips and waited until Derek's and Cambria's footsteps faded into the other room and the volume on the TV kicked up a notch. There'd be no point in bringing Cambria in on this if George wasn't on board. Then again, I didn't plan on giving him much choice. I pulled him against the corner of the counter and whispered, "I think I have a plan. A way to help you. Do you trust me?"

"Of cour—"

"Sshh." I glanced at the doorway.

"Of course," he repeated, his voice barely audible. "But why do I get the feeling no one else approves of this plan?"

I bit my lip. "I'm not going to lie, it could be dangerous. I don't know what we'll be walking into. But this guy is our only option, and I have to try."

His brows knitted. "You're talking about that Astor guy, aren't you? I thought he was crazy, off his rocker or something."

"He might be, but he also might have answers. And we don't have time to wait around for a better option."

He ran a hand through his half-dried hair. It fell over his forehead in shiny blond waves, where it'd grown out the last few weeks. Everything about him looked healthier, sturdier, stronger. It wouldn't be long now. I could sense it on him, like a coiled spring held by a single finger. Any moment, the power inside him would release. I wondered if it wasn't already too late. "All right," he said, breaking into my thoughts. "What do you need me to do?"

In hurried whispers, I gave him the details of our plan for slipping away, and Wes's side trip to retrieve a hard drive that would hopefully have any answers Astor didn't. When I was done, he simply nodded, his eyes sparkling. No doubt he thought of this as simply an adventure. Did he even understand the danger that awaited him once he crossed over into his new life?

When we finished, I let out a breath full of relief and anxiety. I watched George out of the corner of my eye as we finished our brownies and my heart hammered against my chest. I listened to the sounds of an action sequence from the movie in the other room and tried not to imagine it as the soundtrack for my own life.

CHAPTER NINE

Two days later, I stood at the edge of the woods for Bailey's funeral. It was the first funeral—Werewolf or otherwise—I'd ever been to. Werewolves, some in human form and some not, were everywhere. The front yard was packed with cars, but there were several arrivals I'd seen wander up by way of the path out back.

Did Bailey really know all of these people in his short life, or were most paying respects to the organization as a whole?

There were the familiar faces of The Cause members, including some I'd met when Leo had come after me. Jill, a dark-haired Hunter I'd met at that first meeting, walked by and waved. It surprised me that she remembered me or that she would acknowledge it. I'd grown so used to being shunned, friendly gestures made me suspicious.

George's hand tightened in mine. I looked down at our joined fingers and then up at him, squeezing back. I knew he was trying to comfort me against the sight of the dark cedar coffin set before us. I'd yet to actually look at it. I'd seen it briefly when we'd made our way down from the house, but the sight of Derek in wolf form, a solemn sentry standing guard beside it, brought such a surge of tears, I'd purposely averted my gaze ever since.

I'd said my goodbyes already. Cambria and I had come early,

before Jack had sealed up the coffin. I'd sat in the guest room and let the tears come, willing my body to empty itself when no one was around to see. Between sobs I'd repeated, "I'm sorry, I'm sorry," over and over again, until Cambria came in and pulled me away.

Now there was a hole where my heart should've been.

Somewhere in the back of my mind I knew the thing with the hybrids was far from over. Their leader—someone who was not Miles —wanted me. For what, I didn't know. I had no doubt they'd keep coming, or that my friends would keep fighting for me. That knowledge only served to solidify my decision to leave with George. Until he was healed, I couldn't allow myself to focus on the hybrids, or anything else. At least with me gone, the others I cared about were safe.

Except for Bailey.

Cambria nudged me. Each time I looked at her, I had to look away; the vanilla-cream scarf around her neck reminded me so strongly of Bailey's coat. She held a tissue out to me. I shook my head. I was determined to hold it together.

The back door swung open. Sunlight caught Jack's face as he stepped onto the grass. I could see the shimmering trail of wet as tears traced down his cheeks. Then his feet hit the ground and he shifted, a single fluid motion that created a rippling effect in the instant before thick fur replaced his skin. When he'd completed the transition, he raised his head toward the group.

Behind him were Fee, Cord, and Wes. Vera remained inside. She'd come out that morning to remove the wards around the house, allowing visitors onto the property, only to find they'd already dissolved. I'd never seen her so drained or empty-looking. It scared me—someone who had once seemed so strong and invincible reduced to a shell of what she'd been. It made my eyes well with fresh grief for what was to come.

Near the backdoor, Fee watched Jack shift with a longing expression, like she'd rather do the same, but Cord hung on her arm, face downcast, shoulders set. Fee's lips moved in whispered words of comfort. As they neared the woods' edge, Cord stumbled, her heel catching on a pine cone. Wes stepped up and grabbed her elbow to steady her, and I could finally see him clearly.

He'd combed his hair, letting it fall to the side instead of his usual style: gelled into disarray. And he wore a suit—navy blue slacks and jacket with a silver tie. The sun glinted off his hair, exposing the varied hues of auburn. Despite my sadness, and the tight rein I was trying to keep on my emotions, my breath caught at the sight of him.

He led Cord and Fee to the group of folding chairs that had been set up on one side of the coffin and pulled Cord down next to him. He wrapped an arm around her shoulders so his fingertips reached Fee. The other hand dug into his pocket and produced a wad of tissues that he pressed into Cord's hand. Then his eyes lifted to the coffin in front of him. His expression as he stared at it was a mixture of grief and longing so sharp I had to hold my breath against the pricks of pain in my own heart.

I reached over and took the offered tissue out of Cambria's hand. She sent me an understanding smile and squeezed my arm.

Then Jack walked to the podium and began to speak. "Thank you all for coming today. We are here to celebrate the life of Bailey Vincent Ross. A life that started out shadowed by grief and loneliness but ended in joy and a tie to a family so strong, even death cannot break it. Bailey was, and will always be, an important member of our family. He belonged to all of us, just as all of you belonged to him. To all of you who had a hand in shaping him into the man he became, I know he was grateful, as am I. Bailey was special, and he will never be forgotten."

Tears ran unchecked down my cheeks as Jack went on. By the time he'd finished, there were more sniffles than stoic faces in the crowd. George managed to hold it together, but I could see the sheen of tears in his eyes when he shifted his gaze away.

Jack concluded by saying, "Bailey will be buried in our family plot."

He pointed in the direction of the small graveyard Wes had shown me the day before. Small, nondescript headstones sprung up from about a dozen plots in a small clearing, their engravings simple—

names, dates, a short message on each. The newest addition, Jack's father, read: Joseph Wolfe. 1936-1999. Fierce leader, loving father.

"After the burial, all Weres will reconvene here for the pack run," Jack finished.

He nodded to Fee. She and Cord rose to their feet. Wes followed behind and, one at a time, they selected a fresh rose from a bucket near the chairs and laid it over the coffin. Then they made their way back to the house and the crowd broke up. Some wandered away and some approached the coffin, selecting a flower to place on top. I stayed where I was, sniffling and wiping at my eyes with my mascara-stained tissue.

"Tay, what do you want to do?" George asked, his voice low and gentle in my ear. "Do you want to go place a flower?" I shook my head. "Do you want to go inside?" I shook my head again. The thought of four walls made me restless.

Cambria tugged on my wrist. "Come on, let's go for a walk."

I let Cambria lead. She chose a path that cut away from most of the other guests and wound around the edge of the yard toward the front. George and I followed in silence.

"It was a nice service," Cambria said, stopping to sit on a fallen tree.

"It was," I agreed.

Now that it was over, my nerves were quickly drying my tears. Grief was replaced by restlessness and adrenaline. The time to make our escape was almost here. If any part of our plan went wrong, the whole thing would fall apart. I dried my eyes one last time and took a deep breath. I didn't have time to be sad right now. I needed to focus, make sure this worked.

"How are you feeling, Cam?" I asked.

She looked up at me. "Right as rain, unless you count my momma drama."

"Cam …" I sank down next to her.

When I'd first told her the plan, I'd been fully prepared for her to wig out, to scream that I find another way. After her initial refusal, I wasn't sure how she'd respond to my idea to sneak off and find Astor.

But she'd been perfectly willing to go along with my idea—one that left her behind, fending for herself against my mother.

She'd dropped enough comments about Derek that I suspected it had just as much to do with him as it did helping George, Wes, and me escape. But with everything happening with her mom, I needed to know I could count on her.

"If you're not up for this, I understand," I began.

"I got this, Godfrey." She gave me a mock salute. "I'm a soldier." I smiled but it was laced with worry. "Relax, I mean it. I can compel in my sleep. They'll all think you're off flirting—I mean, training with Alex." She grinned. "And wow, your mom was easy to convince, I probably don't even need to charm her. She obviously approves of that choice." She wiggled her eyebrows.

I ignored it—and the way she'd said "choice."

"I think she assumes my life would be easier, less like hers, if I was involved with a Hunter. She's afraid of the complications a Werewolf brings. If she had her way, I'd marry a human and lead Girl Scouts or something. Speaking of Werewolves, how's Derek? He seemed wound pretty tight during the service."

Cambria nodded. "He thinks he has to be strong for Cord and Fee, but he's not letting himself grieve."

It shouldn't have surprised me that she knew so much about him already. Every moment she wasn't with me, she was with him. I had no idea what they talked about, and he still barely said two words to me, but he seemed to have a soft spot for her, and she acted more serious about him than I'd expected.

"Maybe after the burial, you can talk to him. Maybe he just needs someone to listen," I said.

At Wes's insistence, I'd agreed to let Cambria tell Derek where we really were. I hadn't wanted to, but if Wes trusted me with the plan, the least I could do was trust his judgment when it came to his best friend. And Cambria wouldn't agree to compel him.

"Yeah, I'll have to wait until after their run, though," she said. "Sort of a weird tradition for Werewolves. One of your pack members bites it and you run? I don't get it."

"It's a unity thing," George said.

We both looked up at him, surprised. He shrugged. "Wes and Derek were telling me about it yesterday. It's to show unity in the remaining pack, like they're all there for each other and have each other's backs and stuff. And it's a sign of respect toward the deceased, a symbol of family."

Cambria smirked. "So, you're like BFFs with Tara's boyfriend now?"

"Wes isn't a bad guy," he said. "He just makes it hard to get to know him."

"And you don't think that's because you're in love with his girl?"

"Cambria," I warned but George didn't seem bothered.

"Tara's my best friend. Always has been, always will be. I'm happy that she's happy."

"Or you're just waiting for him to screw up," Cambria pointed out.

I glared at her. "Can we talk about something else?"

"Sure," she agreed, ignoring my icy look. "Oh, hey, your mom said to tell you it's family night tonight."

"I thought you were going to use your compulsion thing on her," George said.

"I'm not doing that until later. I want to be home with her for a while, make sure the story sinks in," Cambria said.

"Family night?" I frowned. "How is it family night with Grandma gone and—"

"And me here?" she finished. "I dunno, but she said something about *Beaches* on DVD. You know I don't watch that mushy crap, right?"

"It's something we used to do when I was a kid," I explained. I tried to remember the last time Mom scheduled a movie night but I couldn't. It made me ashamed over what I was about to do. I'd promised I'd meet her halfway, that I'd do my part to repair the distrust between us. And here I was, already sneaking away before we'd even begun.

"Tara? Earth to Tara, can you hear me?" Cambria waved her hand in front of my face.

"Yeah, sorry."

"Are you okay?"

"Just distracted. What was the question?"

"I asked you what the chances are of getting your mom to watch *Kill Bill* instead. I don't even know what *Beaches* is about, except that it's a chick flick."

"Oh, it's sad, actually. I cry every time."

She gaped at me. "And your mom thought we'd want to watch something sad? Tonight?"

"She probably didn't think about it."

"Um, yeah, or she sucks at this game," she said.

"What game is that?" George asked.

"The game of cheering us up," Cambria answered. She pulled her phone out and started clicking buttons.

"What are you doing?" he asked.

"Checking for the closest Redbox. I need a backup plan."

"Let me guess—a romantic comedy?"

Cambria eyed him, clearly not amused. "Action. Fighting. Blood and guts. I'm a Hunter, not a cheerleader."

George chuckled. "Cheerleaders are your stereotype of choice, huh?"

Cambria shrugged. "They strike me as the type to make *eww* faces at the screen when someone gets staked. Plus, their voices annoy the hell out of me."

"Buffy was a cheerleader," I pointed out.

Cambria tipped her head. "Point taken."

"Tara was a cheerleader," George said.

"For three seconds," I corrected, "and I only did it because of you."

"Me?" he asked.

"Tara? Cambria? Are you out here?" Wes's voice rang out from the trail behind us.

"Here," I called, rising to my feet.

He rounded the path, his fingers tugging absently at the tie knotted around his neck. "The pack's assembling for the run. We need to head back."

I ignored the fluttering in my stomach at the sight of him in his suit. Now was not the time. "And they believed you weren't feeling well?"

He shrugged. "After the service, how emotional everyone was … it wasn't a hard sell."

"Won't they be offended you didn't do the run?"

"I told them I'd catch up. They'll wonder about it but not enough to come looking. There're a lot of people here for this one, so it'll be harder to realize I'm not there."

"You make it sound like you do a lot of these," I said.

"Enough to know this large crowd doesn't happen often." His eyes hardened. "Liliana's was a ghost town. The only ones who ran were Jack and Derek."

"No one else?" I asked. I'd never met her before the night she attacked me, but it still made me sad that no one else had cared enough for her to make the run.

"A few others came, but I think it was mainly out of respect for Jack and Fee."

"You didn't run?" I asked.

"No." His eyes flashed in anger, hot and quick. "She hurt you. I didn't run."

I remembered the way we'd met that night, the shock I'd been in. It felt like years separating that moment from this one. I was no longer someone who lost it at the sight of death. Still, the grief over life lost thickened the air just the same. As did the guilt.

Wes looked at Cambria. "Derek was looking for you. He said to save him a seat at the dinner table—and a brownie."

Cambria smiled. "The seat I can do. I make no promises about the brownie."

Wes trailed a hand down my cheek where my makeup had run.

"Am I a mess?" I asked.

"You look beautiful," he said, his voice low enough that it wouldn't carry to where the others stood down the path. "I didn't want to leave without telling you that." The way he stared at me, like could see all the way through to inside me, made me shiver.

"You look pretty amazing yourself," I whispered. I ran a hand over the smooth fabric of his jacket and rested my palms on his shoulders.

"I should dress up more often." He kissed my cheek and then moved lower, pressing his lips to the space between my jaw and neck. He smelled like the woods, a heavy scent that made me think of loose bark being pulled away from a tree. My arms around him tightened.

"Hey, it's all right. I'll see you in a couple days," he murmured. His hand made soothing circles on my back for a moment longer before he pulled away. "I'm only a phone call away," he added.

"I know," I whispered.

"You ready?"

I nodded.

He kissed me on the forehead and took my hand as we headed back.

The front lawn was packed with cars, scattered this way and that, no rhyme or reason. Wes's Aston Martin was parked near the end of the driveway, out of sight of the house. He'd done it on purpose on the hope no one would notice right away that he was gone. George and Cambria hung back as we neared his car.

"I almost forgot. Cord is in with Vera. You should check on her," he said, stopping in front of his door. He opened it but didn't climb inside.

I sighed. I was the last person Cord wanted to see, especially today, but I couldn't say no. And I needed to make sure she didn't see us leave. "All right, I'll see her before we go."

He cupped my face with his hands and pressed his lips lightly against mine. I pressed back hard. He responded to the pressure by deepening the kiss. I needed it that way. Tenderness would only make the goodbye harder.

"I'll see you soon," he said, pulling away and leaning his forehead against mine before finally breaking contact.

"Do me a favor," I said, "and stay clear of Steppe while you're in Washington."

"Got it." He slid sunglasses into place so that I wasn't sure if the look in his eyes matched his spoken agreement.

"And that includes his minions," I added. He grinned back at me, making my stomach tighten into a hard knot.

"Aren't I supposed to be the worrier here?" he asked, arching a brow above the rim of his glasses.

"Be careful."

"You first."

"Wes ..."

"All right, all right." He held up a hand. "I'll be careful." His smile disappeared. "Call me every single day."

"I will."

I watched him climb behind the wheel and pull the door shut with a soft click. I caught his eye in the side mirror and hugged my arms around myself. The car eased forward with barely a sound. He hung his hand out the window, waving at me. I waved back, a single hand raised in the air, and stood there until he reached the end of the driveway and disappeared around the curve of the trees.

When he'd gone, I scanned the spot at the edge of the grass where I'd left my car. I'd wedged it in at an odd angle, just short of double-parking, so that no one could block me in. I'd have to drive between a few trees to get out, where the edge of the woods met the yard, but it was doable.

I joined Cambria and George and headed inside.

"Wes said Cord's with Vera." My voice sounded loud against the absolute quiet.

After the rumble of so many hushed conversations that morning, the silence seemed to echo, like a ringing in the ears. "We should go say hi, make sure she's not planning on coming out anytime soon."

I stopped in the foyer and faced the others. Their tense expressions mirrored my insides.

"See you in ten," said George pointedly. The three of us exchanged a look.

George disappeared up the stairs to retrieve his bag. I followed Cambria back to the library that had now become Vera's hideaway. Cambria's knock was followed by a faint, "Come in."

Vera was in the armchair, her specially brewed tea cooling beside her. Cord stood against the far wall, her arms folded. Sunlight leaked into the window behind her, giving her blond hair a halo effect. She looked up as I came in and the expression on her face struck me as angelic. Not in its gentleness but in its fierce anguish. Then she looked away and all that was left were shadows—under her eyes, across her cheekbones—and drying tears sparkling in the light.

"Hello, girls. Come in, sit down." Vera gestured to the chair across from her. I nodded at Cambria and moved behind it, resting my hands on the back.

"Are they gone?" Cord asked.

"Yes," I said. "They left a few minutes ago."

She nodded and bit her lip. I hoped she wouldn't start crying in front of me. Or that if she did, I'd know what to do.

"Um, how are you feeling, Vera?" Cambria asked, cutting through the awkward silence.

"Better, now that I'm out of that heat," she said. "This is certainly a day I'm glad not to be a wolf. I don't think I could've kept up."

"Yeah, it must be pretty cool to have all that speed," Cambria said. The wistful note in her voice caught my attention. I looked down at her, but all I could see was the top of her head from where I stood. Was it simply curiosity or something bigger that had her imagining what it would be like to be a wolf?

"I was telling Cord what a nice turn-out it was," Vera said.

"Who were all of those people? Did they really all know Bailey?" I asked.

"Some did. Others were here to support Jack and The Cause as a whole."

"So the group is bigger than just you guys?" Cambria asked.

Vera nodded. "We have branches in almost every state. Not everyone came today. Only those who lived close enough and could get away."

"And all of them want peace? They believe it can really happen?" Cambria asked.

"They believe in the right not to fight in a war that isn't theirs," Vera said.

"But they have to realize how impossible it is. Peace, I mean. Especially with someone like Gordon Steppe in charge." Cambria was leaning forward now, like she was hoping Vera would argue, tell her it wasn't impossible. Near the window, Cord made a noise like a snarl at the mention of Steppe.

Vera smiled patiently, as if she'd heard all this too often to be bothered with debating it. "Faith is believing even when you can't see the solution."

I shivered at the same time a knock sounded at the door.

It opened before Vera could call out and George poked his head inside. His eyes were wide, his breathing uneven. "Tay?"

I stiffened. "What is it?

"I don't—" He stopped and clutched at his stomach, doubling over.

I took a step forward, alarm shooting through me. "George, what's wrong?"

He straightened enough to look at me. "I don't feel right," he said in a shaky voice.

"You don't look so good," said Cord.

My stomach dropped. No way. This couldn't happen yet. We had to get away first. Get to Astor. I rushed forward, arms out to steady him. Just as I reached him, he looked straight at me and winked.

I faltered.

The gesture threw me off for only a moment before I realized what he was doing and redoubled my efforts. "Let's get you some water. We need to get you cooled down," I said. I took his arm and led him out.

"You need some help?" I heard Cambria say from behind me. Her tone was off, and I knew she'd recognized the ploy.

"No, we'll be fine. You stay," I called back. I ushered us through the door and pulled it closed. George's bag sat on the floor in the foyer. He grabbed it as we passed.

The front door clicking shut echoed in my ears like a gunshot. My heart pounded, my breathing shallow. Any second, I expected the front door to open and Cord to come running out demanding to know what was going on. Or Jack and Fee to come barreling out of the trees to carry me home and lock me in my room.

I ran to the car, weaving in and out between bumpers and truck beds. George followed, not saying a word. I opened my car door, crawled inside, and eased it closed again. George did the same, only his door slammed. I whipped my head around and glared at him.

"Sorry," he muttered.

I didn't answer except to crank the engine, shift the gears, and drive.

I stared harder into my rearview than I did the gravel driveway in front of me. The woods closed around the view of the house behind us, finally obscuring it. I rolled to a stop where the gravel met the asphalt and forced myself to breathe steadily. In and out. In and out.

George dropped his hand onto mine where I white-knuckled the gearshift. Our eyes met, and he grinned. "We did it."

"We did it," I repeated, surprised and relieved and a little scared as I pulled away.

CHAPTER TEN

At the Tennessee state line, to the sound of Plain White T's singing about feeling like a boomerang, my phone finally rang. George lowered the volume as the screen lit up with a single name.

"It's Wes," I said, filling with anticipation and dread. If he was calling so soon, did that mean something had gone wrong?

The phone rang again.

"Are you going to answer it?" George asked. He reached over as if to take it. I yanked it back out of his reach and scowled at him.

I hit a button on the keypad and pressed it to my ear. "Hello?"

"Tara?"

"Hey. Is everything okay? Did something happen?"

"Nothing happened. I'm fine. Just making sure you got out okay."

"Oh." I allowed myself to breathe. "Yeah, George pretended to be in pain, from shifting or whatever, and we snuck away."

"Good. I'm getting close and I just wanted to tell you I love you. I'll call you when I have the hard drive."

"I love you too. We'll talk soon." I disconnected, a little more grounded, a little more sure. Wes was almost there. In a few hours, he'd have the hard drive. I'd get George to Astor. Cambria and Alex would do their part in making sure no one knew where we were until we'd figured this out. It would've been better to fly, time saving. But I couldn't be sure George wouldn't shift, and that was definitely something I couldn't risk at thirty thousand feet.

The phone rang again. I read the screen.

"Who is it?" George asked, leaning over to see the caller ID. "Damn. I guess you should answer."

I hit the button and brought the phone to my ear. "Hey, Grandma," I said.

"Hey there, favorite granddaughter, how's your day?"

"It's been … tiring. How's yours?"

She sighed. "I've had better. These stupid meetings are wearing on me. Cambria's mom got arrested."

"I know, Logan called."

"Good, he's a nice boy. Listen, I just came from a meeting about the whole thing and its better she knows. CHAS is trying make an example out of her. They want to charge her with treason."

"What? For making a few comments to her therapist?"

"It was more than a few, but yes, it's extreme, even for Gordon."

"If she's found guilty …" I couldn't finish. I wasn't well versed in the Hunter judicial system, but they were big proponents of the death penalty.

"I aim to not let that happen, but I think it's only fair that Cambria be prepared."

I sighed. "I understand. Thanks, Grandma. I'll tell her."

"You do that. I'm fixing to get out of here by tomorrow, I think. Should be home tomorrow night. Let her know I can talk to her about it then."

"I will. Grandma?"

"Yes?"

I hesitated. I wanted to ask her how in the world she could bring herself to work for a man like Gordon Steppe and all he stood for, but I held back. How could I ask her to be honest, to bare her most personal thoughts, when I was lying to her? She had her reasons, I had mine. "Nothing," I said.

"I know you're stressed. I'll be home as soon as I can. How's George?" she asked. "And why does it sound like you're in a car?"

I didn't answer. Our entire plan hinged on our destination remaining a secret, even the pretend one involving Alex. Otherwise, I had no doubt Grandma would hop a plane just to double-check my story.

"Is he all right?" she prompted. She sounded worried now.

I glanced at George. He was staring expectantly back at me in the fading light.

"He's feeling pretty good. Wes and Derek have been hanging out with him, running with him. I'm on my way to buy him some new running shoes, actually." Running shoes? Geez, could I have come up with a lamer excuse?

"Well, that's good he has friends to show him the ropes," she said. "Just be careful. No one in town can know who you're shopping for."

"I know. I'll be careful. Love you."

"Love you. See you soon," she said before disconnecting.

I dropped the phone in the empty cup holder and kept my eyes locked on the highway in front of me. Traffic was light and getting lighter as the sun crawled behind the horizon. Orange streaks lit the part of sky visible through the treetops that bordered the interstate. My guilt was so heavy, my shoulders ached.

DAY GAVE WAY TO TWILIGHT, AND HEADLIGHTS LIT THE PAVEMENT. I stopped for gas not long after my call from Grandma. George hadn't spoken since then. I think he realized I needed to work through it on my own. While George pumped gas, I used ATM to withdraw my meager savings. I wasn't putting it past Grandma to track my credit card footprint and find me once the truth was out. Her resources scared me. From here on, cash only.

Back in the car, George flipped through songs on his iPod and I shook my head "yes" or "no" with each choice. "That one," I said, finally settling on some old *Aerosmith* song I'd heard George play a thousand times. It had an edge to it that matched the way I felt.

My phone buzzed with a text from Cambria. George read it aloud. "Back from the run. No one suspects. Cue the compulsion. Be safe. XO."

The sign above us said "Kingsport, Tennessee 5 miles" when my eyes began to droop.

"You could just let me drive, you know."

I shook my head as I maneuvered us into an empty space. The neon lights from the beaten-down motel glared on the dashboard. A blinking sign propped against a weather-faded concrete wall read "Vacancy." It strobed in and out above us, hurting my eyes. I cut the engine.

"It's too dangerous. I know your stunt earlier was fake but something like that could happen at any time," I told him.

"Then I'd pull over," he argued.

"There might not be time. And if you wrecked the car, what then? My mom would love it if I had to call her for bus money."

He sighed. I was right. He knew it.

We got out, abandoning the argument I was sure we'd have again before it was over, and climbed the metal stairs in search of room 207.

"We'll sleep for a few hours and get back on the road," I said, pulling out the silver key and fitting it into the old-fashioned lock. I stepped inside with George behind me and groped for a switch. Yellow light swathed the dingy room. It smelled stale, overused and under cleaned. My nose twitched and I forced my growing sense of smell back down. I walked to the bed and pulled the covers back, inspecting. George emerged from the bathroom and made a face.

"Don't go in there if you can help it," he said.

"That bad?"

"I'll get my shower at the next one."

"Hopefully, the next one's better."

He grunted and flopped down beside me onto his back. He didn't bother pulling the covers down before reaching for the remote and clicking on the TV. He flipped until he found the sports channel and settled in with his hands propped behind his head. I sat next to him in silence.

I couldn't help but think back to another night, another hotel room. A heated kiss, slow to start, but then spreading warmth as it deepened. The memory of it—and Alex, of waking next to him—stirred the animal inside me that seemed to rise so suddenly to the surface lately. I breathed in and out deliberately and tried to clear my thoughts until it receded. It left behind an ache in my chest I suspected had more to do with missing Alex than quelling my inner wolf.

My inner wolf.

At some point I knew I'd have to face it. Maybe it would be easier to do a thousand miles from home.

"Those are some heavy thoughts you've got going over there." The sound of George's voice was a welcome distraction.

"How do you mean?" I asked, twisting so I could look at him.

"That frown you're wearing droops all the way to your chin."

"Funny." I punched him lightly on the arm.

His smile faded and he seemed to be scrutinizing my expression, trying to decipher the thoughts behind them. "You want to talk about it?" he asked.

"That could take a while."

"I've got time."

I winced. We both knew that was technically a lie, but I didn't argue. "I don't even know where to start."

"How about the phone call from your grandma?"

"You heard?"

He pointed at his ear. "A blessing and a curse, these heightened senses."

"Yeah, I figured." What did that mean, as far as time left, if his hearing was already sharpening? "She's worried about you."

"Do you think she'll be mad when she finds out where we've gone?"

"Yes. I'll be surprised if the cops aren't waiting on my doorstep when I return."

"She'd call the cops?"

"If not her, then for sure my mother."

"But they know you're safe. Or I mean, at least as far as the human world is concerned."

"My mother has a hard time separating the two. She lives very much grounded in the human world. I think she hopes if she focuses hard enough on being human, all the rest of it will just fade away."

"Ignorance is bliss."

"Worse. Denial—and she's a pro. And Grandma, she'd do it simply to use every resource at her disposal."

"So we stick to the plan and keep to the back roads?"

I nodded. "Tomorrow we'll ditch this highway for a smaller one."

"Is there a smaller one than this?"

"I think so. I saw it on the atlas I brought." He opened his mouth to say something, but I cut him off. "Don't ask me to drive again."

He sent me a half-hearted scowl. "Whatever you say, boss."

"I'm serious. We have to be careful. If your senses are heightening, it means you're getting close."

"We'll bring some water. Keep my temperature down."

I laughed. "I made that up. I have no idea if that even works."

He chuckled. "What if Vera or Cord had called you on it?"

I shrugged. "I was banking on Cord's lack of knowledge with this sort of thing. And Vera's not going to say anything."

"What makes you so sure?"

"Vera's sort of … invested. She basically gave me the idea for this whole plan."

"Why? Does she know something we don't about this Astor guy?"

"She used to know him, but I think it's more than that. If I know Vera, she's had some vision or premonition about this working out."

"So she's psychic or something?"

"Sort of. I don't think she gets to pick and choose what she sees, though, and she doesn't ever tell me what she sees. Well, except the first time."

"What did she tell you the first time?"

I hesitated, mostly out of habit. I was very aware that this was George I was talking to, someone who, until very recently, had been high up on my "do not tell about my secret life" list. It felt nice, despite the circumstances that had made it possible, to finally be able to tell someone from my old life all about my new one. Not to mention there was finally someone who knew less than me about this world.

"Well, you know The Cause, the group all of them belong to?"

"Yeah, they want to bring peace to the two sides, Hunters and Werewolves, right?"

"Yes. Vera saw a vision before she ever met me, of me leading The Cause and bringing peace."

"I take it you don't agree?"

"I don't think it's a matter of agreeing or not. It's … pressure. She thinks I'm special. 'Like no Hunter ever seen before,'" I said in a deep, mimicking voice. "They think I'm going to save them."

"From what?"

"I don't know." I threw up a hand. Talking about this always frustrated me.

"Are her visions ever wrong?"

"Not that I know of. I mean, they can be changed, I guess. Free will and all that."

"So change it," he said simply.

"It's more complicated than that. Wes believes it. They all do, but him most of all. And he believes we're supposed to do it together."

"He said that?"

I nodded. "He says Vera saw the two of us as leaders." The memory of it, Wes finally admitting Vera's visions to me, of how excited and hopeful he'd been that night, washed over me. "He used the word *destiny*."

George whistled. "That's a little heavy for someone just finding out about all this. I'm pretty overwhelmed as it is, and I don't have any sort of mission or purpose to fulfill."

"He wasn't supposed to tell me. Jack and Vera ordered them all not to, so I wouldn't get scared away, but he did, anyway." I smiled. "Because of you, actually."

"What do I have to do with it?"

"He told me he saw the way I was with you and he wanted that same openness. He wanted us to be able to tell each other anything." I fell silent. We'd come such a long way since then—for a while, in the wrong direction. "That was the night he told me he loved me."

"And you love him."

I looked up, unaware I'd said the words aloud. "I do. Is that—? I mean, I don't want to hurt you."

"You're not. I do care about you, Tay, a lot. But it feels different as time passes. The longer we're apart, the more it feels … I don't know, *settled.*" He shook his head. "That probably makes no sense."

"It does, actually."

"I guess what I'm trying to say is, we'll always be friends, and more and more, that feels good enough." He smiled slyly. "Don't get me wrong. If you change your mind about Wes, I'm here." I laughed. "But mainly I just want you to be happy. Does he make you happy?"

I looked down at the blanket, at the swirling paisley patterns, and thought about how it was before Wood Point, before Alex, before Wes had become a leader. "He does."

"Happier than that Alex kid?"

I glanced up sharply. "What?"

"I saw the way he looked at you when I was there, and you had a few looks of your own. You can't tell me there's nothing there."

"I—"

"And why did he agree to pretend you'd gone to visit him so we could go on this trip? Doesn't he hate Werewolves?"

I concentrated on tracing the patterns again. "He did it for me," I mumbled.

"So the question remains—who makes you happier, Godfrey?"

My heart hurt. I tried to think of an answer and couldn't. Wes's name was on the tip of my tongue but I held it back. If I said it out loud, it was like closing a door on the other. It felt final, like walking away. Besides, during those first few weeks of school, when Wes and I had been fighting, Alex had made me happier. Is that what it came down to?

My face flushed with the effort of trying to answer. Guilt and frustration flooded me.

"This," I said, biting off the word. "This right here, helping you, making sure you *live*. This makes me happy."

"This makes me happy too. Come here." He reached over, and I let him pull me down next to him. I curled into his side and his arm curved around, cradling me. "Can I ask you something?" he asked.

I stared at a water spot on the ceiling, trying to steady my thoughts. "Depends. Is it a new subject?"

His chest shook with light laughter. "Yes. Your cheerleader comment—what did you mean, you did it for me?"

I smiled a little, which was proof at how far we'd come, George and I. "It was around the time I decided to pursue my feelings for you, or pursue you, I should say. I saw you around other girls and I thought—I thought you only liked a certain type of girl."

"And you thought that type only included cheerleaders?"

"No. Yes. I don't know."

"Was I that shallow?"

"No, you weren't. I was. Looking back, I wasn't confident in who I was. I thought I needed to be someone else to make you like me. Which is silly because I never felt that way when we were just friends."

"It's not silly. I felt that way too sometimes."

"You did?" I couldn't help but feel surprised.

"Sometimes, when you'd talk about a book you read or an article about something interesting, I'd feel completely out of the loop. And completely unworthy. You're so smart, full of ideas and opinions, and I didn't have much of either to offer. I wondered if you ever noticed or felt like something was lacking."

"I never felt that way."

He shrugged. I know that, I mean, logically, but it crept in a few times. So I get it."

The conversation faded. I lay there, enjoying the comfort he provided.

"I'm really glad we're friends again," I said. I didn't say the rest out loud, that we were so much better friends than we'd been as boyfriend and girlfriend.

"Yeah," he agreed, and I had a feeling it was for both the spoken and the unspoken sentiment. "Get some sleep," he whispered.

He hit the volume on the remote and the sportscaster's voice began droning on about football camps and team negotiations. George was right. I needed to sleep. I wanted to be on the road before the sun came up. I twisted my head so I could see the screen and forced myself to focus on the man's voice. Soon, the monotony became white noise and I felt my lids begin to close.

George's shoulders shook, startling me. "Sports Center always does the trick."

I smiled and fell asleep.

AT NASHVILLE, WE WENT NORTHWEST INTO MISSOURI AND ACROSS Kansas. By the following night we'd made it into a town called Colby where the interstate and county highway intersected. The single stoplight was a good indication we were still off the beaten path enough to avoid detection. I found a neon sign identical to the one from the previous night, and pulled into the near-empty lot of the roadside motel.

Momma's Kitchen, the restaurant across the street, advertised today's special as fried chicken and mashed potatoes. Several eighteen-wheelers decorated the lot.

"I'm starving," George said, hurrying to get the seat belt off.

"Let's get a room and then we'll eat."

George opened his mouth as if to answer—and snarled.

My eyes widened and we both froze. Instantly, George's face contorted from the angry snarl to shock and remorse.

"What just happened?" he asked.

"You snarled at me." I stared at him, trying to gauge what was behind his calm exterior. "How do you feel?"

"Hungry. Starving, actually. I think that's why I'm so cranky. Sorry about that."

"George, you snarled. That's more than cranky." I rebuckled my seat belt and started the engine.

"What are you doing?"

"Leaving. I'm not taking you into a motel, or a restaurant full of innocent people."

"I guess that's smart." He leaned his head back against the head-rest. "Can we at least drive-through somewhere for a burger?"

I nodded, trying to get the sound of that snarl out of my mind. It continued to echo long after we'd devoured a bag of burgers and left Colby, Kansas, behind.

"Tara, wake up."

I came awake slowly, blinking against the blaring sunlight as it slanted through the windshield.

"What time is it?" I mumbled.

"Two forty," George said, verifying the time on the dashboard. "You were out for a while."

"You should've woken me sooner. I can drive again." I hated letting George drive, but he'd finally worn me down somewhere around Utah. I couldn't drive on no sleep, and I was too afraid to stop. We'd parked and slept in the car at a rest stop once but George had complained it was such a waste of time. He insisted he wasn't tired at all. I wasn't even sure the last time he'd slept. That worried me, but so far, he'd kept a human frame, and he hadn't snarled again.

"I need to know which road to take," he said.

I looked around, trying to get my bearing, and reached for the map on the floorboard. "Where are we?"

"The sign back there said we just left Great Basin National Park." I looked at him blankly. "Nevada," he added.

I sat up straighter and rubbed my eyes. "We're in Nevada already? Geez, George, how fast are you going?" I caught sight of the speedometer and winced.

George laughed. "It's fine. I haven't seen a single cop. I can see a lot farther than I could yesterday, especially since everything's so flat here."

He was right, at least about the landscape. In the distance, the purple haze of mountains rose against the horizon, but here, and for miles ahead, the highway stretched flat and infinite. Ours was the only vehicle in sight. I tried not to think about the other reason his vision had sharpened.

A sign up ahead advertised a junction for routes 93, 50, and 6. I scanned the map I'd used to mark our route. "You want Route 93," I told him.

He veered left and took the exit for the new highway.

"Your mom called while you were sleeping," he said.

Something about his expression made me pause. "Did you answer it?"

"Would you be mad if I said yes?"

"George! She's not supposed to know you're with me."

"I pretended to be Alex," he said, "but she knew it was me. Don't worry, I didn't tell her anything about where we were."

I glared at him. "What did she say?"

"She knows you're not with Alex. They all do."

I bit my lip. I'd known they'd figure it out sooner or later. I'd just hoped it was later. As in, we'd be there already. I checked the map, calculating. "We should be there in a couple of hours," I said. "Did she say anything else?"

"She sounded pretty pissed off. And worried. She asked how I was feeling. I told her I feel great, because I do. For some reason, that made it worse."

"Of course it did. It means you're going to change soon and that she knows all about it. I can't believe you answered. We agreed two days ago that we wouldn't answer, remember? What if she has some way to triangulate the call or something?"

He chuckled. "You watch way too many movies."

"You don't know my grandma. What else did she say?"

"That she's worried. Your mom called Alex to check on you and he spilled the beans. I guess she basically threatened to kill Cambria if she didn't tell them where you were."

"And did she? Tell them, I mean?"

George glanced at me. "What would you do?"

I sat back. "They know."

"You think?" His tone was sarcastic.

"Has Wes called?"

"No."

That worried me. I'd been expecting a call hours ago. I was too afraid to call him, scared I'd interrupt a secret meeting or ruin his cover. Something in the road caught my attention and I bolted upright in my seat. George was fumbling with the iPod again. It took me a moment to find my voice.

"George, look out!"

He whipped his head around and slammed on the brake.

Up ahead, straddling the yellow lines marking the center of the road stood a man and a woman.

"What the hell? Move!" George eased up on the brake to keep the car from fishtailing. The man and woman didn't move as we careened closer. They stood shoulder to shoulder, staring straight at us, no expression on their faces. I squeezed my eyes shut as I braced myself for impact.

None came.

A moment later the car skidded smoothly to a stop. I opened my eyes. The road in front of us was empty. I whirled and stared out the back windshield. I could see the skid marks left by the tires, but no man, no woman.

I looked back at George. He was watching me with an odd expression.

I glanced down at myself, trying to figure out what he was looking at, and caught sight of my hands. Fur, soft and thin, like down on a puppy, covered the back of arms and trailed down my fingers. My nails, which had been rounded and clear, were sharpened to points. I screamed, shoved open my door, and ran.

George was on me in three seconds.

We went down in a tangle of limbs. My claws scratched at George's bare arms as he wrestled me still. "It's okay, it's okay," he repeated against my ear. He folded himself around me, his hands gripping my wrists hard enough to cut off blood flow. I forced myself to stop struggling against him.

"This isn't happening," I said, only now realizing I was sobbing.

George held me without a word. By the time I quieted, his shirt was streaked with tears and I was out of breath. I pulled back and stole a glance at my hands. The soft fur had disappeared; in its place was smooth skin, rounded nails.

"You want to tell me what just happened?" George asked when I'd managed to sit up.

I pulled my knees into my chest, blinking back the last of the tears, and looked around.

"They're gone," he said, answering the question before I could ask. "Now tell me what the hell just happened to you."

"I told you before, I'm turning."

"I know what you said, but seeing it … So, you can be either one?"

"It's slightly more complicated than that." I gave him the quick version about how my inner wolf had only recently decided to emerge, with no real way to control or contain it. "I think Jack or Wes said something once about having both inside me, but that my Hunter side was more dominant than the wolf. I guess that's not the case anymore."

"But you don't know?"

"It's not like there's a whole lot of precedent for this sort of thing."

"What about Wes? Isn't he both?"

"Yes, but his wolf side was already dominant, and as for a Hunter," I shrugged, "how would he tell if that side was taking over, except that he felt strong and fast in a fight, or extra-sensitive to a nearby Werewolf? He already feels all of those things simply from being a Werewolf."

"I don't understand, though. Why is it so bad if you shift? Wes is a wolf. A lot of your friends are. I will be. Is the idea so revolting?"

"It's not that. If I'd been born with the ability, I'd be fine with it. It's the fact that it's happening now. I shouldn't be able to shift like this and if I can—" I stopped, drew a breath. "If I can, it means all of those things Vera thinks about me are true. I'm different, special. And I have no idea what to do with that. I just wish I knew how to control it."

"That couple in the road, the ones from your school, I think they triggered it somehow."

"You recognized them?"

"I saw them in the clinic at Wood Point. They were unconscious. I couldn't figure out what was wrong with them. What do you think they wanted?"

"I don't know."

"But you know them?" he asked.

I nodded, suddenly exhausted. "Their names are Douglas and Sandra Lexington. They're hybrids."

"How did they get out here? I thought they were at Wood Point, or with your people or whatever."

"I don't know. It doesn't make any sense, but I know it was them. They've been reported missing for a few weeks, but CHAS had to know Kane had them in the infirmary that night."

"Do you think they escaped?"

"Maybe." I shivered. It was cooling down with the coming evening.

"We should get going," George said, pulling me to my feet.

"George, before we go, and no matter what happens when we get there, I want to say thanks."

"Thanks for what?"

"For listening and—"

He held up a hand. "Wait."

"What is it?"

He shushed me and scanned the darkening desert. A few yards away sat the car, still parked on the shoulder, the passenger door hanging open the way I'd left it. No other cars had passed by since we'd been here. George was silent a minute longer, slowly turning side to side to take in our surroundings. I did the same, but there wasn't much to see. A few patches of sagebrush cropped up here and there where the dirt became heavier than the grainy sand. There was no sign of water, greenery, or more importantly, cover for an enemy.

"Did you hear that?" he asked.

"What?" I strained to pick up something, anything, but there was only wind.

"I don't know. It was more a feeling than a sound, but I swear it was—there," he hissed, jerking around to face the desert stretching out before us. He squinted into the grayness. "Something's out there."

"I don't feel anything." As soon as I said it, faint goosebumps washed over me. "I take that back. Werewolf, let's go." I grabbed George's wrist and marched toward the car.

"Where is it?" he asked, craning his neck to see behind us.

"Somewhere," I said, waving an arm, "back there, I think. We're not waiting around to find out."

"But it might be the Lexingtons again."

"You say that like it's a good thing." He didn't answer. "George, they stood in the middle of the road like they had a death wish, either for themselves or for us, and then disappeared into thin air. I never even felt them nearby. Does that sound like they want to be friends?"

"Good point." We reached the car. He held out the keys partway and hesitated. "But we could check it out at least. I wouldn't let anything hurt you."

I softened. "When you turn, there's no guarantee you'll be on my side." I said it gently but I could tell the words had an effect. He nodded and handed me the keys.

Wes called an hour later. I released the death grip on the steering wheel and grabbed for the phone.

"Hello?"

"It's me." He said the words between heavy breaths and my heart rate accelerated.

"What happened? Did you get the drive?"

"No, something … came up."

Anxiety curled in my gut. "What exactly *came up*?"

"The girl, the one I supposed to meet, she wasn't there."

"What do you mean? Like, had the day off?"

"No, I checked into it. She was fired the day before I arrived."

"For what?"

A car door slammed in the background followed by the sounds of an engine turning over and revving. "No one knows. I found an address. All of her stuff is there, but no one's home. No one's been home for a while according to the neighbors."

The anxiety twisted into fear. This wasn't good. "Could it be a coincidence? Maybe she went on a spontaneous vacation? Or went to stay with her mom. If I got fired, I'd be upset and maybe—"

"I don't think so, Tara. Her toothbrush, her car keys, everything is there."

"Someone knew you were coming," I said. "They knew what she was going to give you." It wasn't a question.

He didn't answer me directly, which told me he suspected the worst. "Are you guys there yet?"

"Not yet. We're close. There was a delay."

"What happened?" The worry in his voice made him snap the words out.

I told him about seeing the Lexingtons and my near-shift. "You need to get to Astor's as fast as you can," he said. "No more stops, do you hear me? No matter what."

"All right."

"And remember what I said about the threat being the trigger. Keep your cool."

"Okay."

"But not if you're attacked. If that happens, listen to me very carefully: let it loose. The wolf, whatever's inside you struggling to get out, let it. But only if you're attacked, all right?"

I nodded until I remembered he couldn't see me. "Got it," I said.

"Good. I'm doubling back. I'll be there in a day."

"Wes, it's way too far to be there—"

"A day. Call me when you get there."

I promised him I would and we hung up.

"It's going to be all right," George said quietly.

I shot him a look, knowing my expression reflected my panic. "You know, the more people say that to me, the more I realize how wrong it sounds."

He didn't say anything else.

CHAPTER ELEVEN

George's fingers tapped against his knee to the beat of Linkin Park. "…'cause beyond every bend is a long, blinding end. It's the worst kind of pain I know," he sang, his head bobbing up and down. "Weep not for roads untraveled. Weep not for sights unseen. May your love never end, and if you need a friend, there's a seat here alongside me." His foot tapped out the beat against the floorboard, manic energy radiating from him, his muscles bunched and flexed with the movement.

"Are you all right?" I asked.

"Huh?" He looked over at me as if he'd forgotten I was there. "I'm good." He went back to tapping.

I frowned. He'd been antsy the past few miles, like he'd downed a case of Monster. I wasn't sure what had triggered it, maybe nothing, but it couldn't be good. I pressed my foot harder against the gas pedal and watched the speedometer inch upward.

The song ended but the tapping continued in the silence. The sound of Bon Jovi's "Always" filled the speakers.

"Hey, our song," I said, my tone falsely cheerful. Maybe I could distract him. "Remember that letter you wrote me before I left for Wood Point?"

"Uh-huh." He kept singing and tapping.

"That was really sweet."

"Uh-huh."

"George, are you listening to me?" I reached over and touched his arm. He flinched so suddenly, I swerved.

"Don't. Touch. Me." His eyes blazed with barely controlled fury. I sucked in a breath. His eyes were brighter than normal, somewhere between a very human white and a distinctly hybrid yellow.

"George—"

"Let me out. I need to get out. I want out!" He clawed at the door handle as if he couldn't remember how it worked. When it didn't open, he twisted toward me, his back pressed against the window. "Let me out," he whispered.

I slowed and veered onto the shoulder. By then, he'd gone back to fumbling with the door handle and locks. He managed to roll the window down in short, awkward bursts. I watched as he wiggled out of the opening and fell, face first, onto the ground.

"George!" I got out and ran around the car.

He pushed to his feet and straightened in front of me, his hands fisted at his sides. "Get away from me," he growled. His eyes were wild and glowing. Thick hair sprang up on his arms and legs. It poked through the back of his shirt as he turned and bolted into the desert.

I hesitated for only a second before following. This was George. And I'd made a promise.

Darkness hung like a heavy coat over my face. I couldn't see my hands in front of me, much less George. I followed the sounds of his labored breathing and his footsteps as they pounded against the sandy terrain.

Slowly, the ground underneath my feet changed. It became harder, packed dirt instead of loose sand. I stumbled as my feet caught on low-growing plants. I brushed up against something hard as I raced by. A fallen tree. The bark left a scrape on my shin.

Shadowy shapes sprang up in front of me—narrow trunks and leafy branches. The scent of lilac and nectar filled my nose. George's footsteps became louder as he crashed through brush and branches. Where had all of the trees come from? Everything we'd seen up until this point had been nothing but open desert with the mountains forever framed in the distance, never getting any closer, never fading out of sight.

Up ahead, yellow floodlights glowed, throwing everything into an eerie pool of light. Leafy branches and exotic greenery spanned every direction. My foot landed on something hard and I glanced down. A stepping stone. And then another. A path?

Just ahead, George let out a grunt. It sounded heavy, as if the wind had been knocked out of him, and was followed by the crash of branches. The gray outline of his body slunk to the ground. I raced forward.

"George," I called. I pulled up short at the sight of him, groaning and rolling side to side on black asphalt. A thick hedge bordered by granite stone separated the exotic forest behind us from the hard surface stretching in front. I followed it to its end, several yards away.

A house, enormous and sleek, loomed up out of the darkness. Soft yellow spotlights aimed strategically against the stone lit the structure. I stood on what must've been the driveway, a circular path with a fountain in the middle that trickled a steady stream of water from its spout. A sidewalk leading up to the massive double front door was lit in white pathway lights. The numbers mounted above the door read 1183.

We were here.

I knelt in front of George. He was holding his knee, still rolling side to side. The groaning had stopped but he looked pained.

"George?" I said softly. "Are you all right?"

He didn't answer, just continued rolling and writhing, seemingly lost in his own world. His lips moved in silent mutterings, and his eyes were closed. It scared me to imagine what color they'd be once he opened them.

"George, we're here," I said softly. I touched my hand to his shoulder and he reacted. In a lightning move, he rolled away onto all fours and growled at me. His eyes blazed bright yellow.

"Back off." A snarl rose from deep in his throat, twisting his features.

I resisted the urge to retreat. Instead, I straightened, adjusting my stance to be ready if he attacked.

"Stand up," I said.

He snarled again, but he stood. As soon as he was on his feet, I swung. I put everything I had, all of my weight and training, behind the punch. My fist connected. George staggered sideways. I braced myself, ready to hit him again if necessary, but his eyelids drooped and closed, and he crumpled. I bit my lip against the agony of my throbbing knuckles and walked in circles. After a moment, the pain dulled to nearly bearable.

I eyed the massive double front door of the mansion across the way. Butterflies danced in my gut at the thought of ringing the bell. I glanced down at an unconscious George. I didn't have a choice.

It took me several minutes to drag George close enough to ring the bell. I couldn't leave him in case he woke disoriented and ran off, and I couldn't carry him. Being an all-star athlete *and* a Werewolf hybrid definitely made a person solid. I ended up dragging him by his shoulders and the scruff of his shirt. I propped him against the house and then pressed the doorbell before I could change my mind.

A minute passed. Silence from the other side. No lights shone from the windows. Last I'd checked the clock on the dashboard, it had read close to midnight. I sighed and rang it again.

An echoing click sounded from the door, and I jumped.

The door opened and a man stood there. He wore a formal black jacket over silk pajamas. Both hung off his lean frame and he stooped a little at the shoulders. His dark hair was thin and combed straight back. "Can I help you?" He seemed unruffled considering the time of my visit.

"Um, yeah, I'm Tara Godfrey. We're here to see Astor DeLuca."

"We?" His brow rose, a gesture that elongated his nose.

"Oh, my friend and me. He's there."

I pointed and the man craned his neck to peer around the corner. He didn't register any surprise at the fact that George was unconscious. "Do you have an appointment?" he asked.

"An …? No." I stared at him, trying to decide if he was being serious. "I've come a long way and my friend is sick. It's an emergency."

"Hmm. I'll see if he's available." He started to turn away.

"I'm his niece," I added.

The man turned back, expression still neutral. He peered down at me. "You're Tara, you say?" he asked finally.

"Yes. My father was Jeremiah DeLuca."

"Hrmph," he said. Then he closed the door.

I blinked once, twice. By the third time, heat coursed through me. Tears stung my eyes. I'd come all this way to be turned away at the door? I looked over at George. He was still slumped against the side of the house, unmoving. The entire side of his face was raised and red with the beginnings of what would surely be a nasty bruise.

I heard a noise, the sound of the lock being turned over, and sucked in a breath. The door inched open, and a pair of deep-set eyes set against bushy, white eyebrows peered out at me. "You're Tara?"

"Yes."

He continued to stare.

"Are you Astor?"

He straightened and swung the door wide. "Well, I ain't the Pope. Get in here, then."

I took a hasty step forward and then stopped on the threshold, gesturing to George. "My friend. He's sick."

He waved a hand, dismissing it. "Jeeves'll get him. Come on." He turned in his fuzzy brown slippers and headed down a long, dimly lit hallway spanning left.

I hesitated a second longer. I didn't see "Jeeves" anywhere and I wasn't about to leave George lying on the porch.

"Jeeves!" Astor yelled.

I jumped.

The man who'd first answered the door appeared from a side hallway.

"Get that boy off the porch," Astor told him.

"Where shall I put him, sir?"

"Put him in the east wing and lock the door. I smell something not quite right on that one." Jeeves nodded and headed for the open doorway. "Let's get on with it," Astor said as he resumed his trek down the hall. Behind me, Jeeves was already working at dragging George into the foyer. With nothing else to do but follow, I hurried after the strange man.

At the end of the hall, we turned right, and I found myself in an open room. All of the furniture had been pushed back and stacked haphazardly against the wall. In the center of the room stood an easel speckled with various colors of paint. Beside the easel sat a small side table littered with brushes and jars and rags. What had once been a white cloth covered the floor underneath my feet. It was hard to tell if there was more paint on the easel or the cloth.

Astor closed the door behind me with a decisive click. "How did you find me?" he asked, eyeing me sharply.

"Vera Gallagher, sir," I said.

"Vera sent you here? You mean, you're not here to arrest me?"

"Arrest you?" I echoed, thoroughly confused. "No, I came to ask for your help. I'm your niece, or great-niece, or something. My father was Jeremiah."

"Jeremy?"

"Um, yes, Jeremiah DeLuca, leader of The Cause. Married to Elizabeth Godfrey."

He locked his hands behind his back and chewed his lip, lost in thought. "Huh."

He walked to the easel and began fiddling with the bottles of paint. He selected a bottle and faced the easel, a short distance away. He brought his arm back and, in a look of deep concentration, flung the contents of the bottle at the canvas. Cobalt paint splattered this way and that, mostly on the floor beyond. He grunted and went back to his bottles.

"Sir?" I said when he didn't speak again. "I mean, Astor. My friend George was injected with a serum that's going to turn him into a Werewolf. It's a dangerous mixture and his body can't handle it. If I don't help him, he's going to become a monster, without any humanity or reason. I was told you might be able to help us."

"And who told you that?" he asked without turning.

"Vera … and Miles DeLuca."

A tremor went through Astor, a violent tremble that shook him from shoulder to knees. He raised his hand and pointed a bony finger at me. "Don't you say that name to me. That man is evil and I won't lift a finger to help him. If you're working with him, you can forget it. Get out, get out!"

His demands turned into screams and I backed away, at a loss. I had no idea what brought on the sudden outburst, or how to fix it. Every time I opened my mouth to reassure him I wasn't working with Miles, he only screamed louder.

"Get out, get out!" he repeated. His hands were clamped over his ears, drowning out my rebuttals.

I backed toward the door, trying to remember the way out. Then I remembered Astor telling Jeeves to take George to the east wing. I had no idea where that was. This house was huge. I started to say that to Astor, but he continued to rail at me. His screams drowned out my own. His eyes had gone wild and unfocused and I ducked just in time to avoid taking an orange bottle of paint in the face. I backed up and the flat surface of the door brushed against me. I felt for the latch, afraid to take my eyes off Astor, and ducked another bottle of paint.

I flung the door open, ready to flee, and pulled up short. A familiar figure stood in the hall, blocking my path. Her red hair hung in fiery waves around her shoulders, her petite frame wrapped in a thin robe.

"Hello, Tara."

I blinked. "Professor Flaherty?"

Her gaze flickered to Astor, who'd come up behind me still ranting. "I see you've caught him at a bad time," she said. I nodded, unsure how else to respond. "Give me just a moment, don't go anywhere," she said, sweeping past me.

She went to Astor and gently took his hands away from where he'd held them over his ears. He kept his eyes on hers as she spoke. I couldn't hear the words but her tone was gentle, soft. After a moment, his body went slack, as if he'd given up the tantrum, and he let her lead him away. I stood aside as she guided him down the hall.

"This way, Tara, if you don't mind," she called as they passed. The way she leaned into him, the way he responded to her, were they … a couple? It was too weird, and unexpected, not to mention she was half his age. Then again, after the shock of Vera and Kane, I couldn't discount the possibility.

Professor Flaherty took a different hallway than the way we'd come. This one was narrower and lined with doors, all closed, all the same shade of brown. Some were labeled with small plaques on the wall beside them: "Lab 1," "Lab 2," and "Supply." She stopped before an unlabeled door and opened it. I stood a fair distance away, feeling like an intruder as more whispered words were exchanged. At last, she patted Astor's arm and he disappeared inside.

She walked back to where I waited, smiling. "Sorry about that. He doesn't do well with surprises," she said. "I was just on my way to get some tea. Would you like some?"

"Um, sure."

"The kitchen is this way."

I fell into step beside her as we made our way back through the maze of halls. The sconce lamps became closer together as we walked, and I thought I recognized the main hall I'd come in through. We passed the foyer and the front door and continued on, stepping down into a low-ceilinged room.

Professor Flaherty motioned to the small, high-topped table against the wall and I sat and looked around. Counters, cabinets, appliances—everything was white and modern and made softer by the hanging lights set on dim.

"Are you hungry?" she asked, filling a stainless steel teapot with water.

"Maybe later," I said, ignoring the emptiness in my stomach. "First …"

"First you want to know what I'm doing here?" she finished.

I attempted a smile. "I'm a little curious."

Professor Flaherty continued making tea. Her back was to me but the set of her shoulders was relaxed, as if she'd anticipated my questions or, at the very least, didn't mind them. "He's not entirely insane, you know," she said while she worked. "He has his good days and bad days."

"I'm guessing today was not a good day?"

"Actually, it was, but then, he's not used to having midnight visitors, either. Or visitors at any time, really." She set the kettle on the burner and turned to face me. "Aside from me, you're the first in ten years."

I gawked at her. "No one's visited him in ten years?"

"Close to it. I think it was Millie Hayes from the Baptist Church. Or so Mathias tells me."

"Mathias?" I repeated.

"Yes, he works for Astor, keeping up the grounds and overseeing operations. Tall, thin, stooped shoulders."

"Astor told me his name was Jeeves."

She laughed. "He likes to mess with Mathias. They've been friends since childhood. It's a unique relationship."

"So his name is Mathias?"

"Yes, though he'll answer to almost anything these days, with all of Astor's nicknames. Anyway, Mathias tells me all of the comings and goings when I'm away at school. According to him, that sweet, old church lady was the last."

"Oh." I was trying to piece it together as she talked. Did she mean she lived here—with Astor—

when she wasn't teaching at Wood Point? "So what did he do to her?"

"To whom?"

"The church lady. You said she was the last. Did he … do something?"

"Oh, heavens, no." She laughed. "I just meant no one has come since, from the human world or otherwise. And you can be sure no one will, especially from our world."

"I see." I couldn't help but feel relieved.

"And what about you?" she asked. "How did you get here? And what's so important that it couldn't wait until morning?"

She was poking in the fridge now, assembling the makings of a sandwich. "George, my friend, he's sick," I answered.

She paused to crinkle her brows. "George … is that the hostage Miles used to get to you at Wood Point?"

I hesitated. Coming here to ask Astor for help was one thing, but I had no idea where Professor Flaherty's true loyalties lay. What if I told her about George and she called CHAS? Or Kane? I knew they were friends.

"Tara?" she prompted. Her face clouded. "Whatever it is, you can tell me. I can keep a secret. As evidenced by what you see before you." She gestured to the room around us and slid a plate in front of me: a turkey sandwich, with the works. My stomach grumbled. I caved. On both counts.

"George's sickness isn't … human," I said. "Miles injected him with the serum he used to create the hybrids. Only, it doesn't work the same on humans. They can't handle it. They become something else. Something with no humanity. They aren't themselves anymore." I spoke around mouthfuls of food.

Professor Flaherty didn't seem to mind. Her mouth was drawn and she tapped a finger against her chin, like she was concentrating on the story.

"And you think Astor can help him how?"

"Miles told me there's one way to help George's body adjust properly to the change. He said my blood would heal him. I want to know if that's true. And if not, I want to know another way."

"And where is George now?"

"Jeeves—I mean Mathias—put him in the east wing when we got here. He's sort of unconscious." Her brows rose in an unspoken question. "He was beginning to change in the car, and—oh, my car!" I slapped my forehead. I'd completely forgotten.

"Where is it?" she asked. I told her about George fleeing and how we'd ended up here. "I'll have Mathias retrieve it in the morning."

"Thanks."

"You were saying? About George?"

"Oh, I had to chase him. I tried to get him to stop, but he wouldn't listen. I don't even think he knew it was me anymore. I had to knock him out in the driveway."

"You hit him?" The corners of her mouth twitched.

I nodded and grimaced. "In the face. He's going to kill me when he wakes up."

She chuckled. "You're always a surprise, Tara. Your poor mother …" her smile faded. "Speaking of, does she know you're here? And Edie, your grandmother?"

"Yes," I said, though the hesitation in my voice was obvious.

"And they're okay with you being here?"

"Define 'okay.'"

She clicked her tongue. "I'm calling your mother in the morning," she said sternly. "She's probably worried sick. I know what people say about Astor, and I can't imagine she's all right with you being here."

I couldn't argue with her calling my mom. I'd always known at some point, they'd come to haul me back. I just needed to make sure I had my answers before then. "Do you think Astor will talk to me?" I asked.

"We won't know that until tomorrow," she said. "He's not the sort that can be made to do something against his will. Miles contacted him, you know, a couple of years ago. He wanted Astor to work for him, but Astor wouldn't even let him in the front door. I'm told there were a few letters, a phone call, but he was adamant, didn't even care about the project details. He'd made up his mind."

"That's why he was so upset with me tonight. He thinks I'm in league with Miles. He must think that's how George was injected."

"We'll get it all straightened out tomorrow. In the meantime, let me see that hand." I placed my hand in hers, wincing at the sight of my bruising, swollen knuckles. The pain had dulled to a low thud, but it flared again when she touched it. "This needs ice and some ointment. Tell you what, you finish that sandwich and I'll go get the ointment and check on George." She walked to the door.

"George is going to need some ointment too. His cheek was bleeding."

She shook her head, a wry smile on her lips. "What would your friends do without you?"

CHAPTER TWELVE

A creak in the mattress jolted me upright and goosebumps flared anew across my arms. I looked around, my memory hazy until I felt the soft cushion of the armchair against my back and remembered. Across the room, George shifted restlessly in the king-sized bed. He'd tossed and turned most of the night. The covers were a rumpled mess, knotted around him like a mummy suit.

After Professor Flaherty finished with her dose of first aid, she'd led me into a spare room, fully furnished, the covers turned down. The dark walls and stylish artwork reminded me of a five-star hotel. All I'd wanted was to sink between the sheets and down comforter and fade into oblivion, but I couldn't get past my anxiety over George. He'd almost turned, and I wasn't convinced the process wouldn't begin anew as soon as he woke. I hadn't been able to shake these goosebumps all night, a sure sign George was now more Werewolf than human.

I'd spent the night in the chair, in a corner of George's room, watching him sleep. I'd spoken to Wes twice but he'd made me hang up and promise to rest. Now my hand was numb from propping up my chin while I dozed.

George's blankets rustled again. He rolled over so he was facing me and I saw his eyes were open—and stained with yellow. I swallowed hard. He spotted me and his head came off the pillow. He winced, his progress slowing as he sat up.

"Tay, what are you doing in here?"

I sat forward, shifting my weight in case I needed to get up quickly. "How are you feeling?"

He frowned and seemed to be taking stock. He wiggled his jaw, his fingers pressing against his swollen and already bruising cheek. I hoped he liked the color purple. "Like I got hit by a bus. What happened?"

"You don't remember?" He shook his head. "You started to shift last night, in the car, and then you ran. I had to … subdue you."

He blinked and stared back at me for a minute. Slowly, understanding dawned. "You hit me?" He sounded more surprised than angry.

I nodded, feeling awful. "It knocked you out."

A slow grin spread across his face. "Remind me not to get on your bad side."

I sat up straighter. "You're not mad?"

"Of course not. Yeah, I've got a headache from hell, but I'm still *me*. You saved me, Tay." He sat up, moving carefully, and swung his legs over the side of the bed.

"I didn't think of it like that," I said. I decided not to mention the yellow eyes just yet. Or the goosebumps. I'd give him a moment to wake up. He stood and swayed on his feet. I jumped up to help him but he waved me off.

"I'm good," he said. "Besides, I don't really want an escort for where I'm going. Do you know where the bathroom is?"

"Across the hall."

I followed him as far as the hall and leaned against the doorframe while I waited. Mathias appeared from around the corner.

"Good morning, miss. Breakfast is in the sunroom with Master DeLuca," he said. His pajamas had been replaced by a crisp white shirt and black pants. The suit jacket remained, as did the lack of personality or facial expression.

"Thanks," I said. He gave a curt nod and turned back the way he'd come. "By the way," I called after him. "Where exactly is the sunroom?"

He pointed down the hall behind me. "Go to the end and take a left, then an immediate right. You can't miss it. The lilacs are fragrant this time of year." Then he walked away.

George came out of the bathroom and stared at me. The bruise stood out starkly against his skin, and his hair was wet at the edges as if he'd splashed water on his face. "My eyes …"

"It's going to be fine. We're here now and we're going to figure it out." My tone held way more certainty than I felt, but it did the trick in satisfying his worry. For now.

"All right." He took a deep breath as if setting it aside. The fact that he counted on me so absolutely both warmed and terrified me. "Did I hear talk of food?" he asked. His light tone sounded forced.

"Yeah, the butler said to meet in the sunroom."

He raised a brow. "Dude has a butler?"

"His name's Mathias. He said Astor would be in there, so let's go."

I started off at a quick pace, eager for another chance to get answers, and hoping Astor was a little less insane this morning. "Whoa there, tiger," George called from behind me.

I waited while he caught up, his steps slow and stiff. "Ran over by a bus, remember? What's the rush, anyway? The food will be there when we get there."

"I know, it's just … we don't have a lot of time left."

"You think I'm going to change again?"

I stopped and held my arm out. The small hairs stood straight up.

"I'm doing that?" he whispered. I nodded. "So you can sense me now?" I nodded again. He let out a breath and rubbed the back of his neck. "Okay, yeah, I get it. We need to hurry." We started walking again.

"That … and my mother is probably on her way."

"How do you know?"

I filled him in on the events of the previous night. He looked a little wary when I got to the part about Astor's craziness and frowned when I told him about Professor Flaherty.

"Do you think we can trust her?" he asked. We'd almost reached the sunroom. I could smell the flowers from here, just as Mathias said. I stopped before we reached the doorway and dropped my voice.

"I don't know, but it's not like we've got much choice. We're out of options. We just need to get our answers before my mother tips off the others and sends a posse."

"You're assuming Cambria didn't already crack and tell them our exact location. Your grandma scares me," he said.

"True." Cambria hadn't answered either time I'd tried to call her, which could mean she was afraid to admit she'd failed, or Grandma was torturing her in a basement somewhere. "Either way, we need to make the most of the time we have left."

He craned his neck side to side, as if stretching it. It was a gesture I'd seen him use many times before a game. I heard a small *pop,* and he rolled his shoulders back and straightened. "All right. Let's get in there."

The sunroom was true to its name in a way I hadn't imagined. Somehow, through the maze of halls that made up the house, we'd ended up in the rear. The exposed wall was done entirely in glass that curved upward well past where it met the ceiling. The sunlight against all of the bright green and purples and yellows of the plants was gorgeous. All that was missing was a hammock.

In the right corner, near a wall covered in hanging vines, a table had been set with bowls and platters of what looked like every breakfast food imaginable.

Astor sat in the chair at the head of the table; at least I assumed it was him behind the newspaper. I cleared my throat before approaching, not wanting to startle him. The paper jerked aside and he eyed me sharply. The bathrobe he'd worn the night before was gone, replaced with a long-sleeved shirt, lopsided and misbuttoned, and khaki slacks. He still wore the slippers. His white hair stuck out, as if he regularly ran a hand through it the wrong way.

"Jeremiah's daughter," he muttered. Then louder: "You're still here, I see."

"I was hoping we could talk," I said, taking a tentative step forward.

He didn't have time to answer before Professor Flaherty breezed in, stepping around me and heading for a seat at the table. She sat closest to Astor, looking fresh and ageless in her black pants and flowing halter.

"Aren't you two hungry?" she asked, pouring coffee from the carafe on the table.

That was all the encouragement George needed. He shuffled forward and took a seat. "Starved," he said, digging into the closest bowl.

Professor Flaherty raised a brow at the purple-and-yellow coloring of his face. "Tara?" she prompted, gesturing toward the empty seat beside George.

I sat down and eyed the choices. The table was covered with eggs, bacon, fruit, and dishes with stainless steel tops that, when lifted, revealed pancakes and waffles within. I decided on coffee and toast.

"You must be George," Professor Flaherty said, extending a hand across the table. George dropped his spoon and hastily shook her hand, openly staring as he took his attention off the food long enough to notice her face. "Your heroism in the cave gives you a reputation to be proud of. Friends that loyal are hard to come by," she told him.

He smiled, appreciating either the compliment or Professor Flaherty herself, or both. "Tara's my best friend. I'd do anything for her," he said.

"As it seems she'd do for you." She looked at Astor, who'd gone back to hiding behind his newspaper, and laid a hand gently on his arm. "Darling, Tara's come a long way for your help. Won't you hear them out?"

He lowered his paper barrier and blinked at me. "What?"

I scrambled for words, unsure how long his attention would last; he seemed impatient. At least he hadn't screamed at me yet. "My friend George," I said, nodding at him, "was injected with a serum that will turn him into a Werewolf. The thing is, he's human, so his body can't handle the change. It's hurting him, and if I don't figure out a way to fix it, he'll die, or become some sort of monster. I was told you could help."

"What is it you think I can do exactly?"

"For starters, give me answers. Miles—"

"That DeLuca kid isn't quite right, you know. I'm not getting into bed with the likes of him or his associates."

"Me, either," I agreed. I spoke quickly, hoping to make it clear I wasn't in league with Miles before Astor lost it again. "Miles only injected George as a way to get to me. Miles was evil, and all I want is to fix the damage he's done."

"Anna says he's dead," he said, still eyeing me. His brows furrowed into a thick knot spanning his forehead. He looked half suspicious, half curious.

"He is. One of my friends killed him." I tried not to hesitate over the word "friend," especially referring to Cord. We were something, but I wasn't sure it was friends. "Before he died, Miles told me the only way to save George from becoming a monster was to give him my blood."

"So do it already. What do you need me for?"

"I don't trust him. Everything he ever told me was a lie. He said I should come to you to verify it, so here I am." Astor's frown deepened. He didn't answer. "Look, you're my last hope. I have no idea what else to do, and if I give him my blood, and it kills him, it'll be my fault, not Miles's anymore. I can't live with that. I need you to tell me if it'll work."

"And what makes you think you can trust me?"

I sat back, pausing to consider what was actually a very valid question. Why did I trust him? I didn't even know him. And I couldn't say Professor Flaherty's vote swayed me much, since I still wasn't entirely sure whose side she was on. "Well, for starters, Vera trusts you."

"And that's enough for you?"

I shrugged, frustrated. "You're my family. My father trusted you. That counts for something."

"We'll see if that holds," he said.

I ignored that. "Will you help?"

"Come with me." He pushed back from his chair so abruptly the table shook. The salt and pepper shakers toppled. Professor Flaherty righted them again. He looked down at her, looking ready to issue some sort of apology.

"Go on," she said waving her hand. "I'll tidy this and catch up with you."

"Call Jeeves. He'll handle it." Astor spun on his slipper-clad heel and headed for the door. I motioned to George to follow. He grabbed a handful of bacon before stepping up beside me.

Astor didn't seem to notice, nor did he look back to see if we still followed. He wound through hallways and cut through rooms like a mouse in a maze headed for cheese. He muttered to himself, but I pretended not to notice. Finally, when it felt as if we'd walked the length of the house and back again, he stopped in front of a door marked "Lab" and threw it open.

I stepped inside after him and halted.

It was huge, the size of five of my living rooms. Stainless steel tables ran the length of the room in neat rows, each of them covered in glass beakers, scales, Bunsen burners, and bottles of various liquids. As I passed, I caught sight of labels that advertised types of acid. Buckets lined the shelves bordering the room. These, too, sported labels marked with acid.

"What does this guy do?" George whispered in my ear.

I shook my head. "No idea."

We weaved in and out of rows, peering down at tables and the strange instruments that littered them. Astor stayed in the back of the room, apparently content to ignore us for the time being. I found bowl after bowl filled with clear liquid and metal rods. George met my eyes with raised brows.

Finally, Astor beckoned us to the far end of the room where two large vats stood bolted to a slab of concrete. Connected to the lid were lines of tubing, feeding something in or out, I wasn't sure. A swishing sound similar to a washing machine came from one. Astor opened the lid on the one that wasn't making watery noises and peered inside.

He picked up a pair of tongs and reached into the barrel, extracting a long, shiny piece of silver. He closed the lid and carried the silver to a container on the table. I watched as he dipped the bar into clear liquid and swished it around a few times before picking it up again and holding it out to me with the tongs. "Take it," he said.

"What is it?" I asked.

"A test."

"A test for what?"

"To determine whether or not your blood will help your friend."

He shoved the metal at me, clearly impatient at having to explain himself.

I stared at the shiny, silver bar. It looked like a stake without the point and was made entirely of some kind of steel. I exchanged a look with George, who shrugged. I reached out and took the bar.

I turned it over in my hands, inspecting it, looking for something that made it special, meaningful. I knew all about the way Hunters used metal as weapons, though I didn't fully understand the why. Was this supposed to be some sort of weapon? Did he want me to use it?

I frowned at the same moment Astor laughed. It sounded closer to a giggle, and promptly led into a raucous bout of cackling. I stared at him.

Astor tossed the tongs aside and clapped his hands.

"What?" I demanded.

More cackling laughter.

"Astor!" At my look, his laughter died off. He fumbled with his shirt, trying to straighten up and appear serious, but the grin was there, just beneath the surface. "What's so funny?"

"You passed!" He broke out into a dance, both feet jumping and hopping, arms swinging. No laughter this time, only ear-to-ear grinning.

"What do you mean 'I passed'?"

"The test, the test, you passed the test." His knees rose and fell with the rhythm of his words.

"Altogether now, say it with me, loony." George's breath tickled my neck where he'd leaned in close to whisper to me.

I shushed him and shook my head, frustrated. I was afraid to snap at Astor too hard, in case it set him off like last night. "Astor," I said as calmly as I could, "I've touched metal, or steel, or whatever, many times, so I don't understand why this is a big deal. Can you please explain?"

He danced back over to me, still obviously thrilled. "Of course, of course, but you've never touched *this*." I cocked an eyebrow at him and he went on. "The material you just held is called Unbinilium. It is one of the newer members on the periodic table and one of the purest metals on the planet. That bar is especially pure because of the extra leaching I've given it."

He was hopping in place. I was losing him.

"Leaching?" I repeated. "What is that?"

He sighed, but it was dramatic rather than impatient. "I see I better start from the beginning. You know the weapon of choice against a Werewolf is anything laced with or tipped in metal, yes?" I nodded. He seemed relieved, and I assumed I'd earned a little redemption from my ignorance. "Right-o. And metal works best when it is purified. Now, most metals manufactured by CHAS, or at least the convenient and cost-effective sorts, are comprised of aluminum, copper, or if they feel like splurging, titanium."

"CHAS manufactures metals?" George asked.

"Not the metals themselves. Gah! Why do I always get the clueless ones? CHAS, the powers that be, the head honchos, they manufacture all Hunter-approved weapons."

"I get it," I said. "CHAS pays for the metal and they're cheap spenders."

"Right. And cheap metals equal cheap reactions. You've got to wield it better, stronger, and get a clearer shot for optimum results. Now, if they used the good stuff like iron, gold, silver, that's something else. Stronger metals equal a stronger reaction. On both sides. The Werewolf could be taken out with a less-than-lethal blow because the material would do the work. And the Hunter would feel it too."

I remembered the night I'd fought with Leo and how much it affected me, using that steel beam on him. Then I thought about Liliana. I'd barely felt a reaction then, or at least from what I remembered. "So different materials cause different reactions?"

"Precisely."

"And the metal I just touched is more powerful than any other metal?"

"Right-o."

"And you thought I'd … what? React somehow?"

"You are a perfect mix, are you not? A completely blended cocktail, half of each kind?"

I wasn't sure how I felt about his calling my blood a cocktail, but I answered, anyway. He was finally starting to make sense. Sort of. "Yes."

"And you're Jeremiah's daughter?"

"Yes."

"Then, you're non-reaction is exactly as it should be. You're *her*. The one. Your father succeeded. And more to the point, your blood is exactly what he needs." He pointed at George, then made a face as if he'd only now caught sight of George's colorful jawline. "With your DNA cocktail in his veins, his second spirit will not rule the first."

I shook my head, totally confused despite the fact that he'd just told me what I wanted to hear.

"So, her giving me blood … it will cure me?" George looked torn between relief and disbelief.

"There's no way to stave off the change, if that's what you're hoping for. It will curb the monster, keep your first spirit, your human spirit, in control of your wolf. And what you can't control on your own, the bond will control for you."

"Bond?" I repeated in a weak voice. I didn't love where this was going.

"If you give him the transfusion, it will bond the two of you. Your wolf side is strong. I can sense it."

"You can?" An acidic taste rose in the back of my throat. Panic.

"I sensed it the minute you walked in last night," he said.

"But …" I looked at George. "Do you sense it?"

"I didn't want to say anything," he said, a look of silent apology creeping over his features. "It started yesterday when you almost …"

"What does this bond entail, exactly?" I asked, focusing on Astor again. I refused to think about the fact that I now registered on the supernatural radar as a Werewolf. There'd be plenty of time to freak out later.

"It's similar to a pack dynamic, but stronger, more visceral," Astor said. His voice caught on the last word. His expression was neutral, but I could see him straining to keep it that way.

George looked confused. "What does that mean?" he asked.

Astor sighed, his impatient expression returning. "What do you play, jock? Baseball? Badminton?"

"Football … what's badminton?" he asked.

Astor threw up his hands.

I spoke up, hoping to get the subject back on track. "So, if I give George my blood, it will bond us, giving us some sort of emotional tie to the other, but it will ensure he stays himself, even when he shifts, correct?"

"Someone's finally catching on," Astor said. He shot George a pointed look.

"And that's it?" I asked.

"Hardly," he said, "but it answers your initial question."

"And only leads to more," I shot back.

"I hate questions," he said.

I ignored that. "What did you mean when you said my father succeeded? And how did my non-reaction to that piece of Unbiliu-whatever tell you I was so special?"

"It's Unbinilium. And the best way to explain is to show you." He held out his hand. "The rod, give it to me."

I held out the bar and set it in his hand. His fingers closed around it and almost immediately his hand began to shake. Then his arm. Then his entire torso. What began as tiny tremors quickly turned to violent shakes as the reaction spread through his body, into his legs. One of his knees buckled, and I reached out and snatched the rod away from him.

As soon as his body lost contact with the material, the shaking subsided. He took a deep breath, let it out slowly, and shoved his hand through his disheveled hair. Energy crackled in the air, raw and smelling of ozone.

His voice shook as he spoke again. "As you can see, the purer the metal, the more heightened the reaction. George, on the other hand, well … See for yourself."

I looked where he pointed and found George. He'd wandered away, apparently to nose around at the different containers and instruments littering the tables, and was bent over a see-through tank, sniffing the liquid. As I watched, he reached out and touched whatever was in the tub. As soon as his finger made contact, he pulled back and yelped.

"George!"

I rushed over but George backed away, clearly in pain. I glanced at the tank. Stacked inside, completely submerged in liquid, were metal bars. They looked a lot like the Unbinilium I'd just watched Astor react to.

He held his arm against his chest, cradling it and wincing.

"Are you okay?" I asked.

In answer, he uncurled his hand and showed me his fingertips. The pointer and middle finger were red and blistered, like they'd been burned. He blew on them. "Stings like a bitch."

"Stop touching things, then." I wanted to feel bad for him but was too distracted by what it all meant. "I get it," I said, walking over as Astor dropped the rod back into the vat. He adjusted one of the giant dials on the lid and then stood back to eye the rest. "You're saying I'm immune to metal. But if that's true, then why did I react when I used it to kill a Werewolf a couple of months ago?"

"Had your wolf side emerged yet?" he asked.

"No," I said. He gave me a look that said *well there you go then.* "But it was still in me, right? In my blood?" Astor shook his head. "Then I don't understand."

He rolled his eyes. "You can't expect me to fill you in on a lifetime of research and experimenting in such a short time."

"Try," I said.

"The short version is that your father found something in my research, a genetic coding I'd developed that allowed the bearer of such a code to exude the characteristics of a Werewolf without actually becoming one. Somehow, and I don't know the details as I wasn't exactly in the loop by then, but somehow, he found a way to do the reverse." He paused, brows raised as if waiting for me to understand. "Reversing the code sent a present Werewolf gene into dormancy. When you were born, he injected you with a serum made from this code."

"And that's why my wolf side is only now showing itself," I finished.

He beamed like a teacher might at his star pupil. "Right-o."

"Why now? Wouldn't it have been easier to make it disappear forever?"

"Sure, and while we're at it I'll rope the moon for you," he snapped. "You think something like this is easy?"

"I bit back my retort and focused. "Why do it at all?"

"It was entirely for your protection. There was another ingredient to the serum, a gene-booster if you will. It's what gave you your immunity to metals, precious or otherwise." His words became halting. "No one else in Werewolf history has been able to fight the power of precious metals." Longing flashed in his eyes, coupled with a sudden and unbearable sadness that vanished so quickly, I thought I'd imagined it.

"You were right," I said, "My blood is a cocktail."

Astor blinked, his expression smoothing over. "I'm always right when it comes to science."

"But why would my dad do this? Was he going to turn me into some sort of super-hybrid? For what? Peace?" I couldn't help the sarcasm on the last word.

"How should I know?" Astor shrugged, his voice taking on the singsong quality of earlier. "Lunch, lunch, time for lunch."

Lunch? Already? "Astor, stay with me here," I said. "I'm not finished."

"I'm finished. Terminée. Terminado. Afgewerkt."

"Astor—"

"Tay, let him be." George came up behind me and slung his arm around my shoulder. "He's obviously nutso. And he did kill a girl, remember?"

Astor's eyes flashed and he rounded on George. He straightened to his full height, which was the same as George's now that he wasn't slouching, and stared at him. "You know nothing," he hissed, stabbing his index finger into George's chest.

George's eyes flashed, yellow and angry, and I stilled, my muscles tensing. Something about the way he looked at Astor … his eyes were darker, his pupils dilated. I inched forward, ready to land a blow across his other cheek if need be.

Finally, he threw his hands up in a sign of surrender. "Yes, sir, I know nothing."

The intensity of Astor's expression disappeared as quickly as it had come. He leaned away and smoothed his shirt, his eyes vacant. "I'm hungry, who's hungry?" He dropped the tongs onto the table with a clang.

I scurried forward, unsure what else to do but follow.

"Time to eat. Then time to paint. No more questions," he continued out into the hallway, turning the words into a song. "Jeeves! Jeeves! Lunch!"

Mathias appeared, from where, though, I couldn't tell. "Sir, your easel has been prepared in the lounge."

"Easel?" Astor blinked at him. "Time to paint?"

"Yes, sir."

"Paint. Then eat." Astor looked at me. "Paint. Then eat," he repeated and then left. I caught the sound of him humming as he disappeared around a corner. It sounded strangely like the theme song to *The Addams Family*. Astor reminded me of one of the characters, Uncle Fester. Strange, guarded, always out of left field.

I stayed where I was, unsure where to go in this giant house without Astor or Professor Flaherty to escort me. Mathias cleared his throat. "Shall I show you to the game room?"

George tugged on my arm and I nodded. "That would be great," I told him.

Mathias led us to a new doorway and promised to be back to get us for lunch before disappearing. The room was exactly what the name implied, complete with a foosball table, three different game consoles, surround sound speakers for the big screen, and a pool table. George let out a whoop and picked up a controller to the game console. I fell onto the couch with a look of longing directed at the pool table. My lids felt heavy after the last few nights of broken sleep. Even the revelation about my dormant wolf couldn't keep me awake. The last noise I heard was the revving of George's racecar as he beat the first level of his game.

George shook me awake. Mathias waited at the door when I stood and stretched.

"Lunch is served in the sunroom. I can show you the way if you like," Mathias said. His voice and expression were deadpan, as, I was beginning to realize, it always was.

"Do we have to eat with Astor?" George whispered.

I glared at him, but didn't answer. "Thank you, Mathias. That would be great."

He dipped his head in a nod and we followed him down the hall. I slowed my pace to put distance between us and Mathias. I kept my voice low.

"I want answers, and he's the only one who can give them to me. So, yes, we eat with him," I whispered.

"He doesn't like me. Maybe I should just sit this one out," George whispered back.

My brows lifted. "And pass up a meal?"

His mouth curved. "All right, maybe I'll just keep quiet and sit far away from him."

Apparently, a nap had been what my brain needed to kick into overdrive. A thousand different questions speared through me as we walked. Why had my dad done this to me? Had he really been trying to protect me by deferring my Werewolf gene? From whom? From where I stood, everything my parents had ever kept from me only came back to bite me in the end. And if this was true then I should've been a Werewolf since birth, like Wes. Only, why hadn't Miles ever shifted? He hadn't registered as wolf on my radar at all.

Professor Flaherty was already at the table with Astor. They broke off their low conversation as we entered and Professor Flaherty smiled.

"Tara, George, there you are. Come and sit down. This crab dip is amazing," she said.

George didn't need to be told twice. He took a seat at the far end of the table and began scooping food onto his plate. Astor's head was down, like he was fascinated with the crackers and cheese on his plate. I didn't give a crap about crab dip, but the answers I wanted were trapped inside those who did. I sat.

"It sounds like you had a productive morning," Professor Flaherty said.

"Very," I said cautiously. How much did she know? Could I talk to her, instead of trying to break through Astor's wall of crazy?

Professor Flaherty's expression softened, as if she could read my thoughts. "I told you last night, your secrets are safe with me."

"Secrets are the devil!" Abruptly, Astor shoved back from the table and strode out of the room, sputtering about devils and "the sins of the father."

"Speaking of secrets," I said, giving her a pointed look.

She sighed. "There are a quite a few stored in that brain of his," she said. "Go easy on him. He isn't used to the demands of company."

I wanted to say he didn't seem used to the demands of *sanity*, but I had a feeling that wouldn't have been well-received.

"I spoke with your mother earlier," Professor Flaherty said. "Your grandmother will be here this evening."

"Of course she will," I said.

"I'm sorry, I know you didn't want them to know, but I couldn't let them continue to worry."

"No, I understand. I knew they'd find me eventually. Frankly, I'm surprised it took them this long."

"She did say something about your 'little diversion' and how she'd be speaking to you about that."

I held back a shudder as I thought about how angry they were all going to be. I had no doubt my time for answers would end as soon as that doorbell rang. I needed to hurry. "Professor, how much do you know about me? I mean, about the stuff Astor told me, the genetic coding in my blood?"

"You mean, do I know if he's telling the truth?" I nodded. "I do, and he is."

I slumped back in my chair. I should've been happy to finally understand what was going on with me and how to save George, but hearing Astor's explanation only raised more questions. And the one person who could answer them had died seventeen years ago.

"How about we take a walk?" Professor Flaherty set her napkin aside and stood. "I could use some fresh air."

I looked down at my plate. It was still empty. My stomach felt like it held rocks. I shot a look at George. "I'll be here," he said, the words distorted by a full mouth. He waved at me with his fork. "Go on."

I rose and followed Professor Flaherty out.

CHAPTER THIRTEEN

The door opened into the backyard, in the middle of the bright green garden I'd chased George through the night before. It extended along the entire perimeter of the house. Or, more accurately, it *was* the perimeter, the way it thickened and grew together like a wall at its borders.

We stood on a deck that overlooked descending tiers of greenery and large exotic flowers. The types of plants differed on each tier, getting smaller and smaller closer to the ground. Far below was the desert floor, burnished golden sand that reflected sunlight until your eyes hurt. It stretched for miles until it met the horizon.

"This is beautiful," I said, inhaling the dry desert air mixed with the pungent sweetness of the plants.

"It's my favorite place on the property," she agreed.

We descended the deck stairs that led to a winding path weaving up and down the length of the first tier. Leaves the length of my arms, with droplets of moisture lining their veins, hung over onto the path. The humidity increased as the canopy of plants closed over our heads—a rainforest in the desert.

"Astor says you had no reaction to the Unbinilium," she said.

"Which apparently makes me immune to metal. So … some sort of all-powerful hybrid?" It came out as more of a question than a statement; frankly, I still wasn't sure how much to believe.

She smiled wryly. "I see he wasn't delicate with the details."

"He just didn't give any, really. Besides, is he ever? Delicate, I mean?" She caught my eye, letting me know she understood the real question here; this was my way of asking how crazy Astor really was.

"No," she admitted. "Not really. But he's better at explaining the science than I am, and I knew seeing his work come to life would make him happy."

I thought of the jig he'd done when I'd held onto that rod. Professor Flaherty couldn't be more his opposite, with her calm, cool demeanor, her quiet grace. Even in battle, she carried herself this way, letting what she didn't say speak louder than what she did. She reminded me of Angela.

"How do you two know each other?" I asked.

"Extractive metallurgy." I gave her a blank look, and she laughed. "Yes, it's a mouthful, I know."

"What does it mean?" I reached out and ran my hand over the petals of a bright orange flower, each one larger than my hand. It felt smooth, like velvet, under my fingertips.

"It's the study of processes used in separation and concentration of raw materials," she explained.

"In English?"

"He purifies metal."

"Is that what those barrels in his lab are for?"

"Yes. The liquids are a mixture he concocted himself. I'm not sure what's in it, exactly. Several different types of acids, a solvent, a neutralizer." She looked like she was about to say more, but then stopped at my expression.

"Sorry, I'm sure you're speaking English, it's just not my English," I said.

She smiled. "It wasn't always mine, either."

"What made you interested in it?" I asked.

"I wasn't, not really," she admitted. She paused and the look she gave let me know whatever was coming was personal for her. "The

Cause, the original group, was founded when I was twelve. Back then, I was too young to understand, and they were too small to matter. That changed the summer I turned sixteen. My parents managed to get me an internship with CHAS. I didn't have a specialty or any specific interest yet and they wanted one for me. I think they hoped I'd either run for office or marry someone who held office.

"Instead, I was given the job of lab assistant. I realized pretty quickly why. Astor was very hard to work for and impossible to please, especially since I had basically no knowledge of chemistry or metallurgy." My brows creased as my mouth began to form a question. She answered it before I could ask. "Astor was the head of the department for CHAS. The one who oversaw all of the weapons manufacturing, specifically the metals."

"Astor worked for CHAS?" I said, unable to hide my surprise—and confusion. "How is that possible? I thought they hated Werewolves."

"What makes you think he's a Werewolf?" she asked, a single brow raised in challenge.

"Vera said …"

"Yes, she would remember him that way, wouldn't she?" she said, almost to herself. Then to me, "Astor's been a little of both for a long time."

"He's a hybrid?"

"Not exactly. He's a … cocktail, shall we say." I nodded, not quite understanding, especially after hearing him use that word to describe me, but not wanting to interrupt her again. "Anyway, I didn't know a beaker from a glass jar, and he hated me for it. I almost quit."

"Why didn't you?"

"I met your father. Oh, it wasn't like that," she assured me quickly. "He was nice enough, and handsome, but he and your mother were already an item, and anyway, I was too focused on getting Astor to accept me and making my parents proud than anything else. But the things he said, the peace he believed in and was willing to fight for, stayed with me. The following summer I applied for the same internship, but I found out Astor had left. A new head scientist had been appointed. I realized I didn't want to work for anyone else, so I withdrew my application without telling my parents, and I tracked him down. When it was time to go, I convinced my parents to let me travel alone and instead of reporting to CHAS headquarters, I spent the summer here."

She stopped and let out a heavy breath. "Wow, I haven't told that story in … I can't remember."

"Thank you for telling me," I said, and I meant it. It was the most I'd been told about my father by someone other than my mother in my whole life. I soaked it in. "So, you know about the genetic coding because of your time working for Astor and my dad those two summers?"

She nodded and her mouth pulled taut at the corners. "I worked here three summers in total, but then … it wasn't the same anymore after—" She broke off and I hesitated, trying to decide how much to admit to knowing. Not that I knew anything for sure—only what Grandma told me. And Vera.

"You mean when that girl got killed?" I asked softly.

Her gaze swiveled to mine. "You know about Mary Beth?"

"Not much," I admitted. "I know there was an accident. Astor was held responsible."

"I met Mary Beth the first summer I worked here at the manor. She was brilliant. She was a few years older than Astor and something of a mentor, I think. They were a perfect match, intellectually. Both of them tested off the IQ charts and each was as scatterbrained as the other when it came to the routine of daily life." She chuckled. "I cooked more meals and did more laundry than any actual science that summer. Their research was heavy. I didn't understand most of it. I think that's why I didn't try to stop them …"

"Stop them from what?" I asked when she didn't continue. Her expression was far away, as if she'd returned to the memory she described.

"I remember them coming out of the lab, singing, dancing, yelling all over the place, so excited at what they'd figured out. I heard the words "genetic code" and "metal immunity." That was about all I understood. They told me to call Jeremiah, your father. When he got here, they called us all into the lab for a demonstration. I watched as they pulled piece after piece of metal out of the leaching liquids with their bare hands and tossed it back and forth. Neither one showed any hint of reaction to any of it.

"Your father was beside himself with excitement. He demanded to know how they'd done it. I demanded it, as well, though I wasn't sure I'd understand the explanation. It was like a magic trick. I'd never seen anything like it, never dreamt it was possible.

"Astor explained he'd injected Mary Beth with some sort of genetic mutation that allowed the immunity. Back then, it was short-acting. Nothing permanent. But it was a miracle, nonetheless. We tested it over and over for a week, using the purest metals we could find, leaching them until they were completely stripped, raw with power. Then we called CHAS."

Her expression darkened. I tensed, sensing some detail I'd missed. "Was that bad?" I asked. "Shouldn't they have been happy Hunters could wield metals without physical consequences?" I remembered all of those side effects Logan had mentioned. Surely, CHAS would've employed this technology by now.

"They didn't see it that way. CHAS was furious. They were afraid of what it could mean, so they ordered it shut down and buried."

"I don't understand," I said, glad Astor wasn't here to roll his eyes at my repetitiveness.

"All they saw was that Astor had created a way for Werewolves to protect themselves against our greatest weapon. They won't allow technology that benefits the enemy."

It took a minute to understand. "Mary Beth was a Werewolf."

"Yes."

"The technology blocks reactions to metal."

"Precisely."

I scrunched my brows together. Something had been bothering me since I'd arrived. I hadn't been able to pinpoint it until now. "Why can't I sense him? Astor, I mean." I hadn't felt a single jolt come over me since I'd arrived. No goosebumps, nothing. "I know you said he's a mixture, but I should be able to feel him, right?"

"Do you know what exactly about them triggers our body's warning system?" I shook my head. "It's the wolf DNA that lingers after they've changed. It sends a signal to our brains, letting us know that even though they look human in that moment, they are more. A possible threat. But the wolf DNA only lingers as long as they are capable of shifting. Otherwise, they feel like any other human."

I thought of Miles and how he'd only ever registered as a Hunter. "Are you saying Astor can't shift?"

"I'm saying he hasn't in almost fifteen years."

"Why not?"

"He says it's a byproduct of all the experiments he's conducted on himself. He was born a Werewolf but by the time he went to work for CHAS, he'd manipulated his body into that of a Hunter. His inability to shift was the only reason they hired him."

"So what ended up happening with CHAS? They were mad about the metal immunity stuff, right?"

"Right. CHAS sent Astor a 'cease and desist' letter. Astor refused. Three nights later, the house was raided. They launched tear gas through the windows. I managed to find Astor stumbling toward the lab, but Mary Beth was missing. I forced Astor out the side door and we were detained. When the smoke cleared and the guards emerged, they'd already boxed up the entire contents of the lab—including Mary Beth. We were told they found her there, gathering notes. They approached her, demanded she stop, and she tried to run. They said she tripped and fell into the barrel of leaching liquids. Her body burned in the acid."

"Those barrels are at least three feet high and the lids are closed. How could she have tripped?" I asked.

"A very good question." There was fire in her eyes behind the sadness and the regret.

"I'm sorry," I said.

"So am I. Astor was never the same, as you can see."

"He loved her?"

"Yes, but it became more than that. I didn't realize about the bond until after."

My body stilled. "What do you mean 'bond'?"

"From what I could get from Astor, he injected himself with Mary Beth's blood at some point during their research phase. Something about testing the metal immunity on himself but it didn't work. Instead, it created some sort of emotional link between them. He felt what she felt, and vice versa. It made her death that much harder on him. Sometimes I think he only acts this way to cover up the pain."

I shuddered and stroked the orange flower until it drooped under the weight of my hand. Astor had said George and I would have a bond if I gave him my blood. Would it be this way for us? A link so strong that if one died, the other was driven insane with grief? Could I do that to him? To myself?

I cast about, searching my jumbled thoughts for something, anything, to focus on. The weight of the solution before me was too much. I needed to catch my breath; I needed facts.

"I always wondered why they used metal against Werewolves," I said. I was aware of the way I'd said "they" instead of "we" on purpose. I wasn't willing to put myself into the same category as CHAS any longer. "Is the purifying, or leaching, what makes it harmful?"

"That and the properties already within the material itself." She smiled ruefully. "I forget sometimes how little you know about our culture. Yes, the leaching, or purifying, helps, but mostly it's the fact that metal is a conductor all on its own."

"A conductor," I repeated. I was bombarded with mental images of Ben Franklin wielding a kite in a lightning storm. "Like for electricity?"

"Electricity is one example, but it can be harnessed into many different things. Heat, lights, and what we use it for: power. Think of it more as being a conduit for energy."

"Where does the energy come from?"

"The term is 'band theory.' It's the idea that metal is made up of energy bands, its two major components being electrons and neutrons. Just as a Werewolf is made up of two sides, so is the energy used to destroy them."

"The second spirit," I said, remembering Logan's explanation.

"Exactly. Both forms of energy are highly powerful. So powerful that it's impossible for both to occupy the same space at the same time. One always wins out. The trick is to purify the metal so its energy becomes more powerful than the energy of the Werewolf's second spirit."

"And once you've killed their second spirit, the human spirit immediately follows," I finished.

"Typically, the human spirit is weaker than the wolf's. The lesser the metal used, the more force is needed, or the more precise the wound. The stronger the metal, the less precise one needs with the kill shot."

"And my dad found a way to somehow make me immune to all of it. Does that make me … immortal?"

She laughed. "Not quite. It just makes you harder to kill. It was a way to protect you. I can only imagine what you must think, hearing this for the first time, and without him here to explain himself. I am so sorry for your loss."

We were nearing the deck again, having covered the trail twice over. I was almost glad when the canopy gave way to sunlit sky and the dry air sucked the moisture of the plants away. Without the humidity, the heat felt bearable.

"Thank you for being honest with me, for explaining it," I said. I thought of my mother and her habit of dishing details after I already knew, and Grandma, who was probably already on a plane by now, but not necessarily to stand by me or divulge any truths. "No one else has," I added.

"To be fair, I'm not sure they know. According to Astor, your father's intention was to leave them in the dark as a protective measure. If the information fell into the wrong hands, he knew it could bring you harm. His whole purpose was to avoid that. For you and you mother."

"You think she doesn't know?"

"I think it's worth giving her the benefit of the doubt," she said as she climbed the deck stairs. I joined her at the railing. "He wanted you to follow in his footsteps, to maybe do what he couldn't. Someone born of both sides would gain the ear of the Werewolves for sure, but he knew Hunters were much more stubborn, more close-minded, and more unified in their prejudices. His decision to send your wolf side into dormancy was another layer of protection. Not only would it ensure you'd grow up as one of us, it would protect you from the prying eyes of CHAS and maybe even secure you a place with them before that side of you became known."

She patted my hand. "I'm going to check on Astor. I'll find you after you've had some time."

She began to turn away. I touched her hand and looked up at her. The sun beat down on her hair, making it shine and shimmer so hard, I blinked against it. "Thank you," I said. She nodded, and I watched her disappear inside.

I turned back to the railing, staring out over the golden canvas of the desert. Here and there, small plants rose from the ground, defying the dryness and relentless sun in their will to survive. I felt connected to them for that even as I wondered exactly who I would defy in my desire to live.

CHAPTER FOURTEEN

In the end, the decision was easy. It always would be. I had to save George. Whatever bond or connection we developed as a result, we'd figure out later.

I found George waiting for me just inside the doors. He looked like he was finishing up lunch. "How much did you eat?" I asked.

He stood and patted his stomach. "Do you think Werewolves eat more than humans?"

"I think you just proved they did."

He grinned, but it faded quickly. "How'd it go with your teacher?"

"Good, I guess. At least I know Astor's telling the truth about everything."

"He's crazy, not a liar."

"I'm beginning to see there's a difference."

"So what do we do now?" he asked. Hands stuffed in his pockets, he rocked back and forth from heels to toes.

"Now, we fix you."

He stopped rocking. "Are you sure?"

"Of course I'm sure, don't be an idiot." For some reason, the fact that he'd doubted my answer irritated me.

"But, Astor said we'd bond—"

"I know what Astor said. I don't care if it joins us at the hip. I'm saving you like I promised."

A slow smile spread across his face, the kind that lit his eyes and used to make my heart beat faster. That was then.

"Thanks, Tay."

I smiled too, but it lacked depth. My eyes locked on his, on the eerie yellow emanating from them. Were they brighter than they had been this morning? I was watching him inch closer and closer to the edge. Only now, I could pull him back to safety. "Thank me when we're done." I couldn't allow myself to feel happy yet, not until I knew whatever we were about to do actually worked. "Let's go find Astor."

MATHIAS APPEARED AS SOON AS WE REACHED THE HALL. HE GUIDED US to the lab, where he said Astor had gone, and disappeared again as soon as we'd reached the door.

"How does he do that?" George asked.

I didn't answer. I noticed George's foot tapping against the carpet as I pushed the lab door open.

It took me a moment to spot Astor. He sat on a stool in the far corner, bent over a mess of paperwork. Professor Flaherty stood next to him, calling out figures as he recorded them. She looked up as we approached.

"Hi," I said.

She smiled at me and laid a hand on Astor's arm. He jumped, but she directed her words to George. "George, would you please give me a hand with something across the hall?"

He cocked his head at me, questioningly. I nodded.

"Sure," he answered.

The door closed behind them. Astor looked up at me. "Well?"

"I want to do the transfusion," I said.

He dropped his pen and glared at me. "Why in the hell would you want to do that?" he snapped.

"Because he's my family, my best friend."

"That's the worst reason I ever heard. Worse than the idea itself."

"Saving his life is a bad idea?" I didn't know whether to be angry or confused.

"Tying his life to yours, and yours to his, that's the kick in the teeth." The expression he'd worn earlier, the veil of misery, returned.

"You must have really loved her," I said quietly. I held my breath, waiting for him to change the subject or scream or run away.

"Don't sass me or I won't help you," he said in a gruff voice. I met his eyes and found them alert and steady.

"I wasn't—" I stopped, a smile forming on my lips. "You know, I'm convinced you're not nearly as crazy as you'd like everyone to believe."

"I'll be as crazy as it takes." The moment of clarity vanished, and the mask was back in place. He stuck out his tongue, picked up his pen, and went back to work. I stood there, unsure what to say next. "Well, don't just stand there. Fetch me the boy."

I grinned and hurried into the hallway. Professor Flaherty and George were walking back, their hands full of syringes, clear plastic tubes, towels, and plastic vials. "Ready?" she asked me.

"I—how'd you know?"

"I've known him a very long time," she said. I followed them back inside and watched as Professor Flaherty set everything up. "I may need more room," she said to Astor. He frowned and then with one hand, reached out and swept the contents of half of a table onto the floor. Beakers broke, papers fluttered everywhere. Professor Flaherty just looked at him.

"What?" he demanded. Then he seemed to break under the pressure of her gaze. "Jeeves!" he yelled. I jumped. "Jeeves!"

Mathias appeared in the doorway, a broom and dustpan in hand. Without a word, he swept up the broken glass and replaced the paperwork neatly on another surface. "Will that be all?" he asked. Astor grunted and Mathias left.

"Let's get on with it," Astor said. He motioned to the stool and I sat. The sound of George's foot tapping grew louder.

"I think I need some air," he said abruptly. We all looked at him. His eyes were definitely a darker shade of yellow.

"You're a little on the glowy side, son," said Astor.

"Tara, can you handle this while I walk with George?" Professor Flaherty asked me.

"Sure, go ahead," I said.

George turned to follow her out and I grabbed his arm. I tried to ignore the foreign look in his eyes and searched the rest of his face for signs of the real George. "Just hold on a few more minutes," I whispered. "We're almost there."

He nodded and then he was gone.

I felt the pressure of a tourniquet being tied on my upper arm. "Pump your fist," Astor instructed. I obeyed and watched as he unwrapped a fresh syringe from the packaging and then poked and prodded at the veins in the crook of my elbow. He grunted, apparently meaning he'd found one he liked. He positioned the needle tip and paused with it hovering over my skin.

"No going back after this," he said.

"I'm aware."

He cleared his throat. "In that case, I'd like to take a few extra samples. For research."

I thought about that. "On one condition. You have to share all of your findings with me. No more secrets."

We regarded each other for a moment, his eyes sharper than I'd seen before, and I had no doubt of his lucidity in that moment. He nodded. "Deal."

Then he stuck me.

THE BLOOD DRAWING PROCESS WAS OVER QUICKLY. I STOOD BUT MY knees buckled and tiredness washed over me. Astor shoved a package of cookies at me, demanding I eat them. Halfway through the second stale Oreo, the dizziness eased.

Astor worked quickly, labeling and storing the vials. Three he left out on the table. Four others he labeled and put in a small refrigerator against the wall.

Professor Flaherty and George returned. He didn't look much better, but he was hanging on. His tapping had intensified.

"Have a seat," Professor Flaherty told him, gesturing to the stool. Astor wound the tourniquet around George's bicep and pulled it tight. When his mouth tightened into a hard line, I stepped up to his other side and took his hand.

"You're going to have to sit still, boy," Astor told him, preparing a needle. Professor Flaherty worked on his other side, preparing what looked like an IV bag with clear fluids.

"What's that for?" I asked.

"A way to feed the blood into his system," she said. "Astor will attach an IV and let the blood drip slowly, mixed with fluid. He won't feel a thing after the initial stick."

"You've gotta hold still," I said to George. "Can you do that?"

His hand tightened in mine and his fingers stilled against my knuckles. "For a second."

I nodded at Astor and he slid the needle in.

George jerked a little but the needle stayed in place. I squeezed his hand. He squeezed back, hard enough I had to release my pressure and grit my teeth. I'd probably have a bruise later. I'd forgotten his strength had increased so much.

Professor Flaherty hung the IV bag on a metal hook and cleaned up the work area. By the time she'd finished, so had the bag of fluids.

I looked at George. "How do you feel?"

He yawned. "Tired."

Astor nodded. "The transfusion won't hold off the change. It's coming, sooner rather than later, I'd say."

"But for now," Professor Flaherty said, "you're going to be sleepy. Would you like to lie down?"

He looked at me. I nodded at him. "Might as well," I said.

"Thanks." He hopped off the stool and steadied himself. His eyelids drooped. "I'll catch up with you later," he said.

Professor Flaherty offered to walk him back to his room, and he followed her out. I stood still even after the lab door swung shut behind them. I felt empty, like the crash after a rush of adrenaline. All of that buildup, the days and weeks I'd searched in vain for another solution, the long trip here, and then the truth that had been thrown at me in all directions since arriving—all of it had led here. To a small, silent moment with an empty IV bag. And supposedly, George would be fine.

I did a mental check, trying to sense if any sort of bond existed between us. I didn't feel anything. Maybe Astor had exaggerated. It seemed likely. All I felt was a slight tingle at the back of my neck, a feeling that had started somewhere around West Virginia, I think, and had persisted throughout the trip. I'd grown pretty good at ignoring it.

CHAPTER FIFTEEN

Mathias was, for once, nowhere to be found. I wound my way to the front hall somewhere around the third back-track. . I was tempted to suggest they color-code the carpets. This house was ridiculous. Then again, it *was* sort of perfect for Astor's personality.

Finally, I recognized the entryway and spotted the front door. I pulled it open and stepped out, letting it click shut behind me. Wes had texted during George's transfusion to say he'd be here soon, and I felt anxious. I hadn't wanted to tell him via text about my decision to go ahead with George's transfusion. I'd thought it would be better in person. Now that the time was approaching, I wasn't so sure. What would he think about this supposed bond? Astor hadn't been very specific with the details, but the way he'd lost his grip on reality after losing Mary Beth spoke volumes.

I found my car parked where Mathias had left it and walked around the outside, making sure it hadn't been bothered while it sat roadside. Nothing seemed out of place. By the time I'd circled it, I was already sweating.

I opted for the shade of the manmade rainforest where it bordered the circular drive, walking in no direction in particular. It wasn't that I needed to be outside, particularly, but I had a feeling this might be one of my last chances for a while. After Grandma arrived and hauled me back, I was pretty sure I'd be on house arrest indefinitely. I'd be lucky not to be locked in a closet somewhere.

A noise startled me. The sound was vague, barely reaching the edges of my awareness. I froze. The tingling on the back of my neck turned to an ache. I scanned the trees, peering between oversized leaves and slim trunks. Nothing moved. I chalked it up to a bird or some desert animal seeking the refuge of the oasis. I lifted my foot, ready to resume my pace through the exotic greenery.

There.

Out of the corner of my eye, I detected movement. Slight. Far back in the undergrowth.

I bent my knees, going into the defensive crouch that had become second nature to me. I held my breath. There was danger here.

"Tara Godfrey." The speaker's voice was not one I recognized.

"Who's there?" It came out softer than I'd intended. I swallowed and squared my shoulders. "Show yourself," I said, louder.

I spotted a tall plant with leaves the size of canoes ruffling from movement that didn't match the natural sway of the others. The leaves parted and two figures stepped out from behind the stalks. Two familiar figures.

"Mr. and Mrs. Lexington."

I wasn't sure whether to be angry or confused. Last time I'd seen them, they'd run George and I off the road and then disappeared. Did they follow us?

I opened my mouth to ask them what they were doing here and closed it again. A strange itch began along my rib cage. I rubbed my palms down my sides. I'd felt something similar the last time I'd almost …

No. I wasn't thinking about that now..

"You know who we are?" Mr. Lexington asked.

"Of course she knows, dear," said Mrs. Lexington. "Everyone knows who we are."

Their eyes were a matching shade of yellow and their human forms seemed shaky at the edges, as if appearing this way was a strain for them. The itch underneath my skin intensified.

"I know your daughter," I said, mostly because I wasn't sure what else to say.

"Victoria? How is she?" Mrs. Lexington asked. Her eager expression smoothed out as Mr. Lexington glared at her.

"She's fine," I said slowly, trying to understand. Why were they here? And why hadn't they sought Victoria out themselves? "She's spending the summer with a friend from school."

"Oh, good, she's not alone, Douglas."

"We didn't come here for this," he hissed at her. He looked back at me, his yellow eyes hardening. "You will come with us," he said.

"Um, where?" I asked.

"The location isn't important. You've been summoned. It's our job to bring you. You can either come willingly or by force. It's your choice," he said.

Mrs. Lexington fidgeted at the mention of force. I couldn't tell if it was out of discomfort at the situation or if she was simply preparing herself for a fight. My muscles coiled at the threat. I remained carefully still, and stared back at Mr. Lexington.

If they shifted and attacked, could I take them on my own? I wasn't sure.

"I'm not going with you unless you explain what's going on," I said. "Why have you been following me?"

"It's not important," he said.

"It is if you want me to come with you willingly. Why did you run us off the road? Is this about George?"

"Who?" Mr. Lexington's brow furrowed. "You mean your changeling friend? No. This is about you and I won't ask again. Come with us."

"No." I stood straighter, trying to look like I wasn't anticipating their attack. Maybe if they thought I would go easy, they'd slip up.

"Just tell her what will happen if she doesn't," Mrs. Lexington pleaded. "If she knew, she might come on her own."

Tension emanated from each of them. Mr. Lexington's knees were slightly bent, like he was preparing to spring. His form shook at the edges.

"Tell me what?" I asked, mainly to keep him talking.

"If we don't bring you to her, she'll come after your friends and family, one by one, until you submit," Mrs. Lexington said before falling silent under her husband's furious glare.

"Who will?" I asked, finally focusing on the conversation as more than a means to delay whatever Mr. Lexington was planning.

"We stopped you on the road to save you," she said, her voice shaking. "But then she found us and we had no choice."

I shook my head to clear it. This made less and less sense the more she talked. "Killed who? Who found you?"

"Olivia. Our m-master," she said.

Mr. Lexington punctuated her request with a growl. The sound of ripping fabric followed close behind as his clothing tore and fell at his feet. A bony wolf with extra-long claws stood before me, shaking his head back and forth and squeezing his eyes shut as if in pain from shifting. His eyes opened, blood-shot and yellowed, and focused on me.

I resisted the urge to step back, knowing he'd interpret it as fear.

"Why does she want me?" I asked.

Mrs. Lexington sent me a look of pity, but neither one answered.

I could feel Mr. Lexington's intentions. Any second now. I held his gaze while stretching my peripheral vision, searching for a weapon to grab at. The only things within reach were tropical leaves. They didn't even grow on wooden branches, but stalks of greenery. Nothing that would penetrate wolf flesh.

I tried another tactic. "Why send you?"

"It's not just us. Olivia's dispatched an army to find you," Mr. Lexington answered. He took a step forward, low to the ground, stalking his prey. I stayed still.

"An army …? The hybrids." Finally, things clicked into place. "The one controlling the hybrids is a woman. Olivia. She wants me," I said. It wasn't a question. At least now I knew it wasn't Demi.

"We're not leaving here without you," Mr. Lexington said.

"You don't have to do this. I can help you," I said. I gestured to the house, obscured behind me. "Me and my friends, we could protect you, your daughter—"

"No!" he growled. "There's no going back. No more excuses. Last chance to come willingly."

I opened my mouth to argue further about Astor's house being safe. When I did, my foot inched backward allowing my body to twist and my hand to gesture behind me. I knew the second it happened, I'd made a mistake. Mr. Lexington's eyes narrowed. It was the signal his instincts had been waiting for. My retreat. My fear.

He lunged.

I managed to dodge him but the effort sent me sprawling. I tucked my body, keeping my arms in tight, and rolled to a stop on my back, half-tangled in a massive plant. I blinked, realizing too late he was right there. The air whooshed out of me as his paws came down on my chest. I shoved upward with my hands, barely holding him off as his teeth snapped at the air in front of my face.

"You will come," he snarled.

The itching along my ribs turned to sharp pain, and I cried out. Something alien moved inside me, pressing my bones against my skin, almost as if they were stretching, growing. I bit my lip and tasted blood.

At the same time, from somewhere behind Mr. Lexington, came a high-pitched howl. It ended in a yelp and echoed against the sudden silence left in its wake.

"Sandra!" Mr. Lexington shouted. "Are you all right?"

I pried my eyes open, surprised at the sudden absence of his weight. Mr. Lexington was gone.

It took me a second to recognize my own hands as I lowered them to my abdomen, clutching my ribs against the pain. The backs of my hands and the entire length of my arms were covered in soft fur the color of caramel. It was thicker than it had been the first time, and darker. I stared, wide-eyed, when another spasm hit me and I doubled over again. I knew I should be trying to get up, to escape back to the house while my attacker was distracted, but I couldn't move, except to roll side to side against the mind-numbing agony.

I might've cried out again. I wasn't sure. I could no longer hear past the ringing in my ears.

Hands on my cheeks roused me. They smoothed my hair back from my face and wiped away the loose leaves and dirt. Still, I kept my eyes squeezed shut. The only thing that kept me from panicking was the knowledge they were human hands, gentle and careful. Mr. Lexington wouldn't have been so kind.

The pain pulled back, almost grudgingly, as if it wanted to remain. The ringing in my ears faded. The sound of birds and soft breathing reached my ears. I instinctively rolled toward the hand gently stroking my hair.

"George? Is that you?" I managed.

"Not quite," said a voice achingly familiar.

I'd barely opened my eyes when my hand shot out and closed around his wrist, just in case this was a dream and he'd be gone when I looked up.

"Alex," I said, enjoying the way his eyes softened just a little at the edges when I said his name. The pressure in my chest, the anxiety over what I'd just been through, eased at the sight of him.

He smiled down at me, the worry etched in lines across his forehead and around his mouth. "Did you have a nice nap?"

"I was—" I stopped. How could I possibly explain this to him? *I'm becoming a Werewolf a little more each day, no big deal.* I couldn't bring myself to do it, not with him. I was too afraid of the way he'd look at me. Then I remembered the fur on my hands. I glanced at where I still held his wrist, dropping it like I'd been burned, and inspected my hands. The fur was gone; in its place was smooth skin, as if it had never been there at all.

"Stop debating on which lie to tell me," he said, his smile disappearing. It was the same expression he'd worn the day he found me in the woods on my way to meet Miles. The same one he'd used at the hotel when he'd demanded answers.

"I wasn't going to lie," I said. It sounded weak, even to me.

He rolled his eyes. "Right. Tell me what just happened. Why were the Lexingtons trying to have you for dinner?"

"They're gone?" I twisted around searching for some sign of them. Nothing.

"For now." He frowned. "I thought they were locked in a lab somewhere."

"So did I." I took his offered hand and sat up.

I pulled my knees against my chest and we sat face to face. A rush of warmth spread through me at the sight of him. I had the urge to grin but bit it back as I studied him. His hair was longer than its usual buzz. There were shadows under his eyes, as if he hadn't been sleeping. The rest of him was deeply tanned. He smelled like the outdoors. It made me ache for the days when I'd trained with him, sparring until I'd been so winded I couldn't see straight, sprinting through the forest shoulder to shoulder.

I realized he was studying me just as hard and looked away before he could see what I was thinking. "What are you doing here? How did you find me?" I asked. *I missed you.*

The words hung in the air between us, unspoken and heavy. I could see them forming on his lips and then he seemed to think better of it. "No changing the subject. You first."

I sighed, knowing I wouldn't get anything out of him until I'd given him an explanation. "They wanted me to come with them," I said. "A woman named Olivia is behind the hybrids. She sent them to bring me to her. If I don't come, she'll go after my family and friends."

"And you have no idea who she is?"

"No. Mr. Lexington called her Olivia. That's all I know."

"It doesn't sound familiar. Did he say anything else? Where to find her?"

I shook my head. "He was on me before I could get anything out of him. And then I …"

"Sprouted fur?" I didn't answer. "Talk to me, Tara," he said quietly. "I want to help."

"Yeah, right," I said. "You say that, but I doubt you could really handle it. If you hadn't known it was me, you would've attacked me."

He opened his mouth—probably to argue, though I wouldn't have believed him—but was interrupted by the sound of someone approaching. A strange feeling, something between goosebumps and the tingling I'd felt earlier on the back of my neck, came over me, strong enough that I shuddered. The skin around my arms tightened.

Alex narrowed his eyes, let go of my hand and jumped up. In his other hand he held a stake tipped in metal. Alarm shot through me. I followed Alex's gaze as he scanned, expecting Mr. and Mrs. Lexington to reappear, ready to finish what they started. A Werewolf appeared, its coat the color of golden sunshine.

It halted at the sight of Alex and me, looking momentarily confused. Then it zeroed in on Alex, teeth bared, and hurtled forward. Alex rushed forward to meet it.

"Stop!" I yelled as I recognized the wolf. Panic shot through me and I scrambled to my feet. "Alex! George! Stop!"

At the sound of each other's name, they faltered. I held my breath, sure Alex would follow through with the swipe of his stake. At the last second they each turned away. Alex's stake barely missed catching George's shoulder. They righted themselves and glared at each other.

"Watch it, mutt," Alex said.

George growled. "Attacking you before was reflex. Don't make it premeditated next time."

"George, you shifted," I said. For some reason I slowed when I got close, suddenly unsure at seeing him like this.

He ducked his head. "Do I look …?" He didn't finish. He was more nervous than I was.

"You look amazing." I reached out a tentative hand, and ran it over the back of his neck and down his shoulder. When he raised his head to look at me, we were almost eye to eye. I sucked in a breath.

"What is it? Do I look like a freak?" he asked. He tried twisting his head around to see his torso, and did a full spin. It looked a little like he was chasing his tail.

Alex snorted.

"No, you're not a freak." I smiled. "I was just thinking that for once, we're the same height."

His lips curved, baring a mouthful of sharp teeth, and he let out a growly laugh.

"How do you feel?" I asked.

"Amazing," he said. "I never imagined … is this how it feels all the time?" he asked.

"I don't know. It didn't hurt?"

"Not at all. One minute I was running on two feet, trying to get here and thinking I needed to be faster, and the next I was on four paws. The speed's incredible."

I thought of the excruciating pain of my almost-shift. He hadn't felt any of that?

"And your … um … mind? I mean, do you feel like you?" I asked.

"Yeah, I mean, I can feel something underneath, like a pull. It happened when I saw him." He nodded at Alex. "But then it cleared and I remembered myself. I heard you and I felt … grounded."

"Good," I said, giving him a wobbly smile and relief hit me like a tsunami.

His brows wrinkled together. "What about you? Do you feel different?" he asked.

"Me?" I blinked distracted. We'd done it. George was himself. Humane, compassionate, rational. My blood had saved him. "I'm fine, why?"

"You know, the bond?"

"The bond?" Alex echoed.

"It's nothing," I told him quickly, not wanting to explain just yet. "I don't feel anything," I said to George. "Do you?"

"Nope. Maybe we won't."

"Maybe. Do you think you can shift back?"

"I don't know. How do I do that?" he asked.

"Um." I looked at Alex, but he only shrugged. "Maybe just concentrate on being human," I suggested.

"Okay." He closed his eyes. His wolf form seemed to shimmer at the edges and then he was human again. Two legs, two arms—and completely naked.

"Uh, George." I turned away, my cheeks flaming hot. Alex snickered.

"Oh! Uh … yeah. I think I'll just stay like this for a while longer." I turned back to find him a wolf again. "I guess your clothes don't shift with you," he said.

"They sure don't," Alex said, his voice strained with barely controlled laughter.

George's gaze shifted to Alex and his wolf eyes narrowed. "What are you doing here, anyway?"

"Saving Tara's ass, as usual," he said. He flipped the stake idly in his hand. George snarled at it, which only made Alex laugh.

Alex walked over and touched me lightly on the shoulder. I winced. "What the …?"

"He scratched you," Alex said, his attention on the red lines left on my skin. I hadn't noticed the burn of it until now. It wasn't nearly as bad as past scratches. I wondered if that was due to my wolf side becoming more dominant. Alex's fingers traced the line of them until they disappeared underneath my shirt. I shuddered at the contact.

"Are you all right?" he asked. His voice dropped low, just above a whisper, and for a moment, I forgot all about George and the Lexingtons and nearly shifting.

"I missed you." The words were out before I could stop them. I held my breath for his reply, wondering if I'd crossed a line or broken the rules.

"I thought about you every day," he said. "I—"

George growled and Alex broke off and stepped away. I looked at the scratch marks left by Mr. Lexington, my skin tingling where his fingers had touched me. The red lines had already begun to fade and scab. I stared at my skin, stunned that that I'd just healed five times faster than ever before.

"How'd you know I was here?" I asked, deliberately changing the subject.

"You told me, remember? When you called and asked me to act as your diversion."

Right. I'd forgotten. Or tried to. Because now that it was done, I felt like I owed him, and I didn't particularly enjoy the feeling.

Alex turned to George. "What about you, wolf-boy? If you can't beat 'em, join 'em? Is that it?"

"I told you, it was Miles. He injected George with the serum before I could stop him."

Hurt flashed across Alex's face and was gone again. I clamped down on the guilt of not telling him back at school. I'd done what I had to, to protect George. I refused to feel bad about that.

"You don't trust me," Alex said quietly. It wasn't a question, but I could hear the accusation.

"You're on a scouting team. For Kane. You chose a side," I said.

He looked at me. "It's that black and white? I'm on this side, you're on that side, and that's it? Give me a break, Tara. Our friendship means more than that, doesn't it?"

"Yes," I said quietly.

His words were my own, from our conversation on the hill, all those weeks ago. When I'd screamed at him that it wasn't so black and white, that it was wrong to label someone solely based on his or her DNA.

Alex walked over to me, not stopping until we stood almost toe to toe. "I came here for you. I left Kane's group. I'm not going back."

My head came up. My eyes searched his. "What?" I whispered. "Are you saying you're not going to hunt anymore?"

"I'm saying there are things going on I'm not sure about. And I'm saying I need you to be safe. So I'm here. As long as you need me."

I nodded. It wasn't exactly the answer I'd been hoping for, but it was a more than I'd ever expected.

Behind Alex, George cleared his throat. Or growled. I wasn't sure which. "Tara, it's not safe here."

"We should head back," I said, stepping away from Alex. I needed some distance between us. I needed to think clearly. He hadn't come here for me, not in the way I'd thought. And what if he had? What would I have done? I'd made my choice.

So why did the idea of losing Alex always tug at something deep inside me? And why couldn't I let him go?

I watched him slide the stake back inside a sheath attached to his belt and reminded myself he hadn't committed to anything past this moment.

"You coming with us, Rambo?" George asked.

"If you'll have me," he said, directing the comment to George.

George cocked his head to the side as if considering. "You ran those two hybrids off."

"I did."

George grunted, which apparently meant, "You're in," because Alex fell into step beside me.

CHAPTER SIXTEEN

I made it to the edge of the shade, the exact spot where the pavement met the chemically darkened soil, and stopped. Parked in the circular drive was a familiar-looking pickup truck. Standing on the other side, halfway to the front door, were the last three people I'd expected to see: Cord, Logan, and Victoria.

I didn't have time to react before another car pulled in behind them—a dust-coated Aston Martin.

"What are they doing here?" George asked, stepping around me to get a better look.

Instinctively, I sidestepped, putting space between Alex's shoulder and mine. Cord's frown turned into a scowl as she caught sight of me. I pretended I hadn't seen it but made a mental note not to be left alone with her. She looked furious.

My breath caught in my chest at the sight of Wes as he slid from the car. His jeans and T-shirt were wrinkled, as if he'd been wearing them for a while. It made him look vulnerable. He pulled his glasses off and broke into a smile. His expression, though lined with exhaustion, mirrored the relief and excitement inside me, and I couldn't stand still any longer. I ran to him and threw myself against him, wrapping my arms tight around his neck.

I was dimly aware of Logan and Victoria staring at George in obvious confusion. But then Wes's mouth found mine and I forgot all of them. It was only Wes and me.

And then it wasn't.

Behind me, someone cleared her throat. The lack of subtlety left no doubt who'd made the noise. Wes eased away but kept an arm around me as we turned to face Cord. She glared at both of us, arms crossed. In that moment, I was grateful that she was fond of at least one of us. Hopefully, it would be enough.

The rest of the group wandered up behind her.

"If you two are done sucking face, will someone please explain to me what the hell is going on?" Cord demanded.

"Where would you like me to start?" Wes asked, entirely too calm for the way Cord was eyeing him.

She pointed at George. "Let's see, that one's a full-blown Werewolf, but his eyes are just this side of sane." She pointed at Alex. "He's standing *next to* a Werewolf and not trying to butcher it." Finally, she pointed at Wes and me. "And you two are having some sort of lovers' reunion, which means either you haven't been gallivanting around the country together this entire week or your simple trip to the store awakened Tara's abandonment issues."

"All valid concerns," Wes said.

His eyes roamed the group. First to Logan and Victoria—and I could tell we were all wondering what they were doing here. I didn't dare ask yet. Not with Cord looking ready to punch someone. I winced as Wes caught sight of Alex. His jaw hardened and then twitched as he worked the muscles there. "Alex." He nodded.

"Wes. Nice to see you again." Alex's voice was strained. They didn't attempt a handshake.

"Tara?" Wes's eyebrows shot up. I could tell he was thinking exactly what Cord had just spoken aloud: *What the hell?*

"He just got here," I said. It was the shortest and least descriptive answer I could've given, and obviously not enough, but he didn't pursue it.

"And George?" he asked.

"Turned," I said. "Safely."

"I see that," he said. "How?"

The front door opened, saving me from an explanation just yet. Professor Flaherty took in the scene with a quick glance, her mouth widening into a welcoming smile.

She zeroed in on Alex first. "Alex, what a surprise." She stepped off the porch.

"Professor," he said. Something about his tone sounded off, like he wasn't quite as surprised as one would expect, running into a former teacher here. But then he smiled and shook her hand and said, "What brings you out here?"

"Astor DeLuca, the man who lives here, is a friend of mine. I was just visiting during break," she said. Then she switched her gaze. "Logan, Victoria, a pleasant surprise."

"Professor," Logan said, shaking her hand. Victoria did the same.

"What is everyone doing here?" Professor Flaherty asked.

I couldn't help but redden when every single person except George and I answered with a loud and resounding, "Tara." Cord punctuated hers with a glare aimed at me.

"I see." Professor Flaherty's smile never wavered and she extended her hand to the open doorway behind her. "Let's get you all out of this heat, and we'll get everything sorted out."

"Professor," Alex called. "A word?"

"Of course." She huddled with Alex out of hearing range, both of them casting glances my way. After a moment, Alex jogged toward the trees.

"What's that about?" Wes asked.

"I'll tell you inside," I said, heading for the door.

Logan gave me a quick, one-armed hug on his way inside.

"Hey," he whispered.

"Hi," I whispered back. He moved on when Victoria tugged his hand. I felt her eyes on me but didn't look up as I thought of what I was about to tell her.

George walked inside just ahead of me, still in wolf form, his tail wagging a little. Mathias simply raised a brow at him as he passed.

Halfway down the hall, George turned back. “Tay, I’m going to stop by my room to, ah, change.”

“Come find us when you’re done,” I said as he trotted off.

Wes came up beside me and took my hand. I looked down at our joined fingers and then up at him. He stared straight ahead, his jaw flexing. “I’m glad you’re here,” I said, squeezing his hand. He tugged on my arm until we were a good distance behind the group and then stopped and pulled me close.

“I missed you,” he said, his voice husky. He pressed his lips to mine and then trailed quick kisses over my jawline. He moved back to my lips, lingered there, and then pulled away.

His eyes danced and he looked down at me with a wry expression. “Don’t think this means I’m not going to yell at you later. You were supposed to wait for me before doing anything with George.”

“I don’t think that,” I said, a little dazed. We started walking again. “What *does* it mean?”

“It means I love you, even though you’re impulsive. And I don’t want that moron outside to think otherwise and do anything stupid.” Despite the words, his tone was light, and I could tell he wasn’t nearly as angry as he pretended. Still, I was glad Alex was out of earshot.

“Oh, well, if that’s all.”

I WAS RELIEVED TO FIND THE SUNROOM EMPTY. I WASN’T SURE IF IT was by chance or if Professor Flaherty had carted Astor off somewhere, but either way, it was probably better, at least for now, if he wasn’t present. This many people were sure to set him off, especially with tempers raised like they were.

Logan and Victoria filed in behind Professor Flaherty and sat together on a loveseat by the windows. Victoria whispered something to Logan and he kissed her cheek. They didn’t look over at me. I wondered what they were doing here and how in the world they’d hooked up with Cord.

Wes kept a firm grasp on my hand and led us to a space near the breakfast table where a wicker couch and chairs sat. I stood behind the couch and braced my hands on the frame. I was too wired to sit.

Professor Flaherty brought everyone glasses of water and then drifted back toward the door. I got the impression she was going to let us have it out with one another without interruption.

Cord was the one to speak first. “This is ridiculous. Why is everyone standing around like nothing is going on? George is a Werewolf, except his eyes aren’t yellow and he’s not trying to rip everyone’s throat out like a wolf-zombie.”

She stalked over to me and leaned in, sniffing heavily. She leaned back and made a face. “You’ve been giving me goosebumps since I opened my car door, and you smell like dog.” Everyone’s eyes shifted to me.

“I can explain,” I began.

“She was attacked,” Alex said from the doorway.

He didn’t look at me, but I knew he’d spoken up so I wouldn’t have to. I wondered if he was keeping my secret as a way to prove I could trust him. “When I found her, she was about to be dinner for a couple of Miles-made hybrids. Their scent is probably still all over her, not to mention saliva. He was practically drooling on her.”

“What? Why didn’t you say anything?” Wes asked.

“There hasn’t been time,” I said.

“Perimeter’s clear. I chased them off,” Alex said, settling on a spot against the wall. “Wounded the female, but she’ll recover. There wasn’t time for more.”

“Thank you,” Wes said, nodding at Alex like it pained him.

Alex nodded, though he didn’t quite meet Wes’s eyes. “There was another complication,” he said. “They were familiar.”

“Familiar how?” Cord demanded.

I took a step forward, looking past Cord to where Victoria and Logan sat. They stared back at me, Victoria’s expression as neutral as Logan’s, and for a moment, all I could see was the memory of her, sobbing in our dorm room after her parents had gone missing, and the dejected set of her shoulders when she realized they weren’t coming back.

She edged forward in her seat as if she sensed the words on my lips. I let go of Wes's hand and went to her, lowering myself onto the table so I could face her. The fact that she sat quietly, instead of insulting me or telling me to get away from her, let me know she already suspected.

In that moment, we weren't enemies. We weren't rivals. We were friends—two of a kind, completely understanding of the other, no agendas.

"It was your parents," I said quietly.

"Were they—?" She stopped and bit her lip. Logan took her hands in his.

"They're Werewolves," I confirmed. "They asked about you." The wetness in one of her eyes spilled over onto her cheek. She'd never looked less like a bully.

"They wanted to take Tara to the one in charge of the hybrids now, a woman named Olivia," Alex put in, saving Victoria from the stares of the rest of the room.

Wes rubbed his chin and cheek with the palm of his hand, a gesture of exhaustion. "Do we know an Olivia?" He looked at Cord.

"Not that I can think of. I can't keep up with all of Tara's enemies anymore," she said.

"Give me a break," I grumbled.

"Do you know what this Olivia wants from you?" Wes asked.

"No," I said. "They never told me. All I know is they are determined to bring me in. They called Olivia their master."

"Of course," Cord said. "Heaven forbid we get any peace and quiet."

"Look, this tells us they are going to keep coming," said Alex. "The hybrids in general, and specifically the Lexingtons. We need to play offense instead of sitting and waiting—"

"We?" Wes interjected.

Alex hesitated. "I took a leave of absence from my team."

"How convenient," Wes said.

"Seriously," Cord agreed. "I mean, you just happened to show up here at the same time as a couple of hybrids you've been looking for?"

Alex and I shared a look. He let it pass without correcting her about the Lexingtons' whereabouts these past few weeks.

Logan looked up at him in surprise, probably the only other one besides me who realized what a huge step leaving would've been for Alex. "Why'd you do that?"

Alex pushed off the wall and walked to the window, his hands fisted at his sides. "There's talk between some of the higher-ups … some of the things I've seen lately don't add up. I wanted to take some time to figure it out before I commit." He turned back to face the group, his eyes flickering over Cord and resting on Wes. "In the meantime, if Tara's in danger, I'd like to do what I can to help."

Wes stiffened beside me. I slid my hand into his again, a gesture of reassurance. When Wes didn't offer an answer, Alex turned to Professor Flaherty. "Would it be all right if I stayed?"

"Of course. We have plenty of room," she said.

"And it's understood that my presence here won't be shared with anyone," he added.

"You have my word."

I wondered what that meant. Why would it matter if anyone knew he was here?

"You saved Tara from the attack," Wes said, startling me with the abruptness of his words. He was still staring at Alex.

"Yes." Alex didn't move.

"You have feelings for her," Wes said.

Alex hesitated for only a split second. "Yes."

"Would you die to protect her?"

"Absolutely."

The question itself, and the certainty of Alex's answer, startled me. I didn't know what to say.

"Hmm," was all Wes said.

Cord crossed to Wes and started whispering to him too low for me to hear.

A sniffling sound from across the room drew my attention. Logan had his arm wrapped around Victoria's shoulders. She was leaning into him and trying in vain to keep the tears in check. I went back to the coffee table and sat down in front of her again. Just like that day in my dorm room, comforting her felt awkward. But I couldn't just sit by and watch her cry.

"We'll find them," I said.

She blinked until the tears receded, then stuck her chin out. "If my parents are … violent, and can't be reasoned with, we'll have to deal with them," she said. "You have my permission."

"Victoria …"

"Don't apologize again. It's giving me a headache." Her eyes flashed and for once, I didn't mind her snapping at me if it meant she wasn't falling apart. "All right."

I looked at Logan. "I should've told you what was going on back at school. I'm—" I started to say sorry and stopped when Victoria hissed at me. "I should've told you about George," I said instead. "How mad are you?"

"Not very," he said. "Cambria called after you left and told me most of it. I understand why you did it, although for future reference, I can keep a secret. Besides, for the record, it looks to me like whatever you did worked."

I smiled, relieved and grateful. "Thanks. How did you guys find me, anyway? I thought Grandma was coming."

His brows crinkled, the brim of his hat lowering on his forehead. "I don't know anything about your grandma. Cord called me a couple days ago and asked if Victoria could use her, um, locating skills to find you. Cord picked us up a few hours later, and we drove here."

I looked at Victoria. "You agreed?"

She smirked, looking suddenly like the real Victoria. "Anything to see you catch some heat."

Her words lacked the same acidic coating they usually held, and I wondered if things were changing for us. It felt good telling Victoria her parents were alive, although I still didn't understand how they weren't in CHAS custody anymore.

"Wait, so you … located me? With your gift?" I asked. "Do you think you could use it to find Olivia?"

She shook her head. "I don't know. I'd need something personal of hers to use. Something she's touched. And I've already tried finding the hybrids." She teared up again. "My parents … all of them are off my radar. I think it's their lack of humanity. Whatever it is, they're outside my scope."

Hmm. So much for that idea.

"Wait, what did you use of mine? To find me?" I asked.

Victoria's twisted smile returned. "At least something good came out of you wearing all my clothes. But I have to say … you shed like a dog. All I needed was a strand."

"You used strands of my hair?"

"Try hairballs."

"Knock it off, you two," Cord said, eyeing me. "You still haven't explained how you cured your pet hybrid. And your story better be good, because I drove across the country to hear it."

I stood and faced them. My gaze flickered over them one by one, each waiting for my explanation. Behind them all, Professor Flaherty nodded at me, and further back, shadowed by the open door, Astor stared at me, unblinking.

"I gave him my blood," I said, rushing on amidst raised eyebrows, needing to get it all out. Especially with Astor staring back at me like this was some sort of test, some big moment. "I let Astor draw it and transfuse George with it."

"Why your blood?" Cord asked, making the words sound like a challenge.

"Because it's a mixture of both. My blood is the balancer for the hybrid serum. It allows the human side to control the animal."

"Is it something you could do with the other hybrids?" Victoria asked.

"Probably. If they'd sit still long enough." I frowned. Did that mean I'd bond with any of them I tried to heal? I hadn't felt any different toward George yet.

"Maybe we could get them to come back," Victoria said. We all knew who she meant.

"It sounds like they didn't want to be helped." Logan's tone was gentle but Victoria's face fell and she nodded. I didn't bother correcting him.

I sucked in a breath, looking specifically at Alex. Too afraid to look away, terrified of what I was about to see reflected back at me. "There's something else. I'm immune to metal."

"What are you talking about? How is that possible?" Cord asked. I could hear the skepticism, the suspicion in her voice, but I held Alex's gaze a moment longer.

Shock flooded his features, but it didn't last long. Behind it was an expression that could only be worry.

I scanned the faces in front of me. Professor Flaherty, her hands folded in front of her, watched serenely. Cord stared at me, her expression a mixture of disbelief and awe. Logan, and Victoria, who'd stopped sniffling to give me the evil eye she was so good at. Astor, still hunched in the shadows just outside the door. His eyes sparkled with mischief; he was enjoying the show. And Wes, blinking rapidly over and over again, as if struggling to process the words. Our eyes met.

Then Cord recovered, and so did Logan and Victoria. They all began talking at once.

"I don't believe you," Cord said, though her tone implied she was on the fence. "It's not possible."

"How exactly does it work?" Logan asked. He didn't wait for my answer before he began listing scientific possibilities that sounded foreign to me.

And Victoria: "Your blood can work on any hybrid?"

"Yes." I answered her question since it was the easiest. They all continued to chatter, more to speculate amongst themselves than demand a response. I ignored them and turned to Wes. "You're freaking out," I said.

He looked at me like he'd forgotten I was there. "You're serious. About all this."

"Yes."

"How do you know?"

"Astor tested me. I passed," I said, simplifying it. At some point I'd explain to him how my dad had given me a secret formula to make it all possible. Maybe by then, I'd understand it myself. Wes nodded, still looking lost.

"Astor, can you come in here?" I said.

It took a moment for them to notice him hovering in the doorway. He wore flannel pajama pants and his usual slippers, but over his T-shirt he wore a lab coat that at one time must've been white. Now, it was tie-dyed, splatters of red, blue, green, yellow, and every color in between.

"Painting again?" I asked.

"Chaos is good for the soul."

I laughed. Cord looked at us like we were crazy. "Logan, there's someone I want you to meet." I waited until Logan came up beside me and then made introductions. "Astor, these are my friends, Alex, Cord, Wes, Victoria, and Logan. Logan's very interested in your metal stuff —what's it called?"

"Metallurgy," Logan provided, extending his hand. He stared at Astor like I might an ice cream sundae. "It's an honor, sir. I'm a huge fan."

"A fan, huh?" Astor shook Logan's hand and then wiped his palm on his pants, as if the whole thing grossed him out. "What, in particular, are you a fan of?" The question was meant as a challenge, but Logan answered without hesitation.

"For one thing, your theories about analytical chemistries and how it relates directly to extractive techniques. I did a term paper on the differences between liquid and gaseous leaching, and I think your paper on raw and precious metals is spot on."

"You read that dusty paper? I wrote that thing twenty years ago," Astor said, though he looked slightly pleased.

"Twenty years ago or twenty minutes," said Logan with a shrug, "doesn't matter. It's still the most forward-thinking theory on metal stimulation and second spirit domination I've ever heard."

"Huh. You just might be able to carry on an intelligent conversation. Unlike these nitwits. I've had to explain everything eighteen times till Sunday with them. Come on." Astor turned on his heel and headed for the door. Logan looked back and forth between Victoria and me like he didn't know what to do next.

"Go," I said, waving him out.

"Logan?" Victoria pouted.

"Take her with you," I said.

"I'll find you in a bit," Professor Flaherty told Logan as he left. Victoria hurried after them.

"That guy's the one who told you about your immunity to metal?" Cord asked when they were gone. "He seems like a real stable character. You sure he's for real?"

"He knows about metal. He's the one who discovered how it works in the first place. He used to work for CHAS."

"And he doesn't now because …?"

I scowled at her. I knew she wanted me to say he was insane. I wasn't going to. Not to her, especially now that I'd seen the real Astor, the one behind the mask. "Because CHAS is stupid. And more concerned with killing Werewolves and stamping out the technology that would save them from your weapons, than hiring the smartest and the best." I caught Professor Flaherty's eye as I said the last part.

"Are you saying they fired him because he figured out how to make all Werewolves immune to metal?" Alex asked.

I nodded, trying and failing to read his face. He seemed to believe everything I was saying, and he hadn't stormed out or looked at me with loathing as I'd expected. "Yes, they fired him and then stole his research. He's never quite been able to recreate it since his partner was killed."

"That girl who died was his partner," Cord said slowly, as if putting it all together.

I nodded again, but didn't offer any more of the story. It wasn't mine to tell. At the back of the room, Professor Flaherty's lips were pressed tightly together. She wasn't offering it, either.

"Immune to metal …" Cord walked to the loveseat and sat, sprawling her legs straight out in front of her and slouching against the cushion. She rubbed her hands over her face and for the first time, I noticed the dark circles lining her eyes. She looked tired, but more than that, she seemed exhausted from the inside.

Bailey. I'd been so wrapped up in George and what was happening here that I'd barely even thought of him. He'd been gone, what, a week? And I'd already forgotten. What kind of person forgot someone so fast? Cord obviously hadn't. I knew she wouldn't ever.

I put my hands on the back of the empty chair in front of me, not quite brave enough to sit next to her. "The metal immunity can save others like him, you know," I said quietly.

She jerked her eyes to mine, knowing instantly who I referred to. I sucked in a breath, waiting for her to scream at me. She didn't.

"You're right. Everyone deserves a shot," she said. "Especially when it comes to CHAS. They're corrupt and bloodthirsty. Which is saying a lot coming from me."

I didn't argue with her. At least Cord only killed those who deserved it. Like Miles. Somehow, that actually made her better than CHAS. Definitely better than Gordon Steppe.

"What are you going to do with this, Tara?" Alex asked.

I didn't answer him right away because honestly, I wasn't sure. For the first time, the pressure of leadership that Wes was always talking about weighed on me. It seemed the harder I fought against it, the more I was propelled into leading a cause I wasn't even sure I stood for yet.

"I think we should figure out who this Olivia person is and then we'll talk. One problem at a time."

They all nodded, even Professor Flaherty, and I couldn't shake the feeling a group had just formed.

I stared at Wes, wanting to say a million different things, none of which involved an audience.

"Well." Professor Flaherty unclasped her hands and the energy shifted. Cord rose from the love seat. The meeting was over. "Cord, Alex, I'm going to check on a few things. If you like, I'll show you to your rooms."

They both grunted something resembling a "yes" and filed out.

Cord stopped in front of me, her face a hard mask. "You fixed your friend," she said in a hard voice. Her chin rose and fell so quick, I wasn't sure what it meant. "Nice job." Then she left.

Neither Wes nor I moved, even after the room had emptied. My hands balled into fists at my sides. I pumped them open and closed, needing to channel my nervous energy. I waited for him to say something, anything.

"It's a lot more than just fixing George," he said finally.

"You're telling me," I mumbled.

"It's a lot, Tara."

"I know."

He held his arms out and I practically fell into them. I leaned my cheek against his shoulder and he swayed gently side to side. His hand smoothed my hair. "Everything feels better in this position," I said. He didn't answer. "Are you still freaking out?"

"Maybe. Aren't you?"

"Yes." I straightened so I could look up at him. "But not in the way you think."

"What way is that?"

"The way you're probably freaking out. As in, how did we not know this? What do we do now? What else has Steppe covered up? Stop me when I get one right."

His lips curved. "None of those things bother you?"

I pulled away to pace. I didn't want to end the contact—his arms around me were a steady strength—but I needed to move, especially to tell him this. "Do you know why I don't want anyone to know I can shift?"

"Because you're scared of what they'll think of you."

"It's more like I'm scared of what I'll think of myself."

"You already know you're a Dirty Blood. It doesn't get much worse than that."

"Doesn't it?" I stopped and faced him. The laughter in his eyes faded as he realized how serious I was. "If I can shift, become both a Hunter and a Werewolf, when no one else can—that means something. If my blood can heal a hybrid, give them their humanity back, it means everything Vera said about me is true. I'm special, different. And finding out about this metal thing, that I'm immune, it only makes what she said more real. Is it like she said? I'm supposed to bring peace? Because I have no idea how to do that."

"Even if it does mean something, that you're a part of a bigger purpose or whatever, you have nothing to be afraid of, Tara. You can handle it, whatever it is." He closed the distance between us and cupped my face in his hands. His eyes were deadly serious. "You are capable of anything. Whatever you set your mind to. There's no reason to be afraid. Even if all of those things are true, you being a Werewolf, or immune to metal, or whatever—if you don't want it, I'll walk away with you. We're in this together."

"You would do that? Walk away?"

"Of course I would. Doing something just because you feel like you have to or you're supposed to, that's not destiny. Destiny is doing something because you know you couldn't do anything else."

"For me," I whispered, "that's you."

He smiled a slow smile, transforming his features and shifting them from determined to triumphant. "Being in love with you is more than I ever thought possible. You're my family, my soul mate, the one I was made for. I'm not going anywhere," he said as his mouth met mine.

The kiss was soft and deep, a perfect match for the words he'd spoken. It was a promise of forever. By kissing him back, I'd accepted his promise. Still, reality crept in at the edges, inching me back well before I wanted to. He didn't argue, only raised his hand to smooth my hair and waited for me to go on.

"I could never run, you know," I said. "Not because it isn't tempting, but because I can't outrun *me.* If it were only about facing CHAS, stopping them, or changing them, I'd do it. In a second. Or I'd try. Facing myself is a different story. How can I demand they accept me when I don't know who I am?"

"I can't answer that for you. I can only tell you what was told to me by someone very wise: 'Your blood doesn't define who you are. Your choices do.'"

"Who said that?"

"Fee."

"Very wise," I agreed.

"No one said you had to rush into anything, and no matter what you decide, you have me. You're not alone."

"I know. Thank you."

"One step a time, right?"

"Right. And I think the first step should be to test you against the metal."

"You think I'm immune as well?"

I shrugged. "Our parents were friends. I wouldn't put it past them to experiment on both of us."

"Good point." He rubbed his chin. "Skills, huh? So if I'm immune too, does that mean I have no metal skills or mad metal skills?"

I laughed and took his hand, leading him toward the door. "I think Cambria's vocabulary is rubbing off."

I paused at the doorway and stared up and down the hallway, trying to remember the way to the lab.

"You know where we're going, right?"

I bit my lip and chose a direction. "Right," I said. I really needed to mention my idea about color-coding the carpet.

"I do have one question, though," he said, as we walked. "Did you really have no idea Alex was coming?" His brow rose but there wasn't any force behind the words. Still, I groaned.

"He really did show up just before you. I had no idea he was coming."

"I believe you," he said.

I narrowed my eyes. "You do?"

"Sure, but you had to know when you asked him to lie for you that he'd come."

I stopped walking. We were at a fork in the hallways and I had no idea which way to go.

I stared at him, unable to keep the defensive note out of my tone. "I didn't expect to ever see him again, actually. He had his place with Kane."

He shook his head, his lips curving. "You don't know anything about guys. He was coming to see you from the second you called. I don't care how much he loves killing Werewolves."

I frowned. I didn't want to argue—about Alex, especially.

"It's all right," he said, catching sight of my expression. "I told you, I'm not mad."

I tilted my head. "You're not playing nice about this because you're afraid to fight in front of Alex, are you?" I said. "Because you said you're not mad. So you can't be mad later, either."

"Relax. I'm not playing nice because of Alex," he said. "Not completely, anyway." I glared at him and he laughed and pulled me against him. His lips moved against my ear and when he spoke, his breath left chills where it slid down my neck. "Mostly, it's because I can't stand to be in the same room with you and not touch you," he whispered. "Being angry is counterproductive to that goal."

I shivered as he pressed his lips against my neck, then lower, against my collarbone. Then lower, moving my shirt out of the way to kiss my shoulder, then lower still …

My back hit the wall with a thud, the heated tingling vibrating through me at his touch. My control slipped and passion rose like that day at the lake …

"Wes, we're in the hallway," I managed to whisper.

He sighed and the pressure of his mouth against my neck disappeared. "Dammit. We pick the worst places for this sort of thing." He stepped back and swept his hair away from his forehead. "All right," he said grudgingly, "which way to the lab?"

"I don't …" My words faded away as a strange sensation washed over me.

I looked around, instinct telling me we were no longer alone. I expected to find Mathias lurking, but the hallway was empty.

"What is it?" Wes asked. His expression quickly went from curious to concerned.

"I don't know. I thought someone was there," I said. The feeling in the back of my mind exploded. I squeezed my eyes shut against a searing pain in my skull.

"What is it?" Wes repeated, alarm in his voice now.

My heart raced from the pain. I closed my eyes against the sudden glare of the light. "I don't know. My head hurts," I managed.

"What can I do?"

His voice sounded loud, like the beating of a bass drum. I winced.

"I need to sit." I slid down the wall, eyes closed, and pulled my knees in, trying to block out the glare that burned my eyes through my lids. I could feel Wes hovering in front of me, his fingertips brushing over my legs.

The stillness reverberated, a beat that pulsed and pounded against my skull. Underneath it all was the *presence* of something.

"Tay?" I looked up at the sound of George's voice, breathless and panicked. I pried my eyes open, squinting up at where he stood, his entire body shaking. His form shimmered at the edges, and he looked ready to shift at any second.

"George?" I managed. It came out on a sob. The pain. I couldn't handle much more.

"What's wrong with her?" I heard him ask. I squeezed my eyes shut again, and grabbed Wes's hand, hanging on.

"I don't know. Her head started hurting all of a sudden," Wes said. "Where've you been?"

"It wasn't as easy shifting back as I thought."

I heard George shuffle closer. It sounded loud; everything was magnified—painful beyond anything I'd ever felt, including my bite from Leo.

"Well, do something," George insisted in a shaky voice.

"Back up. And don't you dare shift in here," Wes said to him. "Get a grip."

"I can't help it. I feel protective."

"If you shift this close, you're the one she'll need protecting from," Wes snapped. "Which way back to the others?"

"I don't know. I was in my room."

"Well, how did you find us?" Wes asked, irritated. I squeezed his hand harder.

"I just felt something. I don't know. I knew Tara needed me."

"How the hell would you know that?" Wes's tone was clipped,

bordering on fury. "Never mind, we don't have time. Find Professor Flaherty. Which way to your room?"

"Um, take a left at the end of the hall and its right there," George said. "How about I'll take her and you get the professor? I can't—I can't leave her."

"You can't leave her? What the hell, George! Just get the professor already, and hurry up!"

Wes didn't wait for an answer before scooping me up and hurrying down the hall. I whimpered at being jostled but struggled against the searing pain in my head to keep silent. Something George had said felt important, but around the pounding, I couldn't pinpoint what it was.

Wes laid me down on George's bed—I could smell him on the sheets—and Professor Flaherty came in. I didn't bother opening my eyes. Even with the lights off, it hurt too much.

"Tara, can you hear me?" she asked.

I nodded.

"Your head is hurting?"

I nodded again.

"Can you help her?" Wes asked.

"I mentioned it to Astor. I think I know what's happening." The mattress depressed as she leaned closer. "I think you do too. Honey, you need to let go. George already has and the process wasn't painful for him at all. It's only hurting you because you're fighting it."

I didn't answer. I couldn't. It would've pushed the pain over the edge.

"Fighting what?" Wes asked. He sounded angry—and confused. "Can't you do something to help her?"

"No," Professor Flaherty said. "She has to do it herself. Astor said it's the only way. She has to stop fighting it and let it happen."

"Let what happen? Pain?" Wes's voice rose and I winced and curled the pillow around my ears.

"It would be better for her if we didn't talk for now," Professor Flaherty said, her voice muffled. "We should step out until she's ready."

"I'm not leaving her." Wes and George spoke in unison.

"I'll be right outside if you need me," Professor Flaherty said.

The door opened and closed. Then there was silence.

Someone took my hand. I could tell by the circles his thumb drew on my palm it was Wes.

A second later, I heard a voice near my ear. "You have to let go, Tay," George whispered. His voice was quiet, so low I almost missed the words. "I let go and it doesn't hurt. It's not as scary as it sounds. You can do this."

I sucked in a breath, let it out. I knew what I had to do.

One by one, I relaxed my muscles. Beginning with my feet, my ankles, my legs, all the way up to my neck. Soon all that was left was my head. The pain had begun to recede a little. It was at the edges, ready to flood back in again if I changed my mind.

Only, I couldn't.

I had to do this. I braced myself for whatever came next—and then I let go.

CHAPTER SEVENTEEN

"Tara? Can you hear me?"

I fought my way to the surface, concentrating on the sound of Wes's voice, the pressure of his hand drawing slow circles across my palm.

"Tara, please wake up," he pleaded.

I opened my eyes hesitantly, afraid of bringing back the pain, but there was none. Only calm. And the feeling from before that I wasn't alone, which was completely true, since George and Wes were both hovering over me. They wore matching expressions of drawn brows and worried frowns. George looked slightly less manic, though.

"It's all right, I'm fine now," I said. Things were clicking into place.

"You're sure? Because before …" Wes trailed off as I nodded.

"I'm sure." The pain, the agony, the crushing pounding in my skull—all of that was gone. In its place was understanding. I looked at George. He was watching me with more concentration than worry. I smiled. "Your skills of projection are impressive. I'm calm now," I told him.

"I wasn't sure how much you'd feel," he said.

"Everything. How did you know?"

"When your head started hurting, so did mine," he said. "Almost as badly too. For a few minutes I didn't realize, but then it sort of just hit me. And I knew it was you."

I sat up. "Like I know it's you sending me calm feelings right now."

"Right. It's like you have this signature in my mind—a scent in my brain. Weird."

"Can somebody explain to me what the hell is going on?" Wes stared back and forth between us with wide eyes. He looked torn between confusion and irritation.

"Um, I may have forgotten to mention one of the side effects of the transfusion," I said.

"Well, now might be a good time," he said.

"George and I are sort of, uh, bonded, I guess."

"Bonded," Wes repeated. "As in, a deep friendship?"

"As in, I can feel what he feels, and he can feel what I feel."

"Like read each other's minds?"

I chose my words carefully, because I wasn't sure if Wes was angry, but he didn't look happy. "No, not thoughts, exactly. Feelings. Emotions. George was projecting calmness and it made me feel better."

"And earlier, when you had that headache, he knew to come because he could feel your pain?" Wes asked.

"Right," George answered. Wes looked at him. George smiled, which didn't help.

"So, you guys are a pack now?" Wes shook his head. "That's great."

"We're not a pack," I said, startled at the idea. That would suggest I was a Werewolf, which I wasn't. Not really. Yet.

"The bond you're talking about sure sounds like a pack. Not that it's normally anywhere near this strong, but being in tune with each other, coming to the other's aid. I hate to break it to you, Tara, but you two are most definitely a pack. And by the looks of it, you're the alpha."

"Alpha to whom?" a voice from the doorway asked.

No one answered. Neither of the boys turned to identify the speaker. We all recognized it.

I gulped, my throat suddenly dry. I drew my eyes to the doorway and stared back at Grandma.

"Hi," I squeaked.

Grandma didn't respond. She pointed to the boys. "You, you, out." They left without a word or a backwards glance. Traitors.

Grandma shut the door behind her and dropped her bag on the floor. She sat on the bed near the end, keeping her distance from me. I hung my head.

"How much trouble am I in?"

"With me or your mother?" she shot back. I could feel her eyes burning a hole in the top of my head. I raised my eyes to hers.

"With you," I said. I could handle my mom; I knew what to expect with her. Grandma was a different story. She'd either smother me with guilt until I'd sufficiently punished myself or tie me to a chair.

"Considering you've just registered on my supernatural radar as a Werewolf …" I winced as she let that hang in the air. "I haven't decided yet. Pack your things. We're leaving."

"Leaving? But—"

"Leaving," she repeated, packing a punch in that one word.

"But George—"

"Is cured, I'm told, thanks to his new alpha."

"You spoke with Professor Flaherty?"

"And Astor, for all the good that did. I'm not discussing this right now. We can talk in the car." She rose. "You have five minutes. I'll be in the hall." She didn't wait for an answer before picking up her bag and exiting the room. Through the open door, I could hear her pressing buttons on her phone.

I got up and found my bag in the corner near the chair where I'd slept. Nothing was really unpacked, so even though she'd given me five minutes, I was ready in one.

"Can I at least say goodbye?" I asked.

"I've already thanked Professor Flaherty for her hospitality. The rest of them you can see at home. The car's waiting." She spun and followed a waiting Mathias toward the door. All I could do was follow.

The hall was deserted. I walked as slowly as I dared, hoping for Wes, or George since he had to feel my desperation right now. They could at least wave from a doorway or something. But no one came.

Mathias held the front door for me as I passed. It was, apparently, my only goodbye.

"Later, Jeeves," I said. I could've sworn his lips twitched.

A sleek, black limousine idled in the drive. A man in uniform, complete with white driving gloves, held the car door open. Grandma handed him her bag and climbed inside. I did the same, but I kept my bag with me. I wasn't sure why, but it made me feel better. More in control.

"A limo?" I asked, brow raised. I'd never seen Grandma travel in anything other than her glorified tank.

"It's all they had," she said pointedly. "This trip wasn't exactly planned."

I slid across the leather seat, blinking against the sudden dimness of the interior. Track lighting lit the compartment, like mini-nightlights. I jumped at the sight of another person sitting across from me.

"Alex, what are you doing here?"

I looked at Grandma, who was busy smoothing her bedazzled *Nevada* tee. "Protection," she said.

"He's our bodyguard?" I asked in surprise. "Since when do you need a bodyguard?"

She glared at me. "I have my reasons."

The partition mid-car lowered. Wire-rimmed sunglasses stared back at us through the rearview. "Are we ready, ma'am?" the driver asked.

"We are. Remember to stay off the main roads," she told him.

"Yes, ma'am." The partition slid closed and the car eased forward.

Anxiety crept in, almost blotting out the knowledge I'd left without saying goodbye, without knowing when I'd see any of them again. When the car reached the end of the drive, I twisted around and watched the house disappear from sight.

"My car," I said, catching sight of it just before we turned the corner.

"George will drive it back. I already spoke to him," Grandma said.

"Of course you did." That explained why I hadn't felt any strong emotions through our bond. He was more informed than I was. "Grandma? What's going on?" I asked.

Grandma looked at Alex, eyebrows raised questioningly.

"It's fine," he said.

"What's—"

"Turn the radio on," she said. He hit the power button. A whiny country song spilled out of the speakers. Alex reached to turn it down. "Leave it," she said. His hand fell back to his lap.

"I know you have questions," she said to me, keeping her voice even with the volume of the stereo. I had to strain to hear her. "But I couldn't risk explaining until we'd gotten you out. Alex told me what happened, how you saved George, and how you're starting to shift."

"Alex," I hissed.

Grandma held up a hand between us, like a referee. "We don't have time for that. He was doing you a favor. I can't help you if I don't know the truth." She gave me a look that reminded me I was the one in trouble, not Alex.

"Help me how?" I asked.

"With CHAS. They cannot, and I mean *cannot* know about this," she said. "There are things in place, wheels turning, that you know nothing about. Maybe if you had, we could've handled it better, I don't know. Alex thought maybe we could keep a lid on it, but then Wes showed up and you came here ..." She sighed.

"I don't understand. What's going on with CHAS? Please don't tell me you're going to turn George over to them."

"Why on earth would I do that?" she asked.

"Because you work for them. You're on the council. You're always talking about 'we have to call CHAS' and 'CHAS will want to know about this.'" I shrugged. "Sometimes I wonder who you'd be loyal to if it came down to choosing."

"You listen to me, young lady," she said pointing a finger in my face. "I am loyal to you, first, last, always. The things I'm doing for CHAS are all for you. And you're one to talk about loyalty. When have you ever trusted me with the whole story, huh?"

I didn't argue. She was right. I decided to focus on the first part, the one that didn't have to do with me lying to her. "What do you mean you're doing everything for me? What does CHAS have to do with me?"

"Just tell her, Edie. It's too late to keep it from her," Alex said.

Grandma nodded. "All right, then. Here it is. Alex and I, along with a couple others, have been working to bring CHAS down from the inside. Or more specifically, Gordon Steppe."

"What?" Of all the things she could've said, this I hadn't expected. "But, Alex, you joined Kane's scout team."

"A cover," he said.

Something inside me welled with happiness. I shoved it aside. "You lied to me?"

"I had to. I couldn't tell anyone what I was really doing. As a part of Kane's team, I was able to pass information to your grandmother without anyone suspecting. Then you called and I thought for a second you knew things. It's one of the reasons I agreed to help you. When I found out the truth, I got on a plane."

"Won't Kane be angry? Will he fire you?" I asked.

He shrugged. "Doesn't matter, I'm out." His voice was flat. Something more had happened.

He stared out the window, making it clear his part of the explanation was done.

"I still don't understand what I have to do with all this," I said.

Grandma took my hand and patted it. "Sweetie, CHAS has one mission and one mission only: to stamp Werewolves out of existence. Doesn't matter if they're good or bad. To Steppe, they're soulless, incapable of good. To him, they don't deserve to live, much less have the right to a fair trial and all that. If they knew what you could do … I'm assuming you know about Mary Beth now, the real way she died."

"Yes, Professor Flaherty told me."

"That was Steppe's first run-in with a hybrid. It happened right after he took over as director."

I started to correct her. Mary Beth had been a Werewolf. Then I remembered what Professor Flaherty had said, about Astor and Mary Beth having the bond George and I had. "He made them both hybrids," I said.

She nodded. "Steppe couldn't stand it. The only reason he didn't kill Astor too was because he saw what Mary Beth's death did to him, and he knew Astor would no longer be a threat. But now, with you going to see him, using him to help George, you've painted a target on your own head. We can't let Steppe find out you were there."

"You know he's not dangerous," I said as the pieces clicked into place. "You didn't want me here in case CHAS found out."

"Precisely. If Steppe knows Astor's back in the game, he'll follow the trail. One that leads directly to you. That would be very bad."

"What about George?" Panic leapt in my throat. I couldn't breathe. "If Steppe finds out, he'll kill him. We have to go back for him." I clawed at the armrest, my fingers itching toward the door handle. It didn't matter we were barreling down an empty highway. I couldn't leave him.

"George will be safe," Grandma assured me. "He has Wes and Cord and the others to watch out for him. The best thing was to split you up. No one else knows George was even infected. As long as that remains secret, he's off their radar."

"He's safer away from you," Alex added.

I nodded, feeling numb. "And that's why we had to leave so quickly."

"Yes. I got word Kane's hunting party is close. If they'd seen you at Astor's …" Alex's mouth tightened.

"But how do they know I can shift?" I asked.

"They don't. Not yet, but Steppe knows what you are. He's just waiting for a reason to come after you. Associating with Astor would be all he needs," Grandma said.

"And Wes? He knows what Wes is. Does that mean he's in danger too?" I asked.

"One thing about Steppe, he plays by the rules," Grandma said. "And right now, The Cause is protected as a neutral party."

"Until he finds a way to change the rules," Alex said.

"Which won't be much longer, if he has his way," Grandma added. They shared a look.

"What rule is that?" I asked.

"Steppe is petitioning the council to reverse the amnesty treaty they have with The Cause," Alex said.

"Aren't I protected under the amnesty treaty?" I asked.

"You aren't officially a member of The Cause," Grandma said. "You can't officially join until you turn eighteen, unless a parent or guardian allows it."

"But will CHAS go along with that?" I asked. I looked at Grandma. "Can't you get the rest of the council to vote against it?"

"Most won't go against Steppe. We don't have enough on our side."

"Tara." Alex's voice was careful, controlled. "If they do rescind the law, it'll mean every Werewolf within The Cause and without will be fair game."

Understanding dawned slowly, almost as if my mind could shut it out if I concentrated hard enough. "This is war," I whispered.

Neither of them corrected me.

CHAPTER EIGHTEEN

The airport made me claustrophobic. Between the crowds shoving past with wheeled suitcases in their grasp, beeping golf carts whizzing by with handicapped patrons, and overlapping voices announcing flight arrivals via staticky intercoms, I couldn't think straight. I couldn't breathe.

CHAS was evil. CHAS was the enemy. And they were coming for me and everyone I loved.

I thought about the conversation I'd had with Wes right before I left, about being scared of what it all meant. I'd gone on about not being ready for the responsibility that would come with the choices in front of me. I could barely face who—and what—I was, and now I'd have to fight a war that centered on that very fact. Not choosing was no longer an option. I couldn't run from something like this. It was too big, and way too late for that.

Someone yelled. I was too wrapped up in my thoughts to focus on the words. Alex pulled me out of the way just in time to avoid being run over by a security guard on what looked like a two-wheeled hovercraft.

"Watch it," I said, not that the guy heard me as he zipped down the concourse.

A monotone voice overhead announced our flight. Grandma shuffled us toward the terminal. At the ticket counter, the woman handed us our seat assignments and we filed onto the plane. I felt better when we stepped inside the cabin, like we'd finally made it to safety. Not that we were in danger before, not directly, but the amount of adrenaline running through my veins argued otherwise.

We ended up with two seats together and one three rows behind.

"You guys sit together," Alex said, shuffling toward the seat further back. "I'm going to catch a nap." He stowed his bag and flopped into his seat, his eyes closing before I could respond.

Grandma motioned for me to take the window. As she stowed my bag, I checked my phone. A new text from Wes: *love u. miss u. C u soon.* Probably all I'd get until Grandma said otherwise. Sidestepping my mother was one thing; I wasn't sure he was brave enough to do the same to Grandma.

The prompter hanging above my head blinked on, indicating it was time to turn off all electronics. I closed my eyes, searching for the mental cord that tied George and me together. I felt his mind, calm and steady, as it had been since I'd left Astor's. What was he getting from mine?

Grandma settled in her seat and pulled out a book, the cover of which had bloody-faced zombies being chased by people with large guns. "Looks good," I said.

"Oh, it is," she answered, completely missing my sarcasm.

How could she talk of war and espionage one minute and lose herself in a make-believe story the next? I wished I could turn it off so easily.

I leaned my head against the window frame, trying to distract myself by staring out at the runway. The sun dipped below the horizon, leaving behind a pinkish glow as twilight crept in. It was beautiful in a way that was nothing like home. So much open space, not a tree in sight. It wasn't what I was used to, but I could appreciate it.

It wasn't long before the plane eased forward and the flight attendant's voice droned out over the intercom as he pointed out the emergency exits.

Somewhere between takeoff and thirty thousand feet, I drifted off.

MY MOM WAS ON THE FRONT STEPS WHEN WE PULLED UP. SHE SLAPPED the single bright yellow rubber glove against her thigh to an impatient beat only she could hear. I was suddenly very glad for the Hummer's tinted windows—she couldn't see my fear. Grandma parked and we all got out. I scurried to help Alex with the bags, but he waved me away.

"I've got it," Alex said, swinging our bags over his shoulders.

"You go on ahead," Grandma said with a wave. "Alex and I need to chat."

My shoulders slumped. I swallowed what felt like a lump of cotton balls. Time to face the music.

"Hi, Mom," I mumbled when I got close.

She stopped hitting the glove against her leg. "Hello, daughter," she said. She only called me "daughter" instead of Tara when she was seriously pissed.

"Kitchen?" I asked.

"Oh, yes," she replied.

I led the way.

The smell of bleach hit me before I'd crossed the threshold. My eyes watered and my throat burned. I slid onto the barstool, careful to breathe out of my mouth.

"Geez, mom, how do you stand it?" I croaked.

"If you're in here long enough, you don't notice it after a while."

"You mean your sense of smell burns away."

Her left eye twitched. She gripped the counter with white knuckles. "It wouldn't smell like this if you'd stop running off," she snapped.

"I did it to save—"

"Spare me the 'I'd do anything for my friends' speech, Tara." Her eyes dimmed and instead of angry, she looked exhausted. "I know why you went, who you went to see, all of it."

"All of it?" I repeated. I wasn't sure what those words really meant when it came to my mom. She rarely knew all of it anymore. Maybe she thought she did but—

"Yes," she said, "the bond, your shifting, CHAS. All. Of. It."

I shrank further into my seat. Apparently "all" meant "all." Grandma shuffled in with Alex in tow. He had his hoodie balled up in his hands, covering the lower half of his face. His eyes watered. Somehow, Grandma's remained dry.

"Where are you going?" my mom called to her as she passed. "I thought we were going to do this as a group."

"Elizabeth, I am not doing this in here. It reeks. I told you not to worry."

"This is me not worrying," my mom snapped back.

Grandma shook her head. "Well, I'm not staying in here."

"Where do you want to go? And do not say we can all squeeze into your bedroom," my mom said.

"It is the only fortified room in the house," Grandma said. My mother glowered at her. "Fine, fine, we'll go out to the backyard. Where's Cambria?"

"Out with Derek." My mom glanced at the stove clock. "She should be home soon. I told her you were on your way."

"She'll find us. Let's go." Grandma motioned for Alex to follow. They stowed the bags along the wall below the stairs and headed for the back door.

"Tara, move it," my mother ordered when I didn't follow fast enough.

The backyard was lit by motion-sensor lamps mounted at the edges of the mulch beds. They lit one by one as Grandma passed by. She didn't stop until she reached the gazebo.

"You think it's safe to talk out here?" my mom asked.

"Safer than breathing those death fumes," Grandma said. "I told you not to worry."

"Please, Mother, you of all people should know how impossible that is for me."

"You've got that right," Grandma said.

She zeroed in on me just as I sat on the edge of the wooden bench, nearest the doorway. Even without walls, I felt caged. Mostly by the locked stares I got from the others. "All right, Tara, here's the deal," Grandma said. "You've been keeping us in the dark for a while now. That stops tonight. You're going to start from the beginning and tell us everything. Don't stop until you're finished. We don't care how long it takes, so go slow. We don't want you leaving anything out." When she was done, she folded her hands in her lap, as if patiently waiting. Despite her easy expression, I knew what she'd said hadn't been a request.

"Everything?" I repeated.

"Everything," my mom confirmed. She didn't sound nearly as friendly or patient as Grandma. Across from me, Alex slouched against the wooden bench.

"Starting from when?" I asked.

"The beginning," said Grandma.

My brows went up. "So… birth?"

"How about the night you found out you were a Hunter," Alex said. I remembered the promise I'd made that I'd tell him everything when there was time. His brow rose, daring me to refuse. "You promised."

I sighed. "I promised you. Not them. And for the record, it's not like you've both offered up anything that would help make this easier on me. If I've kept things from you or done things you don't like, it's only because I was forced to find answers on my own."

"Point taken," Grandma said. "I know you think we're making you do this because you're in trouble—" Grandma began.

"I'm not?"

"Oh, you are," my mom put in, "but that's not why we're doing this. Not completely."

"We need to know so we can protect you," Grandma said. "And we're family, which means we're there for each other." I tried not to roll my eyes, but I couldn't help it. "Okay, so maybe we haven't done so hot on the second part before now, but we're changing that tonight." Her voice hardened. "Start talking, girlie."

I opened my mouth, fully prepared to fire back with something about how the women in this family needed to learn to open up, and why did it have to start with me instead of them—but instead, I started talking. The whole story. From the beginning. Just like they'd asked.

Somewhere during my monologue—which took close to an hour—I realized I wasn't looking at my mother or Grandma. I was looking at Alex. Watching him react to all of the wolf stuff should've made it harder but it didn't. It made it easier.

I admitted how I'd killed Liliana more out of confusion and fear than any real malice. How Wes had to erase my memory of it because of how badly I'd freaked out after. I especially didn't look at my mother during that part, too afraid to see the look on her face as she remembered that morning, thinking I'd been sick with the flu.

Then about meeting Jack and Fee and all of the training I'd done with Jack while I waited for Leo to make his move. I heard my mom's sharp intake of breath when I told her about the bite and how Wes had carried and then driven me to Fee. She'd never even known how close I'd come to dying. Realizing that made me feel guilty for all of the things I'd never told her about my new life. When I got to the part about Julie and the bloody message scrawled at the scene, she'd started to interrupt, but Grandma patted her hand and she stayed silent.

I kept my eyes locked on Alex. His expression remained neutral. More than once, I saw emotion creep into his eyes. Concern. Empathy. Anger. But he never looked away, and I never saw the one thing I feared above all: disgust.

Then I got to the part about Miles. How he'd fooled everyone, including me, up until the time he'd come on to me in that warehouse. I'd forgotten about that until today—blocked it out—and the look on Alex's face was pure revulsion. Exactly how I felt inside.

I hurried on in my retelling. On to Wood Point Academy and the weird messages, the hints from Miles that he was creating something that would carve out a place for him and me as leaders. I told them about Miles appearing to me in the woods that day. How he'd held me with his arm around my neck and whispered things that made me feel like no amount of showers would ever erase the grime he left behind. Alex scowled and his knuckles whitened where he gripped the edge of the bench.

Still, I went on. I even mentioned seeing Victoria's parents in the clinic that night, and overhearing Kane insist on secrecy. Alex didn't look nearly surprised enough at how much I'd heard. I'd assumed he'd guessed it. I did leave out the more personal parts. Like Alex's kiss in the woods the day I'd seen Miles and his offer—or threat—to do it again when he thought I wouldn't feel guilty about it after. I faltered in my story as the memory of it washed over me and then quickly hurried on, wondering if he'd been thinking if it too.

Alex's expression was intense, his eyes locked firmly on mine, unblinking, as it had been since I'd begun. I paused, drawing strength from his steady gaze, before describing the next part. Because all of that came easy compared to my massacre in the woods.

Slowly, haltingly, I recounted that night. How they'd attacked first. The countless pairs of eyes, bright yellow with murderous intent, stalking toward us in the woods. How Wes had gone down and something inside me snapped. And when I'd come to, all that was left were bodies. Broken. Bloody. Dead. How I'd reeked of wolf after. And how Wes grudgingly agreed not to tell anyone until I was ready. Until now.

I paused, so sure someone would speak up, unable to remain quiet any longer. But none of them did. Alex didn't waver in his silent intensity, but now I wasn't sure if it was encouragement or simply a loss for words.

I went on. About Bailey and the trip to the lake that began so innocently and ended so tragically. About George, and my promise to him —to myself—that no matter what, I'd save him. Because Miles couldn't be allowed to win.

I mentioned Wes's contact in DC disappearing and told them about my trip to Astor's. Seeing Victoria's parents in the road, almost shifting. The metal testing, his explanation of what my father had done in suppressing my Werewolf gene. And how it was now struggling to break free, especially when I felt threatened. I told them about the bond with George.

Alex's eye twitched at that part, but otherwise he remained immobile as ever.

Finally, I told them about what Victoria's parents had said, about

Olivia—whoever she was—and her using them to get to me, using all of the hybrids to hunt me.

I finished and licked my lips, rubbing my hands back and forth on my jeans. No one spoke. I tried to imagine what Alex was thinking. I stared out into the woods even though I couldn't make out anything but shadowy limbs in the darkness. The crickets and cicadas seemed abnormally loud. As did my heartbeat.

Grandma broke the silence. "Baby girl …" she trailed off. I met her eyes, hearing something in her voice I hadn't expected. Heartbreak.

Beside her, my mother's face caught my eye. Something shimmered there, just under her eye. She reached up and swiped it, and I realized it was a tear.

"Honey," my mother said. She got up and crouched in front of me, the tears streaming freely now.

"Mom, I'm really sorry," I began, sure she must be furious to be so quiet—and crying. Instead, she wrapped her arms around me and smoothed my hair.

"Do not apologize ever again. Not for this. I'm the one who's sorry. I should've been there. I should've tried harder to understand. Please forgive me," she said.

I didn't answer until she pulled away. I didn't know what to say. The last thing I'd expected was an apology. I couldn't help but be a little suspicious that I wouldn't be grounded for life when it was all over. "I forgive you," I said.

"Tara, we appreciate your honesty," Grandma said. It must've been some sort of signal to my mom because she slid back onto the bench. I braced myself. "We know how hard it was for you to tell us all of that. Very brave. And now that we know everything, we can help you." She glanced at Alex. "You're still on board?"

"As long as you need me," he said. The deepness of his voice sent a shiver through me.

She nodded. "Alex is going to train you this summer," she said to me.

"Train me? For what?"

"This thing with CHAS isn't over and we want you fully prepared.

As much as we'd like to lock you away for your protection," she threw a glance at my mom and continued, "we can't do that. At some point, you will face an enemy. That's a given. We want you as prepared as possible."

"As for the wolf side of you, we've got Jack and Fee for that," my mom said. "I've already spoken with them and they'll help you develop it as much as they can, though there's not much precedent for this sort of thing. Vera's checking the *Draven* records to see if some family, somewhere, ever recorded anything like this."

"You've already spoken with them?" I echoed. "So you knew about me turning?"

She gave a small smile, as if sharing a secret. "I've known something's up for a while. Then, when you left, Cambria confirmed some things."

"You seem pretty calm about it," I said.

"I've had a little time to digest," she admitted. "I've been meeting with Jack for a few weeks now. He's been slowly filling me in on what I've missed these past years, helping me ease into it."

"Ease into what?" I asked.

"Being a Hunter again." Her face contorted and I could see her struggling for words. Her eyes glistened again. "After losing Julie and everything with Leo … it's been hard. I never wanted to return to all this." She extended her arms, as if to include this very conversation. I felt a pang at the memory of Julie, my mother's assistant at the shop. Leo had killed her and left a bloody message at the crime scene, addressed to me. My mother went on, "But I have no choice, and I'm willing now, especially if it means protecting you and being a bigger force in your life. I've let you be on your own too long. I don't want to do that anymore."

"So, you're going to what? Hunt again?" I asked. I couldn't help the disbelief. My mother, the Hunter? The mental picture was even more ludicrous than Grandma in a battle. And even that was something I'd had to see to believe.

She twisted the glove still in her lap. Obviously, she wasn't excited about the idea, either. "If it comes to that," she said.

I wasn't sure I believed her, but I let it drop.

"So, back to training," I said. "And in the meantime, what? Are we going to keep looking for the hybrids?"

"The first step is to find out who Olivia is," Grandma said. "I'll get some people working on it."

"What about Victoria's parents?" I looked back and forth between Grandma and Alex.

"What about them?" she asked.

"Last I saw, they were in CHAS custody, heavily sedated. How'd they escape?"

"They didn't." Something about Grandma's tone made me tense. "CHAS had been looking for a way to draw out the hybrids, something that would let us know where they were hiding. They took a vote. It was decided by a 90 percent margin."

"What was decided?"

"They let the Lexingtons go with a tracker device planted inside them. CHAS was hoping they'd lead us to the hideout."

"They let them go?" My first reaction was to be surprised at CHAS going so easy on them, but then I realized their true intent. "They could've been killed. Olivia's obviously done something to them. They called her 'master.'" I shook my head. "I can't believe CHAS used one of their own as bait."

Alex grunted in what I suspected was agreement.

"It was wrong," Grandma agreed. "But CHAS doesn't see them as one of their own anymore. Either way, the plan failed. The tracker was disabled a day into their release. I had no clue where they were until you told me about them finding you."

"And CHAS?" I asked. "What are we going to do about them?"

"CHAS is a little out of our hands right now." Her voice held a note of defeat that hadn't been there a moment ago. "Steppe is garnering support, God knows why. I guess there's more evil than good in our kind anymore. We'll do what we can, use our contacts to try and sway the undecided. The vote is coming soon, though. All we can do in the meantime is keep you off his radar."

"And George," I added.

"And George," she echoed.

"When will they be home?" I asked.

"A day or two. They know to come here, so don't call them. I'll be getting you and George new phones. Until then, no more using yours. I mean it."

I nodded. "Okay. No calls."

"I see that look in your eye," my mom said. She held her palm out.

"I wasn't going to—"

"Hand it over." It was the same tone she'd used earlier, when I'd first gotten out of the car. My hope of avoiding punishment in the face of my honesty was misplaced. I relinquished the phone. She dropped it and stomped on it.

"Mom!" I gawked at the pieces, nothing more than little black shards of plastic.

"I know you. You wouldn't have been able to resist," she said. "Now listen, Grandma's given you the facts, the reality of the situation we're in. None of that is your fault, so you're not in trouble … for that," she added. My shoulders slumped. "For running off instead of asking for our help in the first place, there are consequences, which, I might add, tie in nicely with my goal to keep you safe. Here's how it's going to work: each day, you will be driven to Jack's for training by one of the three of us and then driven back at the conclusion of said training. In addition, you will spend three hours a day training with Alex."

"Three hours? I didn't even train that long at school!"

She went on as if I hadn't spoken. "Except for those two activities, you are grounded to the house until I say otherwise."

"How long can I expect until you 'say otherwise'?"

"Don't hold your breath."

I swallowed and asked the only other question that mattered. "And Wes?"

She frowned, and my calm cracked. "He can come here to see you when you're not training. And you're free to talk to him at Jack's, but no going out."

It was more than I'd hoped for, less than I'd wanted. "Fine," I said.

Grandma and Mom went inside after that. It wasn't so much prison as house arrest; I could do what I wanted, as long as I stayed on the grounds.

Alex started to follow them, but I grabbed his wrist and pulled him down beside me.

"I can't stand not knowing," I said, "especially if we're going to be spending all this time together. Just say it."

"Say what?" he asked.

"What you think of me now that you know … what I am." I looked down at my shoes, kicking them absently against the wooden planks underneath my feet.

"Tara, I've always known what you are," he said. His voice was gentle, but I suspected that was only because he didn't want to hurt my feelings.

"And you've always hated it. You can say it, you know. Get it out in the open. I deserve that, at least."

"I won't disagree—telling you that would make for better combat training. But in the interest of protecting my, uh, *parts*, I'm not going to risk a repeat of our first meeting."

My head came up. He was smiling. It made me want to smile too, but I held back. "Stop joking around. I mean it. Just say what you're thinking. I won't kick you."

His smile faded. The intensity from earlier, the way he'd watched me throughout my story, returned. He looked fierce in the dim moonlight, like a warrior ready for battle. "Listen to me, because I'm only going to say this once." He took my hand, squeezing it hard in his. "You want to know what I thought listening to your story? What I think every time I look at you? Here it is: you are, without a doubt, the bravest girl I've ever known. It doesn't matter what kind of blood flows in your veins. You are a Hunter, in every sense of the word. Your courage and bravery, your desire to protect everything that's innocent in the world, proves it. Whatever physical form you take won't change that." He released my hand. Some of the fire left his voice. "Sometimes I'm jealous of you."

"Jealous? How?"

"The way you can cut right through all the complicating details and simply know what's right. The way you always know exactly what you believe. And you fight for it. Unswervingly. But also without hate. I could never do that."

"Thanks." I swallowed against the lump in my throat. "I'm glad you're here," I whispered.

He smirked, the old Alex coming through. "Are you sure it won't complicate things for you?"

I felt the corners of my mouth twisting. "Only a little. I'm sure you don't mind terribly, though."

He laughed, and a part of the tension inside me eased. "If it gets too crowded, there's always running," he said. "Speaking of, I hope you've kept in shape. I was thinking five miles tomorrow, to start light."

I punched him in the arm. He grinned.

"Well, well, I see I've arrived just in time." Cambria materialized in the darkness, her sandals clunking against the bottom step of the gazebo.

"There you are," I said. "I was beginning to wonder. You missed all the good parts."

"Not all," she said. Even in the darkness, I could see her brow lift.

I smiled. I was too busy enjoying having Alex back in my life to let Cambria's insinuations bother me. I hadn't realized how much I'd missed his friendship—or punching him. "Did you have fun with Derek?" I asked giving her the same look she'd just given me.

She lowered herself onto the bench across from us and leaned her head against the wooden support beam, her hand draped over her forehead in a dramatic swoon. "Gawd, that boy is hot. I mean, sweat in secret places kind of hot."

"Just what I wanted to hear," Alex said. I laughed.

"What about you?" she asked, sitting up straighter. "How did it go with Thing One and Thing Two?"

I could only assume she meant my mom and Grandma. "Is that what you call them?" I asked.

"Have you seen them in action? They can finish each other's sentences. Which is pretty scary in an interrogation, let me tell you."

She shuddered, though I couldn't tell if it was real or for effect. Whatever put that expression on her face was best left unexplained.

"I told them everything," I said.

"Everything? As in … everything?" she asked. "How'd they take it? Should I sleep somewhere else tonight?"

"They took it well," I said. "Better than expected, but then you'd already filled them in on the jaw-dropping parts."

"Sorry about that," she mumbled. "But seriously, you weren't there. There is no good cop, bad cop. There's only scary and scarier." I couldn't help but laugh. It earned me a glare. "Considering I missed all the action, I'd say we're even."

"It's not over yet," I said.

"What do you mean?" She looked back and forth between Alex and me.

"Long story," I said.

"One I've already heard." Alex rose. "I'm going to crash. Big day tomorrow. Get some rest, chief." He patted my knee as he left.

Cambria waited until the back door clicked shut. She eyed me in the darkness. "What in the hello-hottie is going on? What's he doing here, besides making you sweat?"

"Ugh." I leaned back against the wooden pillar, knocking my head against it a couple of times for good measure. "Like I said, long story."

She folded her arms and propped her legs in front of her. "I've got time. Besides, whenever you say 'long story,' it's the popcorn-and-vodka kind."

"Popcorn and vodka?" I echoed.

"Yeah, you know, popcorn for the show and vodka because the only way any of it's going to make sense is if you're halfway sauced. Especially with your stellar decision-making skills."

"Hey."

"I'm just sayin'…"

"Do you want to know the story or not?"

"Proceed." She made the motion of zipping her lips closed and throwing away the key.

Her silence lasted all of five minutes. Right around the time where

I told her about seeing Victoria's parents. "No way. Were they all glowy-eyed and evil? Did they foam at the mouth?"

"The hybrids don't foam at the mouth, Cam."

"But the other stuff, were they weird-looking?"

"No, they looked like … people. They were in human form at first."

She frowned. "I thought the hybrids couldn't shift back and forth."

I thought back to the night Alex had been attacked by the Werewolf Miles sent. How the man returned to human form in death. "I think some can. The ones who cling more to their human side. But it seemed to take a lot for them to pull it off."

"And they're after you?" she asked. "Why?"

"Let me tell the story. No more interruptions." It was bad enough having to retell it.

"Really wishing I had some vodka right about now."

I rolled my eyes and continued. I managed to make it as far as the metal immunity test before she spoke again. "Logan would love this guy. I don't care how crazy he is—maybe because of the crazy."

"Yeah, he took to Logan right away."

"Wait, Logan's there?"

"Let me finish!"

"Okay, okay …"

I managed to get through the rest of it without her interrupting again. It wasn't like her reactions weren't written all over her face, anyway. The "oh" and "what the heck?" expressions she alternated between said it all.

"So, the ice queen's parents are after you—as are all the other hybrids—to turn you over to this Olivia chick, or else she'll kill people."

Bailey's face floated in my mind. "Yes," I said.

"But no one knows who Olivia is or what she wants with you." I nodded. "And in the meantime, you're immune to metal like I'm immune to ugly guys with bad pickup lines. No effect. And now that you've shared blood with Georgie-boy, he's back to his old self.

Humanity, normal eyes, no desire to kill for fun. Unless you count Wes. Who's got his hands full with Alex. Who's here, why, again?"

"Training." I gave her the short version of the situation with CHAS, and Steppe's intention to vote The Cause out of the amnesty treaty. Cambria didn't say anything, even when I'd finished. She sat chewing her lip and tugging on the ends of her hair.

"Cam? Are you thinking about your mom?"

"He's going to lock her up and throw away the key, I just know it," she said. Her tone changed. No more sarcasm. No more flippant humor.

"You don't know. Maybe Grandma can do something—"

"No one can. Steppe has the final word on this stuff. And why do you think your grandma's here and not there? There's nothing else she can do anymore. For you. For my mom. For anyone."

"Then I will."

"Right." She snorted. "You going to charm Steppe into your love triangle—? Or are you up to more of a pentagon now?"

"I'm serious, Cam. For months, everyone's been watching me, waiting, like they're holding their breath. I know I have a decision to make. I've known it since the night Wes told me about Vera's visions, even though I couldn't admit it then. Until now, I haven't wanted to choose, but what good is this sort of power if I don't use it to do something good, something to help people?"

"Okay, I just have to say this. No offense, because immunity to metal is awesome, but it's not really power. You're just a kid. Harder to kill, but still, just a kid. How are you going to help people?"

"I don't know yet," I admitted. "But I'm going to figure it out. And it's not just immunity to metal. There's one other thing."

"Isn't there always, with you?"

I told her about my shifting and the night at school, where I'd killed all the hybrids.

She shrugged. "So, you're becoming a wolf, finally?"

"What do you mean 'finally'?"

"It's been coming for a while now. You don't remember those

crazy mood swings you had back before Miles came around? That night at the bonfire?"

"Well, yeah …"

"PMS is one thing, but those mood swings were something else."

I shook my head. "You're way too calm about this stuff."

She shrugged. "I roll with it."

"I killed an entire pack of hybrids."

"Evil hybrids," she corrected.

"Still …"

"Let's make a deal. You don't morph into a Werewolf and try to kill me, and I'll be cool with the new, furry you."

I rolled my eyes. "Deal.

CHAPTER NINETEEN

The thing about mornings—they always came way too early. Then again, I hadn't had a decent night's sleep in over a week, so I was grateful for the uninterrupted rest, the comfort of my own bed—even if the alarm did begin to buzz long before I would've liked.

"Shut oommphhh," Cambria said from her air mattress. She said some more words I didn't catch. They didn't sound morning-friendly.

I rolled over and hit the snooze button, already grumpy.

My mood didn't improve as I dressed in running shorts and a sports bra and headed downstairs. It wasn't until I walked into the kitchen—and saw the way Alex's eyes took me in—that I realized I probably should've worn something with a little more fabric.

"Morning, chief," he said.

"Whatever," I grumbled and went for the coffee. My mom stood at the stove, moving eggs around in a pan.

"You hungry?" she asked.

"Uh-uh." I gulped from my mug, working through the burn that met my lips and tongue.

"You should eat some of these, anyway. It'll keep your energy up during your workout," she said.

"She's right," Alex agreed. "You look a little … never mind," he said at my murderous expression.

I took the offered plate and fork and sat at the bar with Alex. His eyes lingered on my bare arms before he went back to his newspaper. I scarfed a bite of eggs. "Where's Grandma?" I asked.

"She went to see Vera. She's trying to pin down the identity of this Olivia person," my mom said. She swiveled from the stove to the counter, wiping every open surface with a wet rag. She looked distracted, her mouth turned downward. She'd wiped the same spot three times already.

"What's wrong?" I asked. "Did something happen with Wes and—?"

"No, no, everyone's fine," she said. "They're still on the road. Should be home tonight." I sighed with relief.

I didn't have to ask about George. The bond between us had grown more distinct, and I could feel him getting closer. I could also read his mood a little better than I could yesterday. Calm and content. He was enjoying Wes's and Cord's company, which was a little weird. Some anxiety came through, probably due to the situation and our abrupt separation, but nothing major. Most importantly, he was all right.

"What is it, then?" I pressed. I had a moment's panic wondering if CHAS had already made some sort of move against The Cause.

"Vera's not feeling well. I think she's getting worse," my mom said.

My shoulders fell. Why did everyone have to go bad at once? "Is it —I mean, is she okay?" I asked.

"She'll be fine, for now," my mom said. "But her energy level isn't there, not like it was."

Considering Vera had next to no energy before, it couldn't be good.

My mom shook herself, as if casting off the glumness. Her expression cleared. Some of the shadows remained, but she was back to business. "In the meantime, you've got training, and I need to make some calls to settle the rest of our schedules."

She left us alone after that. I finished my eggs, worried about Vera, and went back to my coffee. I was debating a second cup when Alex folded the paper and pushed off his stool. He placed his dishes in the sink and grabbed a couple of bottles of water out of the fridge.

"You ready?" he asked. It made me grumpy all over again seeing him so awake and refreshed.

"How far are we running?" I asked, sliding off my stool.

He shrugged. "I don't live here, you do, so today, you pick the route."

"I get to choose?" My eyes narrowed. "What's the catch?"

"No catch. Think of it as a day to ease back into things and show me around at the same time."

I chuckled and pushed open the back door. "You know those three stoplights we went through on the way home last night?"

"Yeah."

"Consider your tour complete. That was pretty much 'city center' right there."

"Obviously people don't live here because of the bustling city atmosphere. What about the scenery? Show me what you like about this place."

It was a challenge, that much I knew, and if I was being honest, one too tempting to pass up. "Come on."

I led him past the gazebo where we'd talked last night—where he'd heard everything. Remembering the stark truth of my confession in the light of day did weird things to my stomach. Confessing it to my mom and Grandma had been one thing—their love was unconditional—but this was Alex. I stopped at the edge of the woods on the pretense of stretching.

"About last night …" I began, grabbing my foot and pulling it behind me.

"It was quite a story," he said.

"Is that it?"

"What do you mean?"

"You've had all night to think about it, I just—I don't know."

"I told you last night what I thought."

We'd both given up any pretense of stretching. He was looking at me with the same expression he'd worn last night. It made me more nervous than when he'd checked me out at breakfast. I swallowed. "I know, but maybe you changed your mind."

"I didn't change my mind. Not about you."

His words seemed to reference more than just my blood type and physical capabilities. I purposely ignored that part. "Good," I said. "I was afraid you'd be mad at me for not telling you about George right away."

"I wish you'd told me so I could've helped, but I'm not mad. I mean, I guess we're even, since I didn't tell you about working with Edie."

"Did you only take the scouting job with Kane because of Grandma? Or did you really want it?"

"Both, I guess." His jaw tightened. "I know you don't approve, so don't lecture me. Besides …" He scratched his head in a way that made him look suddenly unsure. "In a way, it wasn't your grandma that made me agree to work against Steppe. It was you."

"Why me?"

"You inspire me. To be better, or something. I don't know. I mean, look at me, I'm not a spy. I'm a soldier. Always have been, always will be. When you really get down to it, the scouting thing is me. Being a Hunter is me, just like it was my dad. The spy thing, the revolution, is you." He looked back at me, his expression carefully clear of any emotion. "Come on, chief, show me these woods."

He broke into a jog, and I followed. His words twisted me up inside. What did that even mean, "the revolution"? I hadn't said anything like that. Is that what he thought? Is that what this was?

And him agreeing to spy for Grandma, had he only done it because he thought it would make me happy? I'd half hoped he'd changed his mind on hunting with Kane, but that obviously wasn't the case. He sounded like he missed it. Like maybe he wished he hadn't left.

Too many emotions, too many conflicting thoughts swirled inside me, and in the end, I was glad for the run. It meant we could be together without the burden of talking. Moments of silence—this was the one, sure time Alex and I could be friends.

I had no idea how far we ran. I stopped estimating after mile four. Our pace was comfortable enough that I wasn't hyperventilating—much. Alex was barely winded, as usual. Still, he motioned for us to stop when we reached a shallow creek.

"It's really nice back here," he said, walking a small circle, admiring the green-leafed canopy that closed us in on the forest floor.

I inhaled deeply, partly to catch my breath and partly in appreciation of the damp, woodsy smell that was inherently home to me. After the dry dustiness of the Nevada air, this was heaven.

"I'd trade the humidity for the desert again, though," he added.

"Mm, not me." I bent down at the water's edge and splashed water over my face and arms to cool off. "Never thought I'd say that, but I missed the humidity right along with everything else. All that dry heat gave me a headache." I rubbed water over the back of my neck.

"Funny how even the stuff we hate about home, we can still miss."

"Are you thinking about anywhere specific?" I asked, straightening and drying my hands on my shorts.

"Monroe, North Carolina. It's a small town near Fort Bragg," he said.

"Like the military base?"

"My dad's family was army. Five generations."

"As in human army? But I thought they were Hunters."

"They are. They were. Doesn't mean you can't kill the old-fashioned way. Human war is just as good as Werewolf war. And when Werewolf war time is slow …" He smiled wryly. "I told you before, I'm a soldier." Despite the smile, shadows framed his expression.

"You're whoever you want to be, Alex. You're not your father."

His eyes clouded. "Yeah, I know that."

"Is that why you think you're like them? You want war?"

"Don't you?" he asked. Fire laced his words, not just passion, but anger.

"No. I don't know."

"Something in you wants to fight. I can see it. It's one of the things I first noticed about you."

"The question is, what are we fighting for?"

"No, that's *your* question. You're bent on protecting the innocent, taking up a cause. Some of us don't care nearly as much about the reason behind the bloodshed."

"Are you referring to Steppe or yourself?" My temper flared, heating my neck and rising into my cheeks. He was purposely baiting me and I couldn't figure out why.

"Do you remember what I asked you in Nevada?" he asked.

"What?" The question threw me off balance.

He strode up, his long legs eating up the ground between us. He leaned down, his breath a warm puff against my face. "When you told us about your metal immunity, do you remember what I said?" His tone was impatient.

"You asked me what I was going to do about it."

"I know you don't want to be involved," he said quietly, "but sooner or later, you're going to have to pick a side."

"So will you," I shot back.

"I thought my presence here made that clear." All I could do was stare back at him. He was right, of course, but I couldn't help but feel this entire conversation had gone completely askew. "My choice surprises you?"

"Well … yeah."

"My purpose is to protect humans from Werewolves. Steppe kills innocent people for the fun of it. There's a difference. I'm not completely evil, Tara."

"I know that," I said. Of course there was a difference. A huge one. "Damn, you make me angry on purpose, and then I can't think straight, and you win the argument."

He grinned, setting me further off balance with the abruptness of the gesture and the butterflies it caused. I hated that grin—because I loved it.

"Why are you smiling?" I snapped. He was still standing way too close and I couldn't breathe.

"Because you're half-naked and angry and your boyfriend would kill me if he could see us right now. I'm enjoying the look on his face while I imagine it."

I punched him in the stomach, hard enough to let him know he wasn't funny. Then I stomped up the trail. "Time to go," I called over my shoulder. When I was far enough ahead that he couldn't see it, I smiled.

ALEX GAVE ME AT LEAST A QUARTER OF A MILE HEAD START BEFORE HE yelled, "Race you!"

"You're on!" I yelled back—only because I was hoping if I left him far enough behind, he'd get lost and I'd win by default.

No such luck.

Somewhere around the two-mile mark, he passed me. By that point, I was too winded to talk smack. He knew it too, because he winked as he passed. The irritation propelled me, but it wasn't enough. He was waiting in the gazebo when I broke through the trees.

"You cheated," I said.

"How did I cheat?" he asked. He stepped off the gazebo and followed me across the yard.

"I don't know." I hung my head between my knees, sucking air and staring at the toes of his shoes. "You just did."

He laughed. "You're out of shape. Two weeks out of school and you're worthless. You know what this means, right?"

I groaned. "No, we are not doing this every day."

"Yup. Every single one until you can at least keep up."

"Alex … I'm warning you. I will kick you if you make me run."

His brow went up, but he didn't look nearly worried enough. "You'd have to catch me first, chief."

That did it. I charged.

We hit the grass at the same time, him on his back and me on my stomach. I tried holding him still with my arm but he wriggled away. Like a snake. I caught his ankle when he wasn't expecting it. He flopped back on the ground and I threw myself over him, trying desperately to get a grip on him before he escaped.

"This part of training doesn't start until tomorrow," he said between blocks.

His torso shook with silent laughter until he couldn't hold it in any longer. Hearing it made me struggle harder. I landed a fist in his gut and he growled. His movements changed from defensive to offensive. Within seconds, he had me pinned underneath him. His hands held mine above my head and he straddled my torso.

"Get off me," I said.

Alex grinned.

"Tara? The others are …" My mother's voice went from neutral, to confused, to decidedly pissed before it trailed off. I stilled. Alex rose and dusted his hands off, looking completely at ease and innocent. I, on the other hand …

"Just finishing some offensive moves," Alex said.

I got to my feet, thankful the flush from my run covered the heat rising in my cheeks.

"Riiight," she said. She didn't sound convinced but she didn't argue. Her lips pressed together in a tight line, and I realized why she'd let it go.

George stood behind her—with Wes.

My mother looked from Wes to Alex and back to me with a smirk. "I'll be inside if you need me," she said, way too cheerfully.

No one said anything as she walked inside. Alex wandered away to retrieve his bottle of water, as if the tension weren't thick enough to cut with a knife.

I watched Wes. "When did you get back?" I asked.

"Just now." His eyes flickered to Alex and then back. "Are you going to hug me or what?" I hurried forward. At first, he held me stiffly, his posture rod straight, but then his arms relaxed and the embrace turned familiar. "Missed you," he whispered in my ear.

"Missed you too," I whispered back. "Oh." I pulled away. "But I'm sweaty. Alex and I just got back from a run."

Wes gave Alex a sharp look. Tension—it took me a moment to

realize it came from George, from the bond—pulled taut. I held my breath, waiting, and Wes broke into a smile and swooped down, planting a kiss on my mouth.

"Didn't bother you last time," he said, his words full of innuendo, and I knew none of it was for my benefit. I sighed and let it go.

"George," I said, turning to him. The tension in the bond dissolved into happiness.

"Hi, Tay." He pulled me into his arms and lifted me off the ground. I laughed, enjoying the uninterrupted relief at seeing him whole again. No twitching, no feet tapping, no yellow eyes. He was more himself than I'd seen him in weeks. It made our entire trip worth it, all of the fear and lying and sneaking—none of it mattered, seeing him like this.

"I'm glad you're back," I said. "I was worried."

"You couldn't feel that I was all right?" he asked. "I felt you the whole time."

"I could, I just … it's not the same as seeing you." Something in my gut twisted when I tried putting my paranoia into words. Ever since the bond had formed, worry hovered like a cloud, threatening to consume me. Astor's story haunted me. If something ever happened to him, especially now … I couldn't live with that. "Some of it is still hard to read."

He frowned. "Are you sure you're not still fighting it? Because I read you loud and clear." His eyes flickered to Alex, then Wes. I didn't bother checking to see if they'd seen it. I knew they had from the way George stiffened, how the connection between us filled with tension.

"I'll work on it," I mumbled. I grabbed Wes's hand and pulled him away.

"Where are you going?" Alex called. "Training isn't over."

"Lunch break," I called back. "I have my rights. There are labor laws, you know."

I felt, rather than heard, George's laughter. Maybe he was right; maybe I had been fighting it.

I chose a path that led back toward the creek where Alex and I had run. I could've gone inside, probably could've used a shower, but I wasn't so sure my mom would've approved of my break from training any more than Alex had. The woods were easier. Calmer. Quieter.

"Where are we going?" Wes asked.

"Away," I said. I slowed our pace but kept his hand. He didn't resist, but his hand felt stiff. "I thought you weren't getting back until tonight."

"George has a lead foot. It was all I could do to keep up."

"And Cord and Logan?"

"Logan and Victoria stayed behind to hang with Astor. We decided it's the best place to hide Victoria for now. Cord's driving to DC to check on her friend."

"The girl you went to see? The one who disappeared?" I asked.

"Yeah. She's going to ask around, maybe check with the girl's family and see if anyone's seen her. I think she's worried about foul play."

"You don't sound very bothered by it."

He stopped walking and turned me to face him. "I was more concerned with being here. Seeing you. After you left … I saw what that headache did to you. Are you sure you're all right?" he asked.

Concern washed his features, just as deeply as it had when the pain had been present. I remembered the terrified look on his face when I'd managed to squint up at him through the pain, and felt horrible for putting him through it—for putting myself through it. All because I hadn't wanted to accept what was happening.

"I'm fine. George didn't explain it to you?" I asked.

"He did, some. I just … I needed to make sure, to hear it from you. Your phone's off."

"My mother killed it." His brows shot up, so I went on. "She and Grandma made me explain."

"Explain what?"

"Everything."

His expression indicated he caught my full meaning. "The night in the woods? The hybrids?"

I nodded. "The hybrids."

"How'd they take it?"

"As expected. My mom cried, then grounded me for life. They've made me a schedule to train with Alex for my Hunter side and Jack for my wolf. They want me to learn to control it, I guess. Apparently, he and my mom have been hanging out so she can catch up on everything she's missed in the past seventeen years."

"I know."

"What?"

"The day Bailey …" His eyes clouded and he blinked it away. "I read it in Fee's mind when I asked her about Jack. He was here."

Vaguely, I remembered a silent exchange between the two of them. "Speaking of Fee, how much trouble are we in for leaving?"

"Derek told her the basics." He grimaced. "I have kitchen duty for a month. You're welcome."

"For what?"

"I told her it was all my idea. She's punishing me for both of us."

I smirked. "Well, thanks. Dishwater hands aren't really my thing."

His expression remained serious. "She knows you're shifting. They all do."

My amusement fell away. "What did they say?"

"Cord said you better not get fleas."

I glared at him. "Of course she did."

He shrugged. "They don't care, Tara. Not in the way you think. You're family. Nothing will change that."

My heart swelled. It was exactly what I needed to hear. "They're my family too."

We shared a smile.

"How are you, really?" he asked.

"Much better now." To prove it, I pushed up onto my toes and pressed my lips to his. This was nothing like the kiss he'd given me earlier. It was heavier, longer, deeper. Everything I'd wanted to do since Grandma pulled me away. The stiffness had melted off somewhere during our exchange. This was us, Wes and me. No one else.

His arms slid around my hips, pulling me closer. It should've been gross, me, sweaty and dirty. But out here, in the woods, all it did was awaken me. I wrapped my arms around him so tightly that he stumbled back, but I didn't care. I pushed harder until we sprawled on our backs, arms and legs tangled. He started to pull away, laughing, but I didn't let him. Whatever had woken inside me needed this too badly.

"Tara ..."

Just the sound of my name on his lips drove me on. My thoughts were hazy. All I could think about was his mouth on mine, his skin, his hands. I was vaguely aware of a sound being made, something like a growl, and then froze when I realized it was me.

"Tara," he said again.

I sat up, breathing heavily, trying to understand what happened. I pulled a leaf from my hair. Wes sat up and I scrambled back a little as something else floated up from the back of my mind. Awareness and then ... embarrassment. Why did I feel embarrassed? It was Wes, I had nothing to be—

"Oh, no," I groaned, covering my face with my hands.

"What is it?" His hands were instantly there, against my back, my neck, soothing.

"The bond," I said. It came out muffled against my hands.

"What about it?"

"I can feel it."

"Okayyy," he said slowly.

He didn't get it. I raised my head to look at him, my expression bleak. "I can feel everything George feels, all of his emotions," I began. He nodded for me to go on. "Right now, he feels embarrassed, because he feels everything I feel too." I waited.

His eyes widened. "You've got to be kidding me." I shook my head. I wished I were. "He knows what we were just doing?"

"Yes."

Unbelievably, he laughed. I gawked at him until he got himself under control and, to my horror, tried to kiss me again. "Wes," I hissed, pushing him away. "Did you hear what I said?"

"Yeah, so what? Sucks for him." He leaned in again. I stopped him with a hand on his chest.

"So, that's weird. I can't just do this with you, knowing he can feel what I feel. It's ... gross."

"He can learn to ignore it," he said.

I pushed him harder, enough that he didn't try to kiss me again. "I don't know if that's possible," I said. "I can't turn it on and off, so I don't think he can, either."

He shook his head. "I'm going to wish you never saved him, aren't I?"

I attempted a smile. "Probably."

CHAPTER TWENTY

Everything hurt. I wasn't sure I'd survive my mom's schedule for long. By the time I got to Jack's, my legs were liquid and my arms were dead weight at my sides. Some of it was my own fault—tackling Alex had consequences. The rest was evidence that two weeks without a workout was too long.

My mom stopped the car next to Jack's truck. She'd insisted on driving Cambria and me, since Grandma and Alex had "things to do," as they'd said before disappearing after lunch.

"I'll be back at four," she said through the open window.

I nodded.

"See you later," Cambria called. She waved as my mom made a loop and started back up the drive.

"Slow down," I said, falling behind Cam as she hurried toward the front door.

"Oh, sorry," she said, eyeing me. "You look like crap, you know that?"

"Thanks." I rolled my eyes and resisted the urge to point out that she'd gotten two more hours of sleep than I'd had. It wouldn't have changed the fact that she was right. "Why are you in such a hurry, anyway?" I asked.

"Derek's taking me out," she said.

"You suck."

"Why, because your house arrest doesn't apply to me? Yeah, I know."

"Only because you were the whistle-blower."

She shrugged "A girl's gotta do …"

"Yeah, yeah." I waved a hand. "Where's he taking you?"

"Some hole-in-the-wall bar we went to last week. He knows the owner. Their pool tables are in pretty good shape, and the music's decent."

I stopped walking to glare at her. "You know, I hate you a little bit right now."

The front door opened and Derek stepped out, his tanned skin a stark contrast to the crisp white of his beater. "Oh, hey, Tara," he said, sounding friendlier with those three words than he'd ever been.

"Hey." My greeting came out guarded and his gaze on me sharpened.

"Listen, about the wolf thing …" I braced myself while he seemed to search for words. Finally, he shrugged. "Pretty cool."

I blinked at him. Whatever I'd expected, it wasn't that. He didn't seem bothered by my lack of response. His eyes lit up as he caught sight of Cambria. I watched him drink in the amount of exposed skin on her body. Between her halter and cutoffs, she showed more than she covered.

"You ready?" he asked. His voice dropped an octave. It might've been funny if my desire to go with them, to slough off all the war talk and impending doom, and pass the day with a pool cue and jukebox wasn't so unbearable.

"Ready," Cambria told him. To me she said, "Babe, good luck." There was sympathy in her words. Derek took her hand and led her to Jack's truck.

I rubbed my hand over my face, resisted the urge to scream, and went inside.

I found Fee first, bent over a pot on the stove. The kitchen was bright and shiny and free of any baked goods, the complete opposite from how I'd seen it last. I caught the scent of something pungent and bitter.

"Hi, Fee," I said.

She turned from the steel pot. Her hair, had come loose from its haphazard tail and wisped over her neck and ears. "Hi, Tara, glad to have you home." There was enough reproach in her words to make me feel guilty.

"I'm sorry about leaving like that."

"I'm sorry too," she said. "I should've been there for you—and George. We all should've. But after Bailey …"

"I understand," I assured her. I hated the haunted look in her eyes. "You don't have to apologize. You had a lot going on. I can't imagine." I swallowed. "It was bad timing, really."

"Yes, it was." She smiled but it looked empty. "I'm glad to know George is all right. You did a very special thing for him."

"I did what anyone would."

"I don't know about that. It's a big sacrifice. Not just the up-front cost, but long term. You'll always be connected."

"He told you about it?"

"Yes. I did a full examination after he and Wes got back."

"How is he?" I leaned forward, suddenly anxious.

"Physically, he's fine. Healthier than when he was human."

"And mentally?"

"Mentally, it's going to be tricky. The bond will take some getting used to, for both of you, I think."

I tried to read her expression, to see if maybe George told her about our shared feelings when I'd kissed Wes.

Not that I'd really spoken to him about it, but I knew after one look at his face that he'd been aware of what had happened between Wes and me. The embarrassment had come flooding back. I'd searched for any sort of jealousy underneath it, but there'd been none. Thankfully.

"Complications aside, he's very grateful for what you did for him," Fee went on. Something in the pot popped and simmered against the lid. The smell worsened.

"What are you cooking?" I asked, trying—and failing—to keep the distaste out of my voice.

She laughed. "It's not dinner, don't worry. I'm brewing some tea for Vera."

"What kind of tea?"

"It's my own recipe, mostly medicinal. She's been drinking it for a few weeks now, but it's losing its effectiveness. I needed a stronger recipe."

The sight of the ever-present teacup made sense. I remembered what Mom said about Vera deteriorating. "How is she?" I asked.

"Not great, not horrible. She hovers at the in-between a lot." For a moment, Fee's mask of careful composure slipped, and I saw the desperation. "I don't know what else to do for her," she said. Her voice broke.

For once, when it came to Fee, I became the comforter. I reached out and wrapped my arms around her. She leaned into the embrace and hugged me back. I felt helpless, like whatever I could do wouldn't be nearly enough. For her, for Vera, for everyone. It made my eyes water, and I blinked it back, wanting to be strong for them all. What would it do to Fee to lose someone again so soon after Bailey? To Jack? To all of them?

"Jack's waiting for you in the back," she said, finally pulling away and wiping her eyes. She smiled and it looked less hollow than before. "Thank you, Tara," she added.

"You're welcome." I left her stirring the tea and headed outside.

Jack was in the backyard, various sparring equipment and weapons strewn about the grass. I paused at the bottom of the steps to take it all in. In all of my time training with Jack before going to Wood Point, he'd always been so hesitant about using weapons or equipment. He'd said you never knew what you'd have at your disposal in a real fight, so better to train with nothing, and be ready for anything. The scene struck me as contrary to that philosophy.

"There you are," he said, dropping a set of arm pads and coming toward me. "I was beginning to wonder about you."

"I got caught up talking to Fee. What's all this?"

"That tea stinks to high heaven doesn't it?" He didn't wait for an answer before going on. "This is my defensive obstacle course," he said, waving a hand.

Wes appeared from around the side of the house carrying a white shopping bag. He set it on the ground beside me and dropped a kiss on my cheek. "Hey, again," he whispered.

"Hey." I smiled at him, enjoying the way my heartbeat sped at the simple "hello," and returned my attention to Jack. "What exactly is a defensive obstacle course?"

"It's a series of stations I've set up to defend myself when you attack," Jack explained.

"You want me to attack you?"

"Not you, your wolf," he explained. As if that made it better.

"Not a great idea." Nausea rolled in, settling itself in the pit of my stomach. I looked to Wes for support. "Remember what happened last time?"

"Don't worry, we're prepared," Wes said. He pointed at the bag at my feet. "I even brought extra clothes, in case you shift all the way."

"This is your idea of teaching me how to control my wolf?" I asked, eyes wide.

"It's the quickest way," Jack said. His tone changed, becoming deeper, firmer, every inch the strict teacher I remembered from before. "And it's not like you left us a lot of time to help you, so don't argue with me."

"Give it a chance," Wes said. He didn't look concerned. I huffed out a breath and followed Jack out into the mess.

He picked up the arm pads he'd dropped earlier, slid them on up to his elbows, and faced me. "I'm ready when you are, kid. Give me your best shot."

"I don't know how to shift on command," I said. The words came out bitten off; my frustration was peaking. "If I did, I wouldn't need you."

"She needs to feel threatened," Wes called from his place against the side of the house.

"Threatened, okay," Jack said. He closed the distance between us and jabbed me in the shoulder. The pad he wore cushioned the impact but it was still enough to drive me back. My shoulder instantly throbbed.

"What the hell?" I snapped, backing away and rubbing my arm.

"I'm threatening you," Jack said. Wes's quiet laughter drifted over.

"You act like you've never done this before," I said, holding my shoulder protectively.

"I haven't," he admitted. "By the time they come to me, they already know what they are."

His words pricked against my pride. "I know what I am," I said. "I'm a Hunter."

I dropped my hand from my shoulder and rushed him, spinning into a side kick, heel out. The momentum as it landed against his hip drove him back a step. He blinked, clearly surprised. I didn't wait for him to recover before swinging out with my fists. They hit the padding more than his flesh. I didn't care. I didn't need to hurt him, only make a point. He took the first few hits and then backed away, his hands up in surrender.

"All right, calm down. I get it. Bad choice of words," he said. "But attacking me that way isn't going to help you rein in your wolf."

"What if I don't want to rein it in?" I said. "What if I just want it to go away?" I folded my arms in front of me, fully expecting his answer to include some form of lecture about it being a gift and responsibility and how I shouldn't be ungrateful. So his response surprised me.

"First, you've got to figure out what brings it out. Then you can make it go away," he said.

We stared each other down for a long moment. His methods struck me as completely ridiculous, but he had a point. I dropped my hands to my sides. "All right. Tell me what to do."

AN HOUR PASSED. THEN TWO.

My wolf never even surfaced, much less took over. I managed to sustain a few bruises from Jack "defending" himself a little too well.

And I knocked him off balance once, but that was it. I was frustrated. At this point, I didn't care whether my wolf emerged. I wanted to be done. I wanted a hot bath. I wanted food.

Jack swatted at me and I kicked out. My foot caught around the back of his knee, making it buckle. He went down like a toppling tree.

"Ugh," he grunted as he landed.

The pads around his arms and back made it hard for him to get up. I reached out a hand, but I wasn't much help. He was too heavy to pull up.

Wes laughed, distracting me. I'd forgotten he was watching. I shielded my eyes from the glaring sun and found him in the same spot as earlier. He leaned against the house, his features concealed by the shade of the rooftop. The set of his shoulders, the way he folded his arms, was completely relaxed. He was enjoying this.

I scowled and gave up my attempts to help Jack to his feet. By the time Jack stood, brushed himself off, and dropped the pads, he was laughing too.

"Are we done?" I demanded.

"For today," he agreed. "Oh, and clean up the equipment."

He clapped Wes on the back and they disappeared inside, leaving me standing in the middle of the mess. I looked up when the door slammed shut and caught sight of a face in the small window. Vera. She retreated and let the blinds fall back against the sill.

I debated leaving the mess for later and seeking her out. It felt unfinished between her and me. Like an interrupted conversation. The sound of footsteps distracted me. George stepped clear of the woods just as the bond alerted me to his presence.

"Where've you been?" I asked. He wore only shorts and sneakers, no shirt, no socks. His hair was matted to his face. "In the woods … alone?"

"Busted." He smiled. "I was practicing shifting."

"Let me guess. No problem, right?" I snatched up an elbow pad and dropped it into the plastic container. "How come it's so easy for you, and so hard for me? Shouldn't it be the other way around?"

He shrugged and picked up another pad, chucked it into the bin. "Maybe you're overthinking it. Trying too hard."

"Trying too hard," I echoed.

"Just a theory. I take it training with Jack didn't go well."

"I knocked him down. Does that count?"

"Umm …"

"Okay, fine, he sort of tripped." I tossed in another pad and flopped down on the steps, my chin in my hand.

"You'll figure it out, Tay, you always do," he said, lowering himself down next to me.

"You really like being a wolf, don't you?"

"Don't you?"

"I don't know." I rubbed at the back of my neck. "Seems like it's one big headache. Literally."

George frowned. "Do you mean your neck?"

"It aches, like a headache, only lower," I said. I caught his expression. "Why are you looking at me like that?"

"You really don't know what it is?" He shook his head. "Wow, never thought I'd see the day I got to give you Werewolf info." He laughed. My patience thinned. "It's your body's way of letting you know there's a Werewolf nearby. Like an alarm system. Every Werewolf has it."

"No," I said, "that's what the goosebumps do for me. This is different."

"I don't know anything about goosebumps, but the prickly feeling on the back of your neck, that's a Werewolf recognizing its own kind. It doesn't bother me as much as it used to. Yours will probably fade."

I thought back to when the prickle first started, during my road trip with George. It was right after he'd almost shifted at that truck stop and hadn't really gone away since. I frowned. If George was right, that meant my body now had a double-alarm system. Great. I got to experience it all twice.

I looked over at George where he sat pulling apart blades of grass. As much as I wished I could've protected him from this, it was nice having him to go through it with.

"You never answered my question," I said. I bumped his shoulder with mine, "about whether you like being a wolf."

"Yeah, I mean, I feel good all the time. I'm strong and fast. Basically everything I've worked at my whole life comes easy now. No dieting. No PT."

"But?"

"I miss my family. My mom is going to worry. I need to figure out what to tell her," he said.

"I know."

"And my friends. Wes, Fee, and all of them are great. But I miss the team." He looked over at me. "Do you ever miss your old life? Your old friends?"

"I still have them," I said. For some reason, the way he asked the question made me defensive. As if I'd abandoned them. "I have you, and Sam, and Angela."

"Yeah, you have me now. But Sam and Angela, it's not the same as it was. They have to know something's up. They barely ever see you anymore."

I wanted to argue, but I couldn't. I remembered the day we'd gone to the mall, the way Angela cornered me and demanded to know what was going on. I still hadn't called her. The thought made me sad—and desperate to focus on something else. "Well, some of them won't be missed," I said.

Our eyes met. "Cindy Adams," we said in unison. Our matching laughter eased my melancholy.

"I'm glad we can laugh about that now," he said. "I mean, I really screwed up. I'm sor—"

"Uh-uh, don't you dare apologize. It's long gone for both of us, so you don't get to bring it up and feel guilty all over again."

"Fair enough. If I'd never kissed her, do you think you and me …?"

"I'd already met Wes," I said quietly.

"Right, I forgot. So, moot point."

"Yeah." Awkward silence descended. I knew we were both

thinking about earlier, the kiss. The weird tension in the bond confirmed it. "Listen, about earlier …"

"You don't have to say anything," he said. He wasn't looking at me, but staring out over the yard. I could tell he felt uncomfortable, but he pressed on. "It's something we'll both have to deal with at some point. Just so happens I get to feel it first."

"That doesn't mean it isn't weird. I won't, I mean, I'll try not to—"

"Tara, don't." He laughed. "Please don't sit here and promise me you won't make out, or worse, with your boyfriend, because of me. Because of this thing that ties us together."

"But I can't," I argued. "Not when it feels like you're in the room or something." I made a face. Because when it came down to it, that's exactly how it felt. In the worst sort of way.

"We'll work on it, okay?"

"How do we do that? I can't get it to shut off unless I'm asleep."

"We'll practice, just like you're doing with Jack."

My brows rose. "Yeah, because my session with Jack was so promising."

"We'll figure it out. I'll start taking naps if I have to. I'm not going to keep you from a love life any more than you'll keep me from mine."

"You have a love life?" I asked, then ducked my head as I realized how it sounded.

He bumped me with his shoulder. "Well, not as hot as yours, apparently. Not yet. But when I do, it would help to know it's only she and I in the room."

"Agreed."

"I have to say, though, after witnessing what I did, even telepathically, Wes is one lucky guy. You were never like that with me."

"George," I warned. "Do not go there."

He went on, pretending not to hear me. "I mean, wow. It was hot. You were hot. If you'd been half that way with me, we'd—"

"George!" I shoved him hard enough to send him sprawling off the end of the step. He might've caught himself if he hadn't been laughing so hard by then.

The door opened behind me, and Wes poked his head out. "What's going on out here? Do I need to separate you two?" George and I shared a look, and he burst into laughter again. He still hadn't moved to get up. Wes looked back and forth between us, confused. "What's so funny?" he asked.

A slow smile spread across my face, and then it bubbled up in my chest and I laughed right along with George, with Wes looking on as if we'd lost it.

"What's so funny?" Wes repeated.

"Kissing … you …" I managed before dissolving into a fit again. For a second, he looked offended, but then he shook his head and disappeared inside.

George and I didn't get up for a long time.

CHAPTER TWENTY-ONE

Five days later, I sat on the back porch, sulking, after another failed training session with Jack. Wes was hiding somewhere inside after his attempts to cheer me up had been met with steady glaring.

George wandered out to sit with me and gave me the obligatory, "you can do it," speech. I didn't respond, and we sat in silence for a while. He tried getting me to practice our bond-blocking thing, but we'd been at it for days with no luck. I wasn't in the mood to fail at anything else today.

The back door creaked open. I looked up, expecting Wes, and found Derek instead. "Living room, five minutes," he said.

"What's going on?" George asked him, already rising.

Derek shrugged. "Cord's back. She's got news."

George dusted his hands on his shorts and extended his hand, pulling me up beside him. The mention of Cord's return had our attention. Jack and Wes tried calling her several times for an update. She rarely answered and when she did, the details were vague. Fee said Cord needed time on her own. I think losing Bailey really rocked her, so we gave her the space she needed.

But if she was back, with news …

George and I hurried into the living room behind Derek. Wes, Cambria, Jack, and Fee were already there. I leaned against the door frame next to George. The front door opened and closed. Cord appeared with Grandma on her heels. The clock on the wall showed my pickup time.

“Perfect timing, Edie,” Fee said.

“I hear there’s news,” Grandma said. She settled herself in the chair near the window.

From my place against the wall, I watched Cord. Her eyes were ringed with circles, her face pale. She’d looked pretty rough before, when I’d seen her at Astor’s, but this was worse. More than tired, her expression reminded me of the one I’d seen on Fee that day in the kitchen—haunted, grim, bereft. It looked even more out of place on Cord.

“Where’s Vera?” Cord asked.

“She’s in her room, resting,” Fee told her. “She’s not up for this.”

Cord’s expression clouded. I knew how she felt. I’d been in to see Vera a couple of times, but it hadn’t been the same. The tea Fee brewed for her wasn’t doing much good anymore. She spent most of her time in bed. She’d taken to watching my training sessions from her window.

“I’ll fill her in once we’re done here,” Fee said. She nodded at Cord. “Go on, what did you find out?”

“You guys know I’ve been looking for my friend, Mal, the one I sent Wes to meet in DC,” Cord began. Everyone nodded. “Well, I found her, and she’s dead.”

“What?” Fee’s eyes widened.

“How?” Wes asked. He slid forward to the edge of the couch. Even from across the room I could feel the tension of coiled muscles from every single one of them. It felt like the moment we’d waited for these past few weeks—the moment it would all begin.

“The paper said she hung herself. They found her in an abandoned building with a sheet tied around her neck.”

“Any witnesses?” Jack asked. Even he looked ready to jump up and rush out.

Cord shook her head, her hair shaking vigorously at her shoulders.

"They interviewed a couple of her coworkers. All of them said she was depressed."

Cambria snorted. "I would be too, working for those asshats."

"What sort of information was she giving us?" George asked.

"I don't know for sure, but it must've been important if they did this to silence her," Wes said.

"It had something to do with the hybrids," Cord said. "Mal made it sound like CHAS knew a way to cure them."

"I'm going to call Logan." Cambria got up and pulled out her phone. "Maybe Astor knows what CHAS doesn't want leaked."

"Good idea," Derek said. He followed her out.

"I have to wonder if it has something to do with all the metal stuff," Cord said. "Mal wasn't suicidal. They got to her. I should've never let her agree to that meeting."

"You said it was her idea," Wes said.

"It doesn't matter. I should've stopped it."

Wes rose and went to Cord. He didn't touch her. She wouldn't have let him. He looked her in the eye, held her gaze. "It wasn't your fault," he said quietly.

We all knew he wasn't only talking about Mal. Cord drew a slow breath. "I know that, but someone has to pay."

He nodded. "They will." I watched her take his hand and squeeze until her knuckles turned white.

"We need proof," I said.

One by one, all of us turned to Grandma.

"I'm already on it," she said, whipping out her phone and striding from the room.

"What do we do now?" George asked.

"We wait," Jack said. He sounded just as impatient as I felt.

CHAPTER TWENTY-TWO

Days passed. Training was slow and painful. The routine with Alex wasn't horrible. I still hated running, but I was better at sparring than before, which made it more enjoyable than it had been at the beginning—when I'd ended up on the ground every three minutes.

Jack's training was tougher. As in, no progress. None.

He seemed clueless as to how to trigger my wolf, using me as a punching bag or saying anything he could to get a rise out of me. All it did was piss me off enough to yell at him—something I'd never have done unless provoked. Even "friendly" Jack scared the bejeesus out of me in a fight. I scowled a lot, and swung my fists, landing a few of them on parts not covered by his padding. All of it was from a body that was decidedly human.

Wes watched and sometimes joined in the baiting. It led to real arguments after, so he'd stopped coming around during the middle of the second week. He'd wait until it was over to show himself, or sometimes he'd stay away until I was home, showered, and fed. I was always in a better mood after that. My mom had started letting him in, under the watchful eye of either herself or Grandma. Alex made himself scarce during those times. I wasn't sure what he did, but I didn't question it. He and Wes in the same room wasn't a pretty sight. Still, they endured it when they had to.

Wes told me he still owed Alex for saving me from Miles and then Mr. Lexington. He said his payback for the debt was to not attempt to murder Alex every time he saw him. I figured that was as good as I could hope for.

Cambria spent all of her free time—which was all day, every day—with Derek. I asked her a few times what it meant, how serious things were, but she brushed me off every time. She'd stopped talking about her mom, even when I asked, so I stopped asking. Despite my promise that night in the gazebo, there really wasn't anything I could do. Not right now.

The routine probably wouldn't have felt so monotonous if it weren't for the hybrids—or, more specifically, the absence of them. Victoria's parents especially. For the first week, I'd looked over my shoulder every time I left the house, on full alert for some sort of attack. None came, and as the weeks passed, I wondered if maybe they'd given up.

Grandma uncovered absolutely nothing about Mal's death. She'd said it was too difficult to work from here and uncover anything useful, so she packed up and went back to Washington. Cambria had put in a call to Logan and he said he'd try to find out what Astor knew, but so far, nothing. Either Astor didn't know, or he didn't want to share. Logan said every time he asked about it, Astor went off the deep end and left to paint. I think the questions reminded him too much of Mary Beth.

Everyone was restless and trying to hide it.

Cord stayed in her room most days. She claimed computer research into her friend's death but I suspected it hurt her to be in the same place where she'd last seen Bailey. I couldn't blame her. I still hadn't gone into the woods behind the house for that reason. I noticed the boys took a new route on their daily run with George. I'd caught Jack staring blankly into the trees one day before practice but pretended not to notice. Fee had lost weight but she put on a brave face.

Grief was the elephant in the room.

Instead of acknowledging it, we spoke of battle. Of justice.

It was only a matter of time until words turned to action, a dam whose foundation was slowly cracking, but it was easier to let it fade from my concern. I had Wes. I had my friends. I had everything I needed.

ONE WEEK INTO JULY, THE DAM BROKE. IT STARTED WITH VERA. She'd taken to watching my sessions with Jack from the window. Fee would prop her bed up and lift the blinds so she wouldn't have to move. I'd only been at it a few minutes, but already I was frustrated.

"Jack, face it, this isn't going to work," I said.

His response—another reassurance to try again, no doubt—was interrupted by a tapping on the window. When I turned to look, Vera motioned at us. I followed Jack inside and through the door to Vera's room.

"What's up?" Jack asked. His broad shoulders took up the entire doorway.

"Both of you, come in here," she said.

"Did you find something?" Jack asked, gesturing to the stack of *Dravens* lying open on the table.

"Maybe. Shut the door."

I did as she asked, and she waved me closer. "All the way over. I need to see something," she said. I walked to the edge of her bed, and she leaned over so her face almost touched my shirt and sniffed.

"What are you doing?" I asked.

"I thought so." She looked up sharply at Jack. "Get George."

"Why?" I asked.

Jack's brow wrinkled, but he left the room.

"Why do you need George?" I repeated.

"I have a theory," she said.

The door reopened. George stepped through, Jack behind him. "What's going on?" George asked.

"I want you to try something for me," she said, directing her gaze at George. "I want you to go outside and shift in front of Tara."

"What? Why?" he asked.

"Because I suspect you're wrong about Tara's trigger," she said. "I don't think she responds to threats or violence. I think it's you." She pointed at George.

"Me?" he echoed, clearly confused with her logic. I wasn't following, either.

"Vera, I've been around George plenty of times and not had the urge to shift," I said.

"Yes, but not when he was a Werewolf."

"I've been around other Werewolves without any reaction lots of times."

"But George isn't just any Werewolf," she pointed out.

"You think my trigger is hybrids?" As soon as I asked the question, I knew.

That night at school with Wes, Victoria's parents in the road, their attack on me at Astor's … Maybe she was right. If so, what about that day on the highway? Coming home from school, when I'd had to run behind the gas station. Had there been a hybrid around?

"You up for it?" George asked. I could feel him probing my mood with the bond. I knew he'd sense my curiosity and more than a little anxiety. Being near a hybrid might be my trigger, but I also had a history of turning on them.

I took a steadying breath. "It's worth a shot," I said.

"Come on, then." Jack started for the door but Vera stopped him.

"Let them go alone," she said.

They shared a look. Something passed between them. He nodded. "All right, I'll be right here if you need me," he said. "But if you manage to shift, I'm coming out."

I nodded. George and I went outside while Vera and Jack watched from the window. I kicked some pads and equipment out of the way and stood in the grass. George stood facing me, not too close. I backed up a few more steps. His brows went up.

"I'm not going to hurt you, Tay," he said.

"I know that."

He shook his head. "You ready?"

"Yeah."

I tried to project the right emotions so he wouldn't see through to my fear. It must've worked because a second later, his form shimmered at the edges, like a pool of water after a rock being thrown. When it settled, he was a wolf. His shoulders were broader than I remembered, his coat lighter.

"You're bigger," I said.

He grinned, flashing a lot of sharp, white teeth. "I've been running a lot. You've gotta try it when you're … you know. It's the coolest feeling ever."

I ignored his reference to my shifting. That weird tingly feeling in the back of my neck returned, leaving a headache. "Your coat is lighter," I said.

"The sun, I think." He took a step toward me and I scrambled back. "What's wrong?"

"Nothing, I—" The tingling in my neck intensified.

"You're fighting it again, aren't you?" he asked.

"No," I argued. I rubbed my shoulder absently.

"Do you feel sort of prickly on your neck?" he asked.

"Maybe."

"That's normal. Just give in to it. You'll be fine."

"It hurts."

"Only because you keep pushing it down. Just let it come."

Tears sprang to my eyes. I blinked them back. He was right; something inside me kept rising to the surface, and each time I pushed it down, terrified if I let it out, I'd hurt someone again. "I'm scared," I whispered.

"I'm not going to let anything happen to you," he said. He took another step.

Alarm shot through me. I backed toward the woods. "I'm not worried about me," I said. "I'm worried about you."

George's expression changed from relaxed to fierce, and for a second, I wondered what I'd said to make him so angry. But then I didn't have time to wonder anymore because he sprang, baring his teeth and snarling. I jumped and rolled out of the way just in time, barely missing his claws as he sailed past me.

I sat up, confused, to the sound of the back door slamming open and the sound of Wes's name being called. I looked up in time to see Jack hurl himself off the steps, rippling into a wolf in midair. He sprinted toward me, his eyes intent. It wasn't until he passed me and launched himself at something over my shoulder that I realized we weren't alone.

This was the real reason for the prickling on my neck.

Behind me, George was surrounded by four Werewolves, each one snapping at his ankles when his back was turned. Jack waded into the middle of their circle without hesitation. His teeth closed around one of the Werewolves' throats. It let out a mangled yelp as Jack bit down.

I got to my feet and grabbed the closest thing I could find. It looked like half of a dowel rod. I wasn't sure what Jack had intended it for, because it wasn't sharp or particularly scary-looking, but I didn't have time to find something better. I rushed toward the fight, weapon—sort of—in hand. The tingling against my neck threatened to distract me. I gritted my teeth and pushed forward.

Wes came barreling out the door, already shifting.

We reached the others at the same time. I barely had a chance to process the yellow eyes of our attackers before a familiar voice called out to me from inside the woods.

"Tara Godfrey."

I faltered, searching for the speaker. Wes pulled up short, his hip shoved against me protectively.

"Show yourself," I called.

Mr. and Mrs. Lexington stepped clear of the trees, both human. Finally, after weeks of wondering how and where they'd find me, I knew. It made me more relieved than afraid. Wes pressed against me, his shoulders bunched, ready to spring. I grabbed him by the scruff and clamped down. "Not yet," I whispered.

"You don't seem surprised," Mr. Lexington said.

"I knew you'd come," I said. "I see you brought friends." I tried to sound unconcerned, but I sensed George's anxiety building. He wasn't experienced with this sort of thing. He was scared.

"Insurance," Mr. Lexington said, waving a dismissive hand. "It will be me who delivers you."

I yanked back against Wes's attempt to run at him. "I'm not afraid of you," I said.

Mr. Lexington's eyes flickered to George and he sniffed. Mrs. Lexington placed her hand on his arm, but she didn't speak.

"I smell fear," he said. "You have twenty-four hours."

Something within the bond shifted. Relief.

Out of the corner of my eye, I watched the last yellow-eyed hybrid fall to the ground in front of George. His muzzle was strained red. None of the hybrids moved where they lay scattered. George and Jack, both winded, turned their attention to the Lexingtons. I read George's intent loud and clear. Attack. I had no doubt Jack intended the same.

"Wait," I called. "What will you do if I don't agree?"

"To you? Nothing. Olivia wants you alive. To your family, your friends ..." He hesitated. I could see the indecision, the battle within him. That, more than anything, made my stomach clench. "They won't be so lucky."

"I don't believe you," I shouted, stuck halfway between pissed and scared.

"And your mother? All alone in her flower shop across town? Can you protect her while you protect your human friends? Samantha and Angela? Can you be everywhere?"

My gut tightened. I couldn't breathe. Wes stilled underneath my hands. I swallowed, trying to find my voice.

"What did you do?" George demanded.

"Nothing yet. Twenty-four hours. We'll be back to collect you then. Cordelia too."

"Cord?" Wes asked. "What do you want with her?"

"Master requested it," he said with a shrug.

Rage, hotter than any flame, welled up inside me at his cavalier attitude. I let go of Wes and took a step toward Mr. Lexington. He narrowed his eyes, suspicious and wary. I didn't care if he saw me coming. "All you've done is issued death threats. Why don't you come over here and I'll show you what it tastes like?"

I couldn't remember making a conscious decision to attack, but that's what I did. One second I was standing still, white-hot anger lacing my veins and bringing them to a boil. The next, I was running at Mr. Lexington, the wooden dowel rod raised over my head. I watched him crouch and then shift to a wolf, the fabric of his clothing falling down around him in chunks. His eyes glowed hotter the closer I got. He opened his mouth and growled, his teeth grimy and pointed.

My insides burned and stretched as I ran. My bones pressed against my skin, straining to lengthen, to change. Canines dropped, breaking the skin along my bottom lip, drawing blood. Still, I ran, wanting only to wrap my hands—which ended in pointed claws now—around Mr. Lexington's throat and squeeze.

I never made it far enough.

"Tara, no!"

A furry body slammed into me, and I went down. My shoulders made a hollow thud as they hit hard earth. The air whooshed out of me and for a moment, the blue sky framed above me danced with pricks of light.

Everything seemed to slow down, as if I'd been sucked into a vacuum. The noise and activity went on around me as if nothing had changed. Only I was affected by whatever force held me still. The rage inside me didn't dull. I still wanted nothing more than to get up and finish what I'd started—how dare he threaten my friends?—but all I could do was lie there, and listen.

I could hear voices now, hurried and harsh in the way they spoke to each other. The first one I recognized was Derek. "… didn't see. They were too fast," he was saying.

"There could be more. Our priority is securing the house," Wes said. "Get Fee."

"Here I am," Fee said. "Where do you want me?"

"You take east and I'll take west. Five minutes. No more," Derek said.

The noise faded, replaced by a sort of rushing sound that was like no sound at all. Rage faded in again, blocking the rest out. I struggled to stand, to fight. At once, a pair of massive paws landed against my shoulders, pinning me.

Voices penetrated.

"... to call them. Cord will go to Sam's. I'll go to Angela."

"What about Tara?" George asked. The worry in his voice leaked through into the bond between us and threatened to overwhelm me.

"She'll be fine. This happened once before ..." Wes trailed off. I could hear him hesitating.

"I know about the attack at school," George said. "She told me."

"Right, that. She'll come out of it eventually. Probably won't remember much, though. Just keep an eye on her."

"I should shift back, call the girls," George said.

"You're not supposed to be here, remember? Get Cambria."

A second later, I heard, "Here I am. What—? Oh. What the hell? She's..."

"Yeah, we know," Wes said. "No time. Get her phone."

Hands groped at my hips. I heard a snarl and realized it came from my own throat. The paws bore down. A hand reached into my pocket and took my phone.

"You're phone leader," Wes said. "Call me if you hear anything. Then call Cord. The rest will check in with you."

"What the hell's a phone leader?" Cambria asked.

Wes huffed once. "Ask Vera. I have to go."

The voices fell silent. I couldn't understand, not like I knew I should. I needed to know what was happening, to me—and to the others. Had they gotten the Lexingtons? Were Sam and Angela safe? My mother?

FINALLY, THE HAZE FELL AWAY, AND I COULD *THINK* AGAIN. I COULD move. The first thing I did was struggle against the pressure of George's paws on my shoulders, but he didn't budge. His weight bore down, making it hard for me to breathe.

"Get off me," I said through gritted teeth.

"Are you … you?" George asked, peering down at me, his eyes wary.

"I'm me," I assured him. He didn't look convinced. "Where's Wes? Where's Mr. Lexington?"

"Gone."

"Gone where?" Panic threatened. George's worry spiked through our bond and I fought to keep my emotions in check. I wanted him convinced. I wanted him off me.

"The Lexingtons split. Jack, Derek, and Fee are trying to track them now. Wes and Cord went to check on Sam and Angela. Cambria's calling your mom."

"I didn't get him." A fuzzy memory of being slammed to the ground mid-attack slid through my mind. I tried to identify the force that had held me still.

"No."

I glared at him. "Why'd you stop me?"

"If you'd attacked, they might've gone after your mom, or one of the girls," George said quietly. "I used the bond to hold you until I could reach you myself."

"The bond?" I blinked up at him. "How?"

"I'm not sure exactly," he said with a shake of his head. "I told you it's powerful. You just aren't using all of it."

"Whatever. Why the heck are we still sitting here? Let's go help." I tried again to push him aside.

"Tara, if I let you up, you can't run off. Jack says we have to stay here. We should probably go inside." He looked around.

"I'm not going inside. My mom—"

"Tara." Jack's voice carried from the far edge of the woods. He bounded up to us and nodded at George who eased up enough to let me sit. Jack towered over me. "Your mom is safe. She's on her way here."

"And Sam? Angela?"

"We'll know in a few minutes." His eyes took in the length of me. "Well, I guess we figured out what it'll take to make you shift."

"What?" I asked. He didn't answer. I looked back and forth between them in confusion.

"Tara, your hands," George said.

I looked down and my stomach dropped to my knees. My hands and arms were covered in down. Gingerly, I reached out and touched it with the tips of my fingers. It was soft, feathery light—and wrong. I jerked my hand away.

"Vera was right," Jack said. "Your trigger is hybrids. The more, the merrier, it seems."

"Did I shift completely?" I asked. It came out a whisper. I couldn't get my voice to work right. I remembered the haze—the voices, the conversation as if heard in a wind tunnel.

"No, just this," Jack said, nodding to my fur.

My abdomen brushed against the fabric of my shirt. More fur. I stilled, not wanting to know how much of me was covered. "Did I—did I hurt anyone?" I asked.

"No, the hybrids were already, uh, taken care of," George said. He nodded toward the edge of the trees where several wolves lay unmoving in the deadened grass.

"The Lexingtons?" I asked.

"They slipped away when you ah, distracted us," Jack explained. "Fee and Derek are sweeping the property for more hybrids. Soon as they're back, we'll try and track them."

"What about … you guys?" I asked, finally voicing my worst fear.

"You think you hurt us?" Jack asked, clearly confused at my question.

"We're fine, Tay."

Relief washed over me, so strong it almost made it all right that I was still covered in fur. Almost.

Fee and Derek appeared from around the side of the house. Their eyes widened when they got close, both of them staring down at me. Neither one commented on the fur covering my arms and legs.

"Anything?" Jack asked. Both of them shook their heads. "Let's get going, then. George, take her inside and lock the doors. Don't come out for anyone. If you hear anything before we're back, go to the back window and howl once. We'll hear you."

"You got it." George started toward the house, but I held my ground.

"Tara, don't be difficult." Jack's tone shifted, becoming decidedly alpha. "I need you here."

"They're my friends," I said.

"And you being safe is the only leverage we have against their lives. Go inside, lock the doors, and talk to Vera."

"Why Vera?" I asked.

"Maybe she can tell you how to fully shift."

"Shift which way?" I said.

"Either forward or back. Doesn't matter. Pick one." He turned and ran for the woods with Fee and Derek at his heels.

CHAPTER TWENTY-THREE

My skin returned to normal within the hour. I couldn't remember if it'd taken that long the other times. I didn't think so. Vera said it was because my wolf was getting stronger. To prove her point, I accidentally growled at George when he complimented me on the soft brown color of my fur.

I swallowed the rest of the snarl that rose in my throat. "Don't," I said.

"I was just saying—"

"I looked like the female version of *Teen Wolf*."

He didn't say anything else after that.

I sat in Vera's room, only half listening while she explained her theory about the hybrids being my trigger for shifting. After what happened out back, I knew she was right—and that I should be more concerned with that fact—but all I could think about were Sam and Angela. Threatened. Possibly hurt—or worse. I couldn't think about "worse."

"Tara, did you hear me?" George asked.

I blinked and shook free of my dark thoughts. "What?"

"The girls are both at Angela's house. Cambria called and told them to stay inside until Wes comes to get them," he said.

"Are they alone?"

"Yeah, their parents are at work. But Wes says there are hybrids in the woods out back. They're waiting for dark—and reinforcements."

"Who exactly …?" I realized it at the same time George answered.

"Alex," he said. "And Edie. I need to signal Jack." I watched as he went to the open window and tipped his head back, letting loose a long, low howl. My skin prickled and something unexpected washed over me. Yearning. My inner wolf strained at the sound. The urge to join him rose in my chest, but I swallowed it back.

I caught Vera watching me curiously and stood abruptly.

"Where are you going?" George asked, turning away from the window after an answering howl. It sounded distant, but there was no mistaking it was Jack.

"I don't know. I can't sit still."

I knew he wanted to stay near the window, to watch. It made him feel useful. I gathered that through our bond—which meant I knew he could feel my restlessness just as clearly. He let me go without following.

I wandered the downstairs until I couldn't look at the same stretch of walls any longer. I went up to the bedroom that had been my recovery room all those times, the room that now belonged to George. I went inside and lay down on the mattress that still smelled like dried leaves and mothballs, but that didn't last long. My brain was working overtime to process all of the worst-case scenarios.

I took a shower, managing to find an old pair of sweatpants that I'd left in the closet, and paired it with one of George's lacrosse shirts from his brief stint on the team sophomore year. It smelled like him—like his scent before he'd turned. Completely human. Then I remembered where I'd seen these sweatpants before. I'd borrowed them from Sam months ago. My breathing hitched and I blinked rapidly.

I heard noises downstairs, then doors opening and closing down the hall. I poked my head and listened to the voices. Jack, Fee, and Derek had returned. Dresser drawers slid open and closed. I imagined them shifting, donning clothes, gearing up to meet Wes and the others. The urge to demand that I be included hit me again. I met Jack as he came out of his room. The hallway seemed narrower with his broad shoulders filling the space.

"You look better," he said.

I tucked my wet hair behind my ear. "I want to come."

"No." He started for the stairs. I followed.

"You said yourself that I'm better," I argued.

"That's not the problem."

"Then what's the problem?"

"We can't expose you," he said. "I'm already taking a risk exposing Cord, knowing they want her too."

I crossed my arms. "In other words, Cord can take care of herself, but I can't."

"I'm not going to argue with you, Tara. You need to stay here. Your mom's on her way. We need everyone together when we get back. To decide what to do." I gave him a blank look. "About the Lexingtons. And their ultimatum. Do you remember anything they said?"

My brow wrinkled as I tried recalling the exact wording. "They said Cord and I have twenty-four hours to give ourselves over to them or they'll kill my friends."

"Right. So until we know what they want with you and Cord, you're not going anywhere." He towered over me, his mouth drawn down in a frown, looking every bit the alpha. Something inside me wanted to challenge him, but the human side of me knew better.

"Whatever," I mumbled. I stood there, staring at the buttons on his shirt until he walked away. Fee came up behind me. Her hand landed on my shoulder.

"You know they won't come back without your friends," she said.

"Jack or Wes?"

"Yes."

I nodded. "Thank you."

She planted a kiss on my forehead and slipped away.

I stood clinging to the banister, listening to the sound of voices drifting up from the direction of the weapons room. Cambria appeared at my side.

"You look sulky," she said.

"They're going without me."

"I called your friends. They're safe."

"You stole my phone."

"You wigged out and grew fur."

Derek walked up, still tucking stakes into various places along his waistline and into his boots. "We'll check in every hour. If we miss a call-in …"

"We've got the Carolina pack on standby. They can be here in under two hours if needed," Cambria said. "I got this. Go kick hybrid ass."

He kissed her long enough that I felt awkward standing beside them. When he pulled away, the expression on Cambria's face surprised me. It was more than infatuation.

Derek nodded at me. "Glad to see you're back to normal," he said.

Jack and Fee waited in the open doorway. He joined them after a final wave. I waved back, even though it was probably directed at Cambria. She blew him a kiss as George closed the door behind them.

"You love him a little bit," I said.

"I might."

I stared at her, shocked that she'd admitted it, shocked it was true.

"Don't look at me like that. Close your mouth," she snapped before marching off.

TRUE TO THEIR WORD, DEREK CHECKED IN WITH CAMBRIA HOURLY. The first time they called, I spoke to Wes, but it was brief. He sounded distracted. Sam and Angela had been alerted to the rescue party. All they knew was that someone was after them, trying to get to me. I hadn't talked to them directly, because I had no idea what to say if they asked for the rest of the story. Vague seemed best at this point. Angela managed to keep her parents away, along with her little brother and sister, so it was just she and Sam in the house.

Wes said he'd counted twelve hybrids, all of them stalking the tree line like they were waiting on a signal of some kind. Hearing that made my stomach clench.

"Are you okay, from earlier?" Wes asked.

"I'm fine."

"I'm sorry I left."

"It's okay. I know you did it to help them."

"Is George taking good care of you?"

"Not as good as you would," I said. "But yeah. I can tell he's tired of playing babysitter. Wishes he were there with you guys."

"He's not ready for something like this."

"I know."

"You wish you were here."

It wasn't a question. I answered anyway. "Yes."

"I'll bring them back."

"I know."

The phone beeped with another incoming call, and I had to hang up. It was Logan. I handed it to Cambria. Not because I didn't want to talk to him, but after delivering the news to Victoria that her parents were alive, and seeing how happy she'd been about it, I really didn't want to tell her we were currently trying to kill them.

My mom arrived in a windstorm of worry and stress. She carried a bag full of disinfectant and rags. I rolled my eyes and left her to it. It's not like Fee would complain once she saw her sparkling house.

George wandered in and out, both of us more and more restless as time went on. At some point during the wait, we found ourselves knee-deep in weapons and padding, and proceeded to reorganize the entire supply room. Jack could thank—or yell at—me later.

At midnight, Derek called and said they were ready to move.

"I think you should lay low when the girls get here," I said, restacking the last of the bins onto the shelves. Jack wasn't going to know where to find anything. I didn't care right now.

"You want me to hide out?" George asked.

"Just until I tell them about you, explain everything."

"It makes sense. They're going to freak as it is," he said.

"I know." The bond between us filled with nervous tension.

The next hour crawled by.

By the time the phone rang again, at four minutes after one, I'd convinced myself they were all dead. I'd torn an entire stack of napkins into little pieces now littering the bar top. My mother glared at me. I pretended not to notice and bored holes in Cambria's back as she spoke into the phone across the room.

"It's done," she said when she hung up. "Sam and Angela are safe. They're on their way home."

I scooted to the edge of my seat. "Is anyone hurt?" I asked.

The hesitation in her eyes gave it away.

"Tell me," I said.

"A few scrapes and bruises. Nothing serious."

"Tell me," I repeated.

"Fee took a hard hit. She's unconscious."

CHAPTER TWENTY-FOUR

The crunch of tires on gravel came just before two in the morning. George took his cue and ducked out. I jumped up, my feet practically coming off the floor trying to get to the door. Cambria reached it first and flung it open. Derek stood on the threshold, wearing nothing but a pair of loose-fitting jeans and a pair of flip-flops. His cheeks were dirty, and I could still smell the animal scent clinging to him—a sign he'd only recently changed back.

Cambria ignored the rest of us crowding around and flung herself into his arms. He barely caught them both from falling backward before hauling her off to the side and holding her against him. The sight of it made my chest ache.

Jack carried Fee in his arms.

She was wrapped in a blanket, hanging limp. Her blond hair hung in tangles and swayed with the movement of his steps. I knew she must be breathing based on Jack's set jaw. I looked away quickly, swallowing hard.

Then I saw Wes.

He walked beside Jack, slow and steady, their pace matched. Like Derek, he was shirtless and I got the feeling he'd only just shifted. His disheveled hair and a single, long scratch down his chest were the only sign he'd been in a fight—that I could see. I searched his body for other wounds. The fact that he was half-naked only registered after I assured myself he wasn't hurt. I wanted to run, to fling myself into Wes's arms like Cambria had done with Derek, but I held back. Right now, Jack needed him more.

Alex walked behind the others, looking out of place in a setting that was so familiar—so Werewolf—to me. His jeans were dirty, and a hole had been torn in the knee and across the right pocket. Blood coated his shin, too thick for me to see the wound. He broke from his hushed conversation with Cord and slipped in beside me, grabbing my hand and squeezing it. I squeezed back and then leaned down to examine the cut on his leg.

"You're hurt," I said. I pulled the fabric away to get a better look and he jumped.

"It's fine. Just a scratch," he said, waving me away.

Jack didn't acknowledge me as he passed through the open door. He looked determined and unseeing.

Wes dropped a kiss on my cheek and glared at Alex on his way inside. "I'll be back after I help Jack get her settled," he said. He stood next to me, but his words—and the threat in them—were directed at Alex.

"I'll keep her company until then," Alex said.

I was hyperaware of Alex's hand in mine, but I didn't let go. It would've felt like admitting guilt of some kind. After a long pause, Wes continued up the stairs behind Jack.

Cord walked in and climbed the stairs behind them. Her shirt had a rip down the back, exposing bare skin that was, thankfully, free of blood or injury. She didn't speak, but her eyes were hard and I suspected seeing Fee injured shook her. Grandma brought up the rear, her hair disheveled and her "Grandmas Rule" tee wrinkled where it had come untucked. Otherwise, she looked no worse for wear.

Sam and Angela walked close beside her, one tucked underneath each arm. When Sam spotted me, she rushed forward and hugged me. "There you are. You have no idea … it was insane," she said. Her voice cracked on the last word.

"I'm glad you're okay," I said. "You're not hurt, are you?"

She shook her head, her voice laced with tears. "No, they didn't hurt us. Wes—I mean, I didn't know it was him at first—he and that girl-wolf got me out. Oh, geez, you're cut." She stared in horror at Alex's arm. Blood seeped out of a wound on his bicep. It ran in rivulets down his arm and dripped onto the hardwood.

"Dammit," he said. "Must've broken open again from the movement."

"What happened?" I asked. "You didn't get bit, did you?"

"No, I ..." he trailed off, looking at Angela. She didn't meet his eyes.

"Angela stabbed him with a butter knife," Sam said.

"What?" I stared at Angela incredulously. "Why?"

She shrugged. "I didn't know he was one of the good guys. He kept trying to grab me and force me to go with him."

"And you stabbed him?" I repeated.

"There were talking wolves, Tara. Wolves! Every-freaking-where. He's lucky it wasn't a steak knife."

"Alex isn't a wolf," I pointed out.

"He startled me." She sidestepped away, and I could see she felt badly, but she didn't back down. I shook my head.

"Come on, you," Cambria said, pointing at Alex. "I'll clean you up." She eyed first his arm, then his knee. "Can you walk or do you need a wheelchair?"

"I can walk," Alex grumbled.

He fell into step behind Cambria as she headed toward the kitchen to find Fee's first aid kit. I started to follow but the look on Angela's face stopped me. She and Sam were still waiting for an explanation—deserved one, really.

"I'll be right there," I called.

"Take your time," Cambria called back, waving a hand without turning.

Before I could say anything, Sam picked up her part of the conversation right where she'd left off. "It was horrible. I mean, talking wolves? I thought I was losing my mind. Maybe I am."

"You're not," I said.

"But it's just unbelievable, really. I mean, wolves? Your Grandma said they're Werewolves?" She laughed and the harshness of it startled me. Her eyes shone and her pupils seemed larger than they should've been. I took her hand and it shook in mine.

"I know it's unbelievable, but it's true," I said, watching her carefully.

"How?" she asked. "I mean, it's impossible, right? Is it magic, or witchcraft, or what?"

I looked at Angela, expecting the same mixture of shock and disbelief and general freaking out I saw in Sam. Instead, Angela stood with arms crossed and a heavy frown. My relief became overshadowed by apprehension. For months, I'd wanted this moment. The moment where I could tell them the truth, share it with them, stop keeping secrets. Now that it was here, what would they think?

"I guess we should talk," I said slowly, my eyes fixed on Angela. I tried to read her, to gauge how much she'd accepted already, but her face was a mask.

"I guess we should," Angela agreed. Her voice was crystal clear, as was the look in her eyes. "You want to explain what exactly happened back there?"

I took a deep breath. "You should sit down first."

We filed in, with Grandma herding Sam—who was now crying—into the living room behind Angela and me. Grandma steered Sam to the couch where she curled into the corner, wedged between the cushion and the armrest. Grandma pulled a blanket around Sam's shoulders and then slipped out.

I lowered myself onto the edge of Jack's chair and clasped my hands together, racking my brain for how to begin. Angela stood with her back to me.

"What are you thinking?" I asked.

"About everything. And nothing. The past few months. Your absence. Your distance even when you were around. My theories you were depressed." She laughed, the sound completely absent of humor. "I wasn't even close."

"I … it's a lot."

"You can say that again." She turned to face me and I was struck by how calm she seemed. "You're happy. I can see that."

"I am. Mostly. It's complicated."

"I can see that too."

"I wanted to tell you."

"At the mall?"

"And other times. Lots of other times. You have no idea how often I picked up the phone, dialed your number, and then changed my mind."

"Here's your chance."

I stood and took a step toward her. She backed up.

Grandma returned with Alex in tow. She looked down at Sam, who was staring blankly at the empty fireplace. "Alex, can you help me with her?" Grandma asked. "I want to take her upstairs. It'll make it easier for Wes."

"You're not taking her anywhere," Angela said. She crossed from the window to block Alex's path. "She's staying where I can see her." She stared up at him defiantly. He didn't argue or move to go around her.

"Ang, it's okay. She can sleep up there," I said.

"She can do that right here."

Alex looked at me, waiting for an answer, and I nodded. "Fine, she can stay here."

Angela crossed her arms, her expression full of challenge and victory. It took me by surprise. This was definitely not the Angela I was used to. I'd expected her to cower, to lose it like Sam had. Instead, she was fierce and fearless. I wondered what had happened to the timid girl I'd known before today.

Alex lingered a second longer, looking down at her curiously, then backed away.

"I'll be right back," Grandma said. She cast one more glance at Sam and left. Alex slipped out behind her.

I listened to the ticking of the clock in the hall and stared at my hands. Why couldn't I think of what to say? Why hadn't I spent the last few hours figuring it out? Now that they were here, and I had free rein to tell them the truth, I felt … stuck.

"Anytime now," Angela prompted.

"What you saw tonight … Wes, and the others, they aren't human," I began.

"Yeah, I got that." Angela's words stung with sarcasm. "They're Werewolves."

"Yes."

"And the others?" Angela prompted. "The ones with the glowing eyes?"

"They're Werewolves, too, just … a different kind."

"Different how?"

"Most Werewolves are born with their shifting ability," I explained. "It's genetic, passed down from their parents. But the ones who came after you tonight were created through an injection. They started off as humans or Hunters, which is what I am, and the serum changed them."

"You mean, like a science experiment gone wrong?" Angela asked.

"Sort of. It messed with their DNA and they aren't the same. They're …"

"Evil?" Angela finished.

Alex appeared in the doorway and my response died away. For some reason, I couldn't bring myself to agree with Angela, though I knew Alex would. I caught sight of white gauze through the hole in his jeans. He'd found a fresh shirt, one that wasn't covered in dirt, drool, and blood. Had he really borrowed a shirt from a Werewolf? A strip of gauze peeked out from under the sleeve. Already, a red stain coated the center. He took a spot on the couch next to Sam.

"No," I said, attempting to answer Angela's question. "I don't know. Some of them, maybe. Whatever it is that creates compassion or a connection to others, they don't have it once they become hybrids. Their conscience is gone."

"They tried to k-kill us," Sam said. She stared at me, bottom lip quivering, and something inside me tightened. This was not Sam. The Sam I knew should've been laughing, joking, cuddling up to the hot guy who'd sat down next to her. This was barely a shadow of that girl. I hated it.

"They're after me," I said.

"They tried to kill us to get to you," Angela said. I wasn't sure how much of it was an accusation, but I felt the guilt.

"Yes."

At that, Sam began crying again. Her whole body shook with the sobs. Her cheeks, already stained with tears and makeup, shone with renewed moisture. Alex scooted closer and put an arm around her. "You're safe now," he said in a low voice. "I wouldn't have let them hurt you."

"Angela almost killed you," Sam said between sobs.

Alex sent Angela an amused expression. "Not even close."

"Why aren't you a wolf too?" Sam asked him.

"I'm a Hunter," he explained. "It's my job to kill Werewolves, to protect humans like you. A butter knife isn't enough to stop me."

"Are you sure, because you screamed really loud when it went in," she said.

Angela snorted. I hid a smile.

"I did not scream," he said. He looked at me. "Do not laugh."

"I'm not."

"She's in shock."

"I know."

Grandma returned and handed Sam a steaming mug. "Drink this, dear."

"Wh-what is it?" Sam asked.

"It will calm you down," Grandma told her. "There you go." She helped Sam steady it as she tipped it back. Sam downed it in three gulps and almost immediately the shaking subsided.

Already, Sam's eyelids looked heavier. Grandma shifted her so that Sam's head leaned on the armrest.

"Sam's out," Angela said. "And I'm still waiting. You still haven't explained anything I didn't already see for myself. Just come out with it already," she said. "I want the whole story."

I nodded at her. "All right."

The ceiling creaked as someone moved around upstairs. My stomach tightened. "Grandma, can you see how Fee is doing?" I asked. "I'm really worried about her." It wasn't a lie, but more than that, I couldn't handle her here. Not now. Not if Angela freaked.

"Sure, sweetie," Grandma said. "Be right back."

When she was gone, I told Angela my story. I started slow, nervous of her judgment more than anything, but as time went on, she relaxed and my words came easier. We ended up cross-legged on the carpet together, her asking questions and me answering. It felt like girl-talk—the supernatural version.

"Wait, so Mason Harding is a Werewolf?" she asked.

"Yup, his whole family."

"Wow. Anyone else at school?"

"I don't think so. I would've sensed them."

She frowned. "What do you mean?"

I told her about the tingling, shivery feeling I always got when another Werewolf was around.

"So every time Wes comes around, you get goosebumps?"

"Not Wes," I said. "He's different."

"How?"

"He and I are hybrids. Not like the ones you saw tonight," I added quickly. "My mom is a Hunter and my dad was a Werewolf. His parents were one of each also. We've been this way since birth. I think that makes a difference."

"You missed out on the glowy eyes," she said.

There was a hint of humor in her words, enough that I smiled. "I missed out," I agreed.

Her amusement faded as quickly as it had come. "You could've told me."

"I wanted to."

"Is that why you went away to school?"

"Sort of. I also really did punch Cindy Adams." We shared another smile.

"Her nose is really crooked now," she said. "Her mom took her to a plastic surgeon, I think."

I groaned. "I feel horrible about that."

Alex looked up from his magazine. "What am I missing?"

"Nothing," we said in unison.

"What else?" she asked.

I told her about Miles and how he'd created the hybrids so he and I could rule with them as our army.

"That's completely creepy," she said.

"Agreed."

"Where is he now?"

"He attacked me and Cord killed him," I said.

"Wow." She shook her head.

"Are you okay?"

"I don't know. It's just … a lot. This is the stuff fairy tales are made of."

"I think you mean nightmares," I said.

"I don't know. You're pretty badass from the sound of it. And we thought Sam was the wild one." I caught her smile just before it faded.

"She's got nothing on me," I joked.

Angela looked over at Alex. "You can take her upstairs now," she told him.

He raised a brow at her. "You sure?"

"I trust you," she said. The look she wore dared him to contradict her. Like before, he regarded her with curiosity before scooping Sam up and carrying her out.

"He's handy," she said.

"When he wants to be."

"He's waiting for me to freak out, isn't he?"

"You are taking it pretty well."

"You realize you're comparing me to Sam," she said. "I'm insulted."

I grinned. "Sorry."

"She's really only sleeping, right?"

"Promise."

Angela smiled. "She's going to be pissed she missed being carried upstairs by someone like him."

I started to smile back, then remembered she wouldn't even know it happened.

Angela's amusement faded. Lines creased her forehead. "You must've been terrified at the beginning, when you first found out about all of this, about what you are, especially doing it alone."

"Ang, it's not your fault, and I wasn't alone." I gestured around me. "But I am glad I can finally tell you."

She shook her head. "If I hadn't seen it with my own eyes …"

"I know."

"Nothing's going to be the same, is it?" I shook my head. Her eyes were sad. "Sam's a mess."

"She'll be all right."

Her eyes narrowed. "Your grandma said something about Wes. What will he do to her?"

"He can make it so she doesn't remember."

Her eyes widened. "He can do that?"

"Yes."

"Can you do anything?"

"Um …" I thought about how I'd almost shifted earlier and my emotional bond with George. George. I still hadn't gotten to that part. Crap. The more I told, the harder it seemed to be.

Grandma came in wiping her hands on a towel. Something about her expression made me sit up straighter. "What is it?" I asked.

"Fee's awake."

I jumped up but Grandma waved me back down. "She was a mess. Lots of pain. I gave her something to drink. She's out again."

"How's Jack?" I asked.

"He's pacing. And grumpy." She scowled.

"Is she going to be …?"

"She'll be fine. She took a bad spill," Grandma said, "dislocated her shoulder and hip. It's too painful to shift right now so healing is slow, but she'll be all right. Wes went to get cleaned up, before you start badgering me about him," she added.

I clamped my mouth shut, pretending I hadn't been about to ask. "Cord's with her too?"

She nodded. “They’re shaken. After Bailey … well, they don’t like the idea of Fee being injured.”

I nodded in understanding. Inside, relief washed over me, sharp and sweet. Fee would be all right.

“How’s it going in here?” she asked. She sent a pointed look at Angela.

“I’m holding it together,” Angela said wryly.

Grandma shook her head. “You’re doing more than that. Most level-headed first-timer I’ve seen.”

“Maybe I’m tougher than I look.” Angela rounded on me. “Or than you gave me credit for,” she added. “So why are they after you? The evil hybrids, I mean.”

I hesitated. I still hadn’t answered her earlier question, but since this one was easier, and right in front of me, I took the opening. “I don’t know,” I said. “They work for a woman named Olivia. She’s the one who sent them, who told them to *use* you and Sam. I have twenty-four hours to give myself up.”

“You don’t know what she wants with you?”

“No.”

She tilted her head. “Are you going to give yourself up?”

I looked over at Grandma. Her expression was neutral, blank. I suspected deep down she’d go along with whatever answer I gave. Alex, who’d returned in time to hear the last question, wasn’t so placid.

“Don’t even think about it,” he said.

I’d known this was coming since the minute they’d walked in from the rescue mission. I’d braced for it. “I can’t ignore them, Alex—”

“You can, and you will. Don’t start with me. I’m serious.”

“It’s not up to you.”

“What’s not up to him?” Wes asked. He stood in the doorway, his hands securing the drawstring on his shorts, his hair still wet from the shower. For once, Alex’s reaction at seeing Wes wasn’t a scowl or muttered curse.

“She thinks she’s going to give herself up to the Lexingtons,” Alex said.

Wes's head came up, and his hands stilled. His eyes on mine were fierce, determined. "Like hell."

"For once, we agree," Alex said.

Cambria and Derek appeared behind Wes.

"What's up?" I asked too brightly. Anything to quell the imminent argument. I didn't like my chances against Alex and Wes on a good day—especially as a united front—and this was definitely not a good day.

"Derek needs a buddy for patrols," Cambria said. Her expression changed as the mood in the room registered. "Or we can come back later ..."

"No, it's fine. I'll go," Alex said, rising.

"I can do it," Wes said at the same time.

Derek leaned in, making a production of sniffing Wes's shoulder. "You smell way too pretty," Derek said. "I can't take you."

Wes swung out, but Derek jumped back, grinning. "Save your energy. You and George have second shift."

"George?" Angela echoed.

Both boys froze. The room went quiet.

"Oops," Derek muttered.

"I thought you told her everything," Wes said to me.

"Baby steps."

"George is here? Where?" Angela's voice rose with each question. "How?"

"I'll explain," I said. I looked at Cambria. "Can you get him?"

"I'm on it." She disappeared down the hall.

Derek looked at Alex. "You ready, man?"

"More than," Alex said, following Derek out. I glared at their backs and listened to the front door open and close behind them. No one spoke while we waited. I could feel Angela's eyes on me.

A second later, George appeared. He'd showered and changed, but there were circles under his eyes. Carrying the stress and worry of two people weighed heavily. I knew, firsthand.

"Hey, Ang," he said quietly.

Angela's eyes bulged. "What are you doing here?" she demanded. "You're supposed to be at football camp."

"Yeah, about that … I'm not."

"Obviously." She glared at him, then me. "How could you tell him and not me? Everything you said about wishing you could tell me for so long, and then you went and told him?"

The hurt in her eyes reflected back, and I realized the reason for her sudden show of anger. She wasn't freaking out about Werewolves or Hunters or anything supernatural. She thought I'd chosen George over her.

"I had no choice," I said. "He was kidnapped and then turned. I had to bring him here to protect him."

"Turned into what?" As soon as she asked the question, understanding dawned. "He's a Werewolf too?" I nodded. "I don't believe this."

George frowned. "I don't have to prove it, do I? Because I just put fresh clothes on."

"Angela?" I asked.

She rubbed her fingers against her temples. "No, please, no more wolves tonight. Geez, Tara. Does it get any weirder? Anything else you want to tell me?"

"Um. I'm a wolf too, now. Sort of. And George and I have this bond thing, where we can feel each other's emotions."

"Of course you do. I need some air." She stalked out.

George went after her, and I let him. I didn't have it in me right now. All I could think about was that I'd had Angela's understanding, and then I'd lost it.

Wes's arms came around me, and I laid my cheek against his shoulder. "She's going to hate me," I said.

"She's not going to hate you."

"She probably already does."

"No, she doesn't."

"She's going to freak out, like Sam."

He paused and then said, "Do you want me to make her forget?"

"Sam? It's probably best."

"Angela."

I sighed. "I don't know. She's taken everything pretty well up until this point."

He didn't answer except to pull me closer. For just a moment, I forced everything else aside and enjoyed the feeling of his body against mine. The way his shoulders curved protectively, the way we fit together—all of it was as familiar, as comforting, as coming home.

"We need to talk about what you said to Alex," he said, and just like that, the feeling slipped away. I pulled back, bracing myself.

"There's nothing to say."

He stared at me incredulously. "There's everything to say."

"Wes—"

"I knew you were going to do this. I knew as soon as they threatened your friends. That doesn't mean I have to stand by and let it happen. It doesn't mean I have to agree."

"Listen, if I can get close enough to the hybrids, figure out how this Olivia lady is controlling—"

"We're back to the hybrids? Is that what this is about for you? They can't be saved, Tara. You need to realize that."

"You don't know that. And we have to at least try. We could save lives."

"I am saving lives. Yours."

"Does that mean others have to suffer? That if it isn't a direct threat to me, we should ignore it, do nothing? They were people before. With lives and families."

"And now they're evil. They killed Bailey, tried to kill you, and tonight they tried to kill your friends."

His words weighed heavily on me. Still, I held on to my argument. "Tonight was a warning."

"The hybrids don't know the difference. You honestly still think you can save them? That they aren't evil, after everything they've done?"

I hesitated, unsure. I couldn't say they were evil. Not when I'd been the one to convince Wes and the others to try and save them in the beginning. Then again, Wes was right. Look where that had gotten us. Bailey was gone, Fee was injured, Sam and Angela could've died.

Were they worth saving?

Especially when the only way to do it might involve forging a bond with them like I had with George? The thought made it hard to swallow. Then I thought of Victoria, of the way she'd looked when I told her I'd seen her parents.

"What if it were our parents instead of Victoria's?" I asked. "Would they be worth it then?"

"It's different."

"Is it?"

"Yes! I couldn't save them—I can save you. I will not lose you like I lost them!" His voice rose to a yell in a sudden show of temper. The air thickened. Something inside him seemed to strain against its hold—his wolf.

My bones ached, my muscles bunched. I stared him down. A part of me—a less-than-human part—knew this moment defined the future. Who looked away first mattered very much. I felt enough sympathy that, had the stakes been lower, I'd have given in. He'd lost so much, rebuilt it piece by piece. No wonder he was terrified of losing it. Of losing me. But the stakes weren't low. To me, to the wolf straining inside me, this moment defined a leadership I thought I'd never want.

He blinked. "This is insane," he said. "We'll find another way."

"And while we figure it out, everyone else is in danger. Sam and Angela … it could've been bad."

"But it wasn't. We saved them."

"And so you're going to what? Let them move in here so you can protect them around the clock? What about their families? What about George's? What about anyone I've ever met? You can't protect everyone forever."

He pressed a hand to my cheek. "Neither can you."

"It's my decision. It's my life."

"It's our life." His voice was instantly fierce. Not angry, but desperate. He leaned in so we stood toe to toe, eye to eye. "We're a team, remember?"

"We are a team," I agreed, "so be on my side. Believe in me. I can do this."

I waited, fully prepared to continue the argument, but he nodded slowly, looking defeated, and pressed his forehead to mine. "I need you to come home," he said. "Promise me."

"I promise."

At five, Wes went to find Alex and Derek to help with patrols. George still hadn't returned from talking to Angela, but Cambria came in and told me they were huddled in the supply room, so I knew she was safe. I wanted to see Fee, but Grandma said she was still sleeping, and I didn't want to sit in a room with a worried Jack—or Cord, worried or not.

I found myself knocking on Vera's door. My mom hadn't come out since the others arrived home. When I poked my head inside, I realized why. She was passed out on Vera's bed. Vera sat sideways on the loveseat, a book propped on her lap. A lamp cast a yellow beam of light across her face, throwing the rest of the room into shadow.

"Tara, come in," she said quietly. "Is everything okay?"

"It's fine. I'm just tired."

"You should get some sleep."

"I will soon. I was waiting for my friend, Angela."

"Your mother speaks highly of her. How's she taking everything?"

"Better than I expected. Worse than I'd like. Mostly, I think she's angry that she was the last to know."

"Betrayal is harder to forgive than murder. My mother said that once."

"Great, so there's no hope."

Vera smiled, a rare, genuine gesture. "You should know my mother was clinically insane by the time she was fifty."

"I see."

She laughed. "Hopefully, you don't." She glanced at my mom. "She was worried about you."

"Me?" I frowned. "I was here the whole time."

"I don't think that matters at this point. She knows what you'll choose."

"With her, I don't have a choice."

"Your fate, your choice." I didn't say anything to that. If my mom had her way, she'd choose for me and lock me in a closet, but I didn't argue it. If Vera said I'd get a choice, somehow I knew I would. "George came earlier and sat for a while. Your bond with him is strong."

"I guess," I said.

"Could come in handy, if you decide to go."

My head came up. I stared at her, suddenly alert. "The bond … he could feel what I'm feeling. He'd know if I was in danger."

"Naturally."

I shook my head, though I wasn't all that surprised anymore. Vera seemed to have a knack for quietly pushing me against the tide. "I'd have to convince them to let me go."

"They'll vote on it."

"Seriously?"

"It's our process. Everyone gets a vote. As I said, your fate, your choice."

"Even George?"

"Especially George."

"What does that mean?"

"You haven't figured it out yet? He's more a part of you than they are. He's your pack."

CHAPTER TWENTY-FIVE

My mind wouldn't shut up. It didn't help that I'd been awake for almost twenty-four hours. Or that everyone else seemed to have a job but me. Wes, Derek, and George were still outside. I wondered if they really expected an attack or if they were too wired to sleep and couldn't stand the thought of being cooped up inside. George's exhaustion was evident through the bond—which only added to my own—so I assumed the first.

Grandma was in the kitchen, cooking more tea for Sam and Fee—just in case. Alex had gone to shower, muttering something about the whole house smelling like dog. I pretended not to hear. Cambria was upstairs, showing Angela to George's room to let her sleep. Sam was there, still under the effects of the drink. I hoped she stayed that way a while longer, for her sake.

Angela still hadn't spoken to me. I wasn't sure what that meant. I didn't go to her when she'd finished talking to George. I couldn't, not until I knew what she thought, where she stood. If, after all of my honesty, and all of the shock, she rejected me because she thought I'd chosen George instead of her … I wasn't even sure what to say to that. So I curled up in Jack's chair and closed my eyes, pretending to sleep.

I AWOKE TO FOOTSTEPS ON THE STAIRS, DISORIENTED BY THE FRESH sunlight streaming in through the blinds. Cambria looked up from the mug of coffee she cupped in her hands. Her lids drooped despite the caffeine. I sat up and twisted back and forth, trying to loosen the kinks in my back for having slept curled in a chair.

Cord poked her head in. "Fee's awake. She wants to see you. Both of you." She spun and left before I could respond.

"What time is it?" I asked.

"Almost noon," Cambria said.

"I was asleep that long? We only have—"

"Four hours, give or take," Cambria said, interrupting my mental math. She rose and held her mug out to me. "Here, this will help the numbers make sense."

I took the mug and gulped. "Nothing helps numbers make sense," I said, following her upstairs.

Fee looked … like Fee. She looked rested—more rested than I did —and her eyes were bright and clear.

"Hey girls," she said, waving us into the room while she rubbed a towel over her damp hair.

"Where's Jack?" I asked, taking a seat on an oversized chair dragged in from one of the spare bedrooms.

"I kicked him out at dawn. He was on my nerves." She rolled her eyes. "It was a dislocation, not a loss of limb."

I hid a smile. It brought a rush of relief and happiness to hear her talk about it like no big deal, like she was completely fine. Then again, Fee always dealt with the medical stuff that way. Jack was the baby.

"Here's the deal," she said, sitting on the edge of the bed, grimacing as she settled herself. "I need to shift so I can finish healing. I'm going for a short run with Jack to check the perimeter. Two birds, one stone, if you will. After I get back, we're having a house meeting."

"To vote," I said, remembering what Vera had told me.

"Right. Everyone needs to be present, so make sure your mom is up. And your friends, Sam and Angela. Wake them too. We need to figure out what to do with them."

"Um, I think Sam is better left out of this," Cambria said.

Fee looked at us questioningly. I filled her in on Sam's reaction to everything, her shock. "Altering her memory is probably the best thing," she said, nodding. "What about Angela?"

I exchanged a look with Cambria. "I'll talk to her," I said.

We rose to leave but Fee stopped me. "I called you girls in here for a specific reason," she said. "You know this thing is going to be put to a vote. The decision will be final. Everyone gets a say, but majority rules. That's how we work. I know you are used to doing things on your own, however you see fit."

She pursed her lips and looked at Cambria. "I also know about your methods," she said pointedly. "So, I'm telling you now, because I won't say it again, the decision is final." I'd never seen Fee so stern. Her disapproving glower weighed heavier than Jack's. She reminded me of my mom, only scarier, since I wasn't sure exactly what she'd do if I went against her.

"Got it," I said.

"Yes, ma'am," Cambria muttered.

"Good. See you in a bit." She opened the door and ushered us out, like we'd just left the principal's office.

George met us in the hall. "Angela's in my room," he said. "And Wes will be up in a few to, um, deal with Sam."

"Does Angela know that's what he's going to do?" Cambria asked.

I nodded. "Yeah. She knows."

"Is she okay with it?"

"I think so. She knows it's the best thing for Sam," I said.

"Are you going to have him do the same with Angela?"

I shared a look with George. "I don't know," I said.

Wes came up behind George and slapped him on the shoulder. "Party in your room," Wes said.

"Looks like," said George. "You ready?"

"Let's do it." He looked at me. "We've got a vote to get to."

George knocked once and pushed the door open. Angela turned

from the window and our eyes met. Everyone stopped, waiting for her response. I watched her glance once at Sam asleep in bed, then Wes. "Let's take a walk," she said to me.

I nodded and followed her out.

We ended up in the front yard, since there wasn't much empty space in the house with everyone wandering around, gulping coffee, trying to wake up.

"That night you broke up with George and called me for a ride … that was the night you killed that wolf-girl, wasn't it?"

"Yes."

"If I'd come to get you—"

"There would've been another Werewolf, another time," I said. "Don't put this on you."

"I'm not, I just … I want to be here for you. I thought about it all night. I know you could have Wes erase my memory, make it so I don't remember—like he's doing with Sam—but I want to know." She squared her shoulders, pulling herself up taller. "I *can* handle this. I think. I want to try."

I resisted the urge to throw my arms around her just yet. "Why?" I asked softly.

"Because we're family, you and I. And because the truth should always be faced, even if it's hard or ugly."

"It's messy," I warned. "And dangerous. This world isn't safe for humans."

"Neither is the one I left behind."

I stared back at her, still contemplating. "All right," I said slowly. "If it gets to be too much—"

"I'll say so," she promised.

She stepped forward and we threw our arms around each other at the same time.

"You know I'd choose you over George any day," I said.

She laughed. "No way. With that bond thing you guys have? Guys are emotionally dead inside. It must be a piece of cake."

I rolled my eyes. "Such a lie. He's just as bad as a girl."

"What do you feel right now?" she asked.

I paused, searching through the mood in my head, trying to separate what was mine and his. "Worry," I said slowly. "For you and Sam. For me. And confidence. He's more sure of himself as a Werewolf."

"Wow. That's pretty good. And what about you?"

"Worry."

"About the hybrids?"

"About the vote Fee called. That they won't let me go." For a moment, neither of us spoke. My thoughts wandered to the coming evening, when Mr. Lexington would show up looking for me. What would he do if I refused to join him? Who would he go after next?

"You're also happy," she said quietly, startling me.

"Happy? Today?"

"Maybe not today, exactly, but in general, with this new life. I've seen it on your face for weeks. Even before you left for Wood Point. It's how I knew something changed. *You* changed."

Any answer I might've given was interrupted by the door opening. Wes came out. "It's done. She'll sleep for a while yet. I think Edie gave her another dose of that tea. Oh, and the vote's in five. We should head around back."

"Outside?" I asked.

"I think Fee's worried about tempers. Everyone has a very specific opinion." His voice took on an edge, and I slipped my hand into his. He held on firmly but he didn't look any more assured.

"Do I get a vote?" Angela asked as we walked.

"Yes," I said, cutting off whatever Wes had been about to say. "You get a vote."

Cord blocked my path as I joined the circle. "You're on board with this, right?" she asked.

Her directness startled me. "With going? Yes. I'm on board."

"You do know they're all going to vote no."

"Wes won't," I said quietly.

That silenced her. Her brows rose at him and then she glanced at Angela. "What about her? She's not going for the Alzheimer's scenario?"

"No," I said. "She's one of us now."

Cord snorted but didn't argue. "Fine, it's another yes, anyway. Let's hope it's enough." She stalked away and stood next to Fee.

"What's her problem?" Angela asked me.

"Life."

"We'll go around the circle, one at a time," Fee began when we'd all assembled. "Give a yes or a no, that's it. When we're done, the vote stands. No arguments." She looked at me, then Cord. "Also, the vote is for both of you. No one is going alone. It's both or neither, understand?"

"Do we know yet why they want both girls?" my mom asked. Her hands twisted nervously. She looked better, rested. I wondered how long she'd commandeered Vera's bed for, because Vera looked ready to collapse. Dark circles ringed her eyes, her cheeks flushed bright pink.

"No. Olivia, whoever she is, hasn't said."

"I think it would be better if we waited, maybe called CHAS—"

Fee cut my mother off with a sharp look. "We are not calling CHAS. I'm allowing you a vote. That's more than fair, Elizabeth, since you want nothing else to do with us."

"Tara's seventeen. She's a minor. Legally, I can make the decision—"

"And any deaths will be on your hands."

My mother pressed her lips together, her face blotchy red.

Fee looked from face to face. "I'll begin. I vote yes." She looked left. "Jack?"

"I vote no," he said.

"George?" Fee prompted.

"No," he said, looking straight at me.

"What?" I stared back at him. "Why?"

Something in the bond spiked. Determination. Protectiveness.

We hadn't spoken much over the course of the night, not since the others had arrived home. I'd just assumed he'd be on my side. I hadn't even had a chance to mention Vera's idea about the bond providing reassurance to the others.

"No explanations. No interrupting," Fee said. "Edie?"

"No."

"Elizabeth."

My mom untwisted her hands and balled them into fists. "No."

"Vera?"

"No."

I sighed. I'd suspected as much. Her support was "under the table."

"Tara?" Fee prompted.

"You skipped Angela," I said.

Fee's mouth tightened. "Angela's here as your guest. She's an observer."

"This affected her as much as the rest of us," I said. "She should get a vote."

"Humans have no place in this world, Tara, as evidenced last night. She's lucky we've allowed her to remember it."

"Are you threatening me?" Angela asked.

I shushed her and turned back to Fee. Her tone had been clipped and short, a clear message to let it go, to stop arguing. But I couldn't. I'd waited too long to tell Angela the truth. I wasn't giving it up easily.

The skin on my hands and arms stretched and tightened. My neck tingled but I ignored it and stared at Fee across the circle.

"Tara!" Wes hissed.

I knew he was trying to warn me, probably to insist I back down in the power struggle I'd ignited, but I wouldn't. More accurately, I couldn't. The wolf in me had woken and it refused to lose.

"Fee, humans are just as much at risk as we are by all this. Those hybrids represent everything humans need protecting from. If anything, they're more at risk than we are. They're frail, easy targets, and they have no idea they're in danger to begin with. Angela should be able to represent them, to speak for a race that has no advocate."

When I'd finished, I clenched my teeth and waited. Despite the fact we stood outside, the air felt sucked dry. I couldn't catch my breath, my skin wrapped tightly against my organs.

Jack leaned over and whispered something in Fee's ear. She shook her head and he whispered again. Her mouth tightened in response, but she didn't argue.

"You raise a valid point. Our war spills over to humans all too often," Fee said slowly. "In the spirit of democracy, I'll allow it. This time."

"And her memories, the decision to keep them, should belong to her. Not us," I added.

Fee stared at me with a fire in her gaze hotter than anything Jack had ever directed at me. I'd been wrong to think he was the only alpha here. So, so wrong.

"That will be discussed at a later time." Fee looked at Angela. "What is your vote?"

Angela cleared her throat. "I vote yes," she said quietly. My mom glared at her.

"Thank you. Tara?"

"Yes," I said.

"Wes?"

Wes's hand tightened in mine. I knew he was hoping his vote wouldn't matter. At this rate, maybe it wouldn't. "Yes."

Someone gasped. I was pretty sure it was my mother. Jack cleared his throat.

"Cambria?" Fee prompted.

"Yes." She grinned at me.

"Derek?"

He looked at Cord like he wanted to hide. "No," he said quietly. Cord's face turned red. "I think there's another way—" he began.

"No explanations," Fee cut him off. He mumbled something too low for me to hear.

"Cord?"

"Yes," Cord said, drawing out the word like it was an obvious response.

For a second, no one spoke. I knew we were all counting—and re-counting—in our heads.

"It's a tie?" Cord asked, disgusted.

"It's not a tie." Alex stepped clear of the shadow provided by the back door and walked toward the group. "I get a vote too, right?" he asked.

The question was unmistakably a challenge. My heart sank. I had no doubt what his answer would be. No more tie. It was over.

Fee nodded. "You get a vote too," she agreed. "What's your answer?"

He walked straight up to me and stared into my eyes. His lashes flickered, not quite a blink, and he sucked in a deep breath as if bracing himself. "Yes."

I practically heard jaws fall open. Mine included.

"Seriously?" I whispered.

He shrugged. "No explanations, remember." Then he was strolling back to the cover of the shadows, and Fee was talking again, and Wes was tugging on my hand.

Fee quieted the group and began dictating instruction on how the plan would work. Across the circle, Cord folded her arms and smiled smugly. Our eyes met, and I knew what she was thinking. Once we got out there, no amount of instruction from Fee would change her course. I knew, because I had the same thought, the same mission. Find this Olivia bitch and kill her.

As soon as Fee's final monologue—full of words like "stay together" and "we'll be close by" and "don't take risks"—ended, I went in search of Alex.

He'd slipped away halfway through the strategic discussion, right after the part where I'd pointed out my bond with George and how it could be a real advantage with what we were doing. I was fairly certain he'd gone back inside, but when I looked, he wasn't there. I went room to room, quietly at first, then calling his name. By the time I circled back to the kitchen, Cambria and George became curious enough to get involved.

"Where could he have gone?" I asked.

"Probably getting some air," Cambria said. "It is a little thick with Werewolves around here."

"We're not exactly his favorite," George agreed. It wasn't lost on me that he'd just officially put himself into the Werewolf category for the first time, but I was too distracted to give it attention.

"He wouldn't just leave," I argued.

"Is he patrolling?" Cambria asked. "Derek and Jack are out now. Maybe they asked for his help."

"Is who patrolling?" Wes asked, coming up behind me and sliding an arm around my waist. He pressed a kiss to my cheek. I barely felt it.

"Alex. I can't find him. I need to talk to him before …" I couldn't decide how to finish it so I let it hang.

Grandma appeared in the doorway. "Tara, sweetie, a word, please." Her tone was a direct contradiction to her words—and warned me to tread carefully.

"What's up?" I asked, breaking away from the group and following her out the front door.

She waved an arm at the front yard. "You tell me."

"Um …" I tried to see what she saw. "Dead grass?"

"My Hummer. It isn't here. You want to explain that to me?"

A sick feeling settled in my gut as I looked at the empty spot where it had been parked since last night. "Alex."

"What about him?"

"He's gone."

"Uh-huh, and you expect me to believe you have no idea where he's gone."

"Me?" I looked up at her. "What about you? I thought the two of you were tight. A spy team."

"Stealing a car is not the sort of thing a teammate does." She pressed her lips together, centering all of her anger on me. It felt like a physical wall of pressure building between us. I realized for the first time just exactly how scary Edie Godfrey could be when she tried.

I took a step back. "I don't know where he is, Grandma, I swear."

"Uh-huh. Doesn't mean it's not entirely wrapped up in what you're about to do." She whirled so abruptly, I scrambled back to keep clear. She stomped inside and slammed the door behind her.

I stayed where I was, deciding it was safer this way. The others filed out a minute later. Cambria looked shaken. Even with the door closed, I could hear Grandma's muffled yelling.

"She's pissed," George said.

"I told you she's scary when she's mad," Cambria said.

"Alex stole her car?" Wes looked at the empty space in the front yard. He shook his head, and I caught the hint of a smile before he adjusted his expression and met my eyes. "He's in deep shit."

"And then some," George agreed.

"Why'd he have to take the Hummer?" Cambria asked. "Does he have a death wish?"

"Because he's an ass," I said. Anger swirled, building into something more. I couldn't believe he'd just left like this, no explanation, nothing. My hands curled at my sides and still the anger churned. Something else lay under it, something I couldn't pinpoint yet.

"I'm sure it was an emergency," George said. He was watching me warily. I knew he could feel my anger. I didn't care.

"This, right here, today, this is an emergency," I said. "What could possibly come before this?"

No one had an answer for that.

The front door opened. I braced myself for Grandma, but Angela stepped out. "Tara, Sam's awake," she said. "She's pretty confused. What do I tell her?"

"I'll go," Wes said. "But someone should take her home. You don't want her remembering this place."

"I'll get my mom," I said. "Sam knows her well enough, it won't bring up anything she should forget."

"It's almost four," Cambria said. "Are you sure you want to ask her to go now?"

"She's gotta be good for something." The words came out clipped and harsh. No one answered. They parted to let me pass.

I found my mom and she agreed to drive Sam and Angela home. Fee offered to go with. I suspected she wanted to be sure Sam's memory loss was complete.

Wes instructed Angela on the story she would feed Sam. A party had gone late. Sam had a few too many and we'd all crashed at my house. My mom had offered to drive them home.

When they were ready, Angela hugged me. "Thank you for fighting for me."

"You're welcome."

"Call me as soon as you can."

"I will."

"In the meantime," she said, looking at George, "can you call with updates? So I know you're all okay?"

"Definitely," he agreed, pulling her in for a hug and holding the passenger door open for her.

"Good luck with Sam," I said.

My mom hugged me and patted my hair. "Be careful," she said in my ear. "Listen to Cord, she's experienced with this sort of thing." I bit my tongue so hard it brought tears to my eyes. There was no use in arguing. Not now.

I stood there waving to Angela until the car disappeared. Wes came up behind me and slid his arms around me. The movement seemed careful, measured.

"He's coming back, Tara." His words were casual, almost off-hand. Anyone else listening would've missed the fact that what he'd said mattered.

"I don't care," I said.

"Yes, you do, or you wouldn't be angry."

"I'm not angry."

"Liar. You're hurt. He's coming back, Tara."

"How do you know?"

"Because I would."

CHAPTER TWENTY-SIX

My mom called at four on the dot to say Sam and Angela were safe. Sam's parents were informed she'd caught a bug while staying the night at my house and should stay in bed. They'd loved Fee—who wouldn't, really?—and even taken some of her tea to use on Sam through the night so she'd be better rested tomorrow. Angela would stay with her to talk her through the blank spots when she woke.

During the phone conversation, the tingling on the back of my neck began. "Mom, I gotta go," I said.

"They're there, aren't they?" she asked.

"I think so."

"Oh, dear." I visualized her wringing her hands. "Have Cambria or someone call me as soon as it's done, okay? Do what Cord tells you. And Tara? I love you."

I shoved from my mind the fact that she in no way believed me capable of this on my own and focused solely on her last three words. "I love you too, Mom," I said and hung up.

I rubbed my neck and stared into the woods. Slowly, two forms appeared. Human, walking side by side.

"Right on time," Wes said from beside me.

"It's the politician in him. He can't help himself," Cord said in disgust.

The three of us stood shoulder to shoulder, halfway between the house and the tree-line. Wes chose to remain human—to appear less threatening, he'd said—and currently had my hand in a death grip. Jack and the others were concealed in various places around the perimeter.

"I see you've decided to come willingly," Mr. Lexington said, his eyes flickering to the small bag on the ground at my feet.

"I've come to make a deal," I said.

"I'm not sure you're in a position—"

"Cord and I will come. No one will harm my friends or family. Ever."

"I can agree to those terms," he said.

"Ever, do you understand? No matter what happens at this little meeting of yours, you can't go after my friends."

"Fair enough." His mouth twitched and his eyes took on a decidedly more yellow hue. He eyed Cord. "Olivia has special plans for you, I hear."

"Isn't that funny because I've got special plans for her too," she said.

His eyes sharpened. Mrs. Lexington shifted nervously.

"They aren't alone," I said under my breath.

"I know," Wes said.

"Whenever you're ready," Mr. Lexington said.

I'd barely reached for my bag when Wes grabbed me and yanked me against him. His arms wrapped around me, squeezing fiercely. "Be careful. You promised."

All I could do was nod. If I spoke even one word the tears would fall. I'd been so wrapped up in the going that I hadn't even prepared for the goodbye.

"Come on," Cord said, pulling my sleeve until Wes and I untangled.

"I won't be far," he said, keeping his voice low. I could see his body shimmering at the edges, on the brink of shifting. For once, I understood the sense of safety it would bring. I felt vulnerable, exposed, with all of my emotions on display this way.

"Just don't rush in too soon. We need to find Olivia first," I said.

"You're first. Olivia's second."

I sighed and let him kiss me. Then Cord pulled on me again, and shoved my bag at me. I didn't glance back as I followed her into the trees. It wouldn't have done any good. I'd already said goodbye to the others, and the only one I hadn't was long gone.

WE WALKED FOR TWO HOURS BEFORE I RELAXED AGAINST THE FEELING of hybrids nearby. They must've increased their following distance because the itching against the nape of my neck faded, and I could finally think straight without worrying every step would land in a paw instead of a foot.

"Are we really going to hike the entire way there?" Cord asked.

She couldn't care less whether we hiked or swam, she just wanted action. And maybe a clue as to where we were headed.

"We're hiking until we're not," Mr. Lexington said.

"Spoken like a true bureaucrat," she said.

We finally stopped as night fell, and Mr. Lexington handed us each a bottle of water. I uncapped mine without hesitation. It was beyond stupid that I hadn't thought to pack water among the few clothes and a hairbrush I'd thrown in my bag, so now that it was in front of me, I didn't hold back.

Cord sniffed hers, eying Mr. Lexington warily.

"You're not thirsty?" he asked. Beside him, his wife gulped her bottle in loud swallows.

"I don't trust you," Cord said.

"You think I put something in it?" he asked. "After you came willingly? We had a deal. I'll honor it."

"Even when you were human, you were rabid. You didn't give a shit about honor then, so why do you now?"

He blinked, obviously taken off guard by her vehemence. Temper flashed and his eyes glowed. "You know nothing about me."

"I know your daughter. Which is more than I can say for you," Cord shot back. "She knows you're alive."

For a moment, his expression softened and he looked compassionate, human. "She's the best of what's left of this family now. I've done what I had to, in order to protect her."

Cord shook her head. "You haven't seen your daughter lately. She doesn't need protecting. She's the one others need protecting from."

The softness faded and his jaw hardened.

She says it's okay to kill you, by the way." Cord's eyes danced as she tipped her water bottle up and gulped the contents.

Cord made it halfway through her drink when it hit me. Sharp pain needled the inside of my ribs, ratcheting from mild to stabbing in a matter of seconds. My eyes widened. I lifted a hand, a silent signal to Cord, but it was too late. My stomach lurched and I retched up what little I'd eaten.

"Finally," Mr. Lexington said. There was a hint of impatience in his voice, nothing more.

I took a step but it landed me on the ground. I struggled to get up past my knees.

Cord finally noticed and lowered her bottle. "What is it?" she demanded. She stalked Mr. Lexington, every inch the predator. "What the hell did you do?" she hissed.

He glared at her. "What was necessary."

I couldn't move. My muscles twitched but it was more spontaneous than deliberate. I opened my mouth to ask what he'd done, and why, but no sound came. My jaw barely moved.

"Olivia wants to kill us, then," Cord said. Fire shone in her eyes. I wondered why she hadn't leaped at Mr. Lexington yet. Then I saw the twitch in her knees, the set of her jaw, and I knew the paralyzing pain had begun.

"The outcome is not my concern, although according to her, a fair amount of retribution is in order," he said.

“Retribution for what?” Cord demanded. Her legs were shaking now. I was surprised she was still on her feet.

“Death, at your hands, the way I heard it.”

“Did I kill someone she cared about?” Cord’s breathing hitched on the last word. She sank to her knees. The fire in her eyes was dying, replaced by agony. My eyelids drooped heavily.

“Indeed. I believe you knew her son.” Mr. Lexington’s voice sounded far away.

“Who is … her son?” Cord managed.

“Miles DeLuca.”

Then it all went black.

CHAPTER TWENTY-SEVEN

Acid coated the inside of my mouth. Acid and cotton. Dirt rubbed against my hands and legs, and I forced my eyes open while my brain screamed resistance. I had no idea how long I'd been out. My stomach felt hollow and crampy. I twisted around, taking in the small space, the closeness of the walls. They were made of wood—pine if my sense of smell was working right—and nailed together in a hurry. Splinters stuck out every few inches where the nail heads had been beaten too far into the grain. Whoever built my makeshift cage had no clue what they were doing.

The access door was on the box's roof and looked as if it was made a little more securely than the walls, since it was steel and iron locked into place by bright, black hinges.

"Cord?" I whispered, trying to see past my cage. "Can you hear me?"

I waited but no answer came. I'd assumed and hoped, really, that she'd woken nearby in a box similar to mine. Somewhere within talking distance. Maybe she was still knocked out. I didn't want to think about the alternative.

I listened for any sound that might tell me where we'd been taken. Birds chirped but they weren't close. Leaves rustled in a breeze. The air carried on the wind might've been fresh or clear but it didn't penetrate my wooden box. Every inhale left a musty taste in my mouth and underneath it, something else I couldn't identify but made me think of rotting fruit.

Movement between the slats caught my eye and I slouched down to see who—or what—it was. The itchiness on my neck was muted. Maybe I'd grown numb to it, or maybe the hybrids were keeping their distance. Either way, I didn't feel ready to crawl out of my skin yet, which was good since I wasn't sure this box would be big enough if I suddenly wasn't human anymore.

Something moved outside my box.

A human hand flashed by, smooth and tanned, then another, also human and thick with muscle. They spoke in low voices, one male and one female. At the sound of the female's voice, Mr. Lexington's last words flashed through my mind. *I believe you knew her son. Miles DeLuca.*

The hollow cramping in my stomach became a heavy brick of dread. I had a moment to wonder what sort of reading George would get from me after so many hours of numbness, and then someone yanked my cage door open from above. A stubbly face with dark eyes peered down at me before moving aside for another. The woman's features were so similar to Miles's it made my breath hitch.

"Get up," she said.

I pushed to my feet. My movements were awkward, my muscles stiff. None of that compared to the smell or the roiling in my stomach as soon as I stood. I crawled upward through the opening onto the box's roof.

I wrinkled my nose and held my arm up to my face, trying in vain to block the stench. If my stomach had held anything, it would've come up as I dry-heaved over the side. Bodies littered the dirt below. Emaciated, shriveled, some already decaying though their chests still rose and fell with labored breaths.

Beyond them were trees as far as the eye could see, the brown of wide trunks interspersed with hues of green. Their leaves extended upward into a thick canopy, blocking out most of the sunlight, shaking in a whispering breeze. The wind wasn't strong enough to carry away the acrid odor leaking from the bodies.

"They smell dead," I said.

"The dead don't smell nearly as bad as those still living."

I turned to her, clutching my stomach. "You're Olivia, Miles's mother."

"And you're Tara, the girl whose rejection got him killed."

"His own violence and insanity got him killed."

Her eyes flashed with rage, wild and unpredictable. She stepped in front of me and leaned toward my face. I scooted back as far as I dared without losing my balance. No railing prevented me from jumping, but the ground was so littered with bodies, I knew I wouldn't be able to avoid them, and the thought of touching them horrified me.

"My son was a visionary, like his father. You are a weak little girl, a mindless puppet. My son's only mistake was compassion. You won't find that here."

Miles had compassion? I didn't want to think what it said about her personality if she thought so. I kept my mouth shut until she retreated enough that I could move my feet away from the edge.

"Let's go. We're wasting daylight, and the smell is giving me a headache." She went to the far edge of the box and began climbing down the ladder mounted there. The man who'd opened my cage door motioned for me to follow.

I hesitated. The reason for coming had been to meet with Olivia, to find out who she was and what she wanted, and to live up to my end of the deal so my friends would be safe. But seeing all of these bodies wasting away, on the brink of death—suddenly getting out of here seemed like a great idea. Except I had no idea where Cord was.

"Chris! Get her down here now!" Olivia screamed.

The man with the burly arms took a step toward me. I put my hands up in surrender and stepped onto the ladder. He hovered over me, watching without a word. This close, I could see his dark eyes were glassy and unfocused. A thin sheen of sweat coated his face and neck. His cheeks held a flush that looked like fever.

When I reached the ground, Olivia began walking without a word.

She wove in and out of trees on a narrow path that was littered with overgrown brush and downed branches. Within seconds, we'd left the scene of bodies behind us and woods closed in. Was I being executed already? Had she already done the same to Cord? The fact that I hadn't seen a sign of her yet made me very nervous.

"Where is Cord?" I asked, picking my way along the trail to keep pace. Chris followed behind. I could hear him breathing.

"You mean my son's murderer? She's none of your concern."

My stomach leaped into my throat. I stopped walking. "What did you do to her?"

"Nothing … yet. Cooperate and keep it that way."

"And Mr. and Mrs. Lexington? Where are they?"

"On vacation," she said. Her words dripped with sarcasm and I wasn't sure if I wanted to know exactly what she meant by that.

Before I could ask, she stopped at a door that I hadn't even noticed, it was so covered in branches and vines, and turned a key in the massive lock. It swung inward and Olivia disappeared inside. I followed slowly.

Only every third bulb worked. All I could see were dirtied walls as we made our way down a narrow hallway. The same smell from the woods lingered here as well—sickly sweet made stale by the confines of the space. Alcohol and disinfectant mixed with it, cutting through the worst of the stench. My chest tightened from the combination of the fumes.

The hallway ended and opened into a larger space. Gurneys, reminiscent of an '80s horror flick with their yellowing sheets and rusted joints, lined the walls. All of them held bodies in the same condition as those I'd seen in the woods. Faces flushed with fever, skin hanging loose around their bones like victims of famine or plague. Some of their eyes flickered to me but none reacted. Here and there, I could hear wheezing, bodies straining to breathe. Not many were conscious. My eyes watered, partly from the smell, partly from the horror.

"What's wrong with them?" I asked.

If the sight or smell of the room affected Olivia, she didn't show it.

She went to a glass-fronted cabinet and rifled through, filling her arms with various medical supplies before she answered.

"They are dying." She said the words so simply, so matter-of-factly, it gave me chills. "Here, hold this." She shoved a handful of empty vials into my hands and readjusted the supplies she held. "Come here."

"Dying from what?" I asked, following her to a small alcove between a wall and a cabinet.

"Sit."

I sat in the scuffed chair she motioned to, barely paying attention to the contents in her hands as she spread them out on the small table in front of her. Her lips moved, but no sound came. I looked over her shoulder at Chris.

He stood like a sentry a few feet away. His eyes darted quickly from spot to spot. I suspected it was more from disease than alertness. The sweat on his face and redness in his cheeks had not diminished since our walk. If anything, he looked worse. He caught me watching him and I noticed for the first time the faded yellow ring around his irises. As he stared back at me, his pupils dilated and the yellow rim glowed. Then he blinked and they returned to normal.

I looked at Olivia again. "What are they dying from?" I repeated.

When she continued to ignore me, I grabbed her arm. She snatched it away and glared at me, her lips pulled back from her teeth like an animal. "Do not touch me," she hissed.

"Answer my question. Why are they dying?"

She regarded me with disgust. "From the change. Now, give me your arm."

"What?" All I could hear was the echoing of her words.

The change.

They were dying from the change. A shadow of the powerful, monstrous hybrids I'd seen in the cave with Miles, a sicklier version of the zombie-like creatures I'd faced in the forest that night with Wes. Human-shaped. Emaciated. Dying.

They looked like … people.

Like a bad infomercial advertising famine-ravaged villages and war-torn countries, looking for "pennies a day to feed an orphan." No image I'd ever seen on TV could've prepared me for this.

"Give me your arm," she said again.

It wasn't until she'd grabbed my wrist and held it still that I noticed the butterfly needle in her hand.

"What are you doing?" I jerked back, holding my arm protectively against my chest.

"It's not what I'm doing. It's what you're going to do. Now give me your arm."

"No. Not until you tell me what this is."

Her eyes flashed with the rage I'd seen earlier. It boiled behind the controlled mask for a few moments before she gained control. "Chris!" He jumped and took a step forward. "Bring out the girl. The other one," she added.

He left without a word, back the way we'd come. I heard a door open along the hallway, then feet scuffling and the sound of something being dragged.

A second later, Chris reappeared, struggling as he dragged a barely conscious Cord behind him. Veins stood out on his neck, deep blue and purple, pronounced against the pallor of his skin.

It was nothing compared to Cord. Her face was a canvas of bloody bruises and welts. One eye had swelled shut, and I could see a trail of blood leaking from the inside of her mouth—her lip?—down her chin. Her arms were dirty and red. I couldn't see her hands where they'd tied them behind her back, but I suspected they would look the same as her arms. Her feet were bare, her ankles bound by plastic cording. She blinked her good eye at me, but it was slow, exaggerated.

I gasped and jumped up to go to her. Olivia shoved me back, the motion so unexpected that I fell back against the chair with a thump.

"What did you do to her?" I demanded.

Olivia didn't answer.

I pushed off again, this time ready to knock Olivia aside to get to Cord. I could take Chris without difficulty. I probably only needed to shove him one good time and he'd topple. I wasn't entirely sure he'd even attempt to stop me. I hadn't seen anyone else that wasn't half-dead since they'd let me out. Escape wouldn't be too difficult. Olivia was the healthiest person here—and she was half my weight.

I made it three steps before the cold sound of a gun cocking stopped me midstride.

I looked at Olivia. Her eyes were crystal clear, calculated, and sure. The gun she held was pointed at Cord. My heart slammed against my chest.

"Get back in the chair," she said quietly.

I hesitated. Surely, George was getting my utter hysteria, my mind-numbing fear. Were they close enough for it to matter? Had they even seen where I'd been taken or had Mr. Lexington lost them somehow? I had no idea if I was alone. For Cord's sake, I had to assume I was.

"Get back in the fucking chair!"

I slid into my seat and Olivia threw the rubber tourniquet at me. "Put this on your arm," she said.

I tied the tourniquet around my bicep and held out my arm, exposing the vein in the crook of my elbow. I waited for Olivia to come forward with the needle. If she lowered her eyes long enough to insert it, maybe I'd have a chance at the gun. Instead, she picked up the needle and threw it over to me.

"Uncap and insert this. When it's in, attach the vial," she said.

"You want me to stick myself?" I asked. "I don't know how."

"You have three minutes to figure it out or I shoot her."

I looked at Cord. She blinked at me slowly, her head bobbing with the effort. I fumbled with the needle, positioning it over what I hoped was the right spot. I'd never done this before. I'd never even watched. Usually, I turned away anytime I had to give blood or get an injection. Somehow, it made the prick less uncomfortable. I couldn't afford to do that now. And I couldn't afford to mess up.

I sucked in a breath, held it, and shoved the needle into my flesh. The pinch was sharp but brief. When I stopped shoving, the pain faded. I held the needle as still as possible and attached the vial to the end of the tubing. Nothing happened.

"It's not working," I said.

"Then it's misplaced. Find the vein. One minute."

I jiggled the needle, wincing at the sting it caused.

"Thirty seconds."

I pulled it out, inserted it again. Blood began to flow into the vial. "I got it."

"Good. When you're done with that one, fill those." She nodded at the rest of the vials I'd dumped onto the table when I'd sat down. My eyed widened.

"There's like fifteen vials there," I said.

"I know."

"What do you need all of this for?" I asked.

The way she looked at me, with her head cocked slightly to the side confirmed what I'd suspected from the moment I'd realized the reason for illness in this place.

"Your blood, as much as it offends me, is the only thing that will make them whole. And I need them whole."

A chill ran down my arms and settled inside my soul. "You're going to inject them with my blood?"

I tried to imagine what it would be like, being connected to that many minds. Feeling the same paranoia and panic over the safety of a hundred instead of one.

I shuddered.

"No. You are," she answered. "I'm going to try not to shoot your friend."

The vials filled quickly. Too quickly. By the time I was finished, I felt lightheaded. Olivia's arm never wavered, never lowered. The gun remained trained on Cord. Halfway through, Chris seemed to lose what little strength he'd been running on and let go of Cord. She folded onto the floor like an accordion. He didn't bother to pick her up and Olivia didn't ask him to. When I'd capped the last vial, I still hadn't thought of a way out. At least not one that included both me and Cord escaping alive.

I tried controlling my emotions enough to send George something specific, something that might help him know to move in, but I couldn't get a handle on my thoughts. One minute adrenaline pumped into me hard enough to rattle my heart against my chest and the next, fear threatened to choke me. Or worse—make me cry. I couldn't be sure he felt any of it, because I felt nothing from him. Maybe he was too far away. Maybe my own frantic emotions blanketed anything I could've gotten from him. I had no idea. I couldn't think straight.

My entire focus was on the vials in front of me and the level of connection it represented once my blood was injected into so many sick bodies. I'd only barely gotten a handle on my connection with George. The knowledge I could lose him one day, even years down the road from old age, scared me to the point of hyperventilation.

And if my mind was suddenly joined with a hundred others—what then? How would I separate my own thoughts from theirs? Would I still be me?

My hands shook.

"Now what?" I asked when I'd removed the needle from my arm and bandaged the area. It ached under the pressure of my fingers and I knew I'd have bruises later.

"Syringe—they're in the cabinet." She pointed with the gun and I stood to retrieve them. My knees buckled and I had to fall back against my chair to keep from collapsing.

"What's wrong with you?" she demanded.

"I … it was a lot of blood and I haven't eaten."

She rolled her eyes. "There are crackers in the next cabinet."

I kept my movements slow and steady. I found the box of syringes and then the crackers. I stared at the mostly empty shelf in disgust. The few wrappers I found lay open; the food was covered in ants.

"Not hungry after all?" I could hear the smirk in Olivia's voice. I turned to face her, doing my best to ignore the sight of the gun.

"No."

"Good. Get to work. You can start in here and work your way back outside."

While I gathered my supplies, Cord moaned from her place on the floor. Olivia strode over, keeping the gun trained on Cord's head, and planted a kick in her ribs. It caused a sickening *thud* where her foot landed against bone. Cord grunted, slumped, and went still.

"Stop!" I screamed. A sob rose on the single word. I choked it back.

"I suggest you get to work," Olivia said, gesturing to the bodies in the room. None of them made a sound the entire time we'd been here.

I walked to the first one: a man with thinning, gray hair matted to his head. His ribs stuck out against his skin. His chest retracted violently in his attempt to breathe. I reached out a hand toward him, then pulled it back. This close, the smell was unbearable. Sweat, urine, death.

"I don't know how to do this," I said.

"Then they will die. And so will she." She kicked Cord again. It was more of a shove, a haphazard poke at something you had no regard for and made me want to strangle Olivia so badly, my hands itched.

Instead, I reached into the box of syringes and unwrapped one. Its spindly metal tip shone dull against the filtered sunlight from the small window overhead. I fumbled with the vial of blood until the needle's tip poked through the rubber stopper and then drew the plunger back to suck crimson liquid into the barrel.

I set the vial aside and inspected the needle, channeling every episode of *ER* I'd ever caught with my mom. I tapped the side of the barrel with my fingers like I'd seen them do on TV and braced myself.

The entire time I worked, I eyed the old man, trying to keep my distance. I recoiled at the knowledge I'd have to touch him for this next part, have to touch all of them before I was done. It was a mixture of disgust and compassion that had me gingerly taking his arm and turning it sideways, searching for a usable vein.

I didn't allow myself time to change my mind or second-guess before I shoved the needle through his flesh. It felt thin and spongy under my fingers. I tightened my grip, depressed the plunger, and yanked it free. I took a full step back and wiped my brow with the back of my hand.

One down. Dozens to go.

"I don't have all year," Olivia snapped.

I stared down at the old man. His breathing remained the same. He didn't move or open his eyes. "Why isn't it working?" I asked.

"It takes time. Keep moving."

I did what she asked and made seven more injections, working halfway around the room before the dizziness washed over me again. I steadied myself on the first thing my hand grasped—and recoiled as my fingers closed around another hand.

This one belonged to a woman, her yellowing eyes open and watchful. She didn't try to speak but her glassy gaze held mine the entire time I worked on her. She didn't flinch when the needle penetrated, only stared back at me with a look of curiosity. When I pulled the syringe free, she sighed. Then Olivia snapped at me and I moved on.

I kept Olivia and Cord in my peripheral vision. The reality of the gun never left my awareness, and as time went on, I had no choice but to accept I was alone. The others hadn't come—weren't coming. Random, errant thoughts flitted through my mind as I injected one person after another. Thoughts of Cambria and what she would've told my mom when they'd lost our trail. Of Wes and Derek and George and how the bond was evidently no help in locating me at this moment. Of Alex, and why he'd voted to let me come, only to disappear. Of these hybrids, caught halfway between death and domination.

What would Olivia do to them if they survived? Was my blood even enough to bring them back, or were they too far gone?

By the time I finished, my arm ached, my stomach rumbled, and my lids drooped with exhaustion. I wasn't sure how I'd make it through the bodies that waited for me in the woods.

"I'm done," I said.

"One more." She pointed at Chris.

He'd slumped over in the chair I'd sat in earlier, his head propped on his hand. He sat up as I approached and held out his arm.

"I need you to stay still," I said, preparing the syringe and setting the vial aside. I approached slowly, wary of the way his eyes tracked my movements. He wasn't nearly as incapacitated as the others. I positioned the needle over his arm and held it there. His arm jerked underneath my hand. I tightened my grip and he snarled.

"Stay still," I repeated.

"I'm trying," he said. It was the first time he'd spoken. The raw desperation in his voice startled me. I'd expected menace, suppressed violence, but not this.

"Just breathe, all right?"

He nodded at me. I could see him fighting for control of his own body under my touch, and I knew he was closer to shifting than the rest of them. His body must've accepted the change a little better. Still, he looked … uncontrolled. More like the hybrids I'd fought at Wood Point. Something in his eyes made me think of the wolf Alex killed when I'd gone to meet Miles that first time. That pack had been hell-bent on killing me, and the order definitely hadn't come from Miles.

"Why are you looking at me like that?" he asked.

"No reason. Here we go." I stuck him before he could pull away, depressed the plunger, and slid the needle free. The whole thing took less than five seconds. He growled but managed to hold his arm in place.

"That hurts," he said, the desperation turning fierce. The muscles in his arm flexed and I took a reflexive step back. I tossed the syringe aside and put the vial back in my box of supplies.

"It's over," I said. Our eyes met and held.

"Almost," he murmured.

I shivered and turned away. Olivia wandered along the gurneys, examining patients. The gun hung limp at her side.

I made it halfway across the room before she noticed me and raised the barrel at my head.

"Don't be stupid," she said.

"I can't help myself," I said.

"Get those vials loaded up. We're taking a walk." She walked back to Cord and began yanking her up. "Chris, help me with her."

Chris stood, looking wobbly and weak, and made his way over to Olivia. She was struggling to lift Cord and still keep hold of the gun. "Carry her," Olivia said.

"Olivia …"

"Carry her, I said."

Chris grabbed Cord and hefted, but he didn't get far before his arms gave out and Cord slid to the ground again.

"Fine, drag her back to her room. I'll deal with her later," Olivia snapped.

With a grunt of relief, he grabbed Cord's ankles and dragged her out. Olivia gestured for me to follow. I felt a stab of regret at leaving Cord like this, but I couldn't do anything else.

"Move," Olivia ordered when Chris had locked the door.

My back tingled where I knew Olivia had readjusted the gun's aim.

CHAPTER TWENTY-EIGHT

Once during our trek through the woods, my pace slowed enough that Olivia got impatient and jammed the gun against my back, prodding me forward. After that, I kept pace with Chris, careful not to let Olivia get too close; I'd take an infected Werewolf over a loaded gun any day. Other than the sound of a faraway bird call, nothing moved or disrupted the stillness around us. I wondered where we were, if we were even in Virginia anymore, but I didn't bother to ask. I knew it would do little good. Olivia wasn't the talkative type, not like Miles had been.

Once we reached the clearing, Olivia stopped and hung back near the wooden cage I'd woken in. Her eyes tracked my movements, as did the barrel of the gun. I could feel her watching me even when my back was turned. She wore her hate and rage under a thin mask of calm. Everything she said, every movement she made, felt calculated, as if she were constantly reining herself in. What would happen to me, to Cord, when my injections were finished? When she no longer needed to hold back? The thought made it hard to keep from shaking as I inserted another needle into another shriveled vein.

None of the people here were conscious. A few moaned when I touched them, no matter how gentle I tried to be, but they did it from behind a wall of oblivion. I'd made it to the outer edges of the group, the furthest from Olivia I'd been since waking, and knelt beside the next body—a man with sagging skin that hung off him in sickening ripples. His jawline was pronounced, his cheeks sunken and dotted with splotchy stubble. I didn't pay much attention. Like the others, his eyes were closed, his breathing labored. I held the syringe to the vial, tipped it up, and slowly pulled back the stopper, letting it fill with red.

Without warning, the man's hand shot out and locked around my wrist. I froze and met his now-open eyes. They were a dull gray, absent of hope.

"It's all right. I'm here to help," I said. He didn't respond or let me go. "This," I said, holding up the syringe and the vial, "this will help you. It will make you better."

"I …refuse to be …a monster." His body heaved with the last word. His chest shook on a silent cough and he gasped for air. I tried to think of something to do but there was nothing, no way to help. All I could do was assure him.

"With this," I said, "you can be yourself."

His eyes flickered to the scene behind me. "Not … with her."

"What do you mean?" I asked. His body shook again, struggling to talk and breathe at the same time. "She controls you somehow, doesn't she? When you're a wolf?" He nodded.

I thought of Astor's theory, that what I'd done with George could work on all of them. And I remembered Vera's words, about George and him being my pack. I looked down at the man and took his hand off my wrist, squeezed it. "After this, you won't be with her," I said. "You'll be with me."

After that, he didn't object to my sticking him, nor did he ask me to elaborate, which was good, since I had absolutely no idea how to explain. Astor said it could work on them all, but was it really as simple as sharing my blood? It had been with George. But George had been healthy, and getting healthier the closer he got to the change. These people had only gotten sicker and sicker. Was a small shot of blood in the arm enough to break whatever hold Olivia had on them? Was I really willing to bind them all to me?

One thing was clear: Olivia didn't know. If she did, no way would she be letting me inject all of these people with my blood. So as far as she knew, it was simply a cure-all for rejecting the change. If I could find a way to use that, maybe—

Urgency, like a flood of adrenaline, washed over me so fast and so hard, I almost dropped the syringe. I managed to finish pumping blood into the man's arm and then threw my used supplies into the box. I glanced back. Olivia was still watching me. She looked bored, but impatient.

The urgency came again.

I paced my movements, desperate not to give it away, and walked to the next body. I crouched and began methodically preparing for the next injection. I kept my head down and scanned the woods out of the corner of my eye. Nothing. No movement, no sound. Even the birds had gone quiet. Still, the urgency in my mind continued to stream. An itchy tingle worked its way down my spine, starting at the back of my neck and spreading.

"George?" I whispered.

No answer. I didn't dare whisper again.

I completed the injection and moved on.

The urgency grew, making me restless. My palms itched and my eyes darted from point to point. I did the next few injections with shaky fingers. At every twitch of a leaf or sway in the breeze, I expected George and the others to come barging out of the woods in rescue. It never happened.

As I circled back around and neared Olivia, the urgency faded. It gave way to a void, an empty feeling that I couldn't push aside. Whether it belonged to me or George, it felt hopeless, final, and I knew one of us had admitted defeat.

When I'd finished the injections, I stood in front of Olivia and handed her back the box. I didn't bother looking at her or the gun. Somewhere along the way, I'd accepted what came next. I didn't even have it in me to summon tears or images of the faces I'd leave behind. I stared at my shoes and waited.

"Let's get going," she snapped. "Chris!"

He snapped awake from where he'd dozed against the wooden slats of my cage. When he saw me standing there, he stood. He looked better than earlier, a little steadier on his feet. She waved at him to lead the way. He glanced at me and my breath caught. His eyes were frighteningly clear and glowed yellow. I fell into step behind him only after Olivia prodded me hard between the shoulders with the point of the gun.

"Why don't you just shoot me and get it over with?" I said dully.

"I have no plans to shoot you," she said. "Unless you give me a reason. Walk faster."

"I saved all your monsters. What else do you want from me?"

"That has yet to be seen. Either way, it was only the first batch."

I stopped walking to look at her. "There's more?"

"Keep walking." She shoved me forward. My feet moved mechanically. Her tone became smug, confident. "I told you, I'm not my son. Nor am I my husband. I do not share their weaknesses. They thought too small. And you. You were a weakness to them, but not to me."

"Miles wanted to take over both the Werewolf and Hunter world, but he thought too small?"

"He thought the only way to do it was with you. That's where he went wrong."

"Because you think you can do it alone?"

"Actually, I don't have to do anything at all except stir the pot. You'll destroy each other in the end with your hatred. When the dust settles, I'll rebuild."

"I didn't hate Miles," I began.

"And yet, he's dead, so it doesn't really matter, does it? Shut up and walk."

I fell silent and kept pace with Chris. He was faster now. It was a struggle to keep up with him. I wasn't sure how much longer I could stay on my feet. We reached the door and Olivia handed Chris the key for the deadbolt. He twisted it in the lock and pushed it open. It swung inward, and I caught a blur of fur and teeth as it whizzed by on its way into the woods. From the dimness of the hallway a wolf appeared and hurtled toward me. Then another and another. I flattened myself against the building to get clear. Eight wolves darted into the trees, their snarls echoing as they spread out among the trees.

"Return." Olivia's voice rang out above it all. The wolves slinked back into view. Their eyes shone with a fevered yellow. Their jowls hung loose and dripped with saliva. The joints in their legs stuck out starkly against their wiry limbs. "You may hunt but return as soon as you've finished. There is work to be done," she said. They blinked and then sprang way.

"Looks like you're the cure, after all," she said to me before shoving me through the door.

CHAPTER TWENTY-NINE

There were seven dead in the clinic when we returned. I wondered if it was because the injections weren't completely successful, or if they'd been dead already when I'd injected them. I hadn't exactly felt for a pulse. Olivia wouldn't have listened, anyway. The rest were in various stages of waking up or moving around. Their attempts were slow and they looked dazed, like suffering from bad hangovers.

Olivia ordered me to dump the box of used syringes into the garbage and then motioned for Chris to move me into what looked like a break room. A faded, once-white chipped-plastic table and two chairs were the only furniture in the space. A mini-fridge sat on a warped green countertop, along with a beat-up microwave, which hummed and whined pathetically in its attempt to heat a bowl of chicken soup.

"Eat," Chris said, dropping me into one of the chairs and setting the bowl in front of me.

I started to lift the spoon to my mouth and stopped again when a water bottle appeared.

I panicked.

The vision of Mr. Lexington towering over me as I lost consciousness took over. I leapt from my chair and swung at Chris without conscious thought but exhaustion slowed me. He ducked aside and landed a punch in my gut. Not hard, but enough to get my attention and let me know he was feeling better. I slumped back into the chair and grumbled at him as he backed away.

Grudgingly, I went back to my soup and water. After closer inspection, I realized the seal hadn't been broken on the bottle. Even so, I sipped slowly, expecting the worst. But it wasn't poisoned. I remained awake.

The food cleared my head, which wasn't entirely a good thing, since I couldn't seem to shut off the panic and desperation that wormed its way in.

Muffled sounds drifted in as I finished. My stomach cramped painfully as it accepted the food. I waited for the dizziness to subside, sure it was due to dehydration and hunger, but it remained. The room didn't spin, exactly, but my vision was fuzzy around the edges. The back of my neck ached.

"Uh-oh," I said under my breath.

Chris looked up, curious, but said nothing. A minute later, Olivia walked in. A half smile twisted her lips. She wiped her hands on a rag. The cloth came away stained red. I couldn't bring myself to ask why. Cord's name echoed in my head.

"They're up." She walked up to Chris, scrutinizing him. "How do you feel?"

"Better, stronger," he said.

"Good." She nodded. Her eyes flickered to me. "Give her a needle and some more vials. I'm going to spend some more quality time with my new friend."

"Don't touch her," I said, jumping from my chair. I wasn't sure if it was the food or the unsettled feeling of my skin, but the anger surging through me was sharp and hot. I couldn't sit quietly any longer. "We had a deal. I give you blood. You leave her alone."

Olivia's head bobbed in an almost imperceptible nod. She stalked toward me, her eyes lit with rage. Chris slid in behind me, grabbing my wrists and twisting my arms painfully behind my back. "You seem to have forgotten who makes the rules," she said. "I told you I wouldn't kill her *yet.*"

The truth of her intentions hit me hard. I'd hoped—maybe because there wasn't any other choice—if I went along, did what she asked, she wouldn't hurt Cord. The look in her eye made it easy to see that had been a lie.

My body went taut. The pain in my arms intensified but it only fed my anger. "I'm not giving you any more blood," I said.

"Then I'll take it."

Chris dragged me toward the door, and I lost it. I kicked out, the first few attempts catching air, but the food energized me and I managed to land a heel in his shin. He grunted and his grip loosened. I wrenched free and tore down the hall. A voice in my mind screamed at me to turn back, that I couldn't leave Cord alone here if I ever wanted to see her again, but I couldn't help her by cooperating any longer.

I made it out the door and to the tree line before I was tackled from behind. Chris's breath blew across the back of my neck and then my body twisted as he flipped me over and pinned me. I blanched at the sight of his face. It was something not quite Werewolf, not quite human. Fur covered every inch of his skin. His eyes glowed hot and yellow, fully hybrid now. I could see the struggle inside him, could feel him shaking. I wriggled but it was no use; his strength was definitely that of a Were.

"Get a hold of yourself," Olivia snapped. I wasn't sure which one of us she referred to.

I couldn't see her over Chris's head but I could smell her. It smelled like the decay of the bodies earlier, sickly sweet and full of death. I wondered how I'd missed that before. Chris flipped me again and began to bind my wrists. I cried out when he wrenched my arm too hard and pain shot into my shoulder. The sharp throb that remained even after he let go made it clear I'd sprained something. He yanked me up, breathing heavily against my back.

"Put her in the box. I need your help with the other one. I'm tired of waiting." Olivia's footsteps faded and the door to the clinic slammed shut. Chris shoved me toward the trail.

"Move," he said. The air around the edges of his body quivered.

"You can't turn, can you?" I said.

"Not yet. It's coming." His voice was strained.

We walked a few steps in silence. I knew this might be my only shot. "My blood saved you."

"You want a medal?"

"You owe me a life."

He didn't answer for a long time. I heard his breathing even out and wondered if he was closer or farther away from his human form—the side of him that allowed compassion, feeling. I searched my thoughts for any sign my blood had connected us in some way, but there was nothing. Only emptiness, like before.

We reached the clearing where my wooden cell stood. He shoved me toward the ladder.

"You could save her," I said.

"You are not my master."

He shoved me through the hole in the roof. I landed on my knee and rolled, trying to absorb the impact. My shoulder twisted at an odd angle from my hands being tied. Pain shot through the arm I was already sure I'd sprained. Black spots danced in front of my eyes. I lay there for a few minutes until the worst of it faded.

I blinked back tears—partly from the pain in my arm and partly from desperation. How had the situation turned so badly? Wes and the others—where were they? I felt nothing from the bond. What did that mean? Had something happened to George?

Every second I sat there felt like an eternity. I tried not to imagine what Olivia was doing to Cord, but it was impossible. I didn't bother trying to hold back the sobs or the tears. They fell against the wood and left watermarks that grew into tiny pools of moisture as more and more fell.

Something moved between the slats and I sucked in a breath, silencing my cries. I caught a glimpse of an arm as someone walked by.

"Hello?" I called.

Then came the sound of feet shuffling, fabric rustling.

"Hello?" I called again louder this time. "Who's there?"

A voice rasped, too low and gravelly for me to hear. Someone coughed. The voice came again. "I'm Curtis. Who are you?"

"Tara. Tara Godfrey." I peered through the crack and saw a pair of eyes ringed in yellow staring back at me. They were wide and alert. My chest tightened.

"What happened?" he asked.

"You were unconscious. I injected you with my blood and it brought you back."

The eyes blinked, processing my words. "Thank you."

His sincerity gave me hope. I sniffled and blinked away the last of my tears. "Is everyone awake?"

"Um ..." The man turned away to survey the clearing and I caught a glimpse of shaggy brown hair that curled at the back of his neck. I held my breath while I waited for him to answer. "Yes. We're all awake." Suddenly, his eyes widened and his features froze in a look of surprise.

"What is it?" I asked, leaning forward.

"I can't stop it ..." he began. His mouth continued to move but the sound was cut off. His form blurred and the popping of bones echoed in the quiet.

Then his body disappeared.

In its place stood a yellow-eyed wolf.

CHAPTER THIRTY

For the first time since my wolf half had woken, I wanted to shift. My skin crawled. My head pounded. My neck and back burned with tingles. Goosebumps slammed into me so hard I convulsed. The clearing was still cluttered with bodies—only they were all Werewolves now. I couldn't see past the first dozen or so, but judging by my body's reaction, I knew many more had survived than I'd expected. Maybe all of them.

I could feel their eyes on me as they paced in front of my cage. A few growled. I could hear a fight breaking out further back. I was glad for the wooden planks that stood between us.

"That's her," one female rasped. "The one we're supposed to bring to the master."

"I can smell her blood," said another.

"I'd like to *taste* her blood." The malice in that one made me shiver.

"Remember what the master said. We can't hurt her."

"We can't *kill* her. We can taste …"

Paws landed lightly on the roof. The iron grated and whined. I held my breath and watched the teeth picking at the latch. The Werewolf snorted when it didn't budge.

"Change back so you have fingers, you idiot," the female said.

A pause and then, "You try to shift back, genius."

"I … can't."

"Exactly."

"Are we stuck like this? Did the master …?"

"Sshh! She's coming. I can feel it."

On cue, footsteps sounded. Human steps. The wolves nearest me let out a whimper and retreated. I watched through the planks as Olivia, then Chris, came into the center of the clearing. Chris was human again and carrying a barely conscious Cord in his arms. At Olivia's direction, he dropped Cord in a heap in the dirt. The wolves growled and pawed at the ground.

"I see you're all up and around," Olivia said. Her voice rang out loudly over the sound of the pack.

I shrank back against the wall as her voice echoed against the pounding in my head. It was as if her single voice had become a thousand others, all competing for room to be heard. I shut my eyes in a vain attempt to block it out.

"When can we hunt?" one of the hybrids called.

"Soon," Olivia said. "First, bear witness. This is the Hunter who killed my son. She has come to apologize, isn't that right, Cordelia?"

Cord said something too low for me to hear. Olivia kicked her and she grunted as the wind left her lungs. I bit my lip against rage and panic. It was easy to see where this was going. Olivia wanted Cord's death public—and slow. I had to do something. But I couldn't get past the rushing in my ears, the buzz in my head.

The door above me creaked open. I had a moment's panic that the two hybrids who'd wanted me for lunch had found a way inside, but then Chris peered down at me. "Get out," he said.

I climbed out at an odd angle, using my head to keep my balance up the steep staircase. Chris waited until I was on the ground and then took my arm and led me forward. I barely felt his hand through the throbbing in my shoulder. Olivia smiled at me, the expression full of malice. "Just in time for the show."

Olivia was relentless. Kick after kick landed in Cord's ribs. I couldn't watch. I couldn't look away. When Cord began screaming, the hybrids howled, their high-pitched voices melting into one. The buzzing in my head reached a crescendo, drowning out the sound in my ears. I squeezed my hands into fists behind my back. My nails dug into my palms, but the numbness from the binds made it hard to feel the pressure. The arm I'd twisted burned from shoulder to wrist.

Beside me, Chris shifted restlessly. "You're hurting," he said in a low voice.

It took me a moment to understand the full implication of his words. I jerked my gaze to his. "How do you know that?"

"I can …" He pressed his lips together, shot a glance at Olivia. "I just do."

He wouldn't meet my eyes, and for a second, the cacophony in my head calmed. I tried to focus on it, separating individual threads. I strained to make out words, voices. They were there, just out of reach. I held my breath. It was too much to hope for.

Slowly, I picked out a single feeling. Like an emotion attached to a vivid memory, the feeling had a taste, a certain flavor, and I knew it was the one I needed. The one that just might save us.

I braced myself for how deeply this would change everything. Then, just like that day at Astor's, I opened my mind and let go.

Chris's eyes widened. He pressed a palm to his forehead. "What's happening?" he whispered.

I couldn't answer him.

Feelings, emotions, some as strong as a thought, poured into me. The wall came down, the buzzing became a roar. My knees gave out. I hadn't stayed fully conscious the first time I'd done this. I wasn't sure how much longer my feet would hold me up with such a crowd inside my head.

It took only seconds for the rest of them to notice. Their eyes shifted from Olivia to me and back, clearly confused. Some of them blinked and shook their heads, pawing at their ears. Was it this loud for them too?

Olivia paused and looked around at her audience, finally noticing their break in concentration. "What the hell is wrong with all of you?" she demanded.

One of them let out a wailing howl. A few others joined it. I welcomed it, since it drowned out the internal noise, but Olivia looked furious. "What are you doing? Silence!" she screamed. A few listened to her, their jaws clamping shut so firmly it looked like Olivia had hit an off switch. The rest continued to wail.

Something heavy pushed against the feelings inside me. They were fighting it. I didn't know how to manage all of the different flavors and feelings, much less push back. Hunger, rage, desperation, pain, heartache, hatred, loathing. The list went on and on.

Olivia marched up to one of the wolves and struck it across the nose. "What is the problem?" she demanded.

It backed up and lowered its head to the ground. "I don't know," it said. "I feel …"

"Feel? You don't feel. You obey." Her eyes cut to Cord, then back. Her voice dropped low and she pointed. "Master says feed."

The yellow eyes dilated. The wolf looked at Cord. Saliva pooled at its jowls.

The hunger inside me became overwhelming. Olivia's eyes gleamed, silently willing the wolf to attack. I swallowed the acrid taste in my throat and concentrated. The wall slid back. The wolf shifted its weight. Our eyes met.

Do. Not. Harm.

I felt the command sink into the wolf's awareness. Its fur stood on end and its form shimmered at the edges. The air crackled with energy. It stared at me.

Olivia followed the wolf's gaze and her eyes landed on me. "You." She covered the distance between us in three strides. Her hands grabbed my face, squeezing and shaking. "What have you done to them?" she demanded.

"I—" Olivia's knuckles struck my cheek and my head jerked sideways.

Something inside the hybrids snapped.

The wall crumbled. Emotions flooded in—and out. The wolf Olivia struck shot forward. Its teeth sunk into her calf and she screamed.

"You did this! What did you do?"

I was too shocked to respond. I hadn't asked for them to attack her, but now that one had led the way, the others followed suit. They stalked toward her. I could feel their hunger.

How would I ever manage all of them?

"Wait," I called, my voice loud and firm. I had to exert authority from the beginning if I was going to make this work.

They hesitated.

"Untie me." I shoved my wrists at Chris and waited, half expecting him to refuse. His fingers brushed my hands as he untied the knots and let the binding fall. I rubbed my wrists gingerly until they tingled with renewed blood flow.

Olivia's face was ashen as she'd bent over to press a hand to the gash in her leg. Blood seeped from beneath her fingers. She watched in silence as I stepped forward to address the hybrids.

My hybrids.

"We aren't going to kill her," I said.

No one argued, but they didn't back away, either.

"Not until I say. Do you hear me?" I asked when no one moved or spoke.

Emotions slid into place. Acquiescence, then certainty, and finally, loyalty. For one moment, the dozens of threads buzzing within me became a single chord.

"We hear you … master."

I nodded like it was the most normal thing in the world to be addressed that way.

"But you're … you're not …" Olivia trailed off.

"A wolf?" I finished for her. She could barely nod. "I'm more of one than your son was, apparently."

"He—he couldn't shift. His father … Leo gave him something to stop it. Stole it from Jeremiah's lab …"

I didn't bother asking her to finish. I retrieved my bindings and handed them to Chris. "Tie her up."

I watched him secure her hands. The other hybrids stood, shifting their weight restlessly. I could still feel their hunger for revenge. I couldn't blame them, but I couldn't allow it, either. If I did, I'd be no better than they were, than Olivia.

"What do you want me to do with her?" Chris asked.

"Put her in the box," I said.

When Olivia was locked up, I went to Cord. She wasn't moving. I couldn't tell if she was breathing until I put my hand over her face and felt the wisp of breath against my skin.

"Cord?"

She didn't respond. I traced the purple circles that covered her arms, blinking back tears. I had no idea where we were, but it was safe to say help wasn't close. I had no idea what to do for her or if it would even matter if I tried. "Cord?" My voice broke.

I sensed someone behind me and turned. Chris stood there, his hands limp at his sides, his expression blank. I didn't feel any particular remorse through the bond, just uncertainty.

"Where are we?" I asked him.

"Warm Springs. It's part of the George Washington National Forest."

"We're still in Virginia?"

"Yes."

"How far to a hospital?"

"An hour's run."

I nodded and swallowed the burn in my throat from the tears. Behind Chris, the hybrids crowded around, watchful, silent. I looked down at Cord again. Blood stained her shirt from underneath. I pulled up her shirt and found cuts across her abdomen from where rocks and twigs had scraped her. Purpling bruises blossomed across her ribs and stomach. Some were knotted and swollen. Some were already black with blood congealing under the skin. The damage was too much.

I couldn't stop the tears. They fell on my cheeks and onto Cord's shirt, splashing wet spots on the fabric. Chris and the hybrids stayed close but no one interrupted. The buzz in my mind dulled in comparison to my grief.

I'd failed.

Cord could die.

Nothing else mattered.

Not the hybrids, or the bond I'd just formed with an entire pack of them, not Olivia, who'd begun ranting and screaming obscenities at me from inside her wooden cage. Her curses were drowned out by my own mental tongue-lashing.

I'd been stupid to come, and Cord would die because of me.

CHAPTER THIRTY-ONE

The yelling and crash of branches came to me in a fog. Tears blurred my vision, making it impossible to understand what was happening until it was too late. The first metal stake buried itself in the heart of a hybrid near the outskirts of the group. Its howl cut off sharply. The sound rocked me to the core. The pain on its heels was worse.

I clutched at my chest and bit back a scream.

Chaos followed.

Bodies—humans wielding shiny weapons—broke into the clearing. Half a dozen at first, then at least three times that surged from the trees. The leaders let loose a battle cry. Their eyes blazed, their expressions a mask of determination and controlled hate.

Hybrids dropped by the handful before the first intruder's face registered. Even then, I wondered if I'd imagined it. No mistake, these were Hunters, but I could swear I'd seen some of them before. I couldn't be certain through the pain—sharp jabs in my chest, twisted pangs in my gut. And my throat burned with invisible flames. I couldn't think, I couldn't move.

A sob escaped. I covered my head with my hands, trying to shield myself against the agony. Nothing stopped it. Like back-to-back tsunamis, the force of it rocked me. I grabbed at my hair, my hands tangling and yanking, searching for something to anchor to—or be swept away into oblivion. I heard my screams, but it felt like someone else wailing and sobbing and clawing at herself.

Then Chris was at my elbow, talking in my ear. "Attack or not? Master?"

Another hybrid fell with an abbreviated yelp. My scream matched his grunt and then we were both silent. I glanced over. His eyes, hard and unblinking, were absent of life. His body shimmered at the edges before fur and paws shifted back to a man with a strong jaw and wiry frame. Blood poured from three different puncture holes in his chest, one still sporting a stake buried hilt-deep in his flesh.

I looked at the rest of them. None were fighting back beyond basic defense. Most looked confused or uncertain and kept glancing at me. The feel within the bond confirmed their hesitation, and suddenly, I knew where the pain had come from.

"Attack," I whispered.

Chris jumped up and gave an order I couldn't hear. It could've been as simple as an expression. The sound of ripping fabric caught my ear at the same time what was left of Chris's shorts hit the ground. His shifting was instant, and I knew he'd been holding it back all this time, waiting for my order.

Master. They kept calling me master.

The pain dialed back after that. The hybrids were relentless and vicious. Through the bond, I could feel their determination, their complete unity; they attacked because the alpha ordered it.

That knowledge made my human side a little sick. It was overwhelming and heady to be followed without question, without hesitation, in every command. Dangerous, really. The wolf in me strained against its chains. It knew its power, now, if not from me, from its pack.

Its pack.

I had a pack. The thought was surreal. Unbelievable. Terrifying.

The pain faded to a prick as my bones strained against themselves. My skin stretched tight. One of the hybrids yelped. The point of a knife grazed its shoulder and tore off a chunk of fur.

My control slipped.

Every nerve ending in my body stood on end. My scalp tingled and the end of my fingers went numb. I shut my eyes against the brightness that seemed to come from inside me. The air flickered, like an electric charge after rubbing your hands too long on your pants—times a thousand. My place in the dirt where I'd hovered protectively over Cord suddenly wasn't the right size for my frame. It felt different. And then I knew: I was different.

My arms weren't arms. I was all legs and nose and … fur.

I couldn't move. I couldn't think—not even to remember why I'd fought this for so long. My mind was empty to everything but instincts and senses. My muscles itched to be stretched. To run. My canines wanted something to sink into. The forest sounds were magnified, down to the simple call of the cicadas. Smells overwhelmed my nasal passage. Sweat. Dirt. Fear.

And underneath it all, pain surged through me.

I stepped back, overwhelmed.

Then, from beside me, Chris grunted. I remembered what had driven me here. My pack. The pain. I had to stop the pain. For me, and for them.

I hesitated, hating to leave Cord exposed, but the second my paws pushed off the ground, my worry faded. The moves were foreign, but even as a beginner, I was fluid, graceful. My muscles coiled and bunched like a spring, and when I pushed off, I sailed. My feet landed silently. I felt weightless—and dangerous. Like a predator.

I shoved myself between Chris and his attacker and bared my teeth. Chris shifted to cover my flank. Dear God, I had a flank.

My attacker slashed out with his knife. His movements looked slow—laughably so. Had he been this bad before I'd shifted? Everything magnified. The trees, the dirt, even the wind. I hadn't even felt a breeze before. The pain I'd felt through the bond wasn't the same, either. It wasn't exactly more bearable, but it became easier to understand. When my chest reverberated with an invisible blow, I knew where it came from. Not just that it came from my pack, but I could identify which pack member and where they were standing—or lying, by then.

Separating the buzz of emotions in my mind took no effort. Everyone had a distinct taste, and some part of me knew instinctively who was who. The connection went deeper. The loss was real, like we'd been friends, though I still didn't even know their names, where they'd come from, what brought them here.

My attacker sliced the air again, this time getting closer to Cord. The threat registered even if he hadn't meant it that way.

"Enough," I said. It came out in a low growl. "I don't want to hurt you, but I will if you don't back off."

The Hunter blinked in surprise, his knife momentarily suspended. "What?" he said.

"I will call them off. Just stop the attack."

"You'll … I can't."

"They aren't bad. It's different now." It was impossible to explain all that had happened in less time than it took another hybrid to fall, but I had to try. I couldn't bear it like this. The pain might've been easier. The grief was not.

"Different how? You're hybrids. Look at the eyes."

"They changed. They don't follow the same master anymore."

He frowned. "Wait a minute—your eyes aren't yellow. Who are you?"

A pang shot through me, tight and hard. I looked over in time to see a hybrid turned human again fall to the dirt in a heap. An arrow protruded from her shoulder. Her pain seized me and I felt the struggle as her heart tried to beat around the pierced tissue. My knees wobbled. My head drooped. Chris scooted in, standing over me. I could feel the protectiveness radiating out of him.

"What's the matter with her?" the Hunter demanded.

"She can feel what's happening to them," Chris said.

"Stop attacking. We'll stop too," I said through a whimper.

The man paused, weighing our words. Someone called to him, and his eyes flickered with renewed determination. "We'll stop when you're dead."

He drew back the knife and thrust it out. Even before my teeth sank into his wrist, I knew the knifepoint had been meant for Chris. I didn't try to reason with or understand the irrational protectiveness I felt toward him. In that moment, he was my pack. I was his. We fought for each other. It was that simple.

The man's flesh gave like tissue paper underneath my canines. His blood seeped into my mouth, awakening something dark and ugly deep inside me. He pulled against the pressure and screamed when my jaw didn't give, and still, I held him there.

Someone hit me from behind, sending me rolling, and my jaw wrenched free. The forward motion, paw over shoulder, disoriented me. I couldn't tell which end was up. My attacker figured it out first and pinned me. This man was faster than the last one had been. I saw the raised stake gleaming in the light, and I reacted.

My teeth closed over flesh. Blood soaked my mouth. I heard the crack of bone under my teeth and released my hold, ready to do it again if necessary. But the stake faltered. My attacker cried out, and I froze. Our gaze locked.

"Alex?" Horror washed over me. I swallowed his blood and my stomach rolled.

"T-Tara?" Pain and confusion clouded his features. He slid off me.

"Oh, God. I'm so sorry."

I sat up and watched him scramble away. "You bit me." His face went white, his lips pressed together in a hard line.

"I didn't know it was you. Are you all right?"

"You shifted," he said, ignoring my concern and his injury to stare at me in disbelief.

"You left me." The words were void of the accusation I'd intended. All I could do was look fixedly at his wrist, bleeding and mangled.

"I wanted to save you from … them," he said. "It's the only way I know."

"They aren't my enemy anymore." *You are*, I thought. "Call your people off."

"What? Why?" He shifted and winced, clearly in pain. His eyes were glassy now.

"They're only protecting me. If you stop, they will too." Another hybrid fell.

I cringed. "Alex, please," I begged. "I can't take this … it hurts."

His eyes narrowed and he seemed to finally realize how much pain I was in. "Fall back," he said, the strain in his voice distorting his words. "Fall back," he repeated louder. He had to say it three more time before anyone took notice. One by one, Hunters ceased their attacks.

"Fall back," I echoed and the hybrids backed away. Some looked disappointed.

Chris appeared at my side. "What now, Master?"

"Guard the prisoner," I told him. He walked toward where Olivia still huddled in the box, shouting orders to the others. I looked back at Alex. "Thank you." The adrenaline in me waned, leaving behind exhaustion.

"Don't thank me. You don't know … I messed up."

"You're shaking," I said.

"It stings a little." He attempted a smile.

I scooted closer, slowly, knowing instinctively he wouldn't want me to hover, but unable to sit by and watch him fade like this. He didn't protest. It scared me to think he was past the point of arguing. One of the other Hunters came forward and knelt beside him, a tall man with broad shoulders. His hair hung in his face, but the scar made him easily recognizable.

"Professor Kane," I said.

"Tara? That you in there?"

"Yes, sir." I wasn't sure the title "sir" was necessary for someone who'd technically tried to kill me, but I went with it. Old habits.

"You're a …"

"Yes, sir," I said.

He looked from Alex back to me. "You bit him?"

"It was an accident."

He frowned and inspected Alex's wound without another word. For me, his silence said it all.

"There's a clinic, a quarter mile that way," I said, nodding toward the trail.

"Not much we can do for him there. Unless you've got a healer."

"No, I … she's not here."

"They're on their way," Alex said through gritted teeth. The guilt in his words, in his expression, stopped me.

"How do you know? Where are they?" He didn't answer. "Alex. What did you do?"

"We don't have time for this," Kane sad. "We'll have to get him to the clinic and hope she shows in time. Show us the way."

He helped Alex to his feet. I rose on four paws and found Chris over the sea of wolf faces. "I'm going to the clinic. Stay here, with *her*." A growl escaped, but he nodded. I looked back at Kane who had an arm under Alex, holding him up.

"Someone else needs to carry her," I said, gesturing to Cord. Kane gave a quick order, and another man stepped forward and scooped her into his arms.

I led the way.

Halfway to the clinic, I shifted. One minute I was limping along on four paws, the next I had two legs and two arms, one of which hung unnaturally from its socket. My knees gave out. The pain washed over me, and I heard myself let out a piercing scream that echoed around us. Before the sound died away, someone lifted me from the ground. They draped a jacket over me, but my relief was small. Being naked was nowhere near my biggest concern. My shoulder throbbed. Stabs of pain shot up and down my arm, from elbow to shoulder. The rest of my body ached and groaned against each jostling step.

I tried shifting back, craving the release of it—I hadn't realized until now the pain had been easier as a wolf—but it wouldn't come.

"You said they're coming?" Kane's voice came from somewhere behind me. "How close?"

"I don't know," Alex answered. "I slowed them down. Here. Speed dial four." Alex's voice was muffled and weak.

I heard buttons being pressed and then Kane's voice muffled by the jacket thrown over me. The jostling continued. A moment passed and the call ended.

"Thirty minutes. Just hang on," Kane said.

Alex grunted.

I wasn't sure if Kane meant him or me.

CHAPTER THIRTY-TWO

"Tara."

My lids fluttered. Even the thought of prying them open made my muscles ache. Could eyelid muscles get sore?

"Tara."

The voice came again, stronger, more insistent. I recognized that voice. The sound of it brought an onslaught of mental images: blood, gnashing teeth, and mangled bodies littering the forest floor.

I wrenched my eyes open to escape it. The face that stared back at me was almost as horrific as the broken ones in my head. But at least this one was alive. Relief flooded me. I sat up and almost toppled out of my folding chair. I lifted myself off the thin mattress.

"Cord! You're alive!"

"I feel like shit. This is all your fault."

I smiled. Yeah. Cord was awake.

"What the hell happened? Where am I?" She looked around the room, wincing at the movement.

"We're in the clinic. Relax, we're safe." Unless something happened to Alex. If that happened, I was pretty sure all bets were off.

"Olivia's in our custody," I added when she blanched and tried to get up.

She lifted a hand as if to touch her face and then lowered it, apparently thinking better of it at the last second. "Fill me in, and make it quick. I feel like I might pass out again."

"Not sure how much you saw—"

"Four walls and the end of a two-by-four was the extent of my view."

"I'm so sorry, Cord."

"Don't be. You took her out. If it weren't for you …" She didn't finish. Her body rocked with a violent shudder.

"I know."

"Where's Olivia?"

"In a cell in the woods. I've got guards on her."

"Wes? Derek?"

"No, they aren't here yet."

"Where the hell are they?"

"I don't know. Alex said—"

"Alex is here? I'm getting a headache."

"Would you shut up and let me talk?" She rolled her eye—the one that wasn't swollen shut—

and made a show of pressing her lips together. "Olivia's been keeping hybrids here, only, they were sick. The change wasn't working on them. They must've been part of Miles's earlier batch. Before he figured out my blood was key. She knew, though, and she made me inject them."

"With your blood?" Cord asked.

"Yes. It healed them. And it sort of … bonded us."

"As in, emotional connection? Soul mates and all that crap?"

"Sort of. I guess. It happened really fast. I broke their connection to Olivia and they turned on her."

"Excellent."

"I managed to call them off before they killed her. We put her in the cell she had me in."

"Damn. Still alive, huh? I almost liked them."

I gave her a look and she fell silent. "Alex showed up. He brought Kane's strike team with him and they attacked. I didn't know it was him, not until after. Geez, Cord, I bit him." I squeezed my eyes shut, trying to block out the image of Alex's mangled wrist.

"You bit him?" She blinked. "Wait … You shifted." It wasn't a question. I could hear the understanding—the full impact of my words—hitting her. "Is he all right?"

"He's sedated, but I can see the infection already spreading. Fee needs to get here soon."

"Where are they? What happened to them?"

"Alex misled them. I'm not sure how. I think he didn't want them walking into the middle of things with Kane's team on rampage."

"Why was Kane's team here? How did they find us?"

"Alex brought them here."

"So nice of him," she said, twisting her lip. The movement reopened one of the cuts there.

"Cord, your lip."

"I know." She patted it with her tongue and swallowed the blood. "Listen, it's getting a little fuzzy around the edges."

"You should sleep some more." I rose from my chair. My backside tingled as feeling replaced the numbness caused by the hard seat. "I'm going to check on Alex."

"Hey, Godfrey … I mean, Tara." I stopped in the doorway and turned back. She licked her lip, her fingers twitching at her sides. "Thanks."

I nodded and left.

A COMMOTION AT THE FRONT DOOR DREW ME. I PICKED UP THE PACE AT the sound of raised voices. My legs ached, protesting the movement, though it was nothing like my shoulder. I tried to hold my arm steady against my side as I walked.

The main door was cracked, a foot wedged in the opening. Chris, in human form, and another Hunter I didn't know blocked the entrance.

"Just tell us if she's in there." The voice came from the other side of the door, muffled and drowned out by Chris's yelling, but I'd know it anywhere.

"Wes!"

I ran forward and shoved Chris aside. "It's all right. He's with me," I told him.

The Hunter moved slower, not quite as submissive as Chris. I bumped him the rest of the way with my hip and wrenched open the door. Wes practically fell over the threshold, grabbing me and crushing me to him. The embrace lasted only a second before he yanked me back, his hands on either side of my temples as he inspected me head to toe.

"Are you all right? Are you okay?" His eyes were wild, unfocused. George, Jack, and Fee shoved through the opening, surrounding me. I could see their confusion as they tried to read the situation. George's relief flowed through me, matching mine.

"I'm fine," I said. "Where were you?"

Wes's jaw hardened and his eyes turned three shades darker.

"Alex's guys jumped us a few miles out. He set us up," George said. He rubbed his head with his palm. "They knocked me out to kill our connection."

I started to ask more but winced at the pressure of Wes's hand on my shoulder.

"You're hurt," George said, the bond between us an open channel now.

"My shoulder was dislocated. They had to pop it back into place."

"What's with the scrubs?" George asked.

"I—my clothes … It's a long story."

"Where the hell are we?" Jack asked, inspecting the room.

I shrugged. "Not sure. A forgotten bunker of some sort—"

"What is that?" Wes demanded. He stared at something over my shoulder.

"This is Chris. He's—"

"He's a hybrid," George said, his voice filled with surprise, confusion. He dropped back, his hands shaking. He looked ready to shift at any moment.

"He's with me," I said, putting enough authority into it, they all turned and stared.

"What?" Jack and Wes echoed in unison.

"Everyone calm down," Fee said. "Tara, explain. Quickly," she added glancing at the Hunter—and the CHAS logo on his jacket.

"If you'll stop interrupting me," I said, looking pointedly at Wes and George, "I will."

I told them everything that happened, beginning with Olivia forcing me to inject the hybrids and ending with Alex. Kane came up behind me as I told them about the bite. "I swear I didn't know it was him," I said. I looked at Fee. "Can you help him?"

"He deserved it," Wes said.

I noticed Fee didn't correct him. Her expression was hard, but she nodded at me, then Kane. "Where is he?" she asked.

"This way," Kane said. "You." He pointed to the Hunter still hovering near the door. "Stay here and guard the door. No one comes in, no one goes out."

Jack took Fee's hand and shot us a look before they both followed Kane down the hall.

"Where's Cord?" Wes asked when they'd gone

"She's sleeping. Olivia beat her up pretty bad," I said. Wes's and George's cheeks flushed a matching shade of red. I didn't need a bond to tell me they were furious. "She's safe now," I assured them. "Olivia's locked up."

"We saw her on the way in," said George. "Derek and Cambria are keeping an eye on the perimeter."

"They're not going to attack any of the hybrids, are they?" I asked, suddenly nervous. I saw Chris take a step forward. Wes noticed it too, and moved so his body blocked mine.

"Why?" George asked.

"They're with me now," I said. "They can't hurt them."

"They won't do anything until we say," George said.

"Are you sure? Because you have to be sure. I can't—they can't hurt them."

They exchanged a look. "All right," George said. "I'll go let them know." He slipped out the door and I relaxed. I wasn't sure how much he suspected, but I knew he'd keep his word.

"And this guy's with you?" Wes demanded. One hand gripped mine with the pressure of a vise. He used the other to gesture at Chris who'd backed against the far wall to give me space. He wouldn't leave unless I ordered it.

"Yes," I said.

"But he's a hybrid." It was an accusation, filled with contempt.

"Yes."

Wes opened his mouth, as if to question further.

A yell pierced the silence. Alex.

"In a minute," I promised, letting go of Wes's hand and running toward the sound.

ALEX LAY ON A COT IN THE OPEN AREA OF THE CLINIC. THE CROWD parted to let me through and my throat closed up at the sight of him writhing on the bed. Only Fee held her ground. Her fingers moved over the wound, poking and pulling at the torn skin around his wrist. Her frown left deep lines around her mouth, her brows drawn together in a single line.

"Alex?" I asked, grabbing his other hand lightly in both of mine.

He didn't answer. His eyes looked glassy, his pupils dilated as he tried to focus on my face. He was breathing heavily.

"Fee?" I asked.

"I don't know, Tara. It's pretty bad," she said quietly.

"You can do something," I insisted. She didn't respond. Panic speared through me; black dots clouded my vision. I leaned against the cot in order to stay on my feet. This couldn't happen. Not to Alex. Not because of me. "Freaking do *something*!"

"Tara." Wes put his hand on my shoulder and tried to draw me back. I jerked away. My eyes stung but I refused to let tears fall. Tears were for death. There was no death here.

"Master?" Chris's voice, the tone of it, cut through the panic that clouded my brain. I found him standing behind me, unimposing but watchful. His hands were fisted at his sides. I knew, to some extent, he felt my panic, my agony. "What about a transfusion?"

"Master?" Wes echoed. I ignored him.

"A …" I couldn't think straight. I couldn't form the words or finish the thought.

"It worked for me," he said. "It can't hurt."

"Yes, yes, I can inject him. Like with you. It healed you. I can heal him." I rushed to the cabinet and flung it open. I grabbed at a tourniquet, a vial—all of the supplies I'd used before. My hands shook and I dropped the vial. I cursed and grabbed another.

"Tara, slow down." It was Fee. "You healed the hybrids from an injection. Alex was bitten."

She stood close behind me, blocking my way. She didn't touch me, which was good. I felt shaky, unsure of my form. I took a deep breath.

"The hybrids were almost dead and my blood brought them back. I get the catalyst is different but the outcome might not be. I have to try. I'm going to inject him with my blood." My voice sounded disturbingly calm. I didn't wait for an answer before I slid around her and sat, working the tourniquet awkwardly around my bicep with one hand. I almost dropped it but another pair of hands appeared and helped secure it. Male hands.

I looked up at Wes. "Thanks," I said.

"What's next?" he asked.

"Unwrap that syringe and hand it to me." He didn't look up as he worked. Fee stood back, watching, thinking. Worry lines came and went in her forehead, but she didn't stop me. I met Chris's eyes across the room. They were steady, an anchor.

"Now what?" Wes asked.

"That vial, get it ready." I stuck my arm without hesitation this time, easing the needle into the vein. I ignored the pinch and watched as blood flowed into the vial. I filled it and pulled it free. "Cap it with this."

Wes complied, then handed it back. I dropped the syringe and took the vial. "Fresh syringe," I said. Wes handed it to me unwrapped and followed me to Alex's bedside without a word. Fee trailed behind, still looking unsure. I ignored her. She'd given up. They all had. All I could do was this. And so I'd do it.

I reached for Alex's arm. He didn't pull away. Instead, he turned his head side to side, as if fighting off a bad dream. I positioned the needle over the crook in his elbow. My hands shook and the point slipped left. My injured shoulder throbbed at the angle I held it. Another pair of hands came around either side of me. I breathed in the scent of Wes as he pressed himself against me and his hands steadied Alex's arm.

"I'm here," Wes said quietly, "whenever you're ready."

I swallowed the lump in my chest. Alex had betrayed me—betrayed us all. An act that almost got Cord and me killed. He'd swooped in with a team of killers, purposely lured away those who would've rescued us, and in the end, had tried to end me with a metal-tipped stake.

Knowing all of that, Wes stood here, his arms wrapped around me, his hands steady over mine, willing to do whatever it took to save Alex's life.

Whatever happened after this day, my choice had been made.

I blinked against the tears that blurred my vision, adjusted the point of the needle against the vein, and pressed down.

ABOUT THE AUTHOR

Heather Hildenbrand lives in coastal Virginia where she writes paranormal and fantasy romance with lots of kissing & killing. Her most frequent hobbies are cuddling with her 100-pound goldendoodle, riding country roads on the back of her husband's motorcycle, and avoiding killer slugs.

You can find out more about Heather and her books at www.heatherhildenbrand.com.

www.ingramcontent.com/pod-product-compliance
Lightning Source LLC
Chambersburg PA
CBHW020247030826
48979CB00030B/2643/J

* 9 7 8 1 9 6 1 4 5 5 2 8 3 *